C000172443

The CHAOS Wielder

BOOK 1 OF THE CHAOS SERIES

A.E. COSBY

CHILL
IT'S ONLY
CHAOS

This is a work of fiction. Names, characters, places, and incidents either are the product of the author's imagination or used fictitiously. Any resemblance to actual persons, living or dead, events, or locales is entirely coincidental.

Copyright © 2023 by Anissa Cosby

All rights reserved. No part of this book may be reproduced or used in any manner without the written permission of the copyright owner except for the use of quotations in a book review. For more information or licensing for official merch contact:
hello@anissacosby.com

Barnes & Noble Press Paperback ISBN: 979-8-3692846-6-7
Paperback ISBN: 979-8-9886591-0-5
Hardcover ISBN: 979-8-9886591-1-2

Book Cover Art by Grandfailure
https://stock.adobe.com/contributor/204918064/grandfailure
Asset ID: #278142794

Cover Typesetting and Interior Book Design by Anissa Cosby
https://www.anissacosby.com

Character Art by Julia Stephens
https://linktr.ee/myplaceforbooks

Edited and Sensitivity Read by Amanda Quade
Alpha Read by Cynthia Armstrong

To the Ancestors for guiding me on this journey.

To the readers who have put their faith in me.

AUTHOR'S NOTE

Thank you for deciding to read The Chaos Wielder!

In this book, you will find two primary languages: Trezoran and Potroyan. They will be reflected in the dialogue as English and Spanish.

There is a portrayal of D.I.D. in this series. While not a part of this community, I did my best with researching the topic. It is done in a fictional and fantastical manner and is not reflective of the community. If you feel that I've done a disservice, please reach out to me so that I can make updates as necessary.

This novel has come from the darkest parts of my soul. Please adhere to the content warnings. If at any point you cannot continue because of any triggers, then please close the book. Your mental health matters more than my novel.

Remember, it's all chaos here...

I cannot be held liable for any therapy you may need afterward.

CONTENT WARNINGS:

If you would like to know the type of ending (cliffhanger or otherwise), you can visit **www.anissacosby.com/the-chaos-wielder**.

General: Implied SA of FMC (not graphic, fades to black, not done by any MMC), mentions of human trafficking, drug use, alcoholism, addiction, murder, gore, graphic violence, dismemberment, graphic language, mass murder, violence against women (MC street fights and is a brawler, fights all manner of people regardless of gender), scenes reminiscent of 9/11, graphic torture, graphic SA (not done to or by MCs or side characters)

Mental health: Fugue states, black outs, waking up in dubious conditions, self-harm, suicidal ideations through cutting, body shaming, self-destructive coping mechanisms, PTSD, sociopathic tendencies, trivializing mental health illness

Romance: Strong sexual content, DS dynamics, dub-con, consensual dub-con, non-con, masochism, sexualized violence, intense language, brat taming, praise kink, orgasm denial, domination/submission, anal, spanking, knife play, blood play, spitting, fisting, MMF scene, MFM scene, pre-necrophilia (vampire feeds while having sex until death)

THE CHAOS WIELDER SOUNDTRACK

(can be found on Spotify)

Music. I see the world through music. Notes fly through the air, creating song and sound for everything I see. Everything has a song. Everything has a theme. Music has always been a part of my soul. It's how I associate with life.

It was crucial for me to create a soundtrack for The Chaos Wielder. Every major scene has a song. Every main character has a song. To add an interactive piece to the novel, when there's a scene with a song, you'll find * with a footnote with the name of the song to listen to.

You can follow **The Chaos Wielder Soundtrack on Spotify**

Theme Song – "Glory and Gore" by Lorde
Muse – "Summoning" by Sleep Token
Xavia's Song – "EAT ME" by Demi Lovato, Royal & the Serpent
Aurelio's Song – "The Grey" by Bad Omens
Quade's Song – "Monster" by Fight the Fade
Chemistry between the three – "Alkaline" by Sleep Token
Aurelio and Xavia's Song – "Yes Ma'am" by Boy Bowser

SCENE SONGS:

"Big Mad" by Ktlyn
"Smells Like Teen Spirit – Alt Mix" by Witchz
"The Beautiful People" by Marilyn Manson
"Self-Destruction" by I Prevail
"Little Girl Gone" by CHINCHILLA
"The Way That You Were" by Sleep Token
"Pullin Up (Extended)" by Soda
"Eat Your Young" by Hozier
"Die Slow" by Soda, Voyage
"Warning" by Martin, Washyb.
"Play with Fire" by Sam Tinnesz, Yacht Money
"Skin" by Rihanna
"Moan" by Sabrina Claudio
"Give" by Sleep Token
"The Ground Below" by Run the Jewels, El-P, Killer Mike, Royal Blood
"Slayer" by Bryce Savage
"Are You Ready" by BAD NINJA
"THE DEATH OF PEACE OF MIND" by Bad Omens
"Hypnosis" by Sleep Token
"X Gon' Give It To Ya" by DMX
"Vixen" by Miguel
"Dangerous Woman" by Ariana Grande
"Sugar" by Sleep Token
"Muñequita Linda" by Juan Magán, Deorro, MAKJ, YFN Lucci
"DOMINATION" by Kayzo, Sullivan King, Papa Roach
"Do or Die" by Magnolia Park, Ethan Ross
"Burn" by 2WEI, Edda Hayes
"Sweet Dreams (Are Made of This)" by Marilyn Manson
"Waiting on the Sky to Change" by STARSET, Breaking Benjamin, Judge & Jury

PRONUNCIATION GUIDE

Characters
Xavia Silveria (zay-vee-ah) (silver-ee-ah)
Aurelio Broderick (ah-rel-ee-oh) (broad-er-ick)
Quade Nassar (kw-aid) (nah-ss-ar)
Jacinto (yah-sin-though)
'Cin (ss-in)
Lex Esson-Tai (s-son-tie)
Rizor (rye-zor)

Locations
Euhaven (you-hey-vin)
Trezora (trey-soar-ah)
      Asherai (ash-er-eye)
      Calñar (cal-knee-ar)
      Melhold (mel-hold)
      Dolsano (dole-sah-no)
      Shayce (sh-ay-ss)
      Adventus (ad-vent-us)
      Mutuba (moo-too-bah)
Potroya (poe-troy-ah)
      Ayobaí (a-oh-bye)
      Malagado (mal-ah-gah-though)
      Milagros (me-lah-grows)
      Vascaria (vah-scare-e-ah)
Gailux (gay-lucks)
      Tuthia (too-thee-ah)
      Ethnies (et-n-eyes)

Temisraine Ocean (tem-is-rain)

Isla del Cuervo (ee-s-la) (d-el) (kwehr-vo)

Deities, Angels, Demons, Realms, Celestial Terms

Melvina (mel-veen-ah) - Deity of Space, Moon, and Women

Axton (ax-tin) - Deity of Death, War, and Rebirth

Tomis (toe-miss) - Deity of Chaos

Etis (e-tis) and Sortis (soar-tis) - Double headed Deity of Love and Sexuality

Aeshma (a-shh-mah) - Angel of Wrath

Kutiel (cute-eh-el) - Angel of Water and Divinity

Sarandiel (sah-ran-dee-el) - Angel of Night and Shadows

Norrix (nor-ex) – Demon of Fear and Pain

Aether (ether) – Upperworld, realm overseen by Tomis

Orcus (awr-kuhs) – underworld, realm overseen by Axton

Anima (annie-mah) - Soul

EUHAVEN

Isla Del Cuervo

Potroya

Faysos

Vascaria

Temisraine C

Loquiza Peaks

Potroyan
Lighthouse

Ayobai

Malagado

Jacar Volcano

Milagros

Horizon Line

 Capital

 Harbor

 Riptide

 Melvina's
Sacrifice

 Silvermoon
Biome

Aeshma's
Impact

Temple of
the Tetrad

Gailux

ithia

Grenivik

Lundr

Ethnies

Trustek Slopes

Trezora

Mt. Vancarres

Crystal Lake

Alburg

Asherai

Othea

vermoon
Harbor

Trevern Mesas

Dolsano Wood

The Badlands

Shayce

Melhold

Adventus

ar

Shayian Desert

Mt. Chimazi

Jilrobi Jungle

outh Asherai

Mutuba

PART ONE

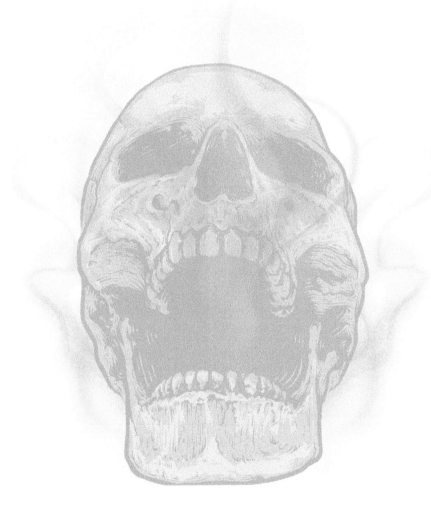

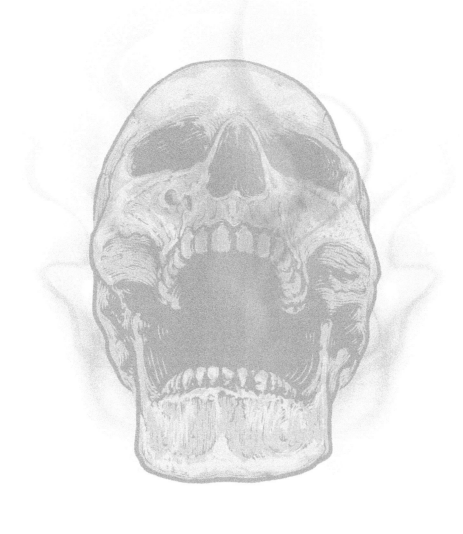

CHAPTER 1

XAVIA

XAVIA CHUCKLED AS SHE took another hook to the chin. Once again, her big mouth earned her another punch to the face.*

"Hit me harder next time." She was in the middle of a street fight, throwing hands and receiving them too. Sweet Tomis, she loved this shit.

Xavia took a deep breath as her head snapped up. She got a glance at the moon that hung lazily in the dark indigo night sky, the waning presence of Ithea in the distance. The planet was so massive that you could see it from Euhaven. Its gaseous body had a strikingly vibrant atmosphere of blue and green swirls, with streaks of yellow lightning throughout. For centuries, scientists tried to gather information about the massive planet, but to no avail. Not one drone or spacecraft could break through the atmosphere.

She looked back at her opponent. A massively tall, beefy ogre towered over her. He stood roughly seven feet tall, with a beer belly that hung over the waistline of his pants. They'd been fighting for twenty minutes now. He took large gulps of air, glaring at her, and he was losing steam. He may have had the power behind his punches, but her agile and curvy body was built for stamina.

It was time to end this motherfucker.

Xavia spat blood before running toward Mr. Beefy. She jumped, landing a knee to his gut before slicing her elbow across his cheekbone, making him stumble backward. His sickly chartreuse skin split almost instantly, blood now pouring from the cut. Moving

♪ "Big Mad" by Ktlyn

quickly, she side kicked him in the chest.

Somehow, he caught her foot, pulling at her, hoping to throw her down. Instead, she used her free leg to swing a roundhouse to his face. He reflexively released her to dodge, and she landed on her feet. She leapt back before he could try to swipe at her again. The ogre swung a jab aimed at her temple. Oh, so he was trying to kill her? Now she was pissed.

Anger fueling her more, Xavia dove under his open legs to come out behind him. Using all of her strength, she jumped and landed, straddling his head. The ogre howled as she rained punches on his bruising head. He grabbed her legs and threw himself backward to slam her to the ground behind him. Stars clouded her vision, the breath rushed out of her lungs. Xavia groaned as she scrambled from under him and got to her feet.

"Come on, you big ugly goat!" she said, goading him. He let out a frustrated yell as he charged at her. "Gotcha..." she murmured before dropping to the ground and swiping out with her leg. Mr. Beefy hit the ground and before he knew it, she was on his back and slamming his head to the concrete. It was lights out after that.

She stood up to the deafening crowd cheering, making her grin with a bow. To those that groaned, she winked and gave the finger. She sauntered her way to the games master with her hand out, the adrenaline still thrumming in her system. She buzzed with it and wondered if she should do another fight.

"Pay up."

The games master, a sniveling thin man with greasy hair, rolled his eyes and slapped five gold credits in her hands. She grabbed her gear and blew him a kiss before she felt a clap on her shoulder.

"Damn Xavia, did you have to go that hard?" Aurelio chuckled. This man was the Deities' gift on Euhaven and Xavia's best friend.

Xavia turned to him, giving him an obvious once-over. Dimples creased his cheeks as he grinned. A jagged scar slid down from his scalp to cheek bone, crossing over one of his silvery gray eyes. She couldn't help but admire the way his ass fit in the blue and navy fatigue pants that he wore. Grey and white Storm Wieldermarks traveled down his muscular arm in a montage of different forms of natural disasters. His dark brown skin and full lips drove all the women crazy, including Xavia. She struggled to move her gaze from his lips and flushed a bit when she realized what she was doing.

Aurelio happened to be one of the rarest level five Storm Wielders to be born in ages. Wielders were non-human mortals capable of harnessing energy and elements. Wielding was classified into five levels with five being the strongest. Their Wieldermarks developed over time on their arms, starting in childhood and completing at maturity.

As the Captain of the Guard's Special Forces, he shouldn't even be here. But he always felt the need to look out for her, even though she found it annoying. Xavia couldn't help but laugh as she started to remove the wraps from her bruised hands. She flexed her fingers, making sure none of them were broken, and winced. He passed her an anti-bruise ointment which only he could get as Captain. Ok, so maybe it was a good thing he always stuck around. She gave him a grin.

"Yes, yes I did. He's from the Suncry Hunter's Guild. I had to show him up and teach him a lesson." Xavia had been a bounty hunter for nearly eight years and had undying loyalty to Axton Hunter's Guild. Named after the Deity of war, death, and rebirth, it was arguably one of the best guilds in Melhold. She wasn't going to let a motherfucker from Suncry try to make a fool out of her.

As they walked toward the local dive bar, she ran a hand through her chin length curly chestnut hair, taking in a fresh breath of air. Nothing like a good fight. She marveled at the sight of her city, Melhold. Sunset orange and mauve skyscrapers rose to meet the horizon, lights in windows beginning to flicker off as the daytime denizens said their good nights. She personally loved the night. It seemed to come alive in ways that the daytime didn't. She loved her city, even in the seedier areas, where they currently were.

"You would've made a great Lieutenant." Aurelio was always sentimental.

In another life, they had attended the Academy of the Guard together. Spent four years enduring brutal and sometimes deadly training. But when it came time for commencement, Xavia decided she didn't want to move forward. She suffered from fugue states, having blackouts and ending up in places she didn't remember going. It wasn't a good trait to have. Special Forces wanted her, despite the fact that she wasn't a Wielder, but she didn't trust herself. Plus, the rules and structures did not sit well with her. She wasn't a fan of the Monarchy and all the bullshit it put the people of Melhold through. Shortly after, she joined Axton and never looked back.

"Yeah, yeah. You always remind me." She hated leadership too. Why lead when you can avoid the responsibility and just do your own thing? She rolled her dark brown eyes. "I wouldn't look as good as you in a uniform." She joked as she elbowed him in the side.

Before they could enter the bar, she felt Aurelio's stare like a brand. Her eyebrow lifted slowly. Xavia looked at herself in the window's reflection, taking in her dirty brown tactical pants, sweaty green tank, and black aviator jacket. She always carried at least one gun on her person that she kept out of sight. There was a nasty bruise blooming across her jaw, marring her deep golden tanned skin. Her chestnut curls were messy and clinging to the sweat on her forehead. She held out her hands and did a turn.

"What? Don't like it?" Now it was his turn to roll his eyes.

"Do you think this is the best way to spend your time?" He said, sobering up a bit.

Xavia let out a groan. She was tired of hearing this. All. The. Time. She knew he meant it as a way to keep her from spiraling. The only time she participated in street fights was when she came out of a fugue state and needed her wits smacked back into her–literally. It's a miracle that Aurelio had stuck around for the last twelve years.

They walked in and up to the bar. Xavia gave a sensuous smirk to the bartender. She was cute with dark brown hair in a ponytail, emerald eyes, and a low cut, form fitting dress that left her deep bronze cleavage on display. Colorful Earth Wieldermarks covered the entirety of her left arm. The bartender flushed, her complexion darkening in a blush.

"Lemme get top shelf bourbon, double," Xavia said with a wink. The bartender gave a small nod and looked at Aurelio who just shook his head. Xavia let out a hard sigh. "To answer your question, yup. I am absolutely sure this is what I should be doing. Why would I need to do anything else?" Life is way too short, she thought.

After growing up an orphan and dealing with a hellish ex, she decided she would live each day like it was her last. No matter that she was approaching thirty-five and most women her age were having children or getting married. "What about you? You haven't settled either. Unless there's a lovely woman I don't know about?"

"So, the bartender can't take her eyes off you." He said, obviously not wanting to be the pot calling the kettle black. Sure enough, as the bartender made her way back to them with her bourbon and water for Aurelio, she was making eyes at Xavia. She was also smart enough to bring the bottle of bourbon with her. The bartender bent over to place the glass and bottle in front of her, giving Xavia a much better look at those bronze breasts.

"What's your name?" She murmured in a husky voice before downing the bourbon. She licked her lips slowly, maintaining eye contact with the bartender.

"Ah. Um. Tiff," she said, clearly flustered. She fussed with the bar towel in her hand, eyes on Xavia's lips. Xavia leaned in, inhaling the sweet floral scent coming off her. She reached out and tucked a brown hair behind Tiff's ear, slowly letting her finger trail down the woman's throat.

"Meet me after you get off." The woman's breathing hitched as she nodded and scurried off. Xavia poured herself another double and turned to find Aurelio's mouth agape. She shrugged and lifted an eyebrow. "What?"

"How do you do that?"

"Do what?"

"That." He said, motioning to her and then to the bartender. Xavia shrugged.

"Don't be jealous that my game is better than yours." She laughed as he huffed at her before standing.

"Whatever. Have fun. Some of us have to work in the morning.

I'm out." He said, shaking his head but with a smile on his face, showing off his deep dimples. Sweet Tomis, those dimples. Xavia wriggled her eyebrows. She chuckled, downing another double. He made a step to leave before watching her gulp down the bourbon. He turned to her, a look of concern on his face. Oh boy.

"Take it easy," he murmured, watching her drink. She shrugged. He always had a problem with her drinking. She was getting ready to down another glass when he gently took hold of her elbow. "Seriously. Slow down." Clearly, he was getting to the edge of his patience with her. She shrugged out of his hold.

"How 'bout no?" she said, feeling the buzz of the bourbon. Good. About damn time. "I'm a grown ass woman. I can handle myself." She promptly took another gulp. Aurelio looked at the bottle of bourbon next to her. She snatched it before he could and shook a finger at him. "Nuh uh. Nope. Not taking it." She grunted before standing up. Oh, how the world tilted. She snorted, shaking her head. Ire bloomed in his eyes as they grew darker, almost blending with the blacks of his pupils. Thunder boomed overhead. Xavia was not impressed and just rolled her eyes, now drinking straight from the bottle.

"I'm surprised your liver still works. I hope I don't find you in a ditch somewhere," Aurelio hissed before storming out of the bar. She hugged the bottle of bourbon to her as she made her way to the bathroom. She took a swig from the bottle, the buzz in her head growing more persistent.

After handling her needs, she stared at herself in the mirror. Tired. She looked tired. She winced as she dabbed the bruise on her chin. Her fingers trailed the long jagged scar on her neck, which began under her ear and continued down to her collarbone. It was the first scar of many to come throughout the years. Fuck. Maybe Aurelio was right. She looked at the bottle in her hand. She took a long swig. That would be tomorrow's problem. Right now, she was tired and horny.

Last call sounded as the bar emptied. Xavia made her way to the bar top, placing the now empty bourbon bottle in front of Tiff. She gave a wink to the bartender, motioning with her chin that she'd wait outside.

As she swayed out into the balmy night, she looked at herself again in the window's reflection. Sweet Deities, she needed a good, hot shower. Thoughts of her time in the Academy came to her, and she half considered just canceling and heading home. But if she did, then she'd only have her hand to entertain herself, and that wasn't what she wanted right now. Right now, she wanted to fuck and forget.

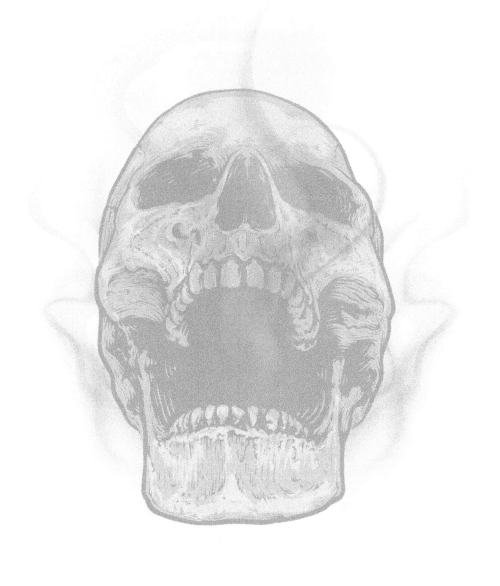

CHAPTER 2

AURELIO

AURELIO STORMED INTO THE Monarch Tower, pissed at Xavia and himself for not sticking around to make sure she got home ok. To say he was furious was an understatement. It was one thing for Xavia to street fight, which he *hated*. It was another when she drank herself into oblivion. He hated that he could do nothing but watch her slowly spiral over the last twelve years he'd known her.

He remembered when they first met at the Academy. She was thin, but not by choice. It was clear she was getting out of a hellish situation and wanted to learn how to protect herself from it ever happening again. She proved her worth during the tests and she mostly kept to herself until she met him. They clicked almost instantly. Young bucks as they were, he thought they'd actually share a life together. But after he learned about her fugue episodes and having it land her somewhere she didn't want to be, she broke his heart by telling him she couldn't commit. Who she was then was drastically different from who she was now. He watched her get harder and harder around the edges and wasn't sure how he felt about it.

Aurelio made a beeline for the Special Forces training unit. The sounds of someone hitting a heavy bag caught his attention, and he could only guess who it was. Only one other person would be training at this time of night. The door snapped open as he entered the room.

The training facility for the Special Forces differed from the general Guard in that there were much more deadly sparring tools.

It was large, at least fifty-two thousand square feet. Different centers were set up for specific skills; archery, knife and sword fighting, strength training, endurance and stamina machines, and a massive sparring ring in the middle. Alongside the far wall, different weapons were shelved or hung, ranging from the current handguns and semi-automatics they used on the regular, to experimental weapons that were bound to glitch and needed constant trial and error. Next to the weapons wall, there was a glass wall where Aurelio could see inside the gun range. In a separate room, there was a Wielding-proof room for Wielders to practice their skills.

The sound of deep breathing drew his attention to the heavy bag swinging to his left. Quade Nassar was his second in command. His best friend, who was more like a brother. They trained together in the Academy and led their Special Forces team for the last eight years. Quade was an asshole. Everyone knew Quade was an asshole. Shit, Quade knew that, but it didn't stop him from being damn good at his job. He was quick-witted, strategic, and had a way to let others know he was not to be fucked with. Because of this, he ran point on interrogations. He was the fire to Aurelio's quiet storm. It was the main reason they worked so well together.

Quade side stepped, burnt sienna eyes snapping to Aurelio. He had ear buds in and was most likely listening to metal of some sort while he continued focusing on beating a hole into the bag. He lifted his chin as a 'what's up'. His normally slicked back, black hair fell forward to his eyes as he continued hitting the bag. He kept it cut short on the sides and left some length in the middle. Where Aurelio had a crisp beard that ran down the length of his jaw and goatee over his lips, Quade had a rough five-o-clock shadow that covered a jaw sharp enough to cut diamonds.

Quade stopped hitting the bag, pushing his sweaty hair back and taking one of his ear pods out. Metal screamed from the pod making Aurelio wince. He didn't understand how people listened to that music.

"Sup, Cap?" Quade panted, sweat gleaming on his golden tanned body. Scars peppered his skin; a price for the line of work they were in. Fire Wieldermarks covered his left arm and pectoral muscle. His eyes were additional evidence of his heritage. He was slimmer and taller than Aurelio, but no less muscular. He was made for stealth and stamina, that much was clear. Dressed in navy sweats and busted boxing sneakers, black wrappings covered his hands.

Aurelio shrugged out of his jacket, tossing it aside, before slipping his shirt off. He bounced in place and nodded to the sparring ring. He needed to spar and get this energy out. Quade hit a button on his watch and the screeching of metal stopped. He stuffed the ear buds into his pockets before heading to the sparring ring without question.

Aurelio gave Quade exactly five seconds before launching at him. First throwing a jab and then a hook, twisting to land a side kick to Quade's gut. Quade effectively blocked each punch and barely dodged the kick then retaliated with his own, which hit Aurelio square in the gut. It knocked the breath out of him momentarily but he recovered with ease, dodging the jab aimed at him and threw an uppercut that made its mark under Quade's chin. The sound of his teeth snapping together was loud in the otherwise quiet gym.

Quade's eyes narrowed, fire dancing in them, and he punched Aurelio with two jabs to his gut. Aurelio grappled with Quade, his hands locking behind his neck. He drove a knee upward, but Quade blocked with his hands. Aurelio let go of one hand to elbow the side of Quade's face. He ate the elbow like it was a snack and maneuvered into Aurelio's guard. Quade hugged Aurelio around the waist and heaved him into the air and behind him in a suplex. Aurelio's teeth chattered as his body connected with the mat, his head making a THWACK sound.

"What's got your panties in a twist?" Quade panted as he rolled up to stand. He held out a hand, which Aurelio gratefully took as he stood, sweat pouring down his body. He took a moment to catch his breath. Aurelio shook his head, heaving a frustrated sigh that ended in a grunt due to his now-sore ribs. The only time Quade ever got one up on him was when he was distracted.

"Xavia." They both said at the same time. Quade had trained with Xavia and Aurelio at the Academy and they've had a mutual disdain for each other ever since. Quade grunted, making his way to the large fridge in the corner. He pulled out two ice packs from the freezer and handed one to Aurelio. Quade held one up to his jaw and Aurelio placed one on his side.

"The risks she takes keep getting worse and worse," Aurelio griped. He grabbed a water bottle, guzzling it down in one breath. Quade lifted an eyebrow, eyes darkening in anger. The male could rival Xavia in the temper department.

"I don't get why you put up with her antics," he said, pointing at Aurelio. "You need to let her go. She destroyed you and you still hang around like a kicked puppy. It's fucking ridiculous." Aurelio got in his face, both men so close their noses could touch.

"Fuck you. You don't know her like I do." He shoved Quade back, snapping a towel off the rack and drying the sweat from his body. Quade tossed the ice pack into the trash, jaw clenched and the muscle ticking.

"I don't have to. I can see how you let her walk all over you. When are you going to man up and stop acting like a bitch?" Thunder rolled outside as Aurelio's temper started to rise. He'd had this conversation with Quade for years. Aurelio would bitch and complain about how frustrated he was with Xavia, and Quade would listen and then cuss him out for it. "You still love her?" Quade asked, tone a bit calmer.

"No." He answered too quickly. "Yes?" He sat on a bench, resting his elbows on his knees, and put his head in his hands. "Fuck man. It's a different kind of love," he murmured. "I would feel this way if you were going off the deep end." Quade snorted, causing Aurelio to look up. Quade had his signature scowl on his face.

"If I went off the deep end, there's not a thing you'd be able to do about it." Fire licked in his eyes again. Aurelio knew that Quade had a darker side to him. He was never hesitant to kill an enemy in the field. Never had to ask him twice when it came to torture. It was ingrained into who he was. He'd been that way for as long as Aurelio could remember. If Quade ever went off the deep end, that would be a disaster.

"Whatever. What I am trying to say is that I feel like I'm watching a train wreck happening and I can't stop it." He ran a hand over his face standing back up. Quade didn't know about Xavia's mental health, which is why he didn't understand why Aurelio stuck around. "I'm worried she's going to kill herself one day."

Quade slapped a hand on Aurelio's shoulder.

"If she does, then that's her own fucking fault." And with that, he exited the gym, leaving Aurelio feeling worse than he did before.

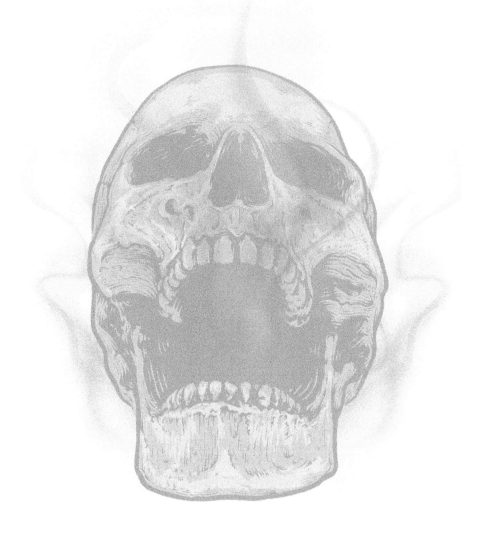

CHAPTER 3

XAVIA

XAVIA WOKE THE NEXT MORNING with a massive hangover. Her pulse slammed in her head like it had an oath against her. She took a peek through aching eyes at the room she was in. Soft yellow walls were trimmed with sea green. One of the walls had a mural painted of Melhold. Xavia realized then that they were in a hotel. She didn't remember getting there, just the fun of the night.

Groaning, she turned to her side to find the luscious bartender lying next to her. Tonya? Tracy? No, Thelma! Xavia didn't understand why she bothered with names. She never remembered them. The bartender opened those emerald eyes and smiled when she saw Xavia. Xavia smirked, thinking of how loud she'd made her moan. "Sleep good?"

Tammy stretched with a nod. No, that wasn't her name either. Xavia leaned over her, kissing her neck and moving toward her breasts. "Shall we continue from last night?" She murmured, hand sliding down the smooth expanse of Tiff's stomach. There it was! Her name was Tiff.

"I have to go," she breathed. "I have a shift soon."

"No, you don't. I want to hear those moans again." Just as Xavia's hand reached its destination, her comm blared to life. Xavia ignored it, suckling on Tiff's neck and making her moan. "That's it sweetheart, louder." The comm blared to life again.

"Shouldn't you get that?" Tiff breathed, hips grinding against Xavia's hand.

"If it's important, they'll leave a message." Xavia huffed,

picking up the pace. The comm blared again. "Fuck!" Xavia slid her fingers out and kept her eyes on Tiff while placing her fingers into Tiff's mouth. "Taste how sweet you are. I'll be back." Tiff wrapped her lips over the fingers, sucking them clean before Xavia stood up. She snatched her comm and headed to the bathroom. The thing blared again in her hand and she hit the button.

"There better be a good reason you ignored my pings." Julian's voice sounded, and the image of her mentor's annoyed face followed shortly after. His dark brown hair and beard were dusted with grays, giving him a roguish, hot older man look. But she never thought of him in that way. He was more like family, which said a lot, considering she didn't have any. His hazel eyes widened as he looked her over. "Sweet Melvina, Xavia, what did you do last night?" She rolled her eyes and could only imagine how rough she looked.

"The usual, plus a hot bartender with great boobs and a fine ass." She shrugged and he let out a bark of laughter.

"If you were a male, I'd tell you to keep it in your pants." He shook his head.

"What's up? Said bartender is waiting for me." She gave a salacious wink.

"Unfortunately, she is going to have to continue waiting." Xavia sighed and sat on the toilet as he continued, "There's a bounty contract with your name on it. Riddick Sham." She perked up. Riddick Sham was a known black market potions peddler. "Apparently, he stole something from someone and they want him back."

"Alright. Where was he seen last?"

"Diamond District." The Diamond District wasn't as snazzy as it sounded. It was the common name for the black market that crawled under the city tunnels.

"Finding a peddler in the Diamond District is like trying to find a needle in a haystack," she grumbled.

"Hence why you were chosen. Best tracker yet!" The smirk on his face made her grumble some more.

"Fine." She sighed. "I'll do it. I'll be at Axton soon." She went to close the comm.

"Don't dillydally." Julian chided. She rolled her eyes, snapping the comm closed. She stepped out of the bathroom to find Tiff still lounging on the bed.

"And here I thought you had to leave?" Xavia chuckled before pouncing on her.

XAVIA BREEZED THROUGH THE AXTON GUILD, looking around at the bustling people moving about. She was in a fantastic mood today. After showering and getting into fresh gear, she was ready for the day, or rather, the evening.

Out of all the guilds, Axton was the biggest and had the best bounty hunters. The facility had an industrial chic feel about it. Walls were covered in murals showcasing different parts of Melhold and Axton bounty hunters of prestige and the floor was deep mahogany, recently swept clean. Tall tinted windows took up the expanse of the front wall. Shelves made of iron covered the remaining walls. She gave a nod to Tyson, the receptionist, as she made her way to Julian's office. Not only was he her mentor, he was also the boss.

She stepped into the office, not bothering to knock. The decor was as manly as it could get. A navy carpet covered the center of the room, a simple mahogany desk on top. The charcoal walls were bare except for a few iron shelves here and there. A wet bar sat beneath a window in a corner and she went straight for it. She poured herself a double of whiskey and turned to Julian, who was standing by the desk.

"I told you not to dillydally," he grunted, staring her down. He was a short and stocky kind of man when compared to other males, but it didn't make him any less dangerous in the field. He wasn't the boss without reason. Wearing black cargo pants stuffed into combat boots and a light tan henley that brought out his dark brown skin, making his hazel eyes shine. Xavia gave him a shit-eating grin.

"Sorry?" She gulped down the whiskey, setting the glass on the bar. "What intel do we have already on Riddick?"

"He's been spending time with Dimitri." Fuck.

"Who'd he steal from?" If he was spending time with Dimitri– an ugly ass troll of a male–then he must've stolen from someone extremely connected.

"Ryder." Julian said with a wince. Double fuck.

"Ryder... Kingpin Ryder? As in, 'I'll toss you off the top of Luna Towers and feed you to the borgs,' Ryder?" She had heard some seriously vile things about him. He was one of the few werewolves who had a taste for mortal flesh. It made him dangerous. Julian nodded. "Why doesn't he just have one of his goons do this job?" She probably shouldn't ask. A contract meanr credits and credits were a thing they needed to survive.

"He wants it discreet. Riddick knows most of the people in Ryder's crew. He'd spot them a mile away." He waved to the tablet, which had the contract. "Ryder's paying fifty thousand credits." Xavia started. Holy Tomis.

"Run that by me again... Fifty thousand credits?" Her eyes widened as she filled herself another glass of whiskey. "What the fuck did Riddick steal?"

"His daughter, Lena." Xavia choked on her whiskey, taking long gasps. Julian laughed, shaking his head. "Yeah, that. Apparently, she and Riddick are in love and Ryder does not approve." Xavia's eyes narrowed. "But personally, I think she was given a potion of some sort. Werewolves mate and Ryder wouldn't keep her from her mate if that was what Riddick actually was."

"Oh, Tomis' tits... Really?" She already knew that if she turned Riddick in, he'd likely die. "So, we're taking on death warrants, then?" Julian shook his head.

"No. The contract for Riddick is so that you can find his daughter. He cares more about bringing her home than Riddick. This whole thing needs to be handled discreetly." He gave her a look in which she shrugged as if to ask What? "The key word is discreet, Xavia." She drank down her whiskey, feeling the beginnings of that lovely buzz.

"It was one time, Julian!" Maybe more than that. She tended to make a show out of her captures. Oops.

"Seriously. Don't piss him off." Julian's tone sobered her up. He was scared. He was sending her out into the werewolves' den and it was clear he didn't like it. She nodded.

"Alright. Let's do it." She marched over and signed the contract.

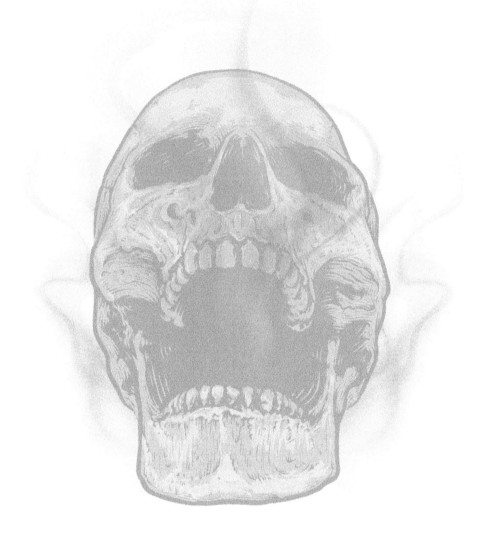

CHAPTER 4

XAVIA

IT HAD ONLY TAKEN XAVIA TWO days to find out where Riddick was staying. She called Aurelio on her comm.

"She lives..." he answered. Her nose flared in frustration as his image popped up. Holy shit, he was sporting a shiner. She only needed one guess on where it came from: Quade.

"Yup, she does," Xavia said with sass. Aurelio rolled his silver eyes, a smirk on his lips. Oh Tomis, those dimples.

"What can I do for you?" She could think of a few things he could do. She pulled her lips in to try and avoid the blush creeping up her cheeks. Aurelio missed nothing, his smirk turning into a full-on grin. "What are you thinking about?"

"Nothing!" She huffed, rolling her eyes. "I need some backup for a bounty and I think you're the perfect one." She winked.

"Who's the pickup?" There was shuffling like he was grabbing his gear.

"Riddick Sham. He kidnapped Ryder's daughter." She snorted when Aurelio looked back at her with wide eyes.

"Ryder, the werewolf kingpin?"

"Yup, the same. So will you help?" she said, buckling her gun belt and vest. She swore as she struggled with the buckle. "I swear, why are these things made to piss me off?" She grumbled to herself.

"Yeah, I can help."

She looked at him, seeing that grin still on his face. She narrowed her eyes and stuck her tongue out at him. "Ok, I'll pick you up."

"No. I can get you," he said, too quickly. He didn't like her driving. He made that abundantly clear to her in the past.

"Too bad. I know where to go. I'm driving," she said before clicking off the comm.

Xavia took the elevator to the underground garage. She whistled as she made her way to her favorite muscle car. She personally worked on it, giving it upgrades over the years. It was matte black with a deep purple strip in the middle that ran from front to back. The tail was also purple with halo glow lights around it. Fluorescent lights glowed under the car and changed color while she drove. She hopped in and shivered in delight when the engine purred as she turned it on. The car was her pride and joy.

Peeling out of the garage, she sped to the Monarch Tower. Speed and danger. It was Xavia's favorite part of driving her car. Aurelio was already outside when she screeched to a halt in front of him. He wore a pained expression on his face, obviously reluctant to get in the car.

"Hey, how much you working for?" Xavia taunted as she rolled the window down.

Aurelio gave her the finger before getting into the car. The dash shone brightly, different types of comms and nav units took over the center console. It was how she learned what was going on and what movements were being made.

"How much have you spent on this car?" Aurelio said, looking impressed. "I don't remember the last time I've been in the passenger seat. It looks great."

"You would've seen it earlier if you'd let me drive." She snorted before hitting the road. Stomping the gas, she whizzed in and out of cars, instincts flawless.

"Where are we headed?" Aurelio asked. She glanced at him, noticing a smile on his face. He could talk shit all he wanted about her driving, but she knew he loved the speed as much as she did. She took a moment to inhale his stormy scent, like the smell of fresh rain after a thunderstorm.

"About two miles outside of the Diamond District," Xavia said as she whipped the car around a sharp corner. Aurelio laughed, making her grin. "I knew you enjoyed the speed as much as I do." She winked.

"Yeah, yeah," he said as he got himself under control. "He's shacked up in the 'Hood?" All cities had a 'Hood. It was the poorer parts of the cities, though not always bad. Sometimes parts of the 'Hood were just ordinary people trying to live their lives. It was all about where someone ended up. The Monarchy offered little to no assistance and they had to fend for themselves.

"Yeah, the bastard is squatting in some abandoned house. Apparently, he's heavily guarded."

"And that's where I come in," he said as Xavia nodded. "Are you sure you weren't looking for an excuse to see me?" He gave her a saucy grin.

Xavia pursed her lips, trying not to quip back. Ever since they broke up, the last twelve years had been like one big tease. They were always making sly comments or flirting with each other. It was a miracle they didn't jump each other's bones. But they knew it would make their attempt at a friendship harder, so they did their best to keep it completely platonic.

"So what if I was? I'm sorry about the other night." Xavia said, sobering up. She put her eyes back on the road, not wanting to see his expression.

"I know I can't keep you from fighting." Aurelio blew out a sigh. "But the drinking... It's getting worse. How long can you go without a drink?"

"A week! Maybe two." The car remained quiet. She winced. "A few days," she mumbled, switching lanes. The streets changed from the bright city lights to dark and dilapidated buildings. Xavia swore as she tried to swerve around the potholes. It was going to give her suspension hell.

"X, I just–" Aurelio stopped mid-sentence as they pulled up to Riddick's safe house. It was a two-floor beat-up shack with the windows boarded up.

Xavia and Aurelio exited the car, doors closing in unison. For as long as they'd known each other, they always moved in sync.

"Let me go first," Xavia said as she skipped up the driveway.

The lack of security or bodyguards surprised her. She pulled her handgun from its holster when she noticed the front door was ajar and blood covered the handle. She eased the door open and felt lightheaded as she took in the scene before her.

Her eyes couldn't figure out what to focus on first. The four male bodies, obviously the body guards, mutilated on the ground. Or the male, Riddick, pinned on the wall. Hooks pierced his hands and impaled his feet, pinning him to the wall. His chest was cracked open as if something punched straight through him and pulled out his heart. Said heart was on the floor by his feet.

"What the fuck?" Aurelio's voice startled her into almost punching him. It would've connected it if he hadn't blocked it.

"Holy Tomis, Aurelio! Don't do that." Xavia breathed before turning back to the scene.

"Please don't hurt me," came a soft feminine voice to her left. Xavia whipped her head to find a female, presumably Lena, huddled in a corner. Xavia knelt before her, taking in her tattered lilac dress that made her orange werewolf eyes glow. Her tawny hair was matted in knots, dirt and grime covered her body, and bruises littered her face, arms, and feet. She had a look in her eyes that Xavia knew too well. Xavia gave a silent command to Aurelio, in which he nodded and headed to the car. She heard the car start before she looked back at Lena.

"I'm here to help you. To bring you back to your father," Xavia said softly. "May I pick you up?" She knew better than to touch a battered female without permission, especially a werewolf. When Lena nodded, Xavia scooped her up to cradle her in her arms. Lena gripped Xavia's shirt, burying her face into the crook of her neck. Her body shook as sobs wracked her. Xavia walked out of the house murmuring calming whispers to the werewolf. Aurelio sat in the back seat, leaving the passenger door open. She placed Lena in the passenger seat of her car before tapping her coms.

"Sup?" Julian's voice came before he took in Xavia's expression. "Talk to me."

"I found Lena." Xavia fumed. "I would've killed that fucker if someone didn't beat me to it." She explained what she saw, body burning with fury.

"Bring her to Ryder." He clicked off and she gripped her comm. She hopped into the car and spooked Lena when she turned it on. Xavia looked in her rearview mirror and mouthed to Aurelio.

Don't say anything or else you'll scare her.

He nodded.

"I'm sorry," Xavia murmured as she put the car in drive and headed for the kingpin's compound. Lena took a deep shuddering breath.

"She slaughtered them as if they were ants." She whispered. Xavia's eyebrow lifted as she slightly turned her head to let Lena know she was listening. "I couldn't see her face; it was covered with a mask and she had purple eyes. But she was obviously female." Xavia grabbed her jacket to place over Lena who was now shivering. "She saved my life. Riddick... He was doing things with the others..." Her voice drifted off and Xavia didn't need her to finish. She knew first-hand what happened to Lena. Xavia laid a hand on her head, smoothing her hair. Lena leaned into the touch before closing her eyes and falling asleep.

After returning Lena to her father, Aurelio followed Xavia as she stormed into her suite at Axton's and searched for her fighting gear. She needed to beat the shit out of someone. Aurelio put a hand on her arm and slightly shook her. Apparently, he had been speaking to her.

"What?!" She barked at him. His nose flared in annoyance.

"I was telling you that fighting should be the last thing you do right now."

"Take your hands off of me, Aurelio." The threat was clear in her voice. Memories of her past bombarded her, him touching her making it worse. Aurelio immediately let her go.

"X, you don't have to." His eyes darkened as he became more frustrated with her.

"Yes, I do. Get out." She hissed, kneeling in front of her bed to find her fighting gear under the bed. Xavia looked up at Aurelio to find that he was looking at her as if she punched him. She sighed. "I need this. Just let me do this." She said, slinging the bag around her.

"I swear to Axton…" Aurelio rubbed the back of his head and shook it. "I'm out." He stormed out of the room, slamming the door with a rattle.

"Fuck!" She yelled to no one in particular. Whenever her past crept up, it drove her to do things that were not conducive to her health.

More memories flashed through her mind, making her vision blur as the familiar blackness edged around her vision. Fuck, not now! She blinked furiously as if it would help push back the blackout that was threatening to take hold. This would be the second in as many days. She didn't need this right now. Fighting her blackouts was a losing battle. She let out a soft curse as her vision completely blacked and she hit the floor with a thud.

XAVIA WOKE, WONDERING WHERE the fuck she was. Her vision was still returning when she recognized the hotel room. There was a soft body next to her and found that Tiff graced her bed. Uh, not good. Xavia didn't spend more than a day with the same person. Tiff turned and smiled at her.

"Hey, you." There was a bruise around her neck and red handprints on her arms. "You were totally different last night." She chuckled, running a hand across her neck. The fuck? Xavia liked it rough, but these blackouts might have her accidentally killing someone one day.

She opened her mouth to reply when the room shook. The tremor ended and Xavia sat up, instinct taking over. Despite the fog still wearing off, she leapt from the bed, nearly losing her footing as a stronger tremor shook the room. The sound of the building shaking was loud enough to almost deafen her.

"What's going on?" Tiff yelled. Xavia shook her head.

"I don't know!" She reached for her gear, grimacing at the

grime on them. But she had no time to worry about it. She threw them on, grabbing her gun. Another quake rocked the building, knocking artwork off the walls and pots to shatter on the ground. "Get dressed and get to the parking garage below, now!"

"Where are you going?" Tiff sobbed while she did as Xavia said.

"To figure out what the fuck is going on."

Another quake shook the building as Xavia flew down the stairs. "Get to the basement!" She yelled at anyone she passed by.

Panicked people started clogging up the stairwell. Xavia looked out the window and saw she only had a floor left before ground level. She stepped back, pulling her semi-automatic handgun from its thigh holster.

"Get back," she yelled as someone darted past her. Once it was clear, Xavia fired three rounds into the window, glass shattering. Holstering her gun, she vaulted over the windowsill and landed on the sidewalk with a grunt.*

"The Luna Towers are collapsing!" She heard someone yell. Xavia whipped her head toward the Towers, freezing for a moment. The Luna Towers were the tallest buildings in Melhold. Its silver and purple double helix buildings were falling away from each other. The Crescent moon that normally sat at the top already slammed into the building next to it.

Luna Towers had been built as a remembrance of those who died during the Deity and Angel civil war thousands of years ago. Melhold wouldn't be here today if it wasn't for Melvina, the Deity of Night and Space, and her revolutionaries. Many were devout to her. Personally, Xavia preferred Tomis, the Deity of Chaos, because of her job and her life as a whole.

A loud boom drew Xavia from her thoughts. The collapsing Towers crashed against the nearby buildings. Other skyscrapers were doing the same. The city was falling apart around her and it struck her as the most confusing thing she'd ever experienced. As far as she knew, Melhold never suffered from quakes. It crossed her

♪ "Smells Like Teen Spirit - Alt Mix" by Witchz

mind that Asherai, the country, as a whole never suffered quakes.

Falling debris made her path tricky as she dodged them. She stopped just in time to miss a body landing in front of her. Her breath hitched as she looked up, seeing people careening off a rooftop café as the building toppled over. Xavia heard more screams and covered her head as more debris fell and more bodies littered the ground. People were jumping in hopes that they'd either make the fall, or perhaps they preferred a quick death over potential suffering. Smoke and dust billowed around her, causing her eyes to water and her throat to dry. Shit! She said a prayer to Tomis and kept running.

Xavia ran toward the Guild District, barely able to keep herself upright as the ground rumbled again. She had to make sure Axton Guild was ok. Dust flew everywhere making her cough as Axton came into view. Sweat mixed with dust on her skin, making her sticky. As she made to run toward it, a loud crack from overhead got her attention. A narrow, twenty story building next to Axton had snapped in the middle and was making a fall toward the Guild. She froze as she watched in horror.

"No!" Xavia yelled before Axton was crushed under the weight of the taller building. She pumped her legs into gear, lungs burning as she ran as fast as she could. Skidding to a halt in front of the rubble, she tried to assess a way in. Someone had to be alive. Xavia found a narrow opening by a blown-out wall and slipped her way into the building.

"Anyone alive?" she yelled into the din. Most of the building had collapsed without any pockets of space to move through. Aside from the sound of rocks falling and rumbles from outside, it was deathly quiet. "Please, Tomis's mercy, no."

Suddenly she heard a rasping cough and she turned toward it, seeing a hand sticking out from the rubble. She ran, sliding on the rocks on the ground and landed on her knees in front of the pile. Her knees sang out in pain but she gritted her teeth and started pulling rocks away.

"What the fuck are you doing here?" rasped Julian's voice.

"Trying to save you. You don't get to die on me, fucker," she panted; her fingers bloodied from the rocks. Julian let out a hiss of a chuckle.

"It's over, girl." He grabbed her hand, stilling her feeble attempt to dig him out. He was like an uncle to her. She couldn't lose him, not like this. Tears welled in her eyes. "Don't cry for me." He coughed as blood bubbled up from his mouth. Xavia shook her head, tears flowing freely. She held on to his hand as tightly as she could as she watched the light die out in his eyes.

The ground shook again, causing more debris to fall from the already damaged building. She slid to her bottom, trying to process what was happening. How did she go from laughter and drinking a few nights ago to despair this morning? *Shit! Aurelio!* Xavia got to her feet. She had to make sure he was alright, especially after their terse words last night. The world shook with the most violent quake of them all, causing a boulder to drop from above and knock her unconscious.

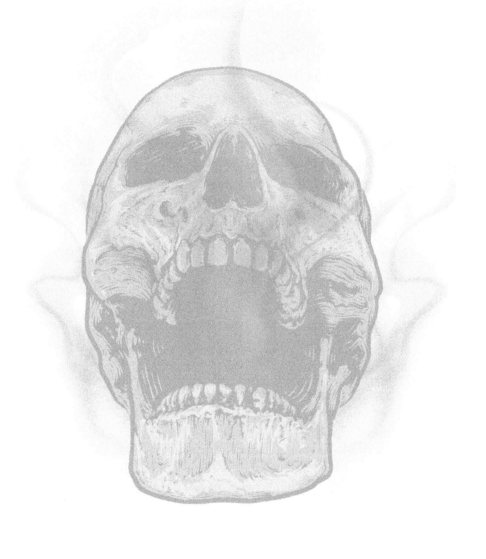

CHAPTER 5

STYX

THE SOUNDS OF SCREAMS OVERWHELMED her as she looked around the brothel. She was finishing up a hit, holding some asshole crime lord's head in her hand. He and his cronies had been abusing the women of this brothel. Brothels and their sex workers were considered an important part of Asherite society and honored Etis and Sortis, the double headed Deity of Love and Sex. However, Melhold was infamous for its crime lords abusing the sex workers. That's why Styx was hired; to keep those assholes in line. Never mind the fact that she took complete pleasure in ripping their heads from their shoulders.

However, the dead body at her feet was not the cause of the screams. The whole of Melhold was falling apart as buildings rained down from the sky. She dropped the head with a wet thud as she zipped her way through the chaotic brothel and outdoors. She lowered the black leather hood that shrouded her but kept her mask on. Her purple curls fell to her face and her inhuman purple eyes peered out from between them. People stopped briefly to stare at her before they continued running. She looked down at herself and let out a curse. Her gray leather pants and black knee-high boots were stained with blood. But maybe that wasn't what they were looking at. A bloodied katana rested limply in her hand. She wiped the blade across her arm before sheathing it across her back.

"Melvina, what is happening?" she uttered to the Deity. A silver pendant in the shape of a crescent moon hung from her neck.

She was a devout worshiper, honoring the Deity's wishes to protect women and those that need help.

The ground quaked again under her feet and spurred her into action. She ran back into the brothel, looking for the Madam.

"Is there anywhere safe underground you can get to?"

The Madam just stared at her, dazed. Fuck. Styx slapped her across the face, bringing the Madam back to the present.

"Do you have a place you can get to safely?" she said again, slower this time. The Madam nodded, body trembling. Styx motioned to the workers. "You have to protect them. By Etis and Sortis, you have to." The Madam nodded, finding the courage she needed to lead her workers to safety.

Styx made another round to make sure everyone was out when a male yell came from behind her. Great, one of the asshole's cronies was still alive.

"You fucking bitch!" He reached to grab her shoulder as she turned to him. She grabbed his wrist before he could touch her, twisting his arm and yanking up to snap his elbow. He let out a holler, using his free hand to punch her side.

"Are we seriously doing this right now?" she huffed, kicking him at the knee to bring him down. "If you haven't noticed—" She grunted and shifted as he made to reach for her knees. "The city is going to shit around us." She dodged another hook. "And I'm much faster than you." She suddenly disappeared in a flash of purple shadows and reappeared behind him. Grabbing his forehead and chin, she twisted until his neck audibly cracked. She let him go so that he could flop lifelessly on the ground.

She made her way back out of the brothel, taking in the sight before her. Buildings toppled over as the ground shook again. A car zipped past her on fire, crashing into a light pole. The cries of pain made Styx turn her head, seeing a mother and daughter huddled together. They were stuck under a collapsed awning and it looked like the mother's leg was badly sliced. Both mother and daughter were covered in dirt and grime, tear streaks on their cheeks. Styx ran toward them, kneeling briefly.

"Keep still," she said softly, looking at the mother. The mother nodded, pulling her crying daughter to her. Styx stood and gripped the awning, thanking Melvina that her hands were gloved. It would've cut her hands like it did the mother's leg. Grunting with the effort, she picked it up and tossed it away from the two. She knelt back down, hovering a hand over the mother's wound. "I can heal this if you let me." Styx removed her gloves and allowed purple smoke to surround her hands.

"Healer," the mother said, South Asherai accent thick. Styx nodded.

"May I?"

When the mother nodded her consent, Styx lowered her hands, touching the wound as gently as she could. The mother hissed, making her daughter clutch Styx's arm tightly. Styx smiled under her mask, hoping it reached her eyes. "It's ok, sweet one, Melvina is with us. I will help your mother." The girl seemed to understand and nodded, letting Styx go.

The glowing purple smoke made its way into the wound and the mother groaned in pain, face straining with a wince. Styx moved her hands in circle motions, willing the wound to knit slowly. Sweat beaded on her forehead as she continued the healing process. It was not a simple task. Her healing differed from the healing that Water Wielders used. Styx's style was raw and more innate. She used it for herself when she could, but found it easier to help others.

"Oh…" the mother breathed, relief slumping her shoulders. Styx finished the healing, panting softly.

"Thank you," the mother said, taking Styx's hands into her own. Tears welled in her eyes as she brought Styx's hands to her mouth. "Melvina keep you blessed," she whispered.

"And you as well," Styx said, softly, before helping both of them to stand. "If you go two blocks that way, you should find a bomb shelter. While I don't think what's happening is a bomb, it'll be safer for you there." She pointed to let them know where to go. The girl tugged on Styx's hand so Styx kneeled to become eye level with her.

"Thank you for helping mama." The voice was more mature than Styx would've thought from a little girl. The girl gave Styx a small kiss on her forehead. "Melvina keep you blessed." She grabbed her mother's hand and ran off toward the shelter. Styx watched them before the ground shook again.

"What in the holy Tetrad is happening?" she murmured, turning toward the Monarch Tower. The municipal district was likely to be safe and have some answers.

CHAPTER 6
JACINTO

BLOOD POURED FROM THE HOMENAJE'S neck as she straddled his lap. Jacinto licked the blood from his lips, fangs glistening. Her blood covered them both. He roughly held on to her, leaving bruising imprints on her hips. His mouth found her pulse above her breast, sinking his fangs in. Her body was pale and almost completely drained of blood. She convulsed as she reached her climax. He pulled back and knotted his fist in her silky black hair, yanking her head back.

Licking a line from her wounded breast to the one on her neck, he sank his fangs into her again. He growled, bucking his hips and bouncing her. Greedily, he drank until her body began twitching as the high of the feeding wore off. A scream left her mouth as the pain of her wounds rose to the surface.

Jacinto chuckled into her throat. He loved it when they screamed. The pain was the best part, as the pain fed him just as much as the blood. His yellow eyes flashed red as he held on while she tried to fight. Homenajes were only human. She couldn't fend off a vampire. As he took the last of her life, he came—hard. He pulled away from her neck and sat there for a moment, reveling in the feel of blood on his body. The homenaje's lifeless body slid off him and hit the floor with a sickly thud.

He rose and made his way to the bathroom. The expansive space was striking, with its charcoal marble floors and countertops. A massive marble jacuzzi was nestled in one corner and a sleek shower stall with a ceiling shower head stood next to it. The toilet, fashioned from the same charcoal marble, blended into the bathroom. On the wall housing the sinks was an enormous piece of graffiti art.

The shower automatically turned on as he stepped toward it, blood dripping down his body still. Jacinto stood under the hot water, hand resting on the navy wall before him, and watched as the water washed the blood off his copper skin and down the muscled expanse of his abdomen.

After he was done with his shower, he made his way to his room. The mahogany floors were smooth under his feet. His bed, which could hold eight mortals, was elevated on a platform with a warm yellow light glowing underneath. An unlit fireplace rose from the center of the room. Shelving made from industrial pipes and wood peppered his walls, books filling them all. Similar to the bathroom, one wall was accented with graffiti art.

He slipped on some boxers and made his way to the large bay windows that took up most of the left wall of his bedroom. Being in the penthouse of the tallest skyscraper in his city, he was able to take in a good look at it all. Malagado, one of the most dangerous cities in the world, spread out before him, and he was King of Potroya, the Dark Continent.

The streets formed a grid throughout the tall, dark steel-colored buildings. Because of the planetary tilt of Euhaven, Potroya was in perpetual night time, making the city full of nocturnals. Car exhaust and the sound of horns permeated the air. The full moon hung heavy in the sky, the only sign that it was true darkness and not the planetary tilt. Ithea glowed magnificently in the distance. For as long as he'd been alive, he always marveled at the gaseous planet. He kept his eyes on the city as the door to his room creaked open.

"We have a problem," came the deep voice of Cyrus, his second. Jacinto turned to him with annoyance. The male had flawless ebony skin with short black hair that was cut close to his temples. He wore a maroon three-piece suit with brown accents; he'd always had a thing for suits. His lean but muscular body came from years as a warrior before Jacinto met him. Yellow eyes spoke to his vampire blood, and they flashed in equal amounts of annoyance. Jacinto had turned Cyrus into a vampire over two hundred years ago and, while Cyrus was a loyal male, he was always trying to put Jacinto in his place. It never worked.

"It must be serious, considering you know I hate being bothered after a sacrifice." Jacinto grumbled, leaning against the wall next to the window. Cyrus rolled his yellow eyes and bent over in a mock bow.

"Oh, I'm sorry, your highness, shall I come back later when Melhold isn't crumbling to pieces?"

Jacinto growled at the sarcasm and would've slammed his head into the wall if what Cyrus said had registered even a moment later. Cyrus crossed his arms with a smug look on his face and raised an eyebrow.

"What the fuck did you just say?"

"Melhold has been destroyed." Cyrus said slowly, as if talking to a child. Jacinto appeared in front of him with a hand at his throat. Cyrus grunted, hand going to Jacinto's wrist.

"Pendejo, what. The fuck. Happened?" Jacinto hissed. Cyrus flicked his eyes to the hand around his neck. Jacinto abruptly let him go, causing Cyrus to stumble back. "Dime. Now."

"There were massive quakes," Cyrus grunted, rubbing his throat. "Apparently they were so severe that most of the buildings collapsed and the loss of life is significant."

What the fuck was going on? Jacinto ran a hand through his shoulder-length brown hair, going to his dresser to grab a pair of jeans and a tee. In his millennia on Euhaven, he never heard of quakes occurring in that region of the planet.

"The reports say that a meteorite crashed not a hundred miles from the border of Asherai." Jacinto's hair stood up, his instincts going on high alert.

"A meteorite? You're sure of this?" Fuck. Fuck. Fuck. He started muttering in his native tongue as he got dressed and made his way out of the room. He walked into his study and hit the touch screen TV. The reports of the incident blared to life with footage of the destroyed city. Cyrus caught up to him, concern written on his face.

"¿Qué es eso?" He asked before realization hit him. "Is it the prophecy?" Jacinto slid a glance to him. "Oh shit, it is." Cyrus slid onto a nearby couch, resting his elbows on his knees. "I didn't believe it was real."

Jacinto only knew parts of a prophecy that many forgot long ago. It foretold an ending to Euhaven, starting with a great ball of fire crashing into the planet. New deadly creatures were prophesied to be unleashed on the world. It was meant to be an end of an era, an end to the very precarious peace between continents. And he remembered one more thing.

"Get the governors together," he said, his strategic mind going to work. "We need to secure this country. They'll be making their way here." He moved to his computer, punching in his password and pulling financial statements. He pored over them, calculating in his mind where to allot funds to beef up his arsenal. "And get the weapons master."

Cyrus was already on his cell making all the proper calls. Jacinto threw on his leather vest, pulling the hood over his head, and grabbed the keys to his motorcycle.

"Wait, why do you think they'll be coming here?" Cyrus said before Jacinto could head out.

"Because I know something they don't."

CHAPTER 7
QUADE

GET YOUR ASS TO THE SHELTERS!" Quade barked as he moved down the streets of Melhold toward the Monarch Tower. The city crumbled around him; buildings catching fire and falling over. People were covered in sticky gray ash, crying, and trying to find family. He snapped his visor down so he could see through the dirt and grime. As far as he knew, Melhold never suffered from quakes.

"Help!" A child's scared voice came from behind him.

He stopped in his tracks to find the source of the cry. Scanning the rubble, he spotted a boy stuck in an upended car. Quade slid to the ground, his Guard fatigues preventing the glass from scraping at his body. He grunted as he leaned into the busted driver's side window. The boy, not older than eleven or twelve, hung by his waist from a stuck seatbelt in the passenger seat. Blood dripped down his face from what looked like a torn collar bone.

"I've got you. What's your name, kid?" Quade assessed the state of the car. The passenger side was shattered; no room to get the kid out that way. He'll have to crawl in through the driver's side.

"Kai." He said softly.

"Hi Kai, I'm Quade," he said, gently. "Where's the driver of the car?" Quade tracked the boy's gaze to a body shredded beyond recognition a few feet away from the car. The person had been tossed from the car.

"Ok, Kai. I'm going to crawl in here to get you. Can you stay still for me?" Kai nodded as Quade shifted his rifle to his back. As Quade shuffled in, belly down, he pulled a knife to cut the seat belt. The smell of gasoline assaulted his nose, urging him to hurry. He grunted as he pulled at the belt, and it finally gave way. Using his free hand, he guided Kai down to land softly. The boy whimpered, obviously trying not to cry. Tough kid.

"My shoulder!" He gasped as Quade tried to help him out of the car. The smell of gasoline pushed him further. Any movement he made put the boy in agony, but he had to get him out of the car if he didn't want to be burnt to a crisp.

"Let's get you out of this car first, then I can look. Can you do that for me, Kai?" When the kid nodded, he took hold again to pull Kai from the car. The glass scraped him up a bit, but it was unavoidable. The kid let out a gasp of pain right before the car blew. Quade threw up a bubble of fire to cover him and Kai. His eyes flared sunset orange as parts of the car battered his shield.

"You're a Fire Wielder!" Kai yelped. Guess the kid couldn't tell because of his dark visors. Quade nodded, drawing the fire back into himself as he looked over Kai.

"Alright, do you want the good news or the bad news?" Quade said, kneeling next to Kai. Kai rolled his eyes.

"Nothing's worse than this." He had a point. The kid reminded Quade of himself.

"Good news your shoulder isn't torn." Quade held on to Kai's wrist while putting a hand on right below the same shoulder. "Bad news, it's dislocated." Before Kai could react, Quade pulled at his wrist while bracing the shoulder. There was a soft *pop* as the shoulder shifted back into its socket. Kai let out a yelp of surprise, followed by slumping in relief and blacking out. Quade scooped him up.

"Don't worry, kid, I'll get you to the shelter," he said to himself as a rumble shook the streets. Fuck, where were the Earth Wielders? Kai woke with a groan as they approached the shelter.

"Shit, you could've warned me, asshole," he snapped as Quade put him down. Quade snorted, patting Kai on the head.

"Be safe Kai, stay in the shelter." Kai nodded in gratitude before disappearing into the shelter.

Quade stopped short in front of the Monarch Tower; now the tallest building in Melhold after the collapse of the Luna Towers. In the shape of an armor piercing bullet, it rose up into the sky at one hundred stories. It was covered in tan tinted windows which glowed magenta during the sunset. The floors were filled with people who lived and worked there. The Guard's compound was at the base of the Tower. While he spent time there every day, the atmosphere was different today. As people ran in and out of the building, grabbing supplies and running into Melhold proper, a body laid motionless on the steps. As he approached, he started to recognize the woman that had passed out, clearly knocked unconscious.

"Xavia?" Quade grunted, reaching for the comm at his ear.

"Talk to me!" Aurelio blared in his ear.

"I'm ok. But your *friend* Xavia is here on the steps." There was a loud boom of thunder and he spotted Aurelio hopping out of a ten-story window to land with a gust of wind next to him.

"Fuck!" Aurelio scooped her up into his arms. "Lieutenant," he addressed Quade. "Come with me." He motioned to the Tower.

QUADE PACED IN THE HALLWAY IN FRONT of the room where Aurelio had taken Xavia. They were in the Monarch's personal guest quarters and he had no idea why. Aurelio finally emerged, looking worse for wear. City grime dusted his cropped black hair, his deep brown skin made pale from ashes, and his gray eyes darkened to steel. Dried blood covered his arms, making it clear that Aurelio's day had been just as hellish as Quade's.

"She's knocked out cold. Either from the quake or…" He didn't finish the statement leaving Quade to wonder what was on the other end of the sentence. Before he could ask, Aurelio motioned to the empty conference room down the hall. They slumped into the chairs, Aurelio leaning forward to rest his elbows on the table.

"What's up?" Quade raised an eyebrow. "Just say it."

"The Monarch has a mission for us and Xavia's going to play tracker."

Quade took a moment to process.

"Are you serious? Why not one of our own scouts?" Quade said, tightly. He was always quick to anger, his temper earning him a fist or two to the mouth. But at the moment, he didn't fucking care. Especially with knowing Xavia was going to be part of the mission—whatever it was. The fire that burned in his veins fought to burst through his skin. Anger was always easy for him, fury even more so. If they were to go on a mission, the last thing Aurelio needed was his ex tagging along.

"She's the best, you know that." Aurelio shot Quade a tired look. "The Monarch will not budge on this and honestly, it's not our place to ask." He rubbed the back of his head, a tell that he was frustrated.

"But do you think it's a good idea having your ex on this mission?" Quade opened and closed his hands, smoke lifting from his palms.

"She's more my friend than an ex," Aurelio snapped. "And yes, if it means getting this mission done to save our continent, absolutely yes."

"Save our continent? What the fuck is going on?" Quade stood up abruptly, chair falling behind him. He could taste the smoke in his mouth as he continued to fume. He hated being in the dark. Aurelio stood up slowly, giving him a pointed look.

"You'll be briefed shortly. Get Alpha Phoenix ready. I'll be down to address you all after the Monarch has spoken to Xavia." Quade's eyes widened, smoke slowly dying out.

"The Monarch is meeting Xavia personally?" He'd never heard of the Monarch meeting with a citizen. Aurelio nodded as he stretched out his neck.

"Yup." His lips popped the P. "Seems that this mission is going to need massive convincing. I already know Xavia is going to say no. She hates the Monarchy." Quade rolled his eyes.

"If she's the 'best'," he threw up quotations, "then she's gonna have to suck it the fuck up." Aurelio returned the Fire Wielder's scowl.

"I know that, asshole." He nodded to the door. "Go get the

team ready. This mission is going to take a month and a half at a minimum." Quade shifted a bit, biting his tongue. He nodded and gave Aurelio a sarcastic salute before leaving.

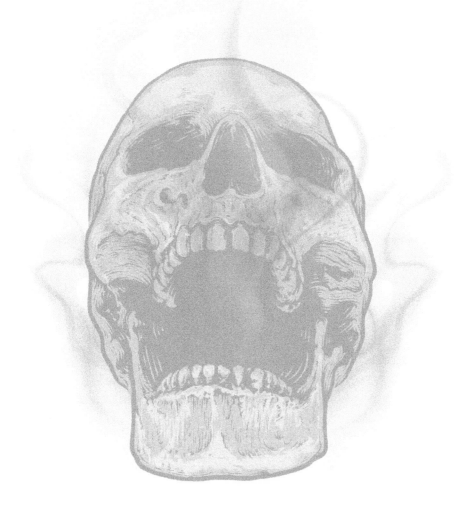

CHAPTER 8
XAVIA

FUCK, XAVIA, WAKE UP!" A familiar voice rattled through Xavia's brain. One thing's for sure, her body hurt. All. Over. She grumbled, wanting to go back to sleep, but the sudden memory of the city and the quakes jolted her awake. She swayed as she tried to sit up.

As her vision cleared, Xavia found Aurelio sitting next to her looking like how she felt. She took in her surroundings and realized she was no longer in the crushed Axton building, but in a private suite. It was lush, silk sheets under her, a four-poster bed around her, and gaudy art and furniture everywhere. Her head throbbed and she wasn't sure if it was the still lingering hangover or the rubble that gave it to her.

"Where the fuck are we?" Xavia managed, her throat raw and dry. Aurelio held up a glass of water and she drank greedily.

He was dressed in his Guard uniform; black under armor shirt with dark brown tactical pants. A bullet proof vest covered his chest and was filled to the brim with all sorts of weapons; guns, knives, grenades, tasers; the works. He had two semi-automatic handguns at his thighs and a bow and quiver on his back. There were different types of arrows, ranging from grenades to armor piercing. Two bowies were sheathed at his lower back. He looked like he was ready to go to war.

"What the fuck is going on?"

"We're in the Monarch Tower." Aurelio held up a hand before she could respond, knowing full well how she felt about the Monarch. "And we need your help. You can't say no to this Xavia.

Not with what is going on." Xavia raised an eyebrow for him to continue before noticing the bags under his eyes.

"How long was I out, Aurelio?"

"We found you on the sidewalk in front of the tower two days ago. I was scared shitless. I thought you were dead." Aurelio's breath hitched, causing Xavia to reach out for his hand. He gripped her hand as if he was afraid that if he let go, she'd disappear.

"Ok. Talk to me. What happened, what did I miss, and why am I needed?" She winced as another throb pierced her head. "And can I get something for this pain?" He held out two pink pills, which she took down with the water. After a moment, the pain subsided, and she took a moment to look down at herself, frowning. She was in clean linen clothes.

"They're getting you new gear," he said, answering her unspoken question and bracing his hands on his vest.

"You mean I'll get to wear those?" Her eyes lit up. Fuck yeah! One thing she missed from the Academy was the tactical gear. Unfortunately, it was regulated to only the Guard and Special Forces so, as a bounty hunter, she could never get herself any. Aurelio let out a soft chuckle, a small grin lifting the bottom of his scar.

"Wait, my car..." Aurelio shook his head. Xavia rubbed her face in dismay, the excitement about the fatigues fizzling out. She'd spent so much time and money on that beautiful machine.

"You'll get a new car and these fatigues, on the condition that you help the threat against Asherai and her cities." What a way to kill the moment even further. Xavia huffed a sigh and crossed her arms, waiting for him to continue. "A meteorite crashed about one hundred miles from the border of Asherai in The Badlands. Well, we thought it was a meteorite." Aurelio rubbed the back of his head, which was a sign he was frustrated. "Apparently it's an Angel."

"An Angel?"

"Yes. An Angel." He murmured. Xavia just stared at him, wondering if this was a joke.

"Oh shit, you're serious?" She asked, feeling the need to lie down again. "Like, wings, halos, and shit?"

"More like wings, battle armor, sword of death, and a horde

army of demons." Aurelio stood, pacing. Oh, he was *really* irritated. "I never thought we'd encounter anything like this. I mean, yes, they taught us about them in history lectures in the Academy, but for them to actually be real?" His thumbs started tapping the straps of the vest. "Her name is Aeshma and she set up camp in the Dolsano Wood."

"Like the Angel of Wrath?" Xavia stood, swaying a little, but otherwise stable. "You're fucking kidding me." She shook her head. No way. There was no way, because what she learned about the Angel was that Aeshma was brutal and locked up by the Deities during the civil war. Melvina jailed her. "So, what do you need me for? Shouldn't you be gathering armies or some shit?"

"We need you to track someone." Xavia's world came to a halt.

"What the fuck do you mean 'track someone'?" She said, mimicking Aurelio. She knew she shouldn't goad him, but she couldn't help it. She wasn't Special Forces. Why send her on a task that could be given to anyone else? She was not equipped for this.

"Xavia, you're the best bounty hunter we know. You would've probably placed second at the Academy if you hadn't left." Aurelio came to stand before her. Xavia looked up at him, fuming. "You can find *anyone*. So, we need your help to find someone that can help us defeat Aeshma." Her eyes narrowed, coming to a realization.

"Who's, 'we'?"

Aurelio had the nerve to look sheepish.

"Well…" He hesitated but Xavia gave him a look that told him he'd better fess up or she'd fuck him up. "I sort of recommended you to the Monarch. I knew you'd be—" She punched him before he could finish. Aurelio took a step back, rubbing his jaw. She wanted to hit him again but instead began her own pacing.

"Why the fuck would you do that? You know how I feel about the Monarchy," Xavia hissed.

The Monarchy was one of the reasons Xavia never learned who her parents were, and probably why she became an orphan. They'd stonewalled her every time she tried to learn the information, and they put up a hell of a fight when she joined the Academy.

She had a feeling they only wanted her in Special Forces to keep her subdued and to stop asking questions. Yet another reason why she didn't go through with it. The Monarchy was a bunch of bullshit anyway.

"I know how you feel about the Monarchy but you're the best person we have." Aurelio opened and closed his mouth, his jaw popping a bit. It gave her a bit of satisfaction knowing that her punch hurt. Xavia was still pissed at him.

"I'm not doing it," she said, looking to see if she could find some shoes she could put on. "I'm leaving." Aurelio stepped in front of her again and she itched to give him a matching bruise on the other side of jaw.

"Where are you going to go? The city is destroyed!" He took her by the arm and led her to a window. Xavia shrugged out of his hold and was ready to snark back when the sight of the city caught her attention. The Monarch Tower was the second tallest building in Melhold and also the furthest away. It would explain why it wasn't affected by the quakes. From her view, she figured they had to be pretty high up because Xavia could see the entire devastated city. More than half of it lay in ruin. Smoke plumed up in the air as some buildings caught fire because of exposed gas lines.

"Any city within one hundred miles of the crash has suffered quakes equally bad," Aurelio said with a soft voice.

As Xavia looked over the city, a different sort of anger bloomed inside of her. It wasn't the normal anger she kept like a blanket around her. This was something else. Massive. Ugly, but oddly comforting. It lit her up, making her blood roar in her ears. Melhold was her home. It was where Xavia ran to when she destroyed her past. It was where she met Aurelio and her fellow Hunters at Axton. A pain seared her heart. Oh, Axton. She could imagine that most of them were dead. Most of them lived in the compound. Shit, she lived at the compound and happened to not be there. That white fiery anger took over Xavia again.

"Who do I need to find so that we can destroy that bitch?"

XAVIA'S ANGER HAD QUELLED by the time she made it to the throne room to meet the Monarch. As promised, she was in full tactical gear almost identical to Aurelio's except instead of a bow and quiver she had two katanas on her back. She couldn't help fidgeting as she stood next to him, waiting to be admitted into the room.

"Relax," he said, nudging her with an elbow. Xavia nodded, stilling her hands. She'd never thought she'd actually meet the Monarch. It was easy to talk shit about someone when they weren't in front of your face. The people did not favor the Monarchy. The petty round of senators did nothing but circumvent each other for power and favor of the Monarch. Unfortunately, the sense of security the citizens received from the Monarch and their Senators was the only reason flat out rebellion hadn't happened already.

The throne room was smaller than Xavia expected; more like a conference room. In the middle stood a large glass table with black curling steel legs, ringed by twenty plush teal conference chairs. Like the city of Melhold, the walls were an amalgam of mauve and sunset orange waves. The dark maroon floor accented the colors of the gold trim and sheer canopies near the ceiling. Overall, it was cozy and not at all what Xavia assumed a throne room should look.

Footsteps sounded to let them know the Monarch was entering the room. Everyone, including Xavia, knelt on one knee as their ruler came into view. No one knew the gender of any of the Monarchs of Trezora, nor what they looked like. Each one wore a silk cloak that hooded over their heads down to the floor and an almost sheer mask in front of their faces. Individual Monarchs wore specific colors to signify their country.

The Monarch of Asherai wore maroon and had an eerie sense about them, almost gliding across the floor. It was uncommon for the Monarch to be without the Senate which told Xavia how secret this mission was. However, their personal Guard was in attendance, and what Xavia assumed was the Spymaster if what she wore was any indication. The woman had a lithe body, black suit with maroon vest on, two pistols at her side, and her blonde hair in a high ponytail. She was absolutely gorgeous.

"Thank you for meeting with me, Xavia Silveria of Melhold." The Monarch's voice had a synthetic tone to it, clearly to keep their gender hidden. "How much has Captain Broderick told you?" The ruler motioned for them to sit. Aurelio and Xavia sat next to each other while the Spymaster stood by the door.

"Just that Melhold is destroyed because an angry Angel crashed into the Badlands, holed up in the Dolsano, and that you need me to help you find someone who can defeat her." Xavia shrugged when Aurelio gave her a look of reproach. *They asked,* she relayed with her eyes. She could tell he wanted to narrow his but he was always better with decorum than she was.

"Yes, but are you aware of the prophecy?" The Monarch turned toward one of their guards who placed an electronic tablet on the table. Xavia looked to Aurelio who seemed just as in the dark as she was.

"I assume not then." The Monarch clicked a few items and a hologram appeared above the table. It showed ancient text in a language no longer used but in the corner was what she assumed was supposed to be a sketch of the Angel Aeshma but it was too blurry to make out.

"There is an ancient prophecy that the Angel of Wrath will return to Euhaven after being locked up for millennia. She is believed to usher in a new era of chaos and enslavement with a horde of demons at her back." Well that much was evident. "However, we have some remaining pieces of the prophecy that speaks to a savior that can destroy the Angel Aeshma." Xavia held back the need to roll her eyes.

The screen changed and an art relief depicting a hooded individual shrouded in chaotic shadows and light popped up. A hood covered their head and held what looked like energetic balls of red and yellow light at their hands. The background showed a destroyed city, giving the artwork a more ominous energy. Xavia couldn't help but reach a hand toward the image before she snapped it back.

"Who is that?" she murmured. The imagery was captivating for something as old as it was. It felt both familiar and foreign to her, as if she'd seen the image before. There was a memory that played on the edges of her mental landscape that she couldn't render.

"The Chaos Wielder." The Monarch stood and began to pace around the table. "In what pieces we could find, the Chaos Wielder is the only known being on Euhaven that can destroy the Angel of Wrath. Not just lock her up, but actually destroy her." The screen switched to what looked like an old map of Euhaven. "We know approximately where the Chaos Wielder can be found but not the precise location. That is where you come in."

"And where do you approximate them to be?" Although Xavia had an idea of where this was headed.

"Malagado." Xavia almost let a nasty curse slip from her lips. Ah fuck. Malagado is the last place on Euhaven that she would ever want to visit.

"Malagado? The City of Vampires? Do you understand how damn near impenetrable that city is?" She winced, realizing she just snapped at the Monarch. Malagado was only accessible by boat due to its overhead shields blocking aircrafts from nearing Ayobaí, let alone the city. Many have tried, all have failed. "We'd have to travel by sea and that can take weeks. Do we even *have* that much time?"

"The Angel Aeshma will need time to gather her forces and resources. We don't anticipate an attack any time soon. Regardless, this urges us to find the Chaos Wielder sooner rather than later," Aurelio murmured, seemingly annoyed. Clearly, he was not told about going to the Dark Continent, Potroya. "If Malagado is where we have to go, then we have to leave as soon as we can. We can take a jet fighter to Silvermoon Harbor and use one of the naval ships. It shouldn't take— ".

"You will not be able to use official transport." The Monarch interrupted. Xavia raised an eyebrow, arms crossing at her chest. Fuck decorum.

"Why not? It would make this whole thing happen faster." She made her disdain clear in her voice. If the Monarch noticed, they didn't show.

"They garner too much attention, especially aircrafts due to the Angel Aeshma's gift of air and flight. She will bring down any aircraft that crosses her way."

Aurelio let a soft curse out of his mouth as realization seemed to dawn on his face. Xavia looked at him now, wondering what he was thinking.

"We have to pass through the Dolsano Wood to get to the coast, which means we have to be discreet and avoid large vehicles." Xavia's breath seemed to get caught in her throat, heart thudding in her chest. No way. There was no way she'd do this. She stood slowly.

"I am not sure why you think I'm the best person for this job, but I value my life enough to not risk it going through the Dolsano with minimal support." She turned to leave before Aurelio took hold of her forearm.

"Xavia, if you don't help, there won't be much of a life left to live once Aeshma takes control."

Xavia shrugged out of his hold. "Then I'll live it to the fullest that I can, as I've been doing for the last eight years." She stormed to the doors, stopped short by the guards in front of her. "Move." She hissed, but they stayed put.

"I'll give you the name of your parents if you help." The Monarch's words rang through her. Oh, that motherfucker. Of course, they would use this leverage against her. They knew how desperate she had been to learn about her parents, how close she'd gotten just a few years ago. "You're the best because you're the only one who almost broke through our firewalls to obtain the very information I will give you." Xavia turned to face the Monarch.

"Are you willing to write and sign an oath to that?" She knew how these things worked. The Monarch gave a curt nod. "And I'd like a copy of the prophecy." She ignored Aurelio's nudge that warned her to stop.

"Yes, I'll have my advisors draft it up for you to sign in the morning." The Monarch swiped the tablet screen, sending the copy of the prophecy to Xavia's and Aurelio's wrist comms. "Afterward, you all must leave. You will be given an unmarked mobile transport and Aurelio's hand selected team." Xavia heaved a sigh and turned away when the Monarch said the next worst thing possible. "And you have to find Lex Esson-Tai in Silvermoon to help you." Xavia bristled as Aurelio made his way to her. She glared at him, opening her mouth to say something, but the look he gave her made her swallow her words.

"May the Tetrad guide you and keep you covered." The Monarch touched their forehead, chin, lips, and then held out the front with their palm outward. It was the quad symbol of the Tetrad. The Tetrad were the four holy Deities of Euhaven: Melvina, Axton, Tomis, and Etis and Sortis.

Xavia clenched her jaw and knelt to the Monarch before finally being able to leave the room. Lex Esson-Tai was a known pirate and thief who had a savior complex, doing the whole 'steal from the rich and give to the poor' mentality. They justified their means and held the trust of the people of Silvermoon. Add to the fact that no one actually knew what Lex looked like and she found herself with a hard person to find. Xavia had to not only find the Chaos Wielder but this fucking pirate too. Great. Just great.

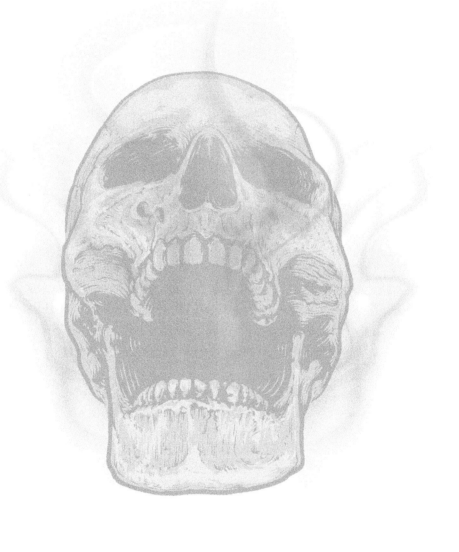

CHAPTER 9
STYX

SHE ADJUSTED HER HOOD AND and face mask as she made her way to the municipal district. Naturally, of all the places in the city, it was the only area that was barely touched. The night sky was filled with light pink clouds, Ithea's swirling mass in the distance. The city smelled of smoke, the fires finally dying out only hours ago. People were already working to start moving rubble to find any survivors underneath. At least the Monarch had set up shelters for the citizens, otherwise they'd have nowhere to sleep.

Styx waited in the shadows of a large oak that sat in the middle of the Municipal square. The grass was lush and the perfect shade of turquoise. The seasons were changing; sea green leaves drifted down from the tree. She had brief memories of her childhood, running in a park and laughing as the leaves fell. She didn't remember much of her younger years, just glimpses like the one she was currently having. The smell of exotic orchids and lilacs rushed to the forefront of her mind as if a bouquet rested in her hands. It was one of the few happy moments she remembered. The rest of her life was dark and far from happy. Styx placed a hand on her hip as she looked at the watch on her free hand.

"This asshole needs to hurry up," she murmured. This was her first time meeting her contact in person so she wasn't sure what to expect. Being late was not optimal for her already tight schedule. She had another assignment to take care of. She didn't have time sitting around.

"What asshole? Me?" A gruff voice came from behind her.

Styx whirled, readying to throw a knife; she'd been too lost in her thoughts to hear the man behind her. The last few days had made her sloppy. She looked at the Guardsman, giving him a long assessment from head to toe. The moonlight made his gray eyes glow and his dark brown skin glisten. A scar made its way from his scalp to his cheek, crossing over one of his eyes and dipping into the face mask he wore. He was in black tactical gear, fully loaded with a slew of weaponry. The male also had a bow and quiver full of arrows at his back. Interesting, she thought. Most Guardsmen hated archery.

"When does the moon set?" She asked the code question.

"Never until Melvina returns," he prompted. She gave a nod. "I'm Leo." He stuck a gloved hand out. Her purple eyes followed it down and back up and remained still. He raised an eyebrow, but nodded in understanding.

"Do you have the information I need, Storm Wielder?" She crossed her arms over her chest to keep from itching at her face. Those stupid face masks always bothered her, but she needed them. It didn't help that the wind blew her purple locks across her face, making her twitch. Leo held out a USB to her.

"This is what I know so far of the mission to find the Chaos Wielder." His eyes glinted. "We have to find them first." Suddenly, he looked exhausted. She could only imagine. They were part of a rebellion that wanted to take down the Monarchy. One person should not have that much power, even with a senate. Everyone knew the senate was just for show. Leo must've been exhausted having to play double agent.

"When do you leave?" Finding the Chaos Wielder first will allow the rebels to hopefully sway them to their cause. Help the rebels defeat the Monarchy.

"Tomorrow, six am sharp," Leo said. He stopped Styx before she turned to leave, his hand catching her wrist. "Wait. I need to explain something else." His tone of voice made her wary. She stared at him and then her wrist before he let her go. Her watch blared, making her sigh with a raised eyebrow.

"What is it? My time is limited," she said, looking at her watch.

"The meteor that crashed wasn't a meteor. It was the Angel of Wrath, Aeshma."

She balked, eyes widening.

"Angel? An actual Angel?"

"Yes, but deadlier. The Monarch wants to defeat her by using the Chaos Wielder, but we both know that's not the only reason. The USB has details with what we know about the prophecy, where our next destination is, and our final destination. I'll contact you when I have more information."

"As if we need anything else to deal with." Styx rolled her eyes and turned to leave. "I'll meet up with you soon." She took off with a run, wrapping a cloud of purple smoke around her before she disappeared.

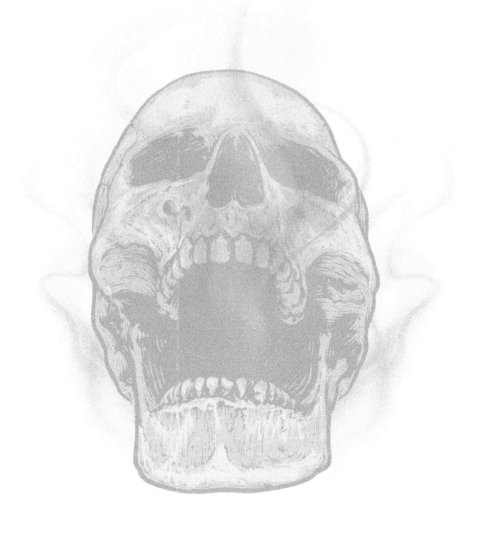

CHAPTER 10

JACINTO

ARE YOU INSANE! ARE YOU** going to let the Asherites come and infiltrate Malagado?" A rotund governor yapped far too loudly and Jacinto contemplated ripping his head from his body.

Jacinto sat at the head of a large conference table where the six governors of Ayobaí sat. They were in charge of the five main nocturnal species that called Ayobaí home; vampires, werewolves, werecats, incubi and succubi, and Shadow Wielders. There were also humans throughout who found they loved the darkness more than the light. The blubbering man child speaking was the human governor who oversaw his own night-loving people. Humans tended to forget that their life was miniscule and that Jacinto could easily replace him. The vampire leaned back, resting his elbow on the arm of the chair, rubbing his temple slightly.

"Who calls themselves King and allows—"

"Show some fucking respect, cabrón!" Jacinto didn't give the man time to speak before grabbing him by the collar and sinking his teeth into the bastards' neck and ripping out his larynx. Fuck it. He'll find someone new. He spat the organ out on the floor, not giving a damn that blood now dripped from his chin and onto his white tee.

The others sank farther into their seats. Each of them was frightening in their own right, but no one was more intimidating than Jacinto himself. Being the oldest at this table, he was also the strongest. But despite it all, he was a very good ruler and he would not tolerate anyone, especially humans, questioning him. He assessed each of his governors, having chosen all of them for their roles. The council consisted of two wereanimals, a succubus, and a Shadow Wielder,

His second in command, Cyrus, rounded them out as governor of the vampires. He was responsible for the more mundane tasks that Jacinto couldn't be bothered with. Always dressed like he had somewhere fancy to be, he was decked in his famous three-piece suit. Today he wore ivory with teal accents that made his ebony skin glow. His dark kinky hair was cropped close to his head. Despite the look, Jacinto knew he had at least two guns and a dagger on his person. Cyrus was the patient one of them both, but it didn't make him any less deadly. Having been a warrior before Jacinto turned him, and then being personally trained by Jacinto after, Cyrus was not one to fuck with.

"Your Eminence, how should we prepare for the Asherites?" Ericka's high, feminine voice rang like bells from the far end of the table. The succubus seemed dainty and quiet but that was part of her ploy when seducing her prey. She was by far one of the most powerful succubi he had ever met, and had proven herself over and over.

Jacinto wiped a thumb across his lips and grimaced, tasting the artery disease in the man's blood. Disgusting.

"Keep your barriers up. For the time being, limit travel. Only citizens can move through their own towns and territories." There was a grumble from Kayne who turned his black angular eyes to Jacinto. Jacinto's eyes flared, "Have something you'd like to share?"

"I think it's fucking reckless that we have to shut down our country when we can prevent the Asherites from landing at all." The Shadow Wielder replied, as he narrowed his angular eyes.

"Only a small team of Asherites are coming on shore. Any more, I'll personally make sure they die," came Cyrus's tenor voice from the end of the room.

"I have heard some rumors about this team. I'm interested in seeing if we can use them as assets." Jacinto looked at each person in the room. "I don't like this any more than you do. But if we blast them out of the water before they even touch our land, we're risking war with Asherai. Our people cannot suffer another war." The civil war with the deities had left Euhaven a torn planet and both continents worked hard to revive their cultures. If not for their peace, their people would've been wiped out.

"Why are they coming to Ayobaí? Is it because of the meteorite?" Lyra, werepanther and Weapons Master, wondered out loud.

Jacinto and Cyrus had kept the truth of the meteorite to themselves. According to the prophecy, the meteor was actually an Angel. He knew that if the Governors learned an Angel had crash landed, they'd be in an uproar. The economy would stop cold and he wouldn't risk that.

"They are seeking relief aid for the destruction of Melhold." He wasn't lying. The Monarch of Asherai had sent a message through their dark network. The Monarch had omitted the real reason they'd sent their team but Jacinto didn't call them out on it. Let them think they were safe. He would show otherwise.

"And why should we help them?"

Jacinto growled deep in his throat at Kayne's question. Kayne was privy to almost everything Jacinto knew except for the true reason for the Asherite visit. He knew exactly why they should help; he was just being pissy for feeling out of the loop.

"To keep the peace. Unless you want to see Euhaven destroyed for good?" Kayne shook his head, letting it go. Jacinto stood, everyone else followed suit. "You all know your orders. The goal is to enhance security, weed out any spies, and lock it down enough to alert the citizens, but not so much that they can't enjoy their sinful ways." He smirked at that last bit. The tension in the room seemed to lighten. He waited as they each filed out of the conference room and lifted his now red eyes to Cyrus. "I need a woman to fuck."

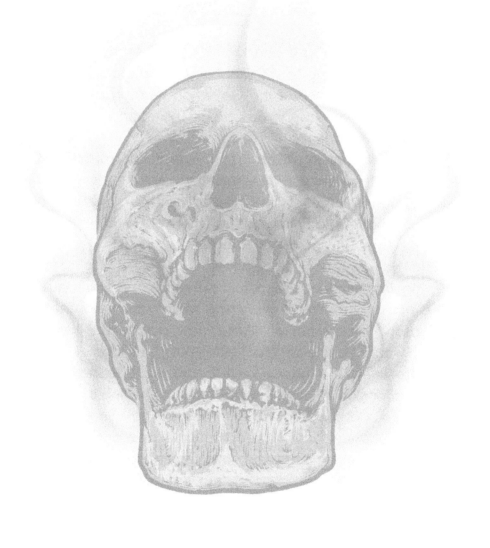

CHAPTER 11

XAVIA

XAVIA SLID HER AVIATORS ON, squinting at the bright sunny day. Despite trying to get some extra sleep, she still felt like hell. Her ass cheek throbbed where she had her birth control injection. Thankfully, Xavia only needed to get it done once every five years. Otherwise, she'd forget if they were in pill form. Children were not in her future. She refused to pass down her issues and trauma.

Xavia made her way across the quad, glaring at Aurelio. "Who calls for a mission start at six in the fucking morning?" she bitched, as she stopped in front of him.

Aurelio just chuckled, his chosen team of six–Alpha Phoenix–behind him. His team consisted of four men and two women, each from different parts of Asherai. They all wore the same tactical gear as Xavia and Aurelio but that is where their differences stopped. Her eyes narrowed as she caught sight of the male in front.

"You remember Quade, right?" Aurelio said in a neutral tone.

Oh, she remembered him alright. From the moment she met him at the Academy she didn't like him. He was an asshole and always seemed to have disdain for her. She rarely saw him over the years since. What she wasn't expecting was how he filled out in that time. He was taller than Aurelio by a head and had a body built for stealth and tussling. Quade's burnt sienna eyes reminded her of the sunset. Too bad he was a jerk, otherwise Xavia would've been interested in learning more about those eyes and body. Quade had a permanent glower on his face; resting asshole face. Where Aurelio had more muscle mass, Quade was leaner but no less muscular. She could see how cut he was through his shirt, even if the rest of him was covered in tactical gear. Xavia held back a grimace. She hated that he was so damn handsome for an asshole. Quade gave her a sneer as she looked him over.

"Yeah, I remember RAF over here," Xavia said with an eye roll. Aurelio lifted an eyebrow. "Resting asshole face," she clarified, earning a growl and a step forward from Quade. She didn't flinch. "Do it, I dare you." Her voice turned deadly. His nose flared, fire licking his eyes. Steam rolled off his arms, indicating he was fuming—quite literally. Aurelio moved his way in between the two to stop them from murdering each other and cleared his throat.

"This is the Alpha Phoenix. Luc, Ryland, Misha, Lilith, and Vivi." Each person gave Xavia a handshake. Each of them wore markings that explained where they were from and if they were a Wielder. They were all built for fighting.

Luc was a silent and serious type, wearing protective eyewear to filter all the light, UV, and other waves that he could see through the air. As a Light Wielder, he had pale beige skin, chin length rainbow hair and crystal blue eyes. The iridescent rainbow hair was a reflection of the primary colors that make up the prism of light. It always shifted and it was never the same pattern for too long. It was quite dazzling and Xavia found herself wanting to touch it. A pinch from Aurelio had her dropping her hand. She didn't even realize she lifted it.

Ryland was Luc's partner. Though he was shorter than the rest of the men, he seemed at ease with himself. He was an Earth Wielder. His skin was a deep bronze, with soil rich brown hair cut close to his scalp, and striking emerald eyes. Luc beamed at Ryland in a way that told Xavia the pair had been together for quite some time.

Misha and Vivi were twins and the only non-Wielders of the group. They both had tawny hair braided down their backs and hazel eyes. Misha was taller than his twin counterpart. They both had rich olive skin although Misha's complexion was slightly darker than Vivi's as if he spent more time in the sun than her. For whatever reason, Vivi clearly didn't like Xavia, and didn't hold back her sneer when she was introduced. Was it because Xavia was a bounty hunter? Xavia just gave her a snarky grin.

When Xavia was introduced to Lilith, she had to keep herself from gaping. Lilith was a stunning, tall, and shapely Shadow Wielder. Her ebony smooth skin practically shined in the sunlight. She was bald with tribal Wieldermarks on her scalp, and her stunning white eyes seemed to pierce right through Xavia. She couldn't help but shudder. Some stories said Shadow Wielders could see your very anima.

"Close your mouth, X," Aurelio's voice rumbled softly as he nudged her. She glared up at him but it was only half serious. She couldn't help but enjoy the beauty in front of her.

After pleasantries were made, Xavia turned to the two tactical jeeps before them. They were loaded with what looked like hiking gear and supplies. She lifted an eyebrow and looked puzzled as she turned to Aurelio. He gave her a look that told her she was not going to like what he was about to say.

"Alright team, here's the Dolsano Wood." A holographic map popped up from his watch, the beautiful wood cascading between Melhold and Silvermoon Harbor. It was large, and filled with hills and trees so tall that they could rival the skyscrapers of Melhold. Aurelio tapped the map and red orbs popped up all over the northeastern part of the Wood, each orb representing a company of ten. "These are where Aeshma and her demons are holed up. They somehow managed to erect a small fortress and camp. The worst part is that they're occupying the only road through the woods." Going by the orbs there were thousands of demons in the forest. Aurelio pointed to the southeastern part, where it seemed the demons were absent. "We will have to hike through the woods."

"What?!" Xavia could feel the blood leaving her face. "Are you fucking kidding me?" She was growing increasingly frustrated with this mission. Quade rolled his eyes and the rest of the team didn't seem bothered at all, but she guessed they wouldn't. This was probably a walk in the park for them. Aurelio scratched the back of his head in aggravation.

"We can't risk taking the road. The jeeps can take us about

twenty miles into the woods but we have to trek it the rest of the way." He sketched out a path on the map. "It'll take us three days to trek it, minimum." Xavia bit down her retort. "Let's get going. We need to get as much daylight as possible."

"Alright!" Xavia clapped before saying, "Let's go fuck this day in the mouth!" She earned a few laughs from Alpha Phoenix, a look of embarrassment from Aurelio, and a scowl from Quade. Of course the asshole couldn't take a joke.

The jeeps could only fit four people each, not including the driver. Aurelio put the twins, Ryland, and Luc in one jeep and Quade, Lilith, him and Xavia in the other. Xavia almost groaned loudly at the thought of Quade joining them. He walked past her and sneered as he got in the jeep. Xavia wanted to strangle him. The only saving grace was that the ebony beauty that was Lilith would be joining them.

THE DRIVE ITSELF WENT BY FAIRLY QUICKLY. The Dolsano was a good two hours from Melhold and then another half hour or so to give a head start into the woods. The ride would've been pleasant had it not been for Quade. He paid her no mind as he went over the details of the mission with Aurelio, and made a comment about why bounty hunters were not the wise choice to bring along. He was trying to get a rise out of Xavia. She wanted to punch him in his perfect teeth and tell him to shut the fuck up. Instead, she leaned her head back and let herself catch some sleep.

Xavia woke with a start as the jeep came to a halt. She found Quade's burnt sienna eyes on her. He had his arms crossed, waiting for everyone to file out of the jeep, her included. She narrowed her eyes at him and gave him the finger as she stepped past him.

"Sleep well princess?" Quade hissed in her ear as he came out behind her. He was a little too close for comfort, making the hair on her arms stand up. She knew he was dangerous and from what

Aurelio had told her of him—logically—she knew that she shouldn't test him. But she couldn't help herself.

"Enjoyed day dreaming about me?" she asked with a smirk. His eyes flared with fire as he pushed past her. Everyone else filed out and started packing on their gear. Aurelio opted for a collapsible bow to keep his back free, however, Xavia was *not* giving up her swords, so she opted to put them in belt sheaths for the time being.

She buckled the harnesses of the large backpacks around her torso and grunted when one of them snagged. Aurelio stepped up to her with a smirk on his face. Sometimes she wanted to just slap him upside his head and see if he'd continue smirking.

"Need help, X?" That had been her nickname since the Academy. Sometimes she hated it, especially in moments like this, where Xavia couldn't figure something out and needed Aurelio's help, but wouldn't ask until he noticed. After nodding, he took hold of the harness, pulling her close as he worked to fix the buckle. Her face flushed at their proximity.

Once upon a time, they thought they'd actually make a life together, but Xavia couldn't do it. Her past brought up too much baggage and she couldn't find it in herself to commit. However, Aurelio still managed to find ways to fluster her. Like this was all a permanent tease as punishment for not committing all those years ago.

"You can shoot a target with the naked eye from miles away but still can't figure out a buckle?" His chuckle rumbled through her, making her skin pebble.

"The target is easy." She grumbled. The buckle was stuck to Xavia's shirt, just above the vest and at the mounds of her breasts. The heat of Aurelio's hands brushing the tops of her breasts seared through her skin. He seemed intent on fixing it, biting his lower lip as he always did when he concentrated. Dimples. Holy Tomis, those dimples. Xavia wondered if Aurelio knew what he was doing or if he did it on purpose. Memories of those hands on her in more intimate places hit her like a slap. *The fuck?* She thought to herself. She shook her head, hoping to shake the thoughts that played handball in her mind.

Xavia must've done a number on the buckle, which shouldn't be surprising considering she always had trouble with these things. Her brain worked differently than others and she was grateful that Aurelio understood that. His hands slowed as he got done with fixing the buckle but they lingered as he raised his eyes to meet hers. They were so close that their chests were lightly touching. Despite maintaining a pretty decent friendship over the years, Xavia knew she'd broken his heart, and she could see the lingering of emotion in Aurelio's eyes. She pulled out of his hold, nodding her thanks, and turning from him. Guilt and shame had no place here, not right now.

"Alright, let's go!" Aurelio's voice boomed and everyone fell into line. They agreed that Aurelio and Xavia would take the front, with the rest filing behind and Quade at the rear.

Xavia faced the massive woods in front of them with awe. It was her first time seeing the almost ethereal woods in person. The leaves of the trees were mixed colors of teal, turquoise, golds, and red. Insects of all kinds were fluttering or crawling about. The largest birds she'd ever seen flew high above, perching on a tall tree here and there.

"Those are scavengers. If you see a swarm of them, steer away. Most like there's something dead nearby," Aurelio mentioned. A small shudder made its way through her. Oh joy, what a way to suck the beauty out of this wondrous place.

Thankfully, they were able to hike for a few hours undisturbed. They would stop occassionally to catch a breath, drink some water, and eat. But they didn't stop for long. They had to make the most out of the daytime hours. Her legs were burning by the time they arrived at their campsite.

"Alright, let's camp here."

The sun had set and the moon and Ithea appeared in the sky. Misha and Vivi scouted the area beforehand to make sure it was secure. Luc, tech genius and explosives extraordinaire, set up a perimeter with motion sensors and small bombs that would light up if something trespassed that wasn't supposed to. Each of them took off their packs, Xavia struggling with the damn buckle again. Before Aurelio could help, Quade walked past her and flicked the buckle so it would unlock. He rolled his eyes when she scowled at him.

"Each of us has half of a tent to combine with someone else for one full tent. It is too much of a risk for everyone to have their own tent." Aurelio looked to Xavia and to her dismay, he said, "Xavia and I will pair up. Quade and Lilith. Luc and Ryland. Misha and Vivi. One person stays up for half the night while the other sleeps and then switch." He was not taking any chances.

They went to work setting up the tents, the center of the camp set up with chairs all around so they could eat together. Xavia watched as Ryland and Luc worked together, smiling and stealing glances. It made her heart clench in envy. She'd always known that having any kind of long-term relationship would never work out. But she couldn't say she'd never dreamed of it or thought about it.

"I'll get the food going," Ryland said as he started to pull out a portable grill, pot, and utensils. Apparently, from the reactions of the others, he was a pretty good cook and Xavia couldn't wait to see what he would whip up. Xavia was a thick woman for a reason; she loved food and food loved her. She wasn't ashamed about it either. Aurelio often joked about how she could out eat him in a hot dog contest. It was true. It had happened. They agreed to never speak about it again. Her stomach was *not* happy with her after that fiasco.

Xavia huffed a sigh, her back and shoulders sore from the bag. She might have trained for this in the past, but in no way did she utilize it in her career. A bounty hunter did not need to hike through the woods for days at a time. She hadn't done this much hiking in years. Xavia knew she was going to feel it in the morning. She noticed how sticky she was so she made her way to the tent she now shared with Aurelio and stepped inside without paying attention.

"So, what do you think Ryland is going to c—" She was cut off by the sight of Aurelio shirtless. He had been in the middle of changing and she couldn't help but give him a once over. It was like looking at him for the first time all over again, as if she'd never seen him naked before. He had built so much muscle over the last eight years he'd been with the Special Forces. The scar over his right eye was fairly new. It happened on one of his ops but he never explained to her what exactly happened. To be honest, it made him hotter but she would never tell him that.

His Storm Wieldermarks swirled in grey and white, depicting a hurricane covered over his right pectoral, storm clouds that formed a tornado wisping from his neck down his shoulder and over his bicep, and ended in a snowstorm that encompassed his forearm. Aurelio's dark brown muscled abs turned into a V above his belt and Xavia snapped her eyes up as he rushed to put his shirt on. He rubbed the back of his head with a smirk on his lips, dimples digging into his cheeks. He made it perfectly clear that he knew she enjoyed the view.

"Ah, sorry," Xavia mumbled before going to her bag to dig out a clean tank and some portable shower wipes to clean herself up. "I can come back when you're done." She made to leave when Aurelio caught her wrist, turning her slowly. She looked up at him he had a good foot in height over her. His eyes were stormy, like rain clouds ready to burst. His eyes dipped to Xavia's lips and slowly back up. She could only blink very slowly, trying her hardest to not lick her lips. When did the tent get so hot? Aurelio let her go, taking a step away.

"I'm done," he said gently. He ruffled her hair, which made her yelp and smack his arm. He left the tent chuckling and she stood there waiting for her body to cool down. *Shit.*

AURELIO

HE KNEW HE FUCKED UP ASSIGNING Xavia to share a tent with him when she walked in on him changing his shirt. The way her brown eyes darkened, almost black, when she saw him made him want to shift his pants but knew he couldn't with her looking. Xavia drove her eyes all over him, like she could see his anima. Aurelio knew she enjoyed the view. But Xavia didn't notice him taking her in as much as she was him.

Over the years, Aurelio noticed that her figure got shapelier as she became more comfortable with who she was. Coming out of that terrible relationship with her vicious ex left her thin and frail. It was clear Xavia had never eaten a full meal when she was with the asshole. But as time went on and she worked on healing, she regained her health and weight. She had curves for days; thick thighs, hips, ass, breasts, stomach. All of it wrapped up in golden tan skin. Her only downfalls were her temper and her drinking. Memories of their nights spent naked plagued his mind. Aurelio got a handle on himself as he left the tent and smelled something delicious.

"I've got a stew going," Ryland announced. Most of the others were cleaned up, wearing tanks or shirts, and their tactical pants. They could never be too cautious, especially out in these woods; each of them sported a gun at their side. Aurelio's stomach growled in response to the tantalizing smells coming from the pot that Ryland was stirring.

"It smells amazing," Xavia said as she came out of the tent. She wore a tank that hugged her body and did nothing to hide her cleavage. He couldn't help but notice the way Quade was looking at her as well. It was almost predatory, and his eyes flared so quickly that if Aurelio wasn't looking, he'd have missed it.

"You can stop staring now," Xavia quipped to Quade as she sat down. Aurelio bit back a snort as Quade narrowed those eyes at her. Xavia was right—he did have a resting asshole face.

"And what will you do if I don't?" Quade sat forward, leaning his elbows on his knees. He was baiting her. Aurelio didn't know why, but Quade was baiting her. Quade's lips turned up in a dark grin. "You're nothing but a bounty hunter. Nothing exceptional about you, despite how hard you try."

He opened his mouth to say something else when his head snapped back. Xavia had thrown a rock that hit him square between the eyes. She'd barely moved, showing just how exceptional she could be. It was a rarity for Quade to be caught off guard. He jumped to his feet, fire bursting from his hands as if he was about to fry her, when lightning struck nearby making everyone jump. Aurelio gave him a death stare that said *don't even try it*. Quade reined himself in and stormed off to his tent.

"Now that's the kind of woman I want at my back," Lilith chuckled, her South Asherai accent thick and lovely. Xavia gave her a smirk with a wink and Aurelio could've sworn Lilith took a moment to remember how to breathe. Nothing ever affected Lilith. Damn Xavia and her seductive skills.

"Food's ready!" Ryland handed everyone a bowl with some sort of potato and chicken stew in it. And naturally it was delicious. They all fought many battles together and they were always thankful that Ryland knew his way around a kitchen. Otherwise, they'd be eating oats and protein bars the entire time. They sat around for a bit, talking shit and all that, and then went about to handle personal matters before turning in for the night.

"I can take first watch," Xavia said as he stepped into the tent. She was lounging on her cot, tablet in her hand and probably reading. It surprised him when he found out she actually enjoyed reading, considering her other recreational indulgences. He grunted as he sat on his own cot, rolling his shoulders.

"Nah it's ok. I'll go first," Aurelio murmured, although exhaustion was weighing on him. Xavia gave him a look that told him to lay down. "Mmk. You win." She smirked as she stepped out of the tent to sit with the others who were on first watch. He huffed as he laid down and let sleep claim him.

CHAPTER 12

QUADE

THE NEXT DAY, QUADE WAS UP RIGHT as dawn crested the sky. He'd always been a morning person. It didn't matter how little sleep he had he was up to watch the sun meet the sky. Being a Fire Wielder, Quade had a special connection to the ball of fire. Oddly enough, it helped him quell the rage that often lived under the surface of his skin.

The camp was quiet as he drank his tea. Coffee was an abomination, never having been something he enjoyed drinking. Grimacing at the thought, he made his way around the camp to check on the others. The second shift had popped back into their tents to wake their partners; the sounds of the camp stirring ruined his peace.

Ryland was the first to pop his head out of the tent, carrying containers of food to make breakfast. The Earth Wielder was an amazing cook and Quade was grateful for it. Cooking was not a skill of his. He could live off peanut butter and jelly sandwiches if it wasn't so destructive to his health.

"Morning Q," Ryland said with a smile. Luc followed Ryland, sitting next to him, thighs touching. The two smiled at each other, Luc's rainbow hair shifting to a lighter hue. Ryland gave him a loving kiss, making Quade shift uncomfortably and look away briefly.

Ryland's emerald eyes glowed as he pulled some roots up from the earth to hold a pot over a portable stove. Folding chairs surrounded the makeshift fire pit. The stove was fire-powered but Wielded to keep smoke from escaping by sucking it out the air. It was an odd contraption, and a bit outdated, but Ryland refused to use an electric stove. He said it ruined the taste of the food, whatever that meant.

"Need a light?" Quade said as he snapped his finger and a flame popped up in between them. The flame floated to the stove, Ryland nodding in gratitude.

"We're going to do some scouting before we head out. Want to come?" Lilith said to Quade as she exited Misha and Vivi's tent. Scouting was not something he enjoyed doing. Torture and interrogation was more his thing. He opened his mouth to respond when he heard a bark of laughter, Aurelio and Xavia exiting their camp.

"Stop bitching. You're gonna have to get up early every day." Aurelio said to Xavia. Of course she wasn't a morning person. Quade was *not* surprised.

"I can bitch if I want to. I hate this shit," she grumbled, going for the coffee that Ryland started.

"So go home," Quade snapped, annoyed. Glowering, Xavia gave him the finger before filling a tumbler with a shit ton of coffee and a dash of cream. How much caffeine did she need?

"It's too early for this shit," Aurelio grumbled, taking a soup mug from Ryland. "What do we have here?" Smelling the contents with a contented sigh, Aurelio plopped down next to Ryland.

"Maple and cinnamon porridge. There are berries if you want them." Summoned by Ryland, a berry bush popped up from the ground. Quade took the mug offered to him plus some berries. As everyone else found a seat first, Quade gritted his teeth when the only remaining seat was next to Xavia. A sneer came across his face as he sat down and she returned it.

"Fucking children..." Aurelio mumbled.

Quade found it hard to focus on his food, practically thrumming with the need to move away from Xavia. There was an odd gravitational pull that he did not feel comfortable with. As everyone wrapped up, Quade was first to get up, taking everyone's mugs to clean them. A hand clapped his shoulder, making him bristle. With a raised eyebrow, he turned to Aurelio.

"We need to go over the prophecy," Aurelio said, motioning to a table that was set up with three chairs. Considering Ryland and Luc were breaking down the tents and packing equipment and Lilith, Vivi, and Micah had left for scouting, Quade could only guess who the third seat was for.

"And by we you mean..." Quade said dryly.

"Aw what's wrong, RAF? Don't want to see my pretty face?" said the Queen Bitch. Eyes narrowing, Quade stormed up to her.

"More like I want to see you on the ground after I fuck you up," he growled, smoke rising from his hands, the taste of it on his tongue. Quade was not naturally inclined to be physically violent to women—unless they asked. However, Xavia seemed to get under his skin. Not only did she tear his brother apart over the course of twelve years, she was a fucking menace. Her attitude and the way she held herself was unlike anything he ever encountered in a woman.

Perhaps it was because she reminded Quade of himself. All fire, all fury, and full of chaos. Despite it all, Xavia could keep a smile on her face while he had a permanent scowl. He wasn't sure how he felt about that. Emotions were hard for him to process. All he knew was that he couldn't help but fall for her goading every single time, and it pissed him off. The feeling of being out of control did not sit well with him.

Xavia gave him a baleful glare, opening her mouth to respond when Aurelio pulled them apart.

"Can we not?" he snapped, pointing at the table as if they were petulant children. Crossing her arms over her ample breasts, Xavia parked it in a chair, looking every bit a child. Her bratty nature was going to be a problem. Resisting the urge to take her down a notch drove him nuts. As they sat across from each other, Xavia's glare answered Quade's scowl.

"Let's act like responsible adults. We have too much shit to deal with," said Aurelio as he dropped a hologram comm on the table. The pieces of the prophecy hovered above the table, a disorganized mess. Xavia made quick work of organizing it like it was a puzzle that only she could figure out. Quade's nose flared in annoyance. Was she actually smart?

"It looks like there's a part missing. When the Monarch said they had pieces of the Prophecy, I assumed they meant it was torn, not that a whole part was missing," she murmured. Quade felt left out and it brought a simmer of frustration under his skin.

"Want to tell me about this prophecy or am I just here to look stupid?" Wincing, Quade realized he set himself up.

"Yes. That's exactly what you're here for," Xavia quipped.

"You set yourself up for that one," Aurelio snorted.

"Then I'll go be stupid somewhere else." Quade went to stand but the Storm Wielder held out a hand, clearly trying not to laugh. It pissed him off more.

"No. We need you." Aurelio's body shook with barely contained amusement.

"No, *Aurelio* needs you. I don't give a fuck." Grinning, Xavia raised an eyebrow, seeing if Quade was going to take the bait. He bit his lip, taking all his restraint to keep from reacting. Xavia's eyes flicked to his lips before quickly turning back to the Prophecy. What the fuck was that?

"What *do* you need me for?" Quade muttered, turning his eyes from Xavia to the Prophecy. He leaned in, looking at the ancient language that was quite poorly transcribed. "That's ancient Angelic." He took no little joy in hearing Xavia's squeak of surprise. "Yes brat, I'm a linguist."

Aurelio snorted, Xavia slapping him on the arm. Who's laughing now?

"As you can see, we need your assistance with making sure this is translated correctly. I didn't want to do it back at the Monarch Tower. I'm not exactly sure I trust them to give us all the details."

Quade's linguistics skills came naturally and made him an asset for Special Forces. Being able to speak virtually every language in Euhaven was the reason he had been elevated to Second to Aurelio. Interrogations went much smoother without a language barrier. Plus it made torture fun because prisoners were always surprised that an Asherite spoke their tongue. There was no way to bullshit.

Quade zoomed in, trying to make sense of the scribbled

language. Being one of the oldest languages on Euhaven, Angelic was notoriously mistranslated. The glyphs often represented letters or sayings that were no longer in the common alphabet. Quade spent the better part of two years getting familiar enough with the language to speak it.

"Roughly, it says that 'The Angel of Wrath will return to Euhaven to seek revenge on those who jailed her.'" Xavia's eyes weighed on him. Trying to ignore her dark brown eyes, he continued, "the Angel of Wrath, Aeshma, was confined to a prison created by the Deities. This prison was supposed to be unbreakable, but Aeshma will find a way out and bring her horde with her." Using colloquial language was usually best when translating. It never went well when he translated exactly how the text was written.

Before he could continue, Xavia interrupted him.

"Does it say anything about The Chaos Wielder?" Her eyes were still trained on Quade. He raised an eyebrow, taking a deep breath and welcoming the taste of smoke in his mouth.

"If you'd let me finish, I could tell you," he said, tightly. When Xavia rolled her eyes, Quade almost lost it. Her attitude was going to get her killed one day and he would be surprised if it wasn't by his hands. She waved her hands as if to signal him to continue. Quade could feel his eye twitching as he turned back to the Prophecy.

"There is a piece missing between the coming of Aeshma and the mention of the Chaos Wielder." He rearranged the pieces just slightly, Xavia having almost put it together perfectly. "After the mention of Aeshma's return, there is an incomplete sentence." He pointed to a piece where it showed a shadow of an Angel hovering above a mountain. A horde of what looked like demons surrounded the base. "'The Angel shall be joined in power by...' And it leaves off there. The question is, what power will she be joined with and what does it mean?" He was more talking to himself as he tried to wrap his brain around it.

Xavia opened her mouth but Quade pressed on, "And," he said loudly, becoming increasingly irritated by the minute, "here it says, 'then the Chaos Wielder, the strongest of them all, shall end them. The Dark Continent is where they will call home.'" The image of the Chaos Wielder was striking. It was evident why it was rumored that the Chaos Wielder was the most powerful Wielder in Euhaven. "It ends there."

"That's it?" Xavia snapped at him. "So we know Aeshma has invaded Euhaven, but we don't know about this power she's supposed to be joined with." She paused. "Joined? Is that the right word? Are you sure it's not combined?" A smug look came over her face. Quade cracked his neck, looking back at the Prophecy.

"Yes… It says Aeshma will combine her powers." As the smoke curled off his hands, Xavia grinned at him. "It was one misread. Care to read it yourself?" he snapped. Her smile grew and he figured she was goading him. Flame licked between his fingers, tempted to shoot a flame and wipe that stupid grin off her face.

"The Dark Continent is huge. Saying the Chaos Wielder finds it home doesn't exactly mean they're in Malagado," Aurelio murmured, inserting himself into the conversation. A cool breeze brushed against Quade's face, helping his temperament. Looking to Aurelio with gratitude, he dissipated the flames in his hands.

"I think the Monarch is either not telling us something or just flat out guessing at this point," Xavia grumbled as she stood and stretched her back. Quade took a good look at how her thick curves moved and snapped his eyes to the hologram.

"That may be possible. For now, we follow the mission and see where it takes us." Aurelio nodded to the team that returned from their scouting. "Let's get going."

CHAPTER 13

XAVIA

THE NEXT NIGHT, XAVIA WOKE WITH a start, when a hand clamped over her mouth. She pulled her gun before she realized who it was. Aurelio held up a hand, signaling her to stay quiet. She nodded and he released her.

Something triggered the detectors but not the bombs, he mouthed to her. Her eyes widened. How was that even possible? Aurelio moved quietly and grabbed his bow and slung the quill full of arrows on his back. His bow unclasped silently and he strung a grenade bomb arrow. He motioned Xavia to flank him as he knelt low and peeled back the tent opening just slightly. Xavia peered over his shoulder to get a better look.

What she saw was not at all what she expected. Among the tents was a dense fog, making its way as if searching for something. Those on watch had gone to warn the others, so the common area was empty. Figures moved on the outside of the perimeter and Xavia figured they must've been controlling the fog somehow. The fog made its way into Luc and Ryland's tent.

There was a heartbeat of silence before Luc stumbled out of the tent, frantically patting his body. Ryland followed soon after. A burst of light flared as Luc lost control of his Wielding. Aurelio tried to signal them to stay put but they were too wrapped up in what was going on around them to realize what was waiting on the outskirts of the camp.

"Get it off! Get it out of me!" Luc yelled frantically. Ryland looked puzzled.

"What are you talking about? Luc, you're freaking me out." He reached for Luc but his partner shook his head violently, starting to mumble incoherently. The others peered out of their tents, weapons at the ready. Suddenly, Luc took off at a run toward the perimeter.

"Luc, no!" Ryland ran after him. Aurelio burst out of the tent, the others following suit. He held the arrow up to Luc, who was closing in on the figures on the outside perimeter.

"Luc! If you don't stop, I'll be forced to stop you!" Aurelio shouted. Luc stopped, almost as if fighting himself. He shook his head again as he inched closer to the perimeter. All it would take was Luc's hand touching the line to temporarily disable it. The surrounding air glimmered as he tried to Wield light. The colors in his hair faded to a paler shade, as if the color drained from it.

"Shit," Aurelio muttered, quickly changing his arrow to a regular steel-tipped one and aiming at Luc's calf. "Turn around. Turn around," he muttered so softly that only Xavia could hear. She hoped Luc would turn, but dread told her he wouldn't. Quade was holding Ryland back when Aurelio let the arrow fly, the point slicing clear through Luc's calf. Luc let out a cry.

"Fuck!" Quade yelped as a tree branch snapped across his face. Ryland started for Luc and time seemed to slow down. As Luc fell, he jolted his body forward just enough so that as he hit the ground face first, his hand barely crossed the perimeter. Light flared around the campsite, temporarily blinding everyone. Then the perimeter dropped and chaos rained down on the camp.*

Xavia balked as she watched everything unfold. The five figures on the perimeter moved forward menacingly, and it was as if she could feel the evil radiating off them from the distance. They wore what looked like tattered red hoodie sweaters with black tactical vests underneath and leather shoulder cuffs. Black leather gloves covered their hands, and gauntlets encompassed their forearms. Vital signs and other weird tech lit up their gauntlets. Their cargo pants fit into large combat boots.

♪ "The Beautiful People" by Marilyn Manson

What bothered her the most were the metallic skull masks that obscured their faces. They must have had a breathing apparatus because she could hear the rasping coming from the masks. There was no way they were human.

One of these metallic masked creatures stepped up to Luc, who was trembling and trying to go for his gun. Having an arrow in his calf wasn't helping his case. He seemed to be out of whatever trance he was in. The light around him flared as he attempted to blind the creature before the light was quickly snuffed out.

Xavia held back a scream as the thing slowly stepped down on Luc's head. Everyone seemed frozen as the boot made its way down, snapping his skull as if squishing a grape. Ryland had screamed, pulling out his guns, but he was not fast enough as the creature kept pushing down until Luc's head cracked open with a sickening crunch. Blood spilled out of his mouth as his eyes popped from the pressure. Xavia gagged as she watched the brain matter leak out of his now crushed skull and coated the large boot that had just done the damage. All of this spanned the course of a minute, but felt like hours. She'd seen a lot of things in her lifetime, but nothing ever like this.

Gun fire brought her back from the devastation. Misha and Vivi shot at the creatures several times but barely made a dent. The creatures broke out into a run toward them, going impossibly fast. Xavia let out a yell as she charged toward them, ducking as one of the monsters swung its foot at her head. It would've surely cracked her head open with its massive boot. She dove into a roll to gain distance before turning toward the tall creature. She threw out a kick but it moved fast enough that she couldn't connect. The thing landed a punch to her gut and she stumbled backward. Xavia did a kick-up, sinking into a fighting stance. Her katanas sang as she pulled them from their sheaths and held one up and the other low, squaring off with the thing.

Moving faster than Xavia was prepared for, the entity appeared in front of her, hand reaching for her throat. She brought one of her swords up and the creature locked the blade in its gauntlets, making an X across its chest. She smirked as she feigned trying to pull away which caused the figure to loosen its hold on the blade ever so slightly. It was enough space for Xavia to force the blade through the space between the vest and mask and into its throat. The thing screeched, ringing her ears like a kettle drum, as she pulled the blade to the left, half decapitating the monster. Before it could react, she sliced with her other sword, cutting through the remaining half of its neck. It sprayed black blood that reeked like carrion all over Xavia, and she gagged at the smell.

Wielding lit up everywhere. Fire, coiled like chains, flared around Quade's forearms as he whipped them across another creature's torso. The creature screeched before moving so fast that she would've missed it if she wasn't looking. It popped up in front of Quade, ramming a fist into his face, causing him to stumble back. His fire stuttered briefly and the being took the opening to lay a kick to his side. The sound of his ribs cracking could be heard across the camp as he toppled over. The monster attempted another kick but Quade let a ball of fire escape his hands, pushing it back. It obviously didn't like fire, howling at the contact. Quade caught on quickly and ran at the entity, fire encompassing his hands as he threw blow after blow. Xavia had to admit the man could fight. Quade slipped behind the beast, back-to-back, and wrapped a chain of fire around the thing's neck. He put weight on the chain, snapping the creature's neck over his shoulder. Quade roared as his fire sliced through the thing's neck.

Another one crept out from behind Quade. A small grenade erupted as Vivi threw it at the creature. It screeched as its leg caught fire and made to run toward her. She hurled another grenade at it, followed by a pop of her gun to make the bomb explode midair. The creature ran right through the explosion, its torso catching flame. Xavia's ears felt like they could bleed at the sound that came from its mouth. The monster managed to dodge a flame ball from Quade but stopped dead, looking around itself as if confused when shadows made their way up the creature's body.

Lilith appeared from a cluster of darkness, thrusting her shadows toward the creature and weaving them into its mask. It made sickly gagging sounds as it became clear that the shadows were making their way down its throat and suffocating it. It landed on its knees with a thud and Xavia bolted her way over to cut off its head. Three down. Two left.

Xavia whipped her head around at Ryland's guttural roar, as he went for the creature that killed his love. Using his Earth Wielding, he uplifted vines and roots, trapping the creature. Misha was quick on his heels to offer support. The both of them worked to bring down the monster in front of them. Ryland managed to spear the thing through its torso, causing it to squirm but not die. Xavia followed his thought process. Keep one alive to ask questions. Ryland wrapped the thing in more vines and roots to keep it from getting free.

Misha evidently didn't get the memo, because he went to slice its neck with his machete before he was forced to stop. He looked down in shocked confusion. The thing's gauntlet had fallen off; black claws now embedded in Misha's torso. Ryland grabbed hold of him and pulled him from the claws, blood pouring from the wounds.

Storm clouds began to swirl and collect overhead, cracking open to let a torrential downpour wash over them all. Thunder boomed and lightning crashed, just narrowly missing the last creature. It faced off with Aurelio, snarling under its mask. It made a beeline for him, tackling Aurelio and clasping its arms around his torso, taking them both down to the ground. The ground slowly turned into mud making them both slip as they wrestled each other. The creature managed to sucker punch Aurelio in the ribs before punching him again in the face. Xavia couldn't hold back her gasp of surprise when Aurelio wrapped his legs around the creature's waist and then hoisted—literally hoisted—the thing over his head. What the fuck? She'd never seen him fight in this sort of capacity. They'd only ever sparred but kept their careers separate. It held her captive, watching the scene unfold before her.

Aurelio grappled with the creature, managing to get on top of it and pulled down lighting to hit it square in the chest. The thing let out one of those awful screeches as the smell of burned carrion made her eyes water. It bucked, throwing Aurelio off of it , and moved with blinding speed, gripping him by the throat and standing. Aurelio grunted as the thing kept hold. Thunder shook the ground as lightning struck next to the creature. However, the creature was prepared this time and dodged the bolt. Xavia could see that Aurelio was starting to lose consciousness, the rain slowing.

Xavia! Do something! A loud voice shouted in her head, startling her. Great, now she was talking to herself. The creature had its back to her so it didn't see her as she ran toward it, leapt into the air, and swung at it with her katana. She landed with a roll at the same time as the thing's head hit the ground with a soft thud. Aurelio dropped from its hand and crumpled on the ground. Xavia slid in the mud as she crawled to him. He wasn't breathing.

"No, fuck, no!" she yelled. Placing her fingers at his carotid, she sucked in a gasp when she didn't feel a pulse. Gently, Xavia tilted Aurelio's head back, opening his mouth to check his airway. Pinching his nose, she breathed into his mouth to force in air to expand his lungs. She began pumping on his chest, counting as she did so. There was no way she was going to lose her only friend, her best friend. Xavia was about to repeat the process before Aurelio gasped and gulped down air. Thankfully Wielders were made of tougher stuff. Had he been human, he likely would've died. His pupils were blown but he regained consciousness as his stormy eyes looked to her, a small smirk on his face.

"Thanks," he said before he promptly passed out.

CHAPTER 14

AURELIO

A THROB ECHOED THROUGH AURELIO'S skull as if someone played a drum on his brain. For a moment, he forgot what happened before it dawned on him. He attempted to sit up but his body said 'NOPE.' He found he was on the cot in his tent. A sharp pain lanced through his side as he took a deep breath, and he quickly realized that he had a few fractured ribs.

Xavia sat next to him, keeping watch. Her knee bobbed up and down, her forefinger and thumb tapping against each other. A tick she did when she was on the verge of a panic attack. All the color had drained from her face and she looked exhausted. She was so focused on the entrance that she didn't even seem to notice he was awake. Her body shook and her eyes darted around.

"Hey," Aurelio rasped. His throat was on fire. Oh, right. One of those creature things had choked him out. Xavia jumped and turned to him. Silver lined her eyes, so she tilted her head up as if to not let the tears fall. Aurelio slogged his way to sitting and swung his feet off the cot. It dawned upon him she'd never seen death up close, except only once in her life. Xavia was shell-shocked.

Aurelio put his hands on her knees to turn her toward him.

"Look at me." The words came out gruff because of his sore throat. He'd have to take something for the pain. Xavia refused to look at him even as her body shook harder. He took her chin between his thumb and forefinger and forced her to look at him. As soon as their eyes met, her breath hitched before she started sobbing. Aurelio pulled her into a hug, practically pulling her onto his lap. His ribs screamed at him, but he held her tighter.

"I thought you died!" Xavia sobbed into his shoulder. "Luc..." she whispered. Her body continued to tremble. "I don't know what I'd do if you died." She sobbed as she gripped his shoulders as if he'd disappear. Aurelio rubbed her back, the smell of tears and hibiscus filling his nose. "You're not supposed to die!" She punched him in the shoulder but it was deflated, no strength in it at all. "If you die, I'll kill you." Xavia rasped, voice now raw from her sobs.

He cradled her, putting his forehead on hers, and breathed in and out, slowly. Soon enough, she mimicked his breathing, looking at him and rubbing her nose against his. Aurelio knew she needed soothing and closeness to help bring her down from an episode.

"Wouldn't killing me defeat the purpose?"

Xavia snorted and attempted to hit him again when he caught her wrist. Her brown eyes were red and puffy from her tears. Aurelio dropped his forehead back to hers.

"I'm here. I'm alive," he whispered. She let out a breath as he ran the backs of his hands over her cheeks to wipe away her tears. Xavia leaned into his touch before standing up abruptly. She shook her hands as she tried to shake out the rest of her nerves. Aurelio let her pace. He knew she hated to cry because it made her feel vulnerable. She always turned inward and scolded herself for something she thought was a weakness.

"I don't think I can do this." Xavia's voice was panicked. "This is way out of my realm."

Shit, she was spiraling again. Aurelio stood up slowly, moving toward her.

"Xavia..."

She put up a hand to quiet him and shook her head. Aurelio narrowed his eyes.

"Xavia," he said, with authority in his voice that he never used with her, only as a Captain to his team. Xavia stopped pacing and snapped her head to him, eyebrow raising. There it was. He needed her to snap out of her spiral and he only knew one way to do that. "You will not run away from this. You will suck it the fuck up and continue on."

Aurelio could practically see the smoke coming out of her ears as she started to fume. Xavia opened her mouth to say something but he cut her off.

"You have a job to do. Don't fuck this up because you're a punk." Bingo! His head snapped back from the ferocity of her punch. Aurelio chuckled as he spit out blood from a now split lip.

"You asshole!" Xavia looked murderous and hot as fuck. "I am not a fucking punk." Before he could stop her, she snatched his shirt as if to shake him. He couldn't help but wince, his ribs screaming again. Xavia dropped her hand, anger fizzling out.

"Oh shit! I forgot." She moved quickly to grab an ice pack and tried to get him to sit back down. "Sit…" she grumbled.

Aurelio shook his head, taking the ice pack and holding it to his side. A loud screech interrupted his thoughts. His eyes widened as she said, "Ryland caught one. We were hoping to get some answers but either it doesn't talk or it's feigning ignorance."

Xavia shuddered. Aurelio patted her shoulder and made to leave, motioning for her to go first but she shook her head. "Nope. Y'all can deal with that all by yourselves." She laid down on her cot and closed her eyes. It was clear she'd stayed up all night to make sure he was ok.

"Alright. Get some rest. I'll let you know what we learn." Aurelio stepped out of the tent, the bright sunlight blinding. He followed the sounds of torture and found Ryland spearing the creature with a tree root, a murderous look in his eyes. He recognized the creature as the one who had killed Luc. Vivi was also there, with an equally murderous look, although Aurelio didn't know why. He didn't see anyone else and he figured they were either resting or starting to pack up. They couldn't stay here for long.

"Talk to me. What's up?" he said, before Ryland and Vivi noticed him. Both of them let out a deep sigh, relief filling their features.

"Hey Captain," Ryland said as he patted him on the shoulder. Ryland and Vivi both looked thoroughly exhausted. Ryland's eyes were red, shadows underneath, and he looked worn through. Vivi had a haunted look about her, which told him something happened that he'd missed.

"So, is it talking at all?" He walked toward the speared creature. Its hands had been cut off and black blood seeped from its open wounds. Aurelio grimaced at the smell coming off the thing. "There's no way this is human."

Ryland and Vivi nodded in agreement. Aurelio made his way around, taking in all the details. If it weren't for the mask and the black blood, he would've thought it was human, Wielder, or at least male of some sort. He stood in front of it, the thing rasping through its mask.

A thought occurred to him as he looked at Vivi. "Have you taken off its mask at all?"

"No. That never occurred to us," she admitted, eyes darkening with frustration. The thing jolted its head back when Aurelio made for the mask. "Does it need it to breathe, you think?"

Aurelio reached out again and the thing hissed. He smirked darkly.

"I am starting to think so," he said, before snatching the mask but not removing it. He held on as the thing tried to get free. "I wonder what would happen if I were to take this off." His voice was deadly, thunder rumbling overhead. The thing froze.

"Stop," it wheezed. Through the breather it sounded raspy and guttural. "Do not remove my mask."

Letting go, Aurelio lifted an eyebrow, hiding the wince as he crossed his arms. "Tell me why I shouldn't after you killed one of my Guards?"

"And maimed another..." Vivi hissed. Aurelio's nostrils flared, now understanding why she was a part of the torture. Something must have happened to Misha. He made to pull the mask off as the thing let out a screech. The three of them grimaced at the sound.

"What do you wish to know?" it rasped through its ventilator.

"What are you?" Aurelio snapped, hand back on the mask.

"Not of human flesh."

"No shit. What. Are. You?" he growled.

"Legion," it spoke.

Aurelio was growing frustrated. "What the fuck does that

mean? Who sent you?" His grip tightened on the mask, making the creature shake under his hold.

"We are legion. Wrath has descended upon Euhaven to devour the animas of mortals," it rasped, laughing. "You will not win."

"Why are you after my team?" Aurelio stepped close, ignoring Ryland's warning. "And give it to me straight before I decide I find you useless and therefore will pull this mask off." He was fuming and could barely contain his anger.

"The Chaos Wielder. We won't let you find them before us." Who else knew about the Chaos Wielder? Who else was trying to get to them?

"You're a demon." Vivi let out a gasp. "How did you find us?"

He and his team had done many covert ops before and had never been spotted. Something about this felt off. The demon laughed harder.

"We are legion. Wrath has descended upon Euhaven to devour the animas of mortals," it repeated. Aurelio clucked his tongue.

"Mask removal it is." He snatched the mask off as the demon began to screech again. He stumbled back, trying to register what he saw before him. Ryland retched from the stench and Vivi went pale.

The demon's skin was a sick pale gray and its eyes milky white as if it had never seen an ounce of sunlight. Black veins snaked their way throughout its face. Two slits in place of a nose rested in the middle of its face. Its mouth was abnormally large as it screeched, its jaw descended and held hundreds of teeth, surely meant for feasting on flesh. Oily strands of hair clung to its nearly bald scalp. It continued to screech as its skin started to burn.

Aurelio moved back more as the skin melted off its face, black blood leaking everywhere. It caught fire, flame starting to engulf the thing. The smell of burnt flesh made Aurelio's eyes water before he turned away to vomit. The stench was overwhelming. The fire died down as quickly as it had started, leaving a smoking mess in the grass. Aurelio wrapped it in wind, forming a small tornado, to push the smoke and scent upward to avoid it traveling. As the wind dissipated, he stepped forward and picked up the mask. He turned it over and noticed it had nostril tubes and other mechanisms to aid in breathing.

"It can't breathe Euhaven air," Aurelio said, realizing what it was. He turned to the others, Lilith and Quade had joined them. Xavia stood in a distance by the tent, arms wrapped around herself. He looked at Vivi. "Where's Misha?"

She led him to their tent.

"Despite what he'll try to tell you, he's not doing good. That thing ran its claws into his side," she murmured, angrily. "I wish I could kill it all over again."

She nodded to the cot where Misha sat before stepping out. Misha looked pale, dark smudges under his eyes. His shirt was tossed in the corner, and gauze and bandages wrapped around his bare torso. He looked up to Aurelio, eyes tired and bloodshot.

"I'm ok Cap," he huffed, attempting to stand. He swayed and Aurelio put a hand on his shoulder to sit him back down.

"You suffered a major injury. I don't care that we're privy to the medi-pills from the Monarch. You still need time." Aurelio's voice was full of authority. Misha sighed, running a hand through his sweaty hair. "Tell me what happened."

Misha ran through the story about how he'd screwed up, getting too close to the demon, and it took advantage of the opportunity to drive its claws into his side. It missed major organs, but the wounds had needed stitches.

"We need to move. We can't continue to stay here." Misha grunted as he stood up and remained steady on his feet.

Aurelio couldn't say that he was wrong. They did need to move, but he wondered how much use they'd be after last night. How far could they go before needing to camp? How could he be sure that another round of those things didn't find them? All these questions played in Aurelio's mind as he stepped out of the tent with Misha behind him. The same questions were on everyone's face. They were all feeling the loss of Luc, with poor Ryland feeling it the worst.

"I know you've all got questions. We don't know what the fuck we're dealing with, but we have to move." Thankfully, no one disagreed. "We are all exhausted. Take a medi-pill. It's meant to increase your healing, energy, and endurance. Start breaking down the tents, get some food and water, and then we move out." The others moved to follow their orders.

"What about making camp later tonight? What if more of these things find us?" Quade looked worse for wear. He had an ice pack at his side, looking like he'd also suffered from some broken ribs. Everyone froze and looked at Aurelio. He massaged his temples, headache blooming across his forehead.

"We take what we learned last night and fortify ourselves better. We are Special Forces for a reason. We adapt and we keep going. Fear has no place here. We don't quit. We're Alpha Phoenix!"

They all shouted together, echoing his sentiment.

"Now, let's get going. We have roughly two more days till we reach Silvermoon." Aurelio looked at Xavia and pointed to the tent. She nodded and began to clear and break it down. Aurelio rubbed the back of his head. Fuck. How was he going to keep everyone safe?

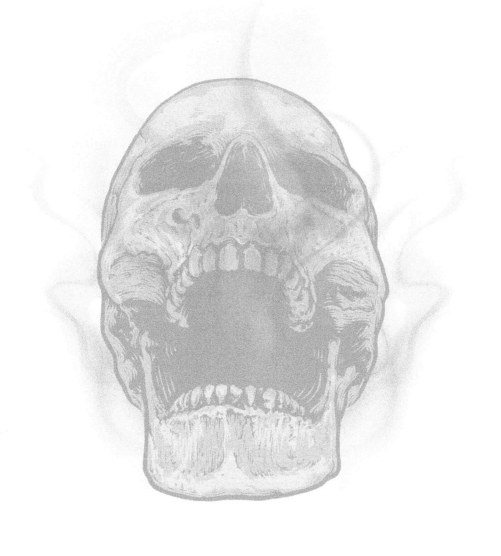

CHAPTER 15

XAVIA

T **HANKFULLY, THEY DIDN'T** encounter any more of those creatures the rest of the day and night. Everyone was on high alert. Misha and Vivi enhanced the perimeters to pick up on smoke, fog, and anything else denser than air. By morning time, it was clear that everyone had barely slept and tempers were rising. Xavia was helping to clean up the campsite when she heard Quade shout.

"What the fuck, Misha!" Quade bellowed as Misha accidentally spilled soup on him. Misha was still struggling with his wounds, even if he wouldn't admit it to anyone. "You need to get your shit together," Quade barked, getting into his face. Misha let out a growl and pushed him back.

"Get the fuck out of my face, Quade." Misha managed to push Quade a few feet back. Quade's face twitched as if he was holding a wince from his bruised ribs. Misha threw his bowl on the ground and stormed off, holding his side, to help his sister with their tent. Xavia made her way in front of Quade before he could go after Misha.

"What the fuck are you doing? You know he's injured!" she barked at him. Quade looked down at her, raising a dark eyebrow.

"As if I'm not?" he barked. She rolled her eyes.

"Go pack up your shit. We have to get moving. We're still a day and a half from Silvermoon, from what Aurelio has told us."

"You don't give me orders." Quade sneered. "*I'm* second in command."

Xavia's hands balled into fists. *Oh, how easy it would be to punch him in the nose right now.* Quade's perfect face would be destroyed with a broken nose. She shoved him and made to grab his shirt but he caught her wrist. Fire lit in his eyes as he pulled her toward him.

"So feisty," Quade murmured. "I bet it makes your pussy wet." Heat rose to Xavia's face at the dangerously smooth way he spoke to her, so softly that only she could hear him. Damn Axton for his sociopaths and their appeal.

Her forehead connected with Quade's nose in a loud crack. He let go of her, hands covering his now bleeding nose. Xavia used the opportunity to grab his shoulders and ram her knee into his gut. He fell to one knee, glaring at her. She raised an eyebrow, practically begging him to get up. She was itching for a good fight.

Reminding her he was Special Forces, Quade stood as he snapped his nose in place, as if it didn't faze him. Before she could react, he punched her, fist smashing into her jaw. Xavia could feel her jaw dislocating briefly before she forced it to snap back. She spat blood at him, egging him on. Fire licked around his hands and she narrowed her eyes, daring him to try. He took a step toward her before being yanked back. Two arms appeared under Quade's arms, hands going to the back of his head, catching him in a full nelson. Lightning blasted a tree apart. Xavia ducked, covering her head, scared shitless of Aurelio's display of anger. It was a rarity that he displayed anger of this magnitude.

"The fuck are you *doing*, Quade?" Aurelio's voice trembled with rage. Xavia had never seen him this furious before. It couldn't be because of the tussle. He'd seen her fight in much worse scenarios. She took a step back, wiping the blood from her lips.

"Don't worry about it, Aurelio. Just two kids having fun," she said, a cocky smirk making its way across her lips. Xavia liked playing with fire, though she took it quite literally in this instance. Quade shot daggers at her with his eyes and let out a grunt as Aurelio abruptly let him go. As Aurelio turned that anger on Xavia, her eyes widened in surprise.

"Stop fucking around!" His eyes turned dark steel gray as lightning struck another tree. "We *have* to get out of this forest and we can't do that if we're fighting with each other."

Xavia's throat bobbed as she gulped, wondering if she'd been pushing him too far. Aurelio motioned for everyone to finish breaking down the camp. She grabbed her bag, heaving it over her shoulders and working on her straps and buckles. Aurelio didn't look her way and she knew she had to figure this out on her own. Xavia started to get angry at herself, that her brain didn't want to work with her on these minute things.

"He cares about you," came a sultry voice, dark ebony hands reaching for her and helping her with the buckles. Xavia looked up to Lilith, the beauty of the wood. Xavia huffed at her. There was no question that Aurelio cared. The problem is that he always felt the need to interject when she could fight her own battles.

"There you go," Lilith murmured, snapping the last buckle in place. "Why do you have such a hard time with these?" The question was genuine enough but Xavia hated having to explain it.

"Um. Ever since I was young, I've had issues with getting my hands to do what my brain is trying to tell them to do." Xavia's cheeks warmed, feeling embarrassment. "It's mostly an issue with buckles, tying my shoes, using utensils, and things of that sort." She shrugged "But I can throw a mean hook, use swords, and shoot a target at a mile away with the naked eye. I don't know why some things work and others don't." Lilith gave her a nod and Xavia was grateful that she didn't receive a look of pity.

They started their hike and Xavia really hoped tonight would be the last night. She needed a hot bath and some bourbon. They remained silent as Aurelio took the front with the holographic map on his wrist cuff. Misha grew paler by the hour, a sweat breaking out over his forehead. He didn't make any complaints but Xavia could see they were going to have to take a break soon. She wondered if she should say something or not. She didn't know him very well and sometimes people took offense when strangers brought up their ailments.

The sun made its way through the sky and started to set. Aurelio signaled for them to start setting up camp. Lilith helped Xavia unbuckle her backpack and Xavia let out a soft sigh as she slid the bag off her shoulders. After putting up their tents, they all grabbed protein bars and water. Ever since Luc died, Ryland had no desire to cook. She couldn't blame him. Luc didn't deserve to go the way that he did. The thought of it brought a shudder up her spine and she tried to suppress it as much as could.

She looked over to Misha to see how he was doing. He leaned heavily on his sister, head resting on her shoulder as they sat and Vivi ate her food. Misha claimed he didn't have much of an appetite. It wasn't good that he refused to eat, but they couldn't force him, so they made sure he at least drank water.

As it got darker and the sun had fully set, an air of dread settled over them all. Everyone was on high alert, hoping that the night would pass as the previous had. Misha sat up abruptly.

"No, stop!" Vivi yelped, trying to keep him from ripping off his bandage

Ryland, being the closest, put a hand on his shoulder but Misha pushed him off, sending Ryland to the ground. Misha put some distance between him and Vivi as if he didn't want to hurt her. His eyes had started to darken, turning blacker by the minute. A sick feeling kicked Xavia in the gut.

"Misha..." Aurelio said as if talking to a rabid animal. He attempted to step toward him when Misha turned toward him abruptly, "Talk to me man. What's up? Can we help you?"

Misha smirked but at the same time his head started to shake as if fighting off something internally. He went back to ripping at his bandages. A dark growl escaped his lips as he ripped the last of it off. Vivi gasped, hand rushing to her mouth. His wound was a sickly black color, veins near it also black. His skin had gotten paler and his breathing increased as the darkness spread along his side. Misha's head shook side to side as he gripped his hair. Another growl passed through his lips as his body continued to shake.

"Misha, talk to me. What's going on?" Vivi said, trying to approach him. He snapped his head toward her, eyes wholly black including the sclera.

"Vivi, back away slowly," Xavia said in an oddly calm voice. Vivi didn't look at her, keeping her eyes on her twin.

"No. I am not leaving my brother." She inched her way closer

THE CHAOS WIELDER | 97

to Misha as he shuddered as if fighting for control of his body. Xavia attempted to pull Vivi back.

"I don't think he's your brother anymore." Vivi snatched her hand away from her.

"Don't fucking touch me!" she snapped. Misha let out another growl. He had somehow gotten closer without either of them realizing. The color of his skin was draining before their eyes. He looked at Vivi with confusion in his dark eyes. She reached a trembling hand for him and placed it on his cheek. "Misha, come back to me," she said, as if realizing that Xavia was likely right.

Misha's breathing increased into pants as he took her hand but then it visibly tightened and hers turned red, and then purple. She tried to pry her hand away but Misha was locked on. The sounds of her bones crunching in his grip had Xavia wincing. Vivi let out a scream as she continued trying to pry her crushed hand from his.

"Misha! What are you doing?" she pleaded as tears fell from her eyes.*

Time slowed down once more. Before Xavia could react, Misha pulled his sister in and tore into her throat, his mouth dripping black saliva mixed with blood. Vivi barely had a moment to scream before her head lolled to the side, eyes lifeless. Xavia, being the closest, pulled her gun. Misha turned his attention to her and before she could think twice about it, she shot him point blank in between his eyes. His body jolted back and fell to the ground with a thud, eyes closing upon impact.

"What the fuck just happened?" Quade yelled, gun out and pointed at Misha. Xavia slowly blinked, taking in the sight before her. Vivi laid lifeless, throat torn and neck almost completely bitten through. The bullet hole in Misha's forehead still simmered, smoke rising from it. Ryland knelt over, gasping for air, trying not to vomit. Lilith stood next to Quade, hand on his shoulder to keep him from getting any closer to the dead twins.

Xavia gripped her guns to keep her hands from shaking. She wasn't sure what she'd just witnessed or how she'd reacted

♪ "Self-Destruction" by I Prevail

so quickly. Aurelio slowly stepped over and knelt to inspect Misha's body. Black veins were spreading from his wound throughout his torso. His skin had gone beyond pale, almost gray-white. The hairs on her arms stood in alarm.

"Aurelio, back away. Please," she cautioned before Misha's eyes popped open. Aurelio let out a shout of surprise, falling backward. He crab-crawled backward, away from his team member, fear filling his eyes. Quade shook Lilith off, holstering his guns and holding his arms out while chains of fire formed around his forearms. Lilith and Ryland followed suit and geared up their Wielding. Storm clouds built overhead as Aurelio wound up his own, right when an inhuman growl escaped Misha's throat. Xavia's mouth went dry as the smell of ozone filled the air while lightning flashed in the sky.

Misha turned toward Aurelio, only moving his head, which bent his neck at an impossible angle. His bones snapped as he twitched and turned his body around. He rose on all fours, hands and feet, as if he was an animal. Xavia's gut dropped, not reacting fast enough, when Misha leapt forward closing the distance between him and Aurelio in just one bound. His hands clasped onto Aurelio's shoulders as he forced the Wielder to the ground. Aurelio let out a grunt before bringing his elbow to slice across Misha's face, snapping his head to the side. Misha let out an inhuman howl when Aurelio brought his forehead to smash against his. He briefly let go and Aurelio rolled out from under him.

"Get the fuck out of the way Aurelio!" Quade yelled as he started whipping his chain of fire overhead. It was clear that Misha was no longer Misha. The fact that the demons could spread their influence through wounds meant this mission just got more deadly. Aurelio dove in time for Quade to whip out his chain of fire and wrap it around Demon-Misha's neck. Misha let out another howl that caused them all to wince. The smell of burning carrion hit Xavia's nose, making her gag. Misha thrashed and jerked, stronger than anyone had expected.

"Quade, pull him over there in that clearing. Away from the camp. Ryland, follow me. Lilith, stay with Xavia," Aurelio ordered.

They nodded while Quade pulled Misha along, stumbling and screeching. Black saliva dripped from his mouth thickly like tar. There was nothing left of the man the team once called brother and companion. Once Misha was at a safe enough distance, Aurelio nodded to Ryland who pulled roots from deep inside the earth to encompass their demonic prisoner. Ryland and Quade moved back, Quade pulling his fire back into himself. They moved smoothly after years of fighting together, and communicated without a word. Misha struggled against the roots around him. Xavia watched, hand over her mouth, noticing the silver lining Aurelio's eyes.

"I'm sorry, brother. Sleep with Axton," he murmured, before the smell of ozone increased. A large lightning bolt made its way down from the storm clouds, and a loud, resounding crack echoed through the trees. It hit Misha dead on, and as the echo faded, there was nothing left of Misha but dust. Aurelio fell to his knees, Quade and Ryland by his side. They each put a hand on his shoulders, lending him strength, before he let out a fierce cry of anger. Thunder boomed and wind picked up rapidly as a funnel cloud started to form in the distance. Xavia made to run to him but Lilith held her back, letting her know that this was a moment between Aurelio and his brothers.

"Cap. You need to calm down or you're gonna bring the forest down on us," came Ryland's deep, calming voice. Aurelio sucked in a breath, clearly reining in his emotions, and while he did so, the tornado dissipated as quickly as it appeared. In the two days they'd been hiking in these woods, they'd lost three Guards. *What the fuck is in store for us next?* Xavia thought.

PART TWO

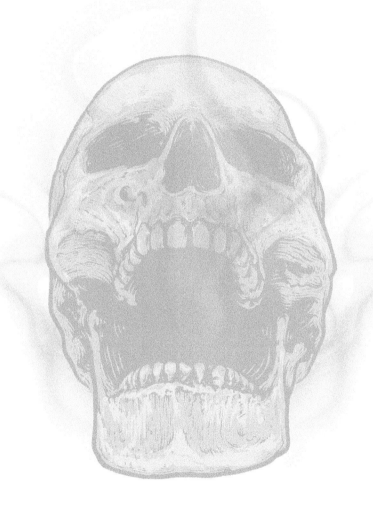

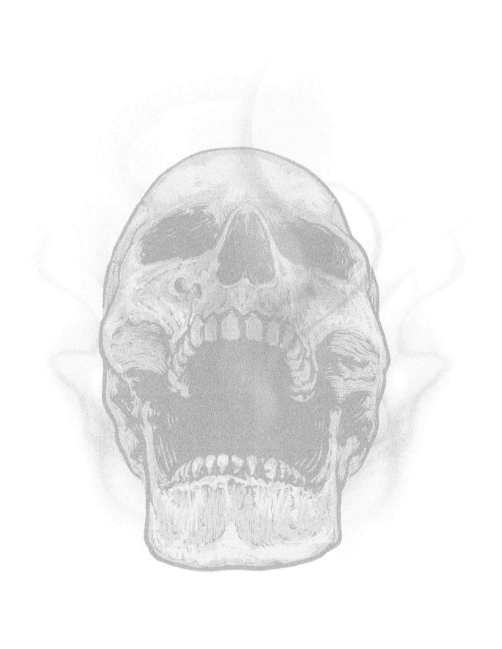

CHAPTER 16
XAVIA

THE NEXT MORNING WAS somber, Misha's and Vivi's deaths hung over them all. Shortly after Misha fell to dust, they burned Vivi's body as well. They didn't want to take any chances that she might also rise. Misha technically died twice; once by Xavia and once by Aurelio. Even if the ends justified the means, it still changed the dynamic of the team.

Ryland was silent and hadn't spoken a word since the previous night. He moved through the motions, helping to take down the tents and pack the supplies. He had taken a jar of the twin's ashes to bring back to their parents when, or if, they made it back home. Xavia could tell that Ryland had already checked out and she would be surprised if he continued on after they arrived in Silvermoon.

Shortly after, they lugged their bags on for the last stretch. If everything went well, they'd be able to reach Silvermoon by nightfall and be out of the woods, no pun intended. To their welcome relief, they made it to the border without further delays. The perimeter shone like a bubble, with rainbow colors and bioluminescence. The harbor city had a natural atmospheric barrier around it. It wasn't magical, just something that the planet conjured.

Once they entered the bubble, the temperature and humidity rose drastically. The warm forests turned into a tropical field. Bioluminescent night-blooming flowers overflowed from different bushes and trees. Fireflies made their way lazily through the air. Annoying stinging bugs bit at her hands and exposed areas of

Xavia's now sweaty chest. She wasn't the only one. If things weren't so somber, she would've laughed. Every one of them slapped away those monstrous bugs, as they were all sweaty, with their hair plastered on their faces. She couldn't have been the only one not used to the humid air.

A pathway made of violet and teal stones lead to a massive gate. Motorcycles waited by the trees lining the gate. Xavia looked at Aurelio with a raised eyebrow.

"I reached out to some contacts before we left and told them to have motorcycles ready for us."

There was one for each of them, including three extras for those who didn't make it out the woods alive. The dark cloud returned over the team as they hopped on their bikes. The gate opened, allowing them onto the official road into the city.

Xavia's mouth gaped as she took in the beautiful, ocean side city in front of her. She'd only seen Silvermoon Harbor on TV as a big vacation and tourist destination. And she could understand why.

As they crossed a brightly lit bridge into the city, the ocean water beneath them swirled in different hues of deep purple, turquoise, and sea green. The beach to their left was pebbled with black and sea green sand. Some grains of sand shone under the moon above. A large boardwalk weaved in the distance, lined with restaurants, hotels, and resorts. The city skyline bloomed with skyscrapers that could rival Melhold's.

Sadness swept through Xavia at the thought of Melhold, reminding her of the importance of her mission. She was pulled from her thoughts when she caught sight of the massive harbor that appeared as they descended the bridge. Sea-going vessels of every color and design filled the harbor. There were boats as small as sailboats and some as large as cruise ships. The view was magnificent.

In the middle of the city, a large turquoise tower shimmered as if the ocean played through it. On the top, it held a statue of a large sea serpent with wings that stretched toward the sky. It was the symbol of Kutiel, one of Melvina's revolutionaries and Angel of

Water and Divination. Xavia could appreciate that it made sense for a coastal city that consisted mostly of Water Wielders to honor Kutiel, even if it was considered taboo by more religious denizens to worship an Angel instead of or alongside a Deity.

They followed Aurelio as he led them downtown. He stopped in what looked like a park in the middle of the city. Xavia admired the large palm trees, the leaves emerald and turquoise. They all got off their bikes, stretching a bit, joints popping.

Aurelio went off in the distance on his ear comm. Now that they were in the city, their reception was back in action and her phone blew up with messages and pings. Any survivors from Axton reached out to her to see if she was ok. She was responding to the messages when she caught sight of Aurelio's furrowed brow. It creased into a V as he grew increasingly frustrated with whomever he was speaking to. He clicked his comm off as he made his way back over.

"Apparently there's a festival going on for the next few days. It's their lunar new year." Everyone groaned. It meant the city was going to be more populated than normal. "Silvermoon is planning on using the funds to offer aid to Melhold so at least they've got that going for them." Aurelio let out a sigh. "Which means that most, if not all, of the hotels are booked solid. Have been for weeks." Was the Monarch trying to ruin them? Xavia was sure as fuck that they would've known about this.

"Is there *anywhere* we can stay? I could use a hot shower," murmured Quade. For once Xavia agreed with him.

"My contact says there's a bed and breakfast not too far from this park. They should have room enough for us all." Aurelio nodded in the direction they would go in before hopping on the motorcycle. They all followed suit and rode about three miles before arriving at the small and quaint building. It looked like it had been standing for at least two hundred years. But despite the age, it was definitely well kept. They parked their motorcycles and made their way up the steps and into the building.

"Wel—" The receptionist at the desk stopped and stared at them as they entered.

Xavia could only imagine the thoughts going through her mind seeing four Guards and a bounty hunter, covered in filth, obviously sweaty and grumpy, walk up to her desk. Aurelio gave her a smile that didn't reach his eyes. She didn't seem to notice as she melted into a puddle in front of him.

"Hey there, sweetheart," Aurelio drawled, making Xavia roll her eyes. "Benjamin sent us over; said you had some space for us?" He leaned partly on the desk and she flushed a bit before looking over her computer.

"Ah yes. I see it here. Five individuals." She handed him keys and motioned to the stairs. "You're on the third floor. Breakfast starts at dawn. We recently updated our facilities so each room has its own bathroom." The receptionist gave him an inviting smile in which Aurelio responded with a wink. She flushed again and he turned around to the team.

They all stared at him. How this man could melt a woman while looking like he just dug himself out of a grave was a shock to them all. Well, all of them except Xavia. She knew what he was capable of. Xavia yawned. She was exhausted and imagined everyone else would be too. Aurelio passed out keys and everyone went into their respective rooms. Xavia held her hand out for her key but dropped her hand when she saw him balk.

"What is it?" she asked, although realization sank in. He looked at her as he held up the last key. Oh great.

"Looks like we're sharing again..." He gave a wry grin as he opened the room and they stepped in. His grin dropped as soon as they entered and she immediately saw the reason. There was only one. Fucking. Bed.

AURELIO

FUCK. THERE WAS ONLY ONE BED. Was Etis and Sortis playing a joke on him? The room wasn't exactly spacious but also not too crammed. It had an ocean montage that leapt from wall to wall, and the rest was a blend of purples, greens, and blues. The king-sized bed was decorated with simple emerald bedding, the carpets a pale lilac. Aurelio didn't understand why sharing a bed with Xavia freaked him out. It wasn't like they hadn't shared a bed before. But... that was when they were a couple, which they weren't anymore.

"I can ask for a cot or I'll sleep on the floor," Aurelio said and took a step toward the door. Xavia slapped his hand from the doorknob and gave him a look.

"What's wrong? Can't share a bed?"

He narrowed his eyes, trying to hold back a snort. She had a way of lightening the mood and knew he needed it. The weight on his chest wouldn't go away anytime soon. Xavia moved toward the window that viewed the city and fumbled with her backpack harness.

"You shouldn't..." she grunted as if talking and trying to unbuckle the damn thing was too much for her brain to process. She momentarily gave up on the buckle. "You shouldn't ask too much of them here. They're already accommodating us." She had a point. Aurelio made his way to her while she still fumbled with the buckles. She managed to get one undone but the top one gave her trouble.

"Can I help you?" he asked, waiting for her nod before proceeding to work on the offending buckle. Somehow, Xavia somehow got the very top of her tank stuck in it. Aurelio didn't understand how this always happened to her, but what he knew was that she often had issues with handling small and minute things.

Xavia started huffing in frustration, causing her cleavage to rise and fall. Aurelio tried not to pay attention to that while he finagled the damn thing.

"What the fuck, X? This is the worst it's ever been," he grumbled, biting his lower lip as he concentrated on getting it undone. He was painfully aware of how close they were, his hands gently touching the tops of her breasts as he tried to get the cloth out of the buckle. Finally, it snapped open and she dropped her bag instantly. Xavia unknowingly pushed herself toward him as she stretched and Aurelio bit back a groan as her chest brushed against his. Suddenly she stopped stretching, realizing how close they were. She blinked slowly before mussing his coily hair, making his nose flare in surprise.

"You stink," she joked, as she made her way to the bathroom before he did. "I'm going first!"

Aurelio made to swipe at her before she squeaked and shut the door behind her. He let out a sigh of relief as he unbuckled and dropped his bag, dumping it in the corner of the room next to hers. His shoulders ached from where Misha threw him on the ground. Shit, his entire body hurt. No amount of bio enhancements or medi-pills would help the soreness.

There was a desk and chair, which Aurelio was grateful for. He pulled out his tech, guns, knives, and finally took off the tactical vest and placed it around the back of the chair. He turned to the air conditioning unit and flipped it on. He'd forgotten how hot and humid Silvermoon was. Aurelio grunted as he slipped his sweaty shirt over his head and dropped it into the nearby hamper. He plopped into the chair and rested his elbows on the desk, his forehead resting on his hands.

"Aurelio?"

He started, realizing he had fallen asleep. Aurelio raised his heavy head and everything became crystal clear, the fog lifting instantly. There Xavia was, standing in the doorframe, with just a towel around her. She had a toothbrush hanging from her mouth. Her chin length curls were barely dripping any water, which made it clear she had been standing there for some time. He narrowed his eyes at her.

"How long have you been standing there?" Aurelio grunted before standing up. Shit, falling asleep sitting up while also being hunched over did nothing for his spine. He noticed how her eyes dipped to his abs before glancing up to meet his eyes. A flush crossed her cheeks. Xavia popped the toothbrush out of her mouth and pointed it at him.

"It was sort of funny watching you snore. I could hear you

before I even turned the shower off." She snorted before moving past him, her hibiscus scent playing with his nose. Kneeling, she dug through her bag and her towel dipped a bit to expose the upper half of her back. A galaxy tattoo started at her left shoulder, moving in a flowing diagonal motion toward her right hip. It was a colorful piece depicting their solar system. The orange sun, colorful Euhaven, Euhaven's Moon, and planet Ithea seemed to move with each breath she took. Aurelio could only see part of it because of the towel. As Xavia stood, he couldn't help but move toward her to gently touch the tattoo. He heard her gasp before she peered over her shoulder.

"This is new…" he murmured.

It never occurred to him she'd get tattoos. But then again, he hadn't seen her naked in years. They actually managed to have a decent friendship, but they also spent little time alone in these types of settings, either. Aurelio trailed the tattoo from Xavia's shoulder to the middle of her back. Her skin raised in goosebumps, which had him smirking. It stroked his ego, knowing that he still influenced her.

"Mhmm," Xavia mumbled. She turned toward him, gripping her towel tighter. She leaned in, noisily taking in an inhale before dramatically coughing and waving her hands in front of her face. "Are you going to shower or am I going to pass out from your stench?" She made as if she'd faint and Aurelio growled at her, tugging at her hair. She slapped at his hands before pushing him toward the bathroom. He couldn't help but chuckle as he headed into the bathroom.

Groaning, Aurelio removed the rest of his clothes before turning on the shower. The hot water was like Aether on his aching body. The steam made its way through his lungs, relaxing his muscles bit by bit. Weighing heavily on his shoulders was the stress from the last few days. He took a deep inhale when the sudden scent of hibiscus made him turn his gaze to the wash cloth hanging from the shower stall.

"Fuck…" he murmured as he felt himself growing hard. The tension with Xavia weighed on him, especially his cock. Trying to ignore her scent, he went about washing his body. Failing, he groaned when he brushed against himself, her tantalizing aroma still assaulting his senses. Memories of their sexual exploits bombarded him as he wrapped his hand around the base of his cock, fingertips barely touching around the girth while he pumped. Aurelio had never been very long but his thickness more than made up for it. An especially hot memory came to mind; a threesome with a sexy female werewolf. Xavia had been in the middle, face full of pussy while he fucked her from behind.

His cock twitched at the memory as his strokes increased in speed. Snatching the rag, he held it to his nose and inhaled. Fuck, he missed her scent on him. He missed how wet she got for him. Biting his lower lip to keep from moaning, he gripped his cock harder, feeling the orgasm building at the base of his spine. *Fucking Etis and Sortis*, he thought as he leaned his free hand on the wall. That hot mouth of hers. All he saw was her full lips wrapped around the head of his cock, dark brown eyes looking up at him. Blood trickled from his lip as he bit down harder and began to come, hot streams of his pleasure painting the wall. He looked at the rag still in his hand, panting. Fucking Xavia and her sweet scent.

He stepped out of the steamy shower a little bit later, wiping the mirror of condensation before taking a good look at himself. Even his dark skin couldn't hide the bruises that littered his body. His ribs were exceptionally purple and green, and he was sure his shoulders would match those soon. He had a bit of scruff forming around his jaw and another healing bruise from when Xavia punched him. Twice.

After brushing his teeth a couple of times, due to the last few days leaving his mouth feeling like sand, Aurelio wrapped a towel around his waist and stepped out of the bathroom to find Xavia completely knocked out on the bed. The blanket was wrapped around her like a burrito. She looked peaceful. No scowl or anger on her face. Aurelio yawned the exhaustion hit him. He slipped on a pair of boxers and eased into the bed slowly so he didn't wake Xavia. He grabbed the spare blanket and pulled it over him. The sounds of Xavia's breathing and her honey hibiscus scent lulled him to sleep.

CHAPTER 17

XAVIA

GENTLE SNORING WOKE XAVIA from her slumber. The last few days caught up with her and she slept like a rock. She shifted to stretch when she realized she had curled up around Aurelio. He was facing away from her, and oddly it reminded her of their times together and how she always ended up being the big spoon. Xavia's arm was draped over Aurelio's stomach, leg over his hip, and her face practically planted against his hard back. Aurelio's arm had hers trapped, hand passively on her wrist. Shit. She had to pee! But she didn't want to wake him. She took a deep breath, inhaling his stormy, fresh rain scent.

"I hope I don't stink anymore," came a soft deep rumble.

Xavia bumped him with her forehead. It was at this moment she realized that she was in nothing but a tee and boy shorts and he was only in his boxers. She was glad Aurelio was facing away so he couldn't see the obvious flush creeping up her neck into her cheeks.

"No, thankfully not," she laughed. "I'm going to grab breakfast. Do you want me to grab you something? Probably something obnoxiously healthy, so I guess no bacon..." Xavia made to pull herself from him but he held her wrist.

"Wait." Aurelio turned slowly to face her, shifting himself so that her arm and leg still remained over his body. Great Etis and Sortis... His eyes were still heavy with sleep, his morning voice gruff. A sleepy smirk played on his lips, the sun making his silver eyes glimmer. Xavia swept her eyes over his face. Aurelio leaned in, resting his forehead against hers. "I'll actually take you up on the bacon." He smacked a kiss on her forehead before popping up on the bed. She stared at him.

"What? Since when?" She raised an eyebrow in suspicion, biting back a chuckle as she watched him move a bit stiffly off the bed and toward the bathroom, not facing her. "Hiding that morning wood, eh?"

Aurelio turned, giving her a nice view of the large tent in his boxers before he gave a cocky grin and stepped into the bathroom. Why did she even say anything? Xavia got up and grabbed her last clean pair of cargo jeans. She was sliding them up when he reemerged from the bathroom.

"The last few days have been rough for us all. I think a little bit of comfort food won't hurt." Aurelio's eyes roved over her. If they kept this up, they were going to end up fucking and Xavia wasn't sure if she could handle that sort of emotional damage right now. She wasn't going to question him on it. She would eat bacon all day, every day if she could. Avoiding his eyes, she popped into the bathroom to take care of her needs before quickly changing her shirt for a blue tank and slipping on her belt holster.

Xavia pulled out two of her handguns and checked their chambers. She made sure they were loaded and the safeties were on, weighing them in her hands. They felt so good and balanced. Her favorite part of the sleek black semi-automatics was that they had minimal recoil and smooth double-action triggers. It made shooting a lot easier, which was a must. Xavia was grateful she had been able to bring them. They felt better at her side than the Special Forces-grade handguns.

She looked up to find Aurelio watching her, already dressed in black cargo jeans and a fitted navy under armor shirt. The navy practically turned his eyes into an ice blue. Before she did or said something stupid, she breezed past him and headed out the room.

The rest of the team were waiting for them in the dining area, food laid out in front of them. While they all looked clean and somewhat rested, the stress of the last few days was clear on their faces. Xavia and Aurelio grabbed their food, extra bacon for Xavia, and sat down. The breakfast spread contained eggs, bacon, fruits, orange juice, coffee, and pastries. She took a bit of everything because her thick thighs wouldn't feed themselves.

Xavia loved food and she desperately needed something yummy and greasy after eating protein bars for almost three days straight. Aurelio plopped an iced coffee in front of her with a light amount of cream and no sugar. She would've said thank you if it weren't for the bacon she'd just stuffed in her mouth. He just gave her a smirk as she washed it down with the coffee. Oh shit, that was good.

"What do you think happened with Misha?" Quade asked, downing a cup of tea. It was probably black, like his anima. "Are the demons contagious?" Xavia groaned as Aurelio nodded.

"It's the only thing that makes sense. It took, what, a day and a half after getting sliced by that demon for him to become whatever he became." He kept his voice low, signaling that they should all do the same. The last thing they needed were civilians listening to their conversation. "If he hadn't..." He stopped short before mentioning Vivi. "I think if he had bitten any of us, we'd have turned too."

"But does that mean we have a potential epidemic on our hands?" Xavia wondered out loud. "Like, if these demons are contagious, what if Aeshma uses that to her advantage?" Quade graced her with a glance, the look in his eyes she couldn't place.

"No. He was completely feral. If it's not something she can control, I don't think she'll allow for it," Lilith said before popping a slice of mango into her mouth. It seemed she was vegetarian since there were no meats on her plate. Aurelio shook his head.

"I don't agree. I think *because* there's a potential for humans to go feral, it will allow her to capitalize on the chaos." What he said made sense. What he said next caused her stomach to drop to her ass. "I don't think she knows yet or else we'd be seeing mass reports about it. I'm afraid of what will happen if she does."

"And the Chaos Wielder is supposed to prevent this?" Quade sounded skeptical; an eyebrow raised as he poured himself another cup of tea. She helped herself to another iced coffee, practically sighing. She had to try to not slurp it down.

"Apparently so. From the prophecies and the Monarch themselves, the Chaos Wielder is the only being on the planet that can stop Aeshma and her horde."

"So, what do we do now?" Ryland spoke after taking a sip of his tea.

"We have to find Lex Esson-Tai," Aurelio said in between bites of eggs and bacon. Xavia still couldn't believe he was eating bacon. He usually stayed away from anything of the sort. "And I have to reach out to my contact to figure out where Lex might be. No one knows what they look like, except that they are very good at their job."

Lex Esson-Tai was a vigilante of sorts, a pirate for sure, and a well-known thief. They were notorious for robbing the previous governor of Silvermoon from right under his nose. The governor was so rich, he didn't notice his funds were depleting until it was too late. Lex had a thing for the poor. They were often seen in the 'Hood bringing food and water to those who needed it most. Over time, they gathered a sizable network of spies and thieves whose sole purpose was to steal from the wealthy and give to the poor. In their eyes, it was about forcing equality that was deserved.

"From what I've heard, Lex usually hangs around the 'Hood, where the fancy urbanites don't go. They like to recruit members from cage fights," Xavia piped up before popping a grape in her mouth. Quade raised an eyebrow in interest. Aurelio just gawked at her and Xavia shrugged. "As a bounty hunter, I am privy to a lot more street intel than you." She winked. Aurelio gave a grunt.

"And what do you suppose we do with this information?" Quade chimed in, looking her over with that dark look in his eyes. She fought and failed to not roll her eyes.

"Roam the streets, find out where the cage fights are, and send me in there." Xavia didn't look at Aurelio as she spoke. She already knew that he would be upset over this. She'd thought about it ever since being told she had to locate Lex. The only benefit from having Lex's help was their ship. They needed the best seafarer they could find, and apparently no one was better than them. "I say we split up and cover more of the city that way." She heard a grunt from Quade's direction as Aurelio nodded.

"Ok, that actually sounds like a good idea," Ryland said, voice soft. "But after this, I'm staying. I'm not going to Malagado with you."

"What?!" Quade, Lilith, and Aurelio all barked at the same time, making Ryland flinch. Xavia called it. She knew this was going to happen.

"I can't. After seeing my love and two of my best friends die... I can't do it." Silver lined his eyes. Xavia felt like she was intruding on the moment that should be between Aurelio and his Guard so she stood up and gave a nod to them before leaving. She headed back to the room to grab the rest of her gear. As she reached for the doorknob, black started to encroach on her vision, head pounding. No, not right now. She made it halfway through the door before blacking out.

AURELIO

AURELIO SHOULD'VE SEEN IT COMING. Ever since that demon killed Luc, Ryland had not been the same. He should've been a better Captain and been there for him. Shit, he should've been a better Captain and protected his team. Thoughts of his last mission came to the forefront of his mind against his will.

"Get that fucking bomb before it explodes!" Aurelio yelled in his comms as he ran into the gunfire. Special Forces had been sent into the den of a rogue militia compound belonging to the Martyrs. They were planning on bombing the Luna Towers in the name of anarchy. Their sole purpose was to tear down the Monarchy and take it over themselves. The Martyrs held extreme beliefs, and they were not afraid to do what was necessary. They were gaining a footing and following, which is why it was up to the Special Forces to stop them. Few of the militia's soldiers had Wielding and almost

all were human. They rarely worked with any non-humans. Aurelio had been sure this would be a simple mission, but he was eating his words now.

Aurelio held up his semi-automatic rifle, locking it in his shoulder for the kick-back. Rain poured down on them and it took everything he had to not slip in the mud. He lost his helmet somewhere in the fray, and while the deluge attempted to blind him, he used his Wielding to keep a constant stream of wind to create a visor. He couldn't stop natural rain from falling, but he could direct the weather. So he let go a bolt of electricity, frying four shooters before they could get more bullets into the air. Most of his team was cornered in the militia's warehouse.

"I'm trying! There are too many of them." Quade's breathless voice came through the comm.

In the distance he could see fire lancing through the air, defying the laws of Euhaven. A bullet whizzed by Aurelio's head, snapping his attention to the militia soldier in front of him and shooting him in between the eyes. There was a soft click from the gun that let Aurelio know he was out of bullets. He slung the empty rifle behind his back and made to run when he noticed two more soldiers making their way toward him.

These two were Wielding the water around them. They were covered head to toe in black with masks covering the bottom half of their faces. From what he could see, one had turquoise eyes and the other deep-sea blue. The one with turquoise eyes formed a whip of water while the other formed a sword and turned it into ice.

What? He'd never known water Wielders who could also Wield ice. Usually, it was only one or the other. Lightning cracked around his hands and made their way up his arms. Storm Wielders could wield lightning in varying methods. Pulling a bolt from the clouds took more energy than Wielding the electricity around them. In a fight, the latter was usually best. Aurelio could tell the one with the ice sword smiled by the tilt of their eyes.

They moved impossibly fast. Aurelio threw a ball of electricity, hitting the one with the whip just barely before the one with Ice Wielding threw up an ice shield in front of them. The Water Wielder retaliated by sending the whip toward his head. Aurelio ducked and threw another ball of lightning almost instantaneously. The Water Wielder hadn't anticipated the second attack and flew back when the lightning hit them square in the chest. Aurelio barely managed to roll out of the way of the crystalline sword that came for his head from the Water Ice Wielder. He held up his lightning covered arm in hopes of shattering the sword but it did nothing against the ice.

"How can you wield both water and ice?" Aurelio grunted, before getting into their guard and landing an electric punch to their midsection. They let out a sharp exhale and brought their elbow across his cheek. He felt hot liquid make its way down his face that let him know he was bleeding. Aurelio shifted back, anger rising within him.

He hadn't heard from Quade and he had no idea if the bomb was safely defused. The Ice Wielder deemed to answer by hurling a sphere of ice the size of his fist toward him. It had spikes around it like a mace, and if it had made contact, he was sure he would've been seriously injured or killed. Acting on instinct, Aurelio turned it into snow in midair, causing it to float down harmlessly.

"Captain! We have a problem." Quade's voice rang in his ear. Before Aurelio could respond, a whip of water made its way around his throat from behind. The turquoise-eyed soldier was standing, armor gaping and smoking in the middle of their chest, the armor they wore had absorbed most of the blast. Although they wheezed and blood poured from their wound, they were not planning on giving up. Aurelio gasped to get a breath of air when water made its way down his throat, thoroughly attempting to drown him. He dropped to his knees, mud splattering. As he fought to keep the water from reaching his lungs, the one with the ice sword made their way menacingly toward him.

Aurelio knew Quade was yelling but couldn't hear what was being said past the roar of his pulse in his ears. Trying to grab the whip was useless and his vision dimmed around the edges. He gathered his Wielding, finding a calm in the impending blackness that was sure to take him. Two could play at that game. He would die by his own means and take them with him if he had to.

Aurelio watched through rapidly tunneling vision as the deep-sea blue-eyed one approached him, ice sword lifted and ready to cut him down. He felt more than saw the sword nearing his face. At the last moment, he pulled down a large bolt of lightning, throwing the Water Wielder back. Pain lanced through him as something hot and searing sliced across his face.

Aurelio vomited up the water that had invaded his throat, vision steadily coming back. As the blackness receded, he saw that the Water Wielder was nothing but a smoking carcass in the distance. The other had a barrier of ice around them but blood was pouring from their former sword hand, now amputated. Aurelio stood on wobbly knees, trying not to pass out from lack of oxygen. Warm blood leaked down his face, burning his eyes. The Ice Wielder dropped their shield and ran, and Aurelio found the strength to run after them. Flames went up in the distance, pinpointing where Quade was. It so happened to be in the direction the Water Ice Wielder was heading.

"Quade, talk to me! There's a Water Wielder heading your way, that can Wield ice—"

"What? How the fuck is that possible?" came Quade's shocked voice.

"Worry about that later. I'm on their heels. Did you get that bomb?" He panted, more blood pouring down his face. He must have been sliced by the sword. Quade's silence worried him. "Quade!"

"Captain, I don't think we can get to them. They have a shit ton of Earth Wielders surrounding the warehouse. I'm trapped behind a row of dumpsters."

This was not good. Since when did The Martyrs use so many Wielders? Aurelio and his team did not anticipate this many. They had gone into this mission thinking they were mostly dealing with humans. He pumped his legs, gaining ground on the Water Ice Wielder.

"I'm almost there. Stay where you are." Aurelio had to figure out how to get his team out. The five members volunteered to join the mission while the others were off rotation. They infiltrated *the warehouse in the hopes of gathering intel on the attack and blueprints of the bomb. Aurelio had been over confident letting them do the job. He should've been the one to infiltrate the warehouse. He should've been in there with them. Instead, he had been on the outskirts looking for the Head of the Martyrs. Aurelio's breath burned like fire in his lungs.*

"Stop!" he yelled, close enough to the Wielder to grab their hood. They managed to swerve and that was when he noticed that in their good hand was a trigger of some sort, blinking red. The closer they got to the warehouse, the faster the light blinked.

"Captain, I think there's an opening!" Quade's voice broke through.

"No! We have to stop that Wielder, they have the trigg—" before Aurelio could finish his sentence the warehouse blew, throwing him back and knocking him out.

Aurelio pulled himself out of his thoughts. He failed his team that night. Was he failing again? They'd already lost three members. He absent-mindedly ran a finger down his facial scar. It was a reminder of what he failed to do that night; save his team. His knee started to bounce up and down under the table, but thankfully no one noticed. Aurelio opened his mouth to speak but Quade beat him to it.

"You're quitting?" Quade was fuming, smoke rising from his hands. Lilith snapped her head to him.

"You want to be less of a dick?" she hissed at him. Ryland seemed to shrink in his seat. Quade slammed his fist on the table, rattling the dishes.

"No! We are Alpha Phoenix. We never quit." He pointed at Ryland. "We have a mission. *You* have a mission." His eyes flared before his tone softened. "I understand that you lost Luc. We all lost people in those woods." Quade reined in his anger. "Shouldn't that give you more of a reason to fight back?"

Aurelio hated to admit it but Quade was right. They'd lost people in the field before. They all knew the risks involved with being Special Forces. Their missions were always dangerous and there was always a risk of someone not making it home. Alpha Phoenix knew that. Luc knew that. So, Aurelio said as much.

"Luc, Misha, and Vivi all knew the risks. We aren't green. We *all* know the risks," Aurelio said, gentle authority in his voice. "We need every person on this. We can't fail." The smoke stopped rising off Quade as his temper fell. Ryland lifted his emerald eyes to Aurelio, silver lining them. "It's not a weakness to cry Ry." Aurelio took Ryland's hand. "We've seen too much to hold it in. Take the time here to properly mourn. We'll gather the intel. When it's time to leave, you *are* coming with us. Why is that?"

"Because we never quit. We never fail," Ryland said softly but with subtle strength. Aurelio patted his hand.

"And why else?"

"Because we're Alpha Phoenix and we get fucking revenge." He gripped Aurelio's hand, letting the tears fall. Quade patted him on the shoulder and Lilith reached over to wipe a tear. They made sure to let Ryland know he was not alone. His team—his brothers and sister—were here for him. Ryland stood up and gave everyone a nod before leaving for his room. Aurelio took a moment, rubbing the back of his head before letting out a breath.

Everyone moved to get started on their assignments. Quade and Lilith were to gather intel on Lex Esson-Tai while Aurelio planned to get in touch with his contact and find out where the cage fights happened. He made his way to his room to grab his gear, hoping to catch Xavia before she left, but she was already gone. Aurelio made his way out when his comm let out a soft beep. His watch showed the meetup place for his contact.

CHAPTER 18

STYX

S TYX WRINKLED HER NOSE AT at the smell of seawater. She hated it and the sticky air that came with Silvermoon Harbor. She loathed how the air made her mask even more suffocating than usual. Yeah, she had breathable mesh, but it didn't mean she enjoyed it. Styx kept her hood up despite the heat, her purple curls frizzing in the humidity. She found herself on the boardwalk, the beach and ocean to her left, and the city to her right. Even the city didn't sit right with her. If she didn't need to be here, she would happily have stayed back in Melhold, helping with the relief efforts.

Styx turned her back to the sea and the happy beach goers, leaning on the railing while she waited for Leo. She caught him walking toward her, wearing a black tee that did nothing to hide his lean muscles, cargo pants, and two guns at his side. His Storm Wieldermarks were on display on his wonderful dark brown skin. Exhaustion weighed heavy in his eyes.

"Long few days?" Styx murmured when he approached her. Leo's silver eyes rolled slightly as he huffed through his face mask.

"Yeah. You have no idea."

She did, but she kept her mouth shut. She'd spent the last few hours gathering information about the cage fights that took place in the 'Hood of Silvermoon. They were held in a seedy area of the city where the criminal underground took up base. The governor let the cage fights happen as a means to keep crime down as much as possible. Apparently, fighting and betting was a good outlet.

"So, Leo. Tell me, when were you going to inform me you're

actually Captain Aurelio of the Alpha Phoenix?" Styx knew she caught him off guard by the rise of his eyebrows, pulling the scar on his face up. She held up a gloved hand. "You're not the only one with sources. How else would I make a living doing what I do?" He chuckled as he took his mask off, taking a deep breath of fresh air.

She lifted an eyebrow of her own, wondering what his role in this was. Aurelio knew she was an assassin and spy. Did he plan to leverage that? If so, she'd kill him right here, right now. She began contemplating the different murder methods when he interrupted her thoughts with a heavy sigh.

"You have nothing to worry about," Aurelio said on the exhale. He rubbed the back of his head–a tell when he was frustrated. Interesting. He was so transparent. "I have my reasons for doing what I'm doing." He leaned on the railing next to her. The wind blew gently, his eyes darkening to a storm gray. "I'm fucking tired of doing the Monarch's dirty work."

"They're a piece of shit. I would be tired too." Styx held up her watch, clicking a button to bring up a hologram map of the city. "Did you know the governor oversees the cage matches?" Aurelio raised a brow. "No? Well, apparently, allowing the matches is better for his pockets and for keeping 'crime down'. He has an overseer, Norrix, who is one hell of an asshole and has something funky going on. I don't think he's a Wielder, but I can't pin what he is, exactly."

"I'm not surprised." Aurelio echoed her sentiment, eyes turning back to light silver. "Do you know where the fights are?"

She magnified the map to a specific block radius in the 'Hood.

"You'll find them somewhere here. They move around and based on the data; it's more than likely the next match is in this radius." Styx motioned for his watch and he held it up to her. "I'm transferring this to you." She bumped her watch against his.

"When is the next match?"

"Tonight." She caught his wince. "What is it?"

"Nothing. I have to find one of my team members. She volunteered to jump in a fight to hopefully find out some more information on Lex Esson-Tai. Do you know anything about them?"

Styx raised a shoulder in a shrug. "Nothing more than that they are a pirate and a vigilante." It was something she respected. Her eyes roved over him, wondering what his thought process was. She stood up straight and made to leave when he caught her wrist. Sparkles of electricity made its way up her arm. She suppressed the shiver that tried to make its way through her body from the odd sensation.

"What are you doing later?" he asked, his eyes now turning steel. His voice had dropped an octave it seemed, causing her eyebrows to lift. Thankfully he couldn't see the bottom half of her face or he'd notice her practically gaping at his boldness.

"Probably murdering someone," she deadpanned. It was her job after all. He chuckled, a smile crossing his lips, dimples creasing his cheeks.

"And after that? How about we have drinks?" He pulled her in a bit but not so much that it would make her uncomfortable.

"You don't even know what I look like," she said. Aurelio shrugged.

"I don't have to," he murmured.

"You don't even know my name." Styx met his steel eyes. He let go of her wrist, stepping away out of respect for her space. He clearly knew how to read the energy and she appreciated that.

"Styx. Assassin and Spy of the Martyrs." Aurelio smirked, dimples digging deep into his cheeks. She froze and he chuckled. "Don't worry. I won't tell anyone. But you and I will have to talk about the Martyrs." For a moment, she considered taking him up on his offer, even for friendly camaraderie, before her watch beeped. She looked down and paled. Shit, she had to go. Time was up.

"Maybe next time Aurelio, Captain of the Special Forces," she said before stepping back into a haze of purple smoke and disappearing.

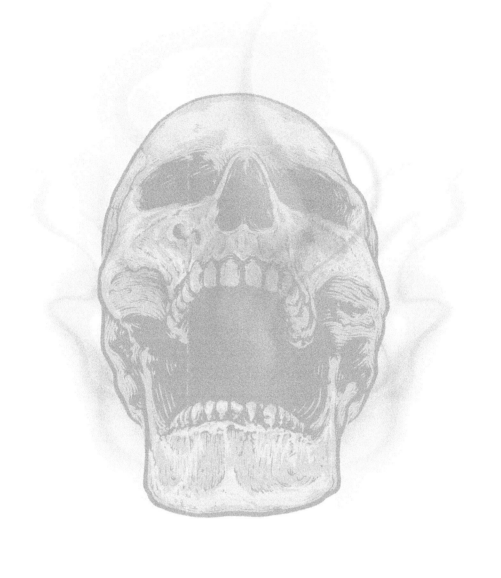

CHAPTER 19

XAVIA

XAVIA GROANED AS SHE RUBBED her aching jaw. Wait. Why the fuck was her jaw aching? The fog covering her brain started to lift as she took in her surroundings. She was in a cage of some sort. The floor was a dusty brown concrete with what looked like blood stains peppering it all over. She had been leaning on the wall of the cage, body struggling to breathe.

Xavia inhaled a large gulp of air, realizing she was in a fighting pit when she heard the cheer of people coming from above her. How the fuck did she get here, of all places? She looked down at herself, tank sweaty and dirt grimed, cargo jeans slightly torn. Xavia was pretty sure there was blood on her boots. Her guns were nowhere in sight. If someone stole them, she'd murder them! She rubbed her jaw again, noticing her hands were wrapped and bloody.*

"Nowhere for you to run, bitch!" came a growl from the other side of the cage. Well, Xavia knew the source of the blood now. The ugly male in front of her was bloodied up, the stuff pouring from his nose, with one eye swollen shut. He was tall and ridiculously muscular, which told her he wasn't human. Shaggy blond hair fell over his face, glowing hazel eyes staring out between the strands. Werewolf. She was almost sure of it. Obviously, he must not have been that great a fighter if she was able to fuck him up the way she apparently did.

"You sure you're not confusing me with you, pup?" Xavia

♪ "Little Girl Gone" by CHINCHILLA

retorted. Fuck, why did she say that? He howled–yep, definitely a werewolf–and ran at her. She ducked before his massive hand could land a blow to her head. Xavia managed to lock her arms around his torso, just barely able to link her hands, and slammed her knee up into his stomach. The male let out a grunt, pushing her to the side. She rolled and swung a leg out in an attempt to swipe his feet out from under him but he jumped over it.

Xavia had no clue how she got here but she damn sure knew she was going to end this fight.

She got to her feet and dodged a punch before landing an uppercut under his jaw. His head snapped back which gave her the room to throat check him with an open-handed chop. The crowd roared at every hit she landed. The werewolf choked, grabbing at his throat as it constricted on itself in defense of the violation. He bent over, heaving, so Xavia grabbed that musty hair of his and forced his head to connect with her knee. A tooth popped out of his mouth with a crunch. On his hands and knees, a growl emanated from his mouth.

"You're dead!" he roared, swiping and grabbing hold of her ankles. She fell backward hard enough to knock the breath out of her. The concrete scraped at her back and arms as he dragged her toward him. She attempted to bring her knee up again when he straddled her, his legs on either side keeping hers locked.

"Afterward, I'll enjoy feasting on your flesh," he growled, reaching for her throat.

Xavia held up an arm but he only grabbed it with his free hand and held it tightly to her side. She huffed when he wrapped his hand around her throat, tight enough to make her see black spots. At first, she struggled against his hold. But she realized that it would only waste energy and oxygen. It only took a few seconds for her to realize she still had her watch on, which held silver darts. Xavia let her body relax, letting him think she was giving up.

Nothing could prepare him for the silver she fired into his left eye. The werewolf howled, tumbling off of her and attempting to scratch at the darts. She stood slowly, body crying out in pain. Xavia heaved a deep breath, throat sore. Fuck, she was going to have a bruise. She stood over him while he slowly pulled the darts out with shaking hands. The look he gave her was now of caution instead of anger. She gave him a hearty, but not deadly, kick to his head to knock him out.

The surrounding crowd stilled for what seemed like forever before erupting into a deafening cheer. She bent over, hands on her knees, as she took big gulps of air. The fight ringmaster came out into the middle of the ring while two ogres made their way to the werewolf to haul him out. He motioned for her and she limped to his side and winced when he grabbed her sore hands.

"Our winner! Xavia of Melhold!" The crowd went wild. Xavia couldn't help but smirk despite how sore her body felt. The ringmaster dropped a bag of credits into her hand and her eyes widened. Holy fuck, that was a lot of credits. She must have found the infamous cage fights. Question was, how?

"Xavia! What the fuck!" Xavia turned to find Aurelio and Quade running toward her. The worry on Aurelio's face caused her smile to drop. He ran up to her, grabbing hold of her shoulders. He touched her face gently, then her torn up arms, held her hands, and then held her face again in his hands. Aurelio's eyes had turned stormy gray, letting her know he was both afraid and angry.

Quade was appraising her as if seeing her in a different light. Xavia wasn't sure if she should be impressed or worried. She was already on his radar as a target, most likely. The last thing she needed was for him to actually find her interesting. His eyes were so dark they were almost crimson.

"What were you thinking? I thought we agreed on doing this together?" Aurelio said through gritted teeth. One of Xavia's eyes twitched, ire growing within her.

"What? Didn't trust me to take care of myself?" she snapped. She turned to storm off, not willing to deal with this when her body deserved a hot bath.

"You weren't yourself in there," Aurelio said, halting her steps. "You were brutal. More so than your normal street fighting. It was like you had murder in your eyes. I honestly thought you were going to kill someone." She didn't know what to say to that. "You fought three werewolves, Xavia." Aurelio stepped toward her but was no longer trying to touch her. She balked. No wonder she was so sore.

"I'll admit, even I was impressed," Quade quipped.

"I don't give a fuck if I impressed you," Xavia snarled before whipping to Aurelio. "I blacked out," she said without hesitation. "I went to the room to grab my gear and that was the last thing I remember. I came to not too long before that jackass called me a bitch."

"Shit..." Aurelio hissed, rubbing the back of his head. His eyes bled back to silver as weariness settled into his eyes and body.

"Wait, what the fuck do you mean, 'you blacked out'?" Quade seethed, stepping in between Aurelio and Xavia. Xavia attempted to shove him off but let out a gasp of pain. Her hands were killing her. "Answer me..." Quade was unmovable, staring down at her as if he deserved answers from her. Xavia stared back at him, refusing to budge.

"I *don't* answer to you. I don't owe you jack shit," she hissed, shoulder checking him as best she could, considering his height, wincing. Aurelio motioned for Quade to wait while he followed Xavia as she made her way toward the locker rooms.

"How did you even find this place?" he asked. Xavia shrugged.

"That's what I'd like to know," she grunted, limping a bit. People patted her shoulder as she passed, and she had to fight a wince each time they touched her or brushed against her. Aurelio walked alongside her, mumbling to himself about werewolves and her trying to get herself killed. As if this was her choice? Just as Xavia got near the locker rooms, she turned to him. "Wait. Do you have—"

"Yes." Aurelio held up her gun belt and her two favorite babies. She let out a sigh of relief before making her way into the grimy room they had the audacity to call a locker room. In the bathroom, she caught sight of herself in the mirror.

"What the fuck did I get myself into?" Xavia mumbled, taking in her bruised jaw, busted eye, split lit, and the growing bruise around her neck. She was filthy. Grime stuck to her and the humidity didn't make it any better. Her hair was in a tight braid with loose curls fraying at the edges of her hairline. Slight cuts littered her arms from obviously being tossed around. She winced, pulling a piece of gravel out of her forearm. She was going to need a medi-pill, or three.

Xavia didn't even want to know the state of her hands. She stared at them, shaking, bruised, and bloodied. How much of it was her blood? How much of it was theirs? Thankfully lycanthropy was not contracted through blood. She wouldn't make a very good werewolf. She let out a huff that was in between a giggle and a sob. Why did this keep happening to her?

"Can I help you with that?" came Aurelio from behind. Xavia looked through the dirty mirror at him. He had slung her belt over his shoulder and was leaning against the door frame, arms crossed in front of him. How long had she been standing in the bathroom? Tears made their way down her cheeks, leaving trails through the grime.

Aurelio remained silent as he walked to her and gently took one hand. He began unwrapping it slowly, the warmth of his hands slowing the shaking of hers. He must be so sick of it by now. Of dealing with her blackouts for so long. Xavia wasn't sure why he still considered her an important part of his life. How much patience could someone have with a person like her? Her life was unpredictable and she could never offer a semblance of stability or normalcy.

"Ow!" Xavia yelped as the last of the wrap pulled a bit of skin with it. Aurelio turned on the sink which groaned through the pipes. There was some lye soap that made her cringe by the smell alone, and he lathered it up to wash her hand. "Mother fucking piece of shit!" It wasn't aimed at him, he knew that, which was why he smirked. Burning lit up her hand. She'd obviously torn her skin in several places. Her middle finger was bruised and dislocated.

"You and that mouth." Aurelio gave a low chuckle, not looking up from her hand. Xavia narrowed her eyes and stuck a tongue out at him. "Very mature." How he knew without looking was beyond her.

After rinsing, he took a gentle but firm hold of her middle

finger. She gritted her teeth and tried not to let loose more expletives when he popped it back in place. A gleam of sweat was beginning to form on her brow as he began working on the second hand, her dominant one. The wraps pulled at her skin and revealed her hand was completely purple. How hard was she hitting these males? Xavia had been in plenty of street fights and cage matches but never had she been this bruised up. She groaned in pain as he washed her hand gently.

"I think it's broken." Xavia gasped as he gently turned it over. Aurelio hummed, nodding his head in agreement. He pulled out two medi-pills and anti-bruise ointment. She swallowed the pills as soon as he passed it to her and couldn't suppress a groan as he massaged the ointment into her hands. He kept going until relief found her and the pain subsided but not completely. It would take at least a day or two for the fractures to heal and the bruising would last longer.

Aurelio grabbed a somewhat clean towel and ran it under the water to clean up her face. With gentle care, Xavia closed her eyes as he cleaned the sweat, blood, and tears from her face. It took everything in her to not break down.

"I don't think I've ever seen you fight like that," he said, softly, helping her with her gun belt. As he tightened it, he yanked her close and it left her somewhat breathless. "You can't be going off on your own," Aurelio said, sucking the air from the room. "I don't know what I'd do if something happened to you." His eyes turned steel as they met hers. Xavia felt like a fish out of water, mouth agape and without words to say.

"I... I didn't mean to." She let out a gasp before his lips met hers. There was something different in the way he kissed her. When they were together all those years ago, it was a young naïve male and a tortured young woman. Now? This was a kiss of a Captain and Bounty Hunter. The ferocity in which Aurelio kissed her left heat burning inside, electricity sliding its way up her arms.

Xavia opened to him, tongues clashing. One hand remained on her belt, the other moved to hold her at the nape of her neck to turn her head up and give him more access. His tongue licked at her lips, teeth grazing her lower lip, before sucking it in between his own. There was a sharp pain from her split lip and he ran his tongue over it soothingly. Xavia pulled away just enough before taking his lower lip in between her teeth, returning the favor. Aurelio let out a growl, hand shifting to wind itself into her hair. She made to wrap her arms around him when a searing pain lanced through her from her broken hand. It brought her back to reality and she broke the kiss.

"No. No." Xavia shook her head, cradling her hand in her arm. She stepped away from him, catching her breath. Aurelio was equally as bothered, a clear bulge straining against his pants. She snapped her eyes up to his face, taking in his bruised lips and heavy-lidded stare. She almost lost it watching him run a thumb over his lower lip, her blood coating it, before licking it off. Who was this man and what did he do with Aurelio?

"We can't do this. Especially right now," Xavia said, voice shaky. He nodded, seeming to get himself under control and motioned as if to say *after you*. She stiffly moved, body aching and not just because of the fight. What in the hell was that?

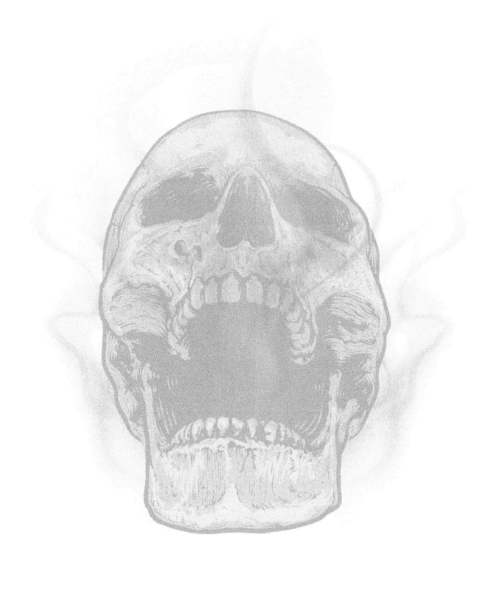

CHAPTER 20

QUADE

FIRE SPURTED FROM QUADE'S HANDS as he paced outside the locker room. A pair of gorgons walked by, eyeing him suspiciously. The look on his face must've told them all they needed to know, because they picked up their pace to the exit. He was pissed at Xavia for her recklessness but couldn't help but respect the hell out of her for her fighting. She was brutal and primal. It reminded Quade of himself in ways he didn't want to acknowledge.

"Fuck..." came Xavia's groan as she exited the locker room, eyes down at her hands. She was royally fucked up. The bruise on her jaw darkened by the minute, along with the nasty one around her neck. Blood crusted her hairline but the grime around her face was clearly washed off. Xavia cradled her punching hand with her opposite arm, her hand clearly broken. It pissed Quade off that she went off on her own and nearly gave Aurelio a heart attack. It was by chance that they ended up here with her in the ring. They weren't even sure if this was going to be the right location.

Anyone would've said Xavia winning was luck. But Quade knew without a doubt that had she stayed in the Academy, she would've placed in the top three behind him and Aurelio. Instead, she was raw fury, filled with wild energy, and an especially skilled brawler. He didn't know if that made her more dangerous.

He glowered at her, thinking of the risk she posed to the whole team; the mission itself. Blackouts? She had blackouts? What the fuck did that entail? Quade stood there as she walked right into him. A current of fire licked its way across his skin and down his hands to her shoulders as he placed them to catch her from falling over. Xavia started, wincing at the flame.

"Shit." Watching her eyes change from bewilderment to anger did something to him that he didn't want to admit out loud. "What do you want?" she snapped.

"*You* walked into me. Not my fault you weren't paying attention," Quade snarled back, letting her go. "You look royally fucked."

Her eyes widened a bit before what he said registered. Xavia snapped them down into a baleful stare. Ah. Something must've happened between her and Aurelio. Just fucking great. Not what they needed.

"Fuck you Quade. Why are you even here?" Xavia winced as she rocked back and forth on her feet.

"Someone had to make sure Aurelio doesn't lose his shit." Quade leaned against the wall, crossing his arms. "You're a fucking liability. His head isn't on straight." She clenched her jaw, the muscle ticking a few times.

"It is not my fault that the Guard has piss poor trackers," she hissed. Quade's nose flared, fire flooding his veins. He clenched his fists to keep smoke from rising off his skin.

"It wouldn't have been a problem if you actually finished the Academy, but you quit. You're a quitter. I'm surprised you haven't run off yet." He took satisfaction in the rising anger he caused in her. Good. She fucking deserved it.

"I am *not* a fucking quitter," Xavia said, stepping up to him, her brown eyes almost black with anger. Quade fought the urge to push her against the wall and make her prove to him she wasn't a quitter. There was something about her brand of fury that called to him but he could not afford to be distracted. It made him even angrier at this succubus of a female.

"You're right, I could've run away, but I didn't because I have a mission to complete. Just because I'm not a Guard doesn't mean I'm not up to snuff." They kept eyes on each other, steaming. Quade's eyes flared deep orange like the sunset as fire licked his fingers.

"I think that's exactly what it means." It wasn't that he had an issue with bounty hunters. It was the fact that one was assigned to this mission. "Other than the Academy, you've no experience with these types of missions. So not only are you a distraction for Aurelio, you're a liability because you don't know how to work with a team."

Xavia rolled her eyes, being the one to break eye contact.

"I know how to work with a team. We wouldn't have gotten this far if I couldn't!"

Quade could tell he'd hit a sore spot by her reaction. She stepped away to bounce on her feet again, presumably impatient because Aurelio hadn't stepped out of the locker room yet. She must've done a number on him—again.

"What do you call going to a cage fight on your own? Teamwork? Because none of us knew where you were. As I said, it was by chance that the intel Aurelio received matched up." Quade watched her bristle as his words hit home.

"*That* wasn't my fault," Xavia said without as much fire. Quade pointed to her.

"And *that* is why you're a liability."

AURELIO

AURELIO RUBBED THE BACK OF HIS HEAD, watching Xavia exit the locker room. He took a few minutes to bring down the energy that was building in him and calm his raging hard on. What was wrong with him? Only just a couple of hours ago he was hitting on Styx and now Xavia? Maybe he just needed to get laid. But fuck, he hadn't expected that kissing Xavia would have that much of an effect on him. Sure, it had been years since they'd been together intimately, but he was sure she'd never kissed him like *that* during their time together.

"Do you know who runs this place?" Xavia asked as Aurelio

finally stepped out of the locker room. It was as if they'd never even touched. Quade eyed them, blind to nothing. There was an energy between the two of them that told Aurelio that they had gotten into an argument.

"Yeah, Norrix Aimes." Aurelio nodded to what looked like an office overlooking the pit. "My source says that no one knows exactly what he is. He's not a Wielder, but he's not human either. He's an asshole, a murderer, and intelligent. Apparently, the governor is just a puppet. Norrix is the one pulling the strings." They made their way toward the steps that lead to the office. "Hopefully he might know something about Lex."

"If Lex is the savior that everyone thinks they are, why would they work with someone like Norrix?" Xavia seemed apprehensive which was understandable. But it was the only lead they had to work with. Quade and Lilith had come up with nothing on Lex, hence why Quade was with them tonight.

"Well, Norrix commandeered Lex's ship once." He shrugged when Xavia whipped her head to him. "That should be good enough to go on."

In front of Norrix's office were two large ogres. They wore black shirts and jeans, with guns in holsters under their arms. They were meant to be intimidating, but it did not impress Aurelio.

"We have a meeting with Norrix," he said to them, "Leo and Xay." The ogre on the right spoke into his comms before nodding. He opened the door to the office and Aurelio followed Xavia in. Quade was to stay outside with the ogres to make sure there were no surprises during their meeting.

The office was pristine; a contrast to the fighting ring and area below. Aurelio almost felt bad for stepping onto the mahogany floors with his muddy boots. The walls were charcoal with wine trimmings. Papers and books covered the ornate ebony desk in front of them. Rising from the leather chair was Norrix. The aura that came from this man was pure evil. There was a smirk on his face as he stood. He wasn't tall, maybe an inch or two shorter than Aurelio, but the energy coming off him more than made up for it.

Norrix wore black dress slacks with ruby pinstripes, a black long sleeve button up that was rolled to his elbows and a ruby vest over it. His skin was pale as snow, eyes a crimson color, and his face angular with high cheekbones. Short and cleanly cut wine hair covered his scalp. Even Aurelio could admit that this male was good looking. He would've thought Norrix was a vampire but the vampires never visited the Trezora continent. Norrix's smile grew as if he read Aurelio's thoughts.

"No Mr. Broderick. I am not a vampire." Aurelio paled. "Yes, I know who you and Ms. Silveria are." Norrix motioned to the chairs in front of the desk.

Xavia let out a sigh as she sunk into the chair. Aurelio didn't let his eyes off Norrix as he made his way over. If Xavia felt what he felt, she didn't let on. Aurelio opted to remain standing, keeping his hand rested on his gun belt.

Norrix's eyes flashed as he turned to Xavia. "And you, Ms. Silveria, are the human who defeated not one, not two, but *three* of my werewolves." Aurelio bristled at the tone of Norrix's voice, as if Xavia was a prize that he wanted to keep as a pet. Xavia shrugged, waving a hand at him.

"Yeah, that's me." She rubbed her temple. "Sorry to cut the chit chat before it even begins, but we need your help.". Norrix raised an eyebrow, waiting for her to continue. "We need to find Lex Esson-Tai, ASAP." She continued to rub her temple, letting Aurelio know she absolutely felt the same as he did about Norrix.

"And why would I help you?" Norrix said smoothly, making his way to a wet bar made of the same ebony wood as the desk. He picked up a decanter of whiskey and poured three rocks glasses. He brought them over, Aurelio shaking his head at the offer. Xavia took both of them, downing them without hesitation. Aurelio bit back his retort when Norrix laughed. "You're a bold one, aren't you?" He leaned against the desk, closer to Xavia than Aurelio was comfortable with. She sat up, resting her elbows on her knees.

"I just beat down three of your werewolves. I put on a good fucking show and I bet you raked in the credits for it too." Xavia, always the eloquent one. "I figure it would only be fair to give us the information we need." She shrugged. Norrix raised the decanter still in his hand as if in question and Xavia nodded. He poured a double, which she sipped this time around. She was smart enough to not get drunk around him.

"The sooner you can give us the information, the sooner we can get out of your hair," Aurelio said, ice lacing his voice.

Norrix looked up at him slowly, with that glint of evil in his eyes. He fought a shudder at the look. Aurelio didn't scare easily but this male had all his instincts telling him to run. Norrix looked back to Xavia as if Aurelio was just a nuisance. Aurelio bristled, opening his mouth to say something unsavory.

"You only served to prove that I need better fighters," Norrix said as he placed the decanter on the desk behind him. "I hardly call that a profit. Do you know how much they cost to replace?" He tilted his head to the side, assessing Xavia as if looking at ways he could profit off her skills.

"So, what do you want then?" Xavia sighed as she sat back, obviously tired and ready to get this over with. Aurelio stood there, letting himself be the presence and strength she needed. Clearly Norrix was going to ignore him.

"You—"

Aurelio took a step forward but Xavia held up her hand for him to wait. Norrix smiled, eyes flashing.

"I want you to go to dinner with me. One night. And I'll give you the location on where to find Lex."

Aurelio wanted her to say no. He figured they could find another way to get the information. She didn't need to sell herself out for them, for the Monarchy that she hated so much.

"Xavia, you don't—"

"Ok," Xavia said, standing up. Aurelio could feel the color drain from his face as he looked at her in shock. She grunted. "I'd shake your hand but mine is sort of broken right now."

"Wonderful. Meet me at The Harlequin." Norrix plucked a card off his desk and wrote down the information. "I'll send you a dress," he murmured, again raking those eyes over her. Aurelio wanted to pluck those crimson eyes out of his skull and feed it to a basilisk. "I wouldn't want to do that Mr. Broderick." Norrix said, malice coating his tongue. Did the male read his mind? "Yes, it's a gift of mine." Norrix responded. It was impossible, or at least he thought it was. Wielders in Special Forces are trained to block against mental attacks and mind reading. There was something off about Norrix and it made him add another layer to his mental shields.

Thunder boomed outside. Aurelio could feel electricity pulsing in his veins, even if he couldn't Wield it indoors.

Xavia turned tired eyes to Aurelio which dampened his anger. She needed to rest or she would collapse from exhaustion. He gave her a nod, offering his arm. Aurelio would be lying if he said he wasn't surprised that she actually linked her arm in his. She didn't do well with accepting help in public. Quade trailed them as they walked out of the fight club. He took in every cut, scar, and bruise that made her who she was, externally and internally. Aurelio knew she had a dark past that she never spoke of. But he would ride or die for this woman. Whether they were lovers or platonic. He wasn't going anywhere and he hoped she knew that.

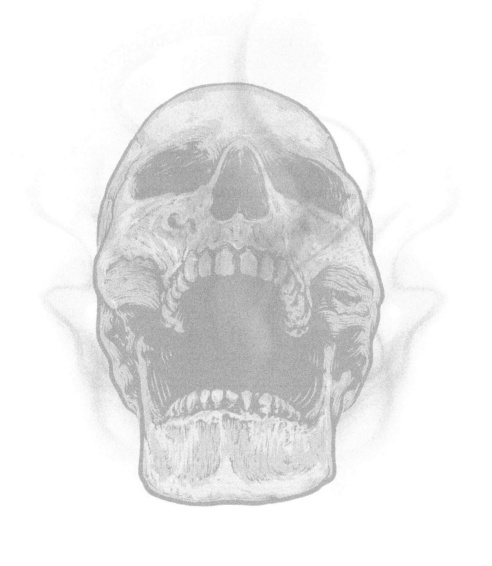

CHAPTER 21

XAVIA

SHE WOKE UP WONDERING IF LAST night was a dream. But she quickly crashed back to reality when the soreness of her body sang through her.

"Fuuuck," she groaned, noticing that she had ointment all over, fresh bandages on her hands, and felt a butterfly stitch on her cheekbone. Snoring came from the corner of the room; Aurelio had completely passed out in an armchair. Purple shadows lingered under his eyes as if he tried his hardest to stay awake all night. She'd slept like a rock, barely remembering much after the fight. Xavia shifted to sit up and let out a groan that was louder than she wanted, causing Aurelio to jerk awake.

"You're up," he murmured, rubbing his eyes. She gave him a *no shit* look which made him smirk. "You remember much of last night?" he asked, crossing his foot onto his opposite knee. Xavia shrugged and fought to sit up against the headboard. Her foot hit a box on the bed and she arched an eyebrow. "That's for you." Aurelio's eyes turned stormy, a crack of lightning crossing the otherwise clear sky.

"What..." The memory hit her like a slap. She'd agreed to go on a date with a crime boss. Xavia groaned, pulling the blanket up to her face. She felt the bed move, and the blanket slipped from her hands.

"No, you don't get to hide." Aurelio's gaze burned through her. She hadn't forgotten the searing kiss they'd shared, how could she? But now was not the time to think about it. He opened his mouth to say something.

"I'm sorry I agreed to the dinner without contemplating it first," she blurted. His mouth snapped shut, eyes still stormy. "I was exhausted. Coming out of a fugue state fucks me up. And I wasn't thinking clearly. But…" Aurelio's jaw clenched, the muscle ticking. "It's a necessary evil if we can get this information. Obviously, Lex is not an easy person to find. Clearly, they're good at their job."

She groaned again, inspecting her hand. The fractures had already healed, but the bruising remained. As if he could read her mind, Aurelio stuck out two medi-pills and anti-bruise ointment for her.

"Thank you," Xavia murmured before popping the pills in her mouth. She rubbed the ointment on her hands, sighing in relief. They stared at each other for a breath and she sighed. "G'head… Have at it."

"Do you realize that you have put yourself in the hands of probably the most dangerous crime boss in Asherai?" Aurelio blew up, as if he'd been holding it in since last night. He popped up from the bed and paced. "I looked him up. Norrix Aimes. Crime lord, murderer, terrorist… You name it." He rubbed the back of his head. "And the worst part?" Xavia's stomach dropped, knowing what he was about to say before he said it. "He's a trafficker," he practically growled.

"Fuck," was all she could say. Xavia's world was spinning. She felt like she was failing in the job that was given to her. *She* was supposed to be the one finding this intel, instead she was blacking out, her body making its own decisions. He stopped dead in his pacing.

"Fuck? That's all you have to say?" Aurelio glared at her. If it wasn't for the soreness in her body, she'd pop right up to his face. Instead, she threw the anti-bruise ointment at his head. He caught it before it could connect, making her even angrier.

"Yes! I need more than a few minutes to process things, Aurelio. Not everyone is a genius like you." His gaze softened slightly and this time Xavia threw her comm, connecting with his forehead. "And don't you fucking pity me either!" She took no small amount of pleasure from the grunt that left his mouth and the look of shock on his face. Aurelio rubbed his forehead and sat on the bed heavily.

"I need you to cancel." He spoke so softly that she almost thought she misunderstood.

"Want to say that again?"

He was doing nothing to reduce her temper.

"I *need* you to cancel," Aurelio said, adding authority to his tone.

"Fuck you! You don't get to tell me what to do. You think I can't handle it?" Xavia was fuming now. "Why?" Tears pricked her eyes, but she refused to cry. She'd cried enough these last few days. She finally managed to get herself to her feet, moving around the bed to look him head on. Even on the bed, he met her height, maybe even a little taller than her. "Because I've got a fucked-up brain? Is that it? Do you think I'm so incapable that—".

"Xavia, shut. up." Aurelio growled, before grabbing her from her nape and pulling her into another one of those searing kisses. What was going on here? She pushed away, shaking her head.

"No. No, we're not doing this. Don't try to distract me." Xavia panted, turning away. "This isn't the first time I've had to go under to get intel." She crossed her arms at her stomach. "I need you to trust me."

Aurelio stood, turning her toward him. He lifted his hand to her face, thumb trailing her jawline where a bruise was healing.

"It's not that I don't trust you." He tilted her head so he could turn those silver eyes on hers. Xavia bit her lower lip which drew his eyes to them. "I don't trust *him*." He leaned in, placing the softest of soft kisses on her forehead. She pulled away from him again and he dropped his hand like a weight. "Xavia..."

"No. What are we doing? What's going on here?" She motioned between the two of them. "Is it adrenaline from Axton's forsaken mission?" Xavia shook her head, eyes snagging on the box on the bed. She pointed to the door. "Just get out. I need a shower and some time to myself. I'm sure you can come up with a game plan with the team for tonight." Xavia dismissed him, heading into the bathroom and snapping the door shut.

She leaned on it, listening to Aurelio fuss before he finally left. She practically slumped to the ground but started to undress instead. Catching sight of herself in the mirror, she saw the healing bruises covering several places on her body. The medi-pills had been doing their job, healing her body at an accelerated pace. She still felt like shit and needed food as soon as possible.

Xavia let out a sigh as she stood under the steaming hot water. It seemed to relax every aching muscle. Thoughts of the last eighteen years of her life rushed at her. How did she get to this point?

Nicolai was absolutely the yummiest male she ever saw. Xavia couldn't take her eyes off the grown man before her. The fact that he wanted her attention made her blush. How was it that she, a seventeen-year-old, had the attention of this hot businessman? Sure, he was probably fifteen years older than her, but what did that matter? Nicolai always told her that age was nothing but a number. He said she was mature for her age and she believed him. She was half sitting up on the bed and giggled as he pulled her to him by her feet and began kissing her up her leg. He was her first and only.

"You are so beautiful," Nicolai murmured, hazel eyes darkening as he took her in. He slicked his shoulder length tawny hair back, revealing a serpent tattoo on his ivory neck. His shoulders were broad, muscles straining against his button up. He had a soft midsection but it didn't take anything from his sex appeal or strength. Xavia laughed again.

"Am I really?" The innocence in her voice made her wince. She didn't want to sound like a child. "I mean, I guess I am, aren't I?" She said with more confidence than she felt.

Nicolai nodded, moving to kiss her lips. His kiss left her breathless, reminding her of why she dropped out of high school. Around her ankle was a diamond studded anklet, a matching one around her neck. He'd promised to take care of her and had done so for the last two years they'd been together.

"Yes. I can prove it to you." He kissed her neck before standing up and opening the bedroom door. Xavia pulled the lower half of her dress down when she saw one of Nicolai's friend enter the room. He gave a smirk, a heated look in his eyes. Xavia looked to Nicolai

who gave a nod to his friend. "Mikael here thinks you're beautiful too."

Mikael looked to be about the same age as Nicolai, but where Nicolai had a mostly muscular body, Mikael was not. It wasn't that he wasn't attractive, but he was not Nicolai. Xavia didn't want anyone but Nicolai, so why was Mikael here?

"Um. Thanks," Xavia said, unsure of why it mattered.

"Didn't I say I'd prove your beauty?" Nicolai said, unbuttoning his shirt. She started to feel nervous, unsure of what was going on. Mikael followed suit, his brown eyes slowly roving over her. A body full of tattoos was displayed as he took his shirt off. Xavia sat up and moved herself to the headboard, away from him. She looked to Nicolai.

"Nicolai, what—" Nicolai moved to her with a glass of vodka in hand.

"Shh. Here, drink this. It'll help calm your nerves," he said, as he sat on the bed next to her, Mikael sitting on the other side. Xavia was already a bit buzzed but she took the glass, trusting him, and started to drink it slowly. He tipped the cup in her hand, forcing her to gulp down the burning liquor instead. She winced as the fire of the vodka made its way down her throat. Nicolai refilled the glass, nodding to her to drink. A tear slid down her face as she gulped it down, Mikael now placing a hand on her thigh. The room started to spin.

"Mikael thinks you're so beautiful, he's willing to pay me to have you for a night." Nicolai chuckled. Heat rushed up to her face in embarrassment. She didn't want to be with anyone other than Nicolai and she wasn't comfortable with Mikael touching her. Xavia tried to move her leg out of his touch but he grabbed her thigh instead. She gasped; his grip was rough enough to bruise.

"I don't..." The room spun again. "I don't know what to say." Her glass was refilled and Nicolai nodded to her to drink some more. She shook her head. Her stomach was already doing flips and she didn't want to vomit.

"You say yes," he said roughly, grabbing her chin and tipping the vodka into her mouth. Xavia couldn't do anything but *drink unless she wanted to choke and cough on the vile stuff. She attempted to move again but found her limbs not working the way she wanted them to. Her head was foggy; the edges of her vision darkening. Nicolai laid her back, hand running up one leg while Mikael ran his hand up the other. Together they pushed her dress up, exposing her. Tears fell from her eyes. Xavia tried to fight again as her vision blurred and got darker. As she started to black out from the alcohol induced coma, she could feel her hands being tied above her head. Why would Nicolai do this to her? She thought he loved her.*

Xavia gasped, pulling herself out of the memory, finding herself on the floor of the shower and huddled in on herself. It felt as if her limbs were concrete, weighing her down. The water had gone cold, tears flowing from her eyes. She fucking hated traffickers. She was a victim herself. Why the fuck did she agree to a dinner with Norrix? Maybe she deserved it. After getting free from Nicolai, all she did was dive deeper into pain and anger, fucking things up over and over again. It was a wonder Aurelio ever put up with her.

Xavia's body began to shake as sobs escaped her mouth. She was so fucking stupid. She grabbed her hair, ignoring the pain of her still healing hands, and began to rock back and forth. What was she doing? Why was she here? Who would let a fucking psycho on their team? Maybe it would just be easier for everyone if she wasn't here. The implications of where her thoughts were going were dangerous.*

"Fuck!" Xavia yelled, grabbing her hair tighter. Suddenly the door knob clicked and Aurelio burst through the door. She looked up to him, sure that she looked like pure shit. Her hair was plastered all over her face, eyes red and splotchy. Xavia was shivering, the water ice cold, but it didn't stop him from hopping into the shower to gather her in his arms. She shook her head, making to smack him away.

"No! No! All I do is fuck things up," she cried, banging her fists against his immovable body. Aurelio held her tighter, pulling her

♪ "The Way That You Were" by Sleep Token

face to his chest. "Why do you stay around? Your life would be so much better without me." Xavia's voice was hoarse, throat raw. Aurelio remained silent as he turned off the shower and brought her to stand. "Life would be easier for everyone if I didn't exist." She was mumbling, letting the words out that she never verbalized before. She stood there as Aurelio patiently dried her body and then wrapped the towel around her. "Why am I so cursed? What Deity did I piss off?" Xavia put her hands to her face to scrub at it, rubbing the back of her hand against her forehead over and over. Aurelio gently took her hands to ease them from her forehead.

He moved her to sit on a stool. He grabbed a hair oil provided by the B&B and put some in her hair. The lavender scent started to ease some of her pain. Xavia let her hands drop to her lap, closing her eyes to the tears that kept falling. Aurelio combed out her hair, like he always did when she had a meltdown. All feeling seeped out of her body, spiraling like a black hole.

"Why do you care about me? Why did you love me?" she whispered. "I'm not worth it." Her lip quivered, threatening another sob.

Xavia felt Aurelio move away before he was kneeling in front of her, hands on either side of her face, lifting to look up at him. She opened her eyes slowly to find that he was soaked and his silver eyes held his own tears. Xavia felt like Aurelio could see her anima. She'd never said these things out loud to him. He never truly knew the turmoil in her head. His thumbs glided gently across her jaws before moving to capture her tears. His silver eyes searched her own, saying everything she needed without him ever having to speak a word.

"I'm not going anywhere. No matter where you go. No matter how dirty life gets. You will never be alone again. You're worth breathing for. You're worth loving and living for."

Aurelio's words blew her mind and made her sob again. He wrapped his arms around her, pulling her close. Xavia grabbed his shirt, clinging on to him, her lifeline. He had always been her rock. She just hadn't realized it until now.

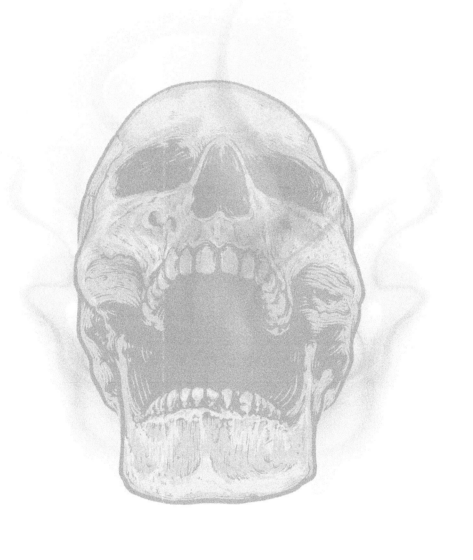

CHAPTER 22

AURELIO

AURELIO SLUMPED INTO THE CHAIR beside their bed. Xavia was out cold, body exhausted from her episode. He watched as the moon shone over her beautiful face, the peace she found in sleep a stark contrast to her waking moments. He had a feeling this dinner with Norrix triggered her episode but he wasn't sure why. Xavia had a dark past that she didn't even talk to him about. Judging from the ragged scar on her neck, he knew it was rough.

Aurelio had never known the extent of the turmoil that went on in Xavia's head. Sure, he knew she had her clinical diagnoses, but he never understood how bad it got for her. Has she been suffering from this her whole life? He'd help her through meltdowns, helping her bathe or towel off, brushing her hair. Anything he could do to help her come down from an episode and bring her some semblance of peace. But each time, Xavia always remained silent. She would shed tears quietly and then drift off to sleep.

His knee bobbed up and down as he worked to fit the pieces together. She didn't seem to mind going to dinner with Norrix to get intel. *That* shit pissed off Aurelio, but Xavia was fuming as usual until...

"Trafficking..." He murmured to himself. After Xavia found out that Norrix was a trafficker, her mood shifted. She went from angry, to shock, and then to fury, before breaking down in the shower. The pieces of the puzzle fell into place.

Xavia had been trafficked.

Anger like he'd never felt rose in his anima. Lightning struck across the sky, a clap of thunder on its heels. He stood slowly, the storm building in fury inside his body. Its barely contained swirl of chaos made him tremble. Keeping his hand still, he cupped Xavia's face and gave her a kiss on her forehead. Electricity hummed under his skin, threatening to sear him from the inside out.

Fuck this.

AURELIO STEPPED OUT OF THEIR ROOM, dressed head to toe in black. He wore a leather jacket that hung over his gun vest and belt. Four guns didn't feel like enough, so he had two bowie knives strapped to the back of his belt with another, smaller, knife at his ankle. He slipped on leather gloves, and his combat boots barely made a sound as he made his way down and out of the B&B without being seen. He hopped onto his motorcycle and made a beeline for the 'Hood.

Aurelio was going to get answers from Norrix, even if it meant that he'd have to kill the damn male himself. He would *not* put Xavia in that situation. He weaved in and out of the cars. The sounds of the Lunar Festival were all over, pedestrians taking up the sidewalks. He hit a sharp turn, approaching the large warehouse where the recent cage fight was held. Aurelio knew Norrix moved with the fights but he had no other lead than the warehouse. His tires squealed as he hit the brake and pulled up in front of the building.

Two ogres were standing outside and began eyeing him up when Aurelio stormed toward them. Lightning cracked across the sky, gray clouds forming, filled with rain. Electricity sang through his body, sparking at his hands and crackling up his arms. The ogres rested their hands on the guns at their sides, waiting for his next move before deciding theirs.

"Where is Norrix Aimes?" he growled. The ogre to the left raised an eyebrow, stepping forward to lay a hand on Aurelio's shoulder.

"You don't find him, he finds you," the wiseass said before

lightning cracked down from the sky and burnt him to ash. Aurelio brushed the ash from his jacket, turning his now storm gray eyes to the remaining ogre. The ogre immediately lifted his hands.

"He's at The Harlequin. Checking his girls." It took everything in Aurelio to not turn that ogre to ash as well. Norrix was going to have Xavia show up at a mother fucking brothel? Aurelio sped off on the motorcycle, earning a few honks and curses from the people he cut off. He barely put it in park as he hopped off, ignoring the valet as he made his way toward the restaurant entrance.

The Harlequin was touted as a fine dining establishment. Leading up to the doors were stunning black marble stairs, red velvet carpeting running down the middle. Above the wine-colored doors was a large obsidian Harlequin mask with a red fleur-de-lis under each eye like tear drops. The lips were red and white flourishes decorated the cheeks and forehead. There was a gold trim around the mask that he was pretty sure was actual pure gold and not just paint. Aurelio couldn't help but roll his eyes. The doors had matching elements of the mask, swirls in white throughout.

If he thought the mask was gaudy, the inside of the restaurant was even more ostentatious. The floors were made of black marble with red and gold veins throughout. Each table had black tablecloths with red linens, the glassware gold. Gold silk curtains flowed down on each red painted wall. It was like they only used three colors and refused to add anything else. There was a wide elegant staircase in the middle made of, you guessed it, black marble. The gold rails seemed to float if he hadn't saw the thin wires holding them up. No one stopped Aurelio as he went up the stairs two at a time. As he entered the second floor, he noticed the atmosphere on the second floor was very different from the first.*

The light was dimmer here, casting a red hue around the black booths. There was a fog covering the floors, music with heavy bass playing. Many of them were occupied by masked men with women in their laps. All the women wore golden mesh veils that obscured their identities. They were either completely nude or with

♪ "Pullin Up" by Soda

gilded straps in between their breasts, across their waist, and in between their legs. Some of the men didn't bother to get a room and were openly having sex at the booths.

"You're new," a husky voice said. Aurelio turned his attention to the naked woman before him. He couldn't see her face but her figure was gorgeous, full of curves, soft belly and heavy breasts. Her light brown hair fell to her waist in sheets of waves, the red lights casting a hue over her umber skin. While beautiful, his gaze only lingered for a moment before he pulled his gun from his hip. He held the gun at his side, tapping her thigh to let her know it was there.

"Where is Norrix?" Aurelio hissed. She lifted a shaking hand toward a door at the far side of the floor. "Consider yourself done for the night," he said, dropping enough credits for her to retire if she wanted.

She let out a gasp and he left before he could hear what she had to say. Aurelio holstered his gun before moving across the floor. He grabbed a shot of whiskey from a waitress, ignoring her squawk of surprise, and downed it. He tossed it aside before pushing through the door and into the lion's den.

The sounds of sex and torture rang out as he made his way down the hallway. Red doors leading to sex rooms lined each side. Aurelio didn't have to guess which door led to Norrix; it was the most obnoxious one of them all. He aimed for the lone black door that had a large gold harlequin mask on it and a heavy-set werewolf in front of it.

He pulled out one of his bowies and before the werewolf could register that he wasn't a patron, Aurelio was on the male and slicing his throat. The werewolf didn't have the time to yell before Aurelio caught him from landing on the floor with a thud. After easing him down, he checked to see if the door was locked. It was not.

He burst into the office, taking a moment to process the sight before him. Norrix was sitting at his desk, a ridiculous grin on his face. His face was bruised and it looked like someone beat Aurelio to the punch. Norrix rolled his eyes up to Aurelio, seemingly tired.

"If you're here to beat Lex's location out of me, Mr. Broderick, your friend already did so." Norrix stood, moving around the desk. Aurelio's confusion must have shown on his face because he added, "The purple haired one," with a voice full of ire. Styx must've fucked him up badly.

"Did you really tell her Lex's location? No lies?" Aurelio's eyes narrowed with suspicion. Anger flared in his eyes, looking around the room. It was then that Aurelio noticed the slew of bodies littering what should've been a pristine white floor.

"She killed my men," Norrix growled, crimson eyes flaring. "She shouldn't have been able to do that," he admitted. Aurelio nodded, considering the scene before him.

"So, I have no need of you." It was the only warning Norrix had before Aurelio clicked the safety off the gun that was hidden in his hand and shot Norrix right between the eyes.

STYX

STYX WAS ON HER WAY OUT OF THE second story window of the adjacent room when she heard a gun fire in Norrix's office. She back tracked and burst into the office from its second entrance to see Aurelio standing over Norrix, smoke still simmering from the bullet wound in his forehead.

"Aurelio!" she yelled, snapping his attention to her.

Anger filled his eyes, turning his silver eyes into a dark stormy gray. Fury rolled off him in waves so thick it was almost palatable. Spotting the blood on his hands, she looked toward the office entrance, and saw the werewolf with a slit throat. She wondered what pissed Aurelio off so badly to make him snap, and eased closer to him, as if walking toward a ticking time bomb. Who knew, maybe he was. He watched her, feral look in his eyes.

"Want to explain to me what you're doing here?"

She held her hands out to her sides, just in case she needed to reach one of her many weapons.

"He's a fucking trafficker," Aurelio growled.

"Yes. I know that." Styx remained calm.

"He had information I needed but he told me you already beat it out of him." He was panting, and thunder cracked outdoors before rain hit the windows in a downpour. "I didn't need him anymore." He snapped the safety back on his gun and holstered it.

Styx tracked his movements. There was more to this story. She had learned about Norrix through her network of spies and considering his type was the flavor she preferred murdering, she'd let him live because she felt she wasn't done with him yet. Aurelio had stolen that from her.

"Did you stop to think he may have had more information we needed?" Styx said, with ire. Aurelio closed his eyes, pinching the bridge of his nose. Nope, he didn't think about that. "What made you snap? What made you see red?"

He just shook his head in dismissal and it irked her more. She opened her mouth to question him further when Norrix's body twitched. Aurelio's eyes snapped to Norrix, and Styx's own eyes widened.

"Did he just move?" The way he asked Styx let her know he'd seen something like this before. She looked down to Norrix and noticed black blood dripping from the bullet wound.

He twitched again, causing Aurelio to mutter, "Fuck." He pulled out a big ass fucking knife and went to kneel.

"What aren't you telling me?" Styx asked before Norrix's eyes popped open. They were completely black, corneas included. She stumbled on a nearby body as she stepped backward in haste. "What the fuck!"

Aurelio skittered backward as well, and they both watched in horror as Norrix sat up slowly, dug the bullet out of his forehead, and stood. The sound of the bullet clinking onto the floor rang in the silence. Norrix proceeded to fix his suit, pulling at the sleeves and fixing his collar. He turned those black eyes on her.

"Mr. Broderick, I'd appreciate it if you'd refrain from shooting me." The malice in Norrix's voice was enough to send shivers down her spine and she'd seen some real evil shit in her lifetime.

Styx could sense Aurelio shifting closer to her. He kept his knife close to his side. A grin spread across Norrix's face as he looked at Aurelio.

"Tell me more about these feral beasts."

Aurelio's eyes widened just a smidge to let her know he was caught off guard before slamming a mask back over his face. Rain poured harder, lightning crackling outside. He wouldn't be able to wield indoors unless the window was open. She slowly slid a hand behind her, going for the gun she had holstered at the small of her back.

"Not sure what you're talking about," Aurelio bluffed, now at Styx's side.

Could Norrix read minds? Norrix gave her a knowing look, answering her question. Something slithered in her mind, like a wet worm. Pain seared across her frontal lobe as he dove into her head to extract memories. She bent over, hands clawing at her temples. No. He would not violate her. Styx let out a yell as she took all of her power to slam down walls around her mind, effectively shutting him out. Norrix's head snapped back as if he had been slapped. He inspected her as if she were a new toy.

"Interesting…" he murmured.

Norrix threw up a hand, halting Aurelio from attacking him without even touching. Thunder sounded loudly before the rain slowed. Dark energy crackled around Norrix's hands, licking up his arms.

"You will tell me what I wish to know, Mr. Broderick." He sent a bolt of that dark energy into Aurelio. Aurelio gritted his teeth, refusing to yell. Styx had her gun out and pointed.

"You know that won't work on me." Norrix laughed, sending more of that dark energy into Aurelio causing his eyes to roll. Still, he didn't yell.

"It may not work but it'll keep you distracted enough." Styx made to shoot when she realized her body was frozen, as if stuck in cement. The most she could do was move her eyes. Norrix's laugh made her cringe as he sent that dark energy into Aurelio.

"I see Mr. Broderick needs more convincing," he said before opening his mouth and letting out a dark smoke that wafted into Aurelio's nose and mouth. There was nothing that Aurelio could do to stop the smoke. Styx struggled to move her body, frustration lacing through her. She watched as Aurelio gagged and choked. Norrix must have been slithering his way through Aurelio's mind like he did hers.

"By the way, Queen Aeshma sends her regards," he said, before sucking the smoke back into him. Aurelio fell to his knees, gasping for air. The storm outside raged again. A thought came to Styx as her eyes tracked Norrix while he paced around her.

"You. I know something about you," he said, so softly that only Styx could hear. "Something you don't want anyone knowing." He chuckled, tapping the watch that was starting to beep furiously. "I think I'll keep you."

She used that moment to phase which allowed her to break the psychic hold he had on her. Norrix backed up with a hiss as purple smoke coiled around her. Styx couldn't phase often and she was already feeling a drain. Before Norrix could react, she shot the window, blasting glass everywhere, and grabbed a handful of Aurelio's jacket. A bolt of lightning made its way through the window to hit Norrix square in the chest. Without a second thought, Styx phased them both out of the building.

CHAPTER 23

XAVIA

THE SOUND OF XAVIA'S DOOR banging jolted her out of her sleep. She was face first on the floor in her favorite cotton shorts and a tank. This wasn't the first time she'd found herself on the floor after a rough night's sleep or blackout. She pulled herself up, noticing the bruising on her hands had gone down more.

"Xavia! Get up!" That was Ryland's voice on the other side of the door. How long was she out? She scrambled to open the door, and did not like the look on Ryland's face. "It's Aurelio…" Xavia started. "He's in Lilith's room."

Lilith being the medic, it made sense he was there but for what reason? She practically pushed Ryland to get to Lilith's room down the hall. She pulled up short when she saw him in the bed, shirtless, pale and with an IV drip in his arm. Quade was fuming in the corner, as always, smoke lifting from his skin.

"What happened?" Xavia looked at Lilith who was focused on the vitals on the hologram above Aurelio's head.

She moved into the room further and covered her gasp with her mouth. It looked like he'd been struck by black lightning all over his torso and neck. It wasn't like when Misha had turned feral. This felt malicious but every second she was in the room, the less that feeling got. Xavia could've sworn she saw sections of the wounds healing before her eyes. She gently sat on the bed, putting her hand on his. In reflex, Aurelio grabbed her hand, although he looked like he was still unconscious.

"What. Happened." She looked around the room, Quade

finding her eyes first.

"He fucking went rogue," he said, jaw ticking as he stood. "He did it for you. Because of whatever the fuck you got going on in your crazy head, he went rogue and tried to take down Norrix by himself."

Xavia looked at him incredulously. First, no one called her crazy but herself. Second, she didn't tell Aurelio to do anything. With an effort, she put those thoughts aside as it settled on her that he risked his life for her.

"We found him in front of the B&B, nearly passed out. He managed to tell us that Norrix is a demon, works with Aeshma, and now knows about the ferals." Quade put up a finger for each statement. She had no energy to fight back and it seemed to surprise him.

Xavia's head began to swim, lightheadedness taking over. Dark spots filled her vision before she had to lay down next to Aurelio. She lined her arm up to his, resting on it softly. The more she touched him, the more those dark scars disappeared and his vitals improved. She laid her head on his shoulder. Xavia could feel Quade's eyes on her and she looked at him. She couldn't find a definition for the expression on his face. Curiosity? Ryland stepped out nodding to Quade to do the same. He wasn't happy about it but he followed Ryland, staring holes in her head. He was probably thinking of the many ways he could burn her to a crisp.

"Why did he go after Norrix alone? I was supposed to…" The answer found her before she finished her sentence. Xavia squeezed her eyes shut, resting the back of her hand on her forehead. Aurelio risked it all for her because of her meltdown. Guilt ate her up inside. As if she didn't already feel like shit that he cared about her, that she wasn't worthy of his attention. She wiped a tear that threatened to fall before turning on her side and resting her head on his shoulder again. Xavia slid her arm under Aurelio's to lace her fingers with his. She sniffled louder than she wanted to, knowing Lilith was still there monitoring his vitals.

"Whatever you feel right now, regardless of Quade's anger, know that you have no place to feel guilty." Xavia peered over

Aurelio's shoulder to look at her. "Aurelio is a grown man. He makes his own decisions. And he wanted to keep you from suffering any more than you already have." Lilith motioned to Xavia's still bruised body. Xavia closed her eyes and curled into Aurelio more. "Whatever you're doing, keep doing it because his vitals are improving immensely," Lilith said with awe, making Xavia pop her eyes back open. She looked down at Aurelio's body and saw that those black splotches had disappeared altogether.

"I'm not doing anything," Xavia whispered. All she did was hold him. She was too devastated by the thought of him risking his life. Aurelio could've died and she would've never been able to forgive herself if he had. Lilith unhooked the IV and turned the hologram off. She marveled at the rate Aurelio was healing. Wielders were already naturally gifted with quick healing, but from what Xavia understood, it wasn't to this extent.

"He should wake soon," Lilith said, with a nod, before leaving the room and shutting the door.

Xavia wrapped herself around Aurelio, head on his chest, top arm across his waist, bottom arm still under his with their hands laced. She rested her leg on top of his and inhaled slowly, taking in his gunpowder and fresh rain scent. She wasn't sure how long they laid there, but she would lay here with him forever if it meant that he'd live. A breeze from an open window played with her hair, wisps tickling her nose. Xavia sniffled, tears dripping from her eyes while she thought about the last few days. Taking a deep breath, she tried to ground herself.

"I hope I don't stink," Aurelio murmured, exhaustion and humor in his voice. She jolted up, peering into his silver eyes. He lifted a hand to wipe her tears but she hit him lightly on his chest which made him huff out a breath mixed with a chuckle and wince.

"It's not funny!" Xavia said before letting out a shuddering breath. He held on to her hand, keeping it over his heart. She felt his pulse, strong and sure, her eyes not leaving his. "Why did you go after Norrix? Why couldn't you have waited?" Her voice was soft but held a tinge of anger. "I could've handled it." The hand Aurelio held tightened into a fist, her nails digging into her palm. She sat up, staring down at him. "You…" She tried to find the words. "I'm not…" Xavia heaved a sigh, not wanting to repeat the words she said last night. She was not worth his life, even if he felt she was.

"It was my choice." Aurelio's voice was slightly hoarse. "I saw red. The Harlequin was a front for a sex trafficking dungeon." Anger laced his tone. Her jaw dropped, not sure what to say about that. "That bastard was probably going to spirit you away and fuck…" He let go of her hand to rub his head, mussing up his growing coily short hair. "And then he turned out to be a fucking *demon*." Aurelio attempted to sit up but fell back on the bed, obviously exhausted. She let him vent, watching the emotions storm in his eyes. A boom of thunder rattled the B&B. "Aeshma knows about the ferals and where we're heading."

"I know… Quade so politely told me." Xavia grimaced when Aurelio growled.

"Do I need to fuck him up?" He propped up on his elbows, trying but failing to hide a wince. She shook her head, her lips tilting into a smirk, and patted his chest, letting it linger.

"Easy now, tiger." Aurelio took her hand and placed a kiss on her still healing hand. His lips left a sear on her hand, heat running through her body. He let go of her hand to trail the back of his hand across her cheek. Shivers made their way down her spine when his eyes dipped to her lips. Heat flushed to her face.*

"Aurelio…" Xavia barely whispered before he cupped her face and pulled her in for a hot, molten kiss. Aurelio's tongue played along her lower lip and she opened for him. Their tongues danced, sending heat down to her core. He hiked himself up more which allowed him to deepen the kiss. She took his bottom lip between her teeth, grazing gently before sucking it in. Aurelio let out a low groan, pulling her to straddle him. She let out a yelp.

"Wait, no, you're hurt," Xavia gasped before he kissed her again.

"Not enough to stop this," he murmured against her lips. She could feel her resistance crumbling. Her hands found either side of

♪ "Eat Your Young" by Hozier

his face, one gripping the back of his head, the other tracing his neck in the way she remembered he liked it. Aurelio gripped her hips before moving down to the swell of her ass. A moan escaped from her lips into his mouth. She barely broke the kiss to take a deep breath before he captured her lips again. His kiss turned fierce, sucking in her lower lip, tongue running over each nip and bite that he took. He squeezed her ass again causing her to break the kiss in a moan. Xavia ground against him, feeling his hardening length through his pants.

"That's not a gun, right?" Leave it to her to say the wrong thing or make things awkward. Aurelio barked out a laugh, dimples piercing his cheeks, before gripping her ass again and making her rock her hips against him. Liquid heat spread down between her legs, her arousal probably slicking against his lower abs. She only had on her cotton shorts, no underwear.

"No baby, that's all me." His voice was pure male. Xavia took a moment to look him over, all the ways he changed over the years. She traced the scar across his face, sliding down to each of his scars on his chest and abdomen. She lingered on his chest, bigger and firmer than when they were younger. Aurelio shuddered when she explored his arms, following the Wieldermarks and moving back to his abs. His hands slid her shorts up so that he could grip her bare ass firmly before flipping her on her back with him on top. He rested on one elbow while caressing her thick, soft thighs. Aurelio gave her another breathless kiss before lifting her chin up to nip at the flesh under her ear. Xavia let out a soft moan as she slid her hands slowly down his abs, closer to the V that dipped into his pants.

Aurelio's breathing hitched as he rested his forehead on hers to watch as her hands found the waistband of his pants. Xavia's heart thudded in her chest so hard that she thought he could hear it. She popped the button and slowly dragged the zipper down. She paused, fingers at the top of his boxers. Deliberately toying with him, she dragged them along the waistband, pulling a shudder out of him.

"We probably shouldn't do this," Xavia whispered, before licking his lips. She let out a soft yelp when his hand moved to the nape, tangling his fingers in her hair, and tilted her head back further to bare her neck to him. She let out a moan while Aurelio nipped and lapped at the sweet spot below her ear. He moved to her lips, sucking in the lower lip, biting it with a bit more force. He let go with a pop sound.

"I don't care," he growled.

A loud pounding at the door startled them both. He dropped his forehead against her at the same time she huffed a sigh. Maybe it was for the best. Honestly, if they had kept going, she wasn't sure how'd she feel afterward.

"I think the woman's right. I don't need you two fucking on my bed," came Lilith's voice on the other side of the door. Xavia could feel the heat rising to her cheeks and she slapped Aurelio's shoulder when she saw the shit-eating grin on his face. She pushed him to the side, ignoring his groan, and left the room. Fuck, she needed a cold shower.

CHAPTER 24

XAVIA

FUCK, XAVIA, HOLD ON!" AURELIO SNAPPED, hot on Xavia's heels. She wore tight green cargo pants with a black tank which hugged her body. Two guns were holstered at her waist and two katanas at her back. It had been three days, and they finally had a lead on Lex, thanks to Aurelio's contact and further sleuthing by Lilith.

Xavia spun around, poking Aurelio in the chest. "No! You knew where Lex was and you weren't going to tell me. I'm not waiting around anymore."

"I just told you! What makes you think I wasn't going to tell you?" Aurelio snapped, obviously annoyed. He wore loose cargo jeans and short-sleeved under armor, and had his bow and quiver slung across his back. He still sported bruises as did she. They moved further down the street, following a GPS hologram glowing from Aurelio's watch.

"Aurelio, I don't think they're going to be here. It's too easy," she said as they turned down an alley toward a known safe-house. She paused, looking at Aurelio, who gave a slight nod. The air shifted just slightly to her left, beyond the shadows of the streetlight. Xavia snapped her hand out into the darkness and came back with the collar of the great vigilante Lex. "Gotcha!" Thanks to Lilith, they found out the pirate had been trailing them throughout the city. All it took was a trap.

Lex grunted as they shrugged out of Xavia's hold. Black skin-tight body armor covered their torso, tucked into loose fitting cargo pants that were also light enough to let them move freely. They wore a hooded vest, zipped up and loaded with knives, a grappling hook, lock picks, smoke bombs, and C4 strips. A black and turquoise scabbard was sheathed at their side. A mask obscured their identity. Lex narrowed dual-colored eyes, one turquoise and the other sea green at her.

"You're a hard person to find." Lex's gloved hands grabbed onto Xavia's wrist, noticing that they were almost the same height, Lex maybe having an inch on her. "Let's chat, we—"

Lex pulled Xavia in to smash their forehead into Xavia's nose. Xavia let out a yelp but without hesitation threw a hook that would have connected if Lex hadn't ducked. They turned and attempted to land a side kick but Xavia blocked it with her forearms, pushing Lex away. They squared off, Xavia putting a hand up to tell Aurelio to not intervene.

The two of them ran at each other, Lex attempting a round house which resulted in Xavia catching their leg in between her hip and arm. She yanked Lex's leg toward her but they jumped off their free leg to push kick Xavia in the gut. The kick connected, causing Xavia to grunt as she let go of Lex's leg. They quickly recovered in a kick-up, staying crouched low and running toward Xavia to clinch their arms around her waist. Hooking their foot behind Xavia's, Lex brought her to the ground, Lex on top. They laid a blow to Xavia's midsection before Xavia almost knocked their teeth out with an elbow to their jaw. Lex stretched their jaw, popping it back into place. Before they could get their bearings, Xavia grabbed their vest, managed to get her feet tucked in and kicked Lex over her head. They landed flat on their back, breathless. Xavia turned over, equally as breathless.

"Are we..." Xavia took a deep inhale. "Are we gonna do this all night?" she gasped, pulling herself up to a seated position, sweat causing her hair to frizz and stick to her forehead. The damn pirate knew how to fight, that's for sure. Xavia stood and held out a hand but Lex ignored her, standing with a grunt. Aurelio pushed off the wall he was leaning on and walked toward them.

"We need your help." Lex looked him over, as if waiting for

him to continue. "Have you heard about what happened outside Melhold?" Lex shrugged. Aurelio went on to tell them about the meteor that wasn't really a meteor but was, in fact, an Angel.

"Look, if what we've been told is true, you're the best seafarer in Asherai." Xavia read the questions in their eyes. "You are our best bet to get to Malagado. Will you help?"

Lex sighed and shook their head.

"Do you talk? Like at all?"

Lex rolled their eyes and made to walk away, when Xavia grabbed hold of their wrist.

"Are you seriously going to walk off? After what we told you?"

Lex shrugged her off and gave her the finger. Xavia pushed back her curls, hot and grumpy. Xavia was both impressed and frustrated with Lex.

"So, does that savior complex not carry over to Melhold? Or is it all a lie?" Lex stiffened. "I mean, all I've ever heard about you was that you're a 'Robin Hood' to the people. If you were, you'd help us. But I guess you're too much of a punk."

Xavia barely dodged the jab that aimed for her nose. Aurelio slid in between them. She grunted as she managed to push around him and grabbed hold of Lex's hood before they could react. As the hood fell, the mask fell with it. Xavia's eyes widened into orbs as she looked Lex over.

"You're a woman?" Xavia stared.

Lex had flowing multicolored dreadlocks that fell past their shoulders and had a silver septum piercing and eyebrow ring. Their skin was light brown with a hint of red undertones, making their multicolored eyes stand out even more. The loose-fitting cargo jeans and utility vest easily covered their body to hide their gender and identity. Lex snatched the mask from Xavia.

"I am not a woman," Lex said, their voice was honeyed sweet, a lilt that was slightly higher than Xavia's

"What pronouns should we use?" Aurelio said, surprise lighting up Lex's eyes.

"They, them, theirs," they said. The ire in Lex's eyes grew and they opened their mouth to say something.

166 | A.E. COSBY

"Before you say anything..." Xavia interrupted. "We won't tell anyone your identity." Lex relaxed slightly.

"That's nice and all. But I can't help you." Lex made to turn away again and Xavia grabbed their wrist. Lex's eyes slowly drifted to the hand. "Homie, you're making a habit of grabbing me and you're going to regret it if you don't let go."

Xavia raised an eyebrow wondering if Lex would follow through with their threat. They seemed to consider it before Aurelio's hand landed on Xavia's forearm, causing her to break her hold on Lex. She practically growled at him.

"We don't have the time for this," he said with a huff. He looked at Lex. "Why won't you help us?"

"I have *my* people to worry about. I don't need to get swept up in typical Melhold drama. You always seek out help from others because you can't help yourselves." Xavia fumed when Aurelio chuckled.

"You sound just like her." Aurelio pointed a thumb behind him to indicate Xavia, who let out a squeak, eyes narrowed. Lex raised an eyebrow, nose flaring, causing the septum ring to glint in the low light.

"I'll tell you the same thing I told Ms. Bossy over here..." Xavia let out a frustrated groan. The side of Lex's lips twitched, visibly holding back a smirk. "What's the use of trying to keep Silvermoon safe if it's bound to get destroyed if Aeshma unleashes the Chaos Wielder?" Lex let out a frustrated sigh, pulling their locs up into a loose bun, seeming to come to the same conclusion Xavia did when she was first approached.

"Give me two days. Meet me at pier three, and make sure you bring your sea legs." Lex looked to Xavia who was still standing there with her arms crossed in front of her chest. They narrowed their eyes and pointed at her. "And you bet' not touch me again, you hear?" Xavia gave them a salacious smirk.

"You won't be saying that for long."

Lex only rolled their eyes before pulling their hood up and placing their mask back on.

"I can already tell that I'm going to like you." Lex's voice was now muffled and masculine sounding due to the mask. They chuckled before pulling out a grappling gun and launched themself skyward toward the rooftops.

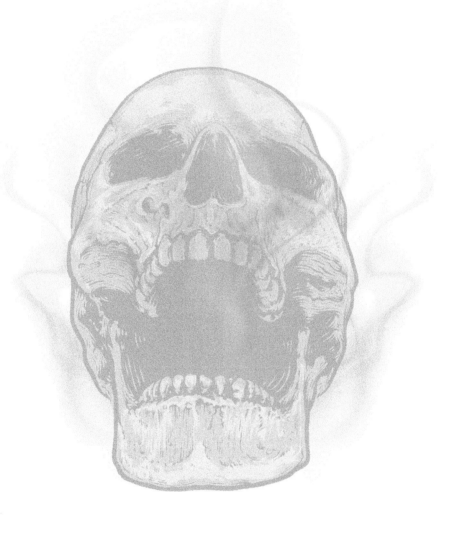

CHAPTER 25

JACINTO

C IN, WE HAVE A PROBLEM."

Jacinto growled into the homenaje's throat he was currently latched to. Lately, Cyrus had had the worst timing. Jacinto withdrew his fangs from her neck, blood pouring down her naked body. He had her against a wall, her legs wrapped around his waist. He turned to Cyrus, still pumping into her as he felt her life draining by the second.

"It better be important, pendejo." Jacinto narrowed his reddening eyes. Cyrus's eyes flicked to the bloodied homenaje and then back to Jacinto. Jacinto smirked, fangs dripping.

"Want to join?" he said darkly. Cyrus was not feeding enough lately. He felt the need to put the entire weight of the world on his shoulders and the rising issue with Asherai and Aeshma only added to his stress.

"No, thank you," he lied smoothly. Jacinto could smell the lie wafting from the male. He snarled before Cyrus could speak further. He returned to the homenaje, latching onto her neck again as he fucked her harder. She let out a whimper before convulsing in pleasure. Jacinto could feel Cyrus's stare on him as he came while the woman died. He pulled his fangs out to glare at Cyrus.

"¿Que paso?" he snapped.

"A demon was revealed in Silvermoon Harbor."

Jacinto abruptly pulled out and ignored the woman as she dropped lifeless to the floor. He muttered several slurs in his native tongue, making for the shower and motioning Cyrus to follow.

"Dime," Jacinto said as he showered the blood from his body.

"Apparently two members of the Asherite special forces team approached him to find someone they needed to get overseas. It didn't go well, thus the demon revealed himself." Cyrus's eyes flashed red.

"Is he still breathing?" Jacinto growled as he toweled off. Cyrus gave him a curt nod. "I didn't think the higher-ranking demons would come out of hiding so soon. Which demon is it?" He had slipped on a pair of jeans and a black tee, along with a pair of black sneakers. Jacinto pulled his wet hair back into a low hair tie, searching for his leather vest.

"Norrix, demon of pain and fear." Jacinto looked up to Cyrus who was looking at his phone. His nose flared, eyes widening. "He's making his way here." Jacinto's body shook with anger and he slammed a fist on the dresser, splitting it into two. "The overseas trip is about a month. Think we can stop him before he gets here?" Cyrus asked, with an eyebrow raised. Jacinto shook his head, growing increasingly frustrated that he couldn't find his vest.

"There's no point. He'll have lower-level demons with him and they are not so easy to kill like the rest of the species on this planet." He turned to find Cyrus holding the vest. Jacinto's eyes flared as he snatched it from him and stepped out the room. They entered the conference room and Jacinto pulled up a hologram of Ayobaí with Malagado at the coast. "No, we have to be strategic about this."

"Strategic how?" Cyrus looked over the map before understanding dawned on his face. "You want to invite him as a guest." Jacinto gave a nod.

"Yes. If the Asherites are not too far behind, then they'll arrive a week or so before Axton's Eve." The sabbath was to honor the Deity of the dead and those who have crossed over into the Otherworld. It was a riotous time where people dressed up in costumes, scare others, and did the most sinful of things. "We host a party, a ball." He figured that it would be better to dine with his potential enemies and keep an eye on them.

"How do we keep Norrix and the Asherite team from trying to obliterate each other?" The hologram changed and showed the grand skyscraper that was the tower he called his Palacio. It was not as gaudy as the Monarchs in Trezora, but still magnificent on its own.

The Palacio rose in the sky as the tallest building in the city. It was at the far reaches of the city; the furthest from the harbor without going into the city next door. The exterior was solid black, the windows gleaming and tinted. It was in the shape of a hexagon, sharp angles making it stand out from the other buildings. While he lived at the very top, all the floors below him held offices, apartments of his closest advisors and officials, and a grand ballroom on the second floor. A highly advanced medical unit took up two floors. Underground, there was a complete military unit that held trainings, weapons, trucks, and the barracks. Jacinto made the building into a well-stocked compound so that if his safety was jeopardized, he'd have a fortress.

"We'll make it a masquerade." Cyrus gave him an exasperated look. Jacinto's grand soirees tended to get very hot, very fast. "What do we know about the Asherite team?" Jacinto said with an eyeroll. Cyrus pulled up what looked like files of each person, all but the bounty hunter had images. Cyrus pointed to the male with dark brown skin, storm gray eyes, and an interesting scar across his eye.

"This one is the captain. He's from the Broderick line." The strongest Storm Wielders in Trezora. He pointed to the next one, another male with black hair and a malicious glint in his burnt sienna eyes. Interesting. "This one is the second in command, a Fire Wielder." He went to name each of the others and their skill sets. When he landed on the bounty hunter, the file didn't have much. "We don't know much about the bounty hunter." Frustration colored his voice. "We don't know if they're male or female, if they're a Wielder or something else. Their information is practically wiped. All we know is they're a damn good bounty hunter and have a near one hundred percent track record."

"Safe to say that they brought the bounty hunter in because

they don't have a good enough tracker." Jacinto almost laughed at that. It reflected poorly on Asherai's Guard and Special Forces team. Cyrus stared at the file as if it would bloom to life. Cyrus was trying, and failing, to hide the slight shaking in his hand. Jacinto closed the hologram, ignoring Cyrus's confusion. "You need to feed." He pointed at him.

"I told you I'm fine," Cyrus growled.

Watching Cyrus now, Jacinto knew that if Cyrus didn't feed soon, the bloodlust would drive him berserk and he didn't want to have to put down his second-in-command like a rabid dog. Jacinto grabbed Cyrus by his perfect collar.

"I am ordering you to feed." Jacinto let him go so abruptly that Cyrus stumbled back a little. Cyrus growled, eyes going completely red before he snapped his teeth at Jacinto. Jacinto stood there as Cyrus proved his point.

"You and me, now." Jacinto made to leave the conference room but Cyrus stayed rooted to the spot. "As your maker, I can compel you. Don't make me." Jacinto eased his tone a bit as Cyrus reluctantly followed him out.

THE MUSIC IN THE DEN WAS LOUD and heavy on the bass. EDM music scratched an itch that Jacinto enjoyed. The music thrummed through his body, writhing bodies crowding around him. Glow paint covered almost everyone in some way or another. He was thankful he had left his shirt in the car and wore only his vest.*

The Den was both a club and a feeding brothel. Jacinto never had to pay because all his victims came willingly. Cages hung above the crowd with a near nude dancer in each. There was a stage at the far end of the dance floor with three poles, one left, one center, and one right. It was reserved for the top dancers

♪ "Die Slow" by Soda, Voyage

who brought in the most credits.

Jacinto made for the bar, a beautiful and majestic thing to behold. Six shelves of liquor graced the back wall of the bar area. Each shelf was lit with different colored glow lights, making the bottles seem as if they were floating. The bar itself was made of solid obsidian, giving it a sleek and dark look. The lights reflected off the bar, which added to the glowing allure. He pulled up to a barstool and motioned to Cyrus to take a seat.

Cyrus grunted as he sat next to Jacinto. He had changed into a tan henley that hugged his muscular body, dark navy straight jeans and brown loafers. It complemented his ebony skin and Cyrus was oblivious to the number of people that stopped to stare at him. Cyrus was handsome in his own right, in a quiet and reserved way. His body was rigid, obviously working to contain himself.

"Try as you might to hide it, I can smell the hunger and arousal coming off you." Jacinto smirked when Cyrus growled deep in his throat. The bartender made his way over and startled when he saw Jacinto.

"Your Eminence. Thank you for coming back," he gave a slight bow with his head. The bartender, Royal, was also the owner of The Den. Despite the wild success of the club, he enjoyed working the floor still. It was part of the appeal, Jacinto guessed. A blush crossed Royal's face when he addressed Cyrus.

"Governor," he murmured, softly, through heart shaped lips. Cyrus appraised him, having only met Royal a few times in the past. Royal hopped on the bar ladder to climb up to the fifth row to grab one of the most expensive tequilas in Ayobaí. He jumped off, landing with a soft thud before procuring two rocks glasses and placing the bottle of tequila between the two. Jacinto gave him a nod, dismissing him.

"I'd let you give Royal a go but we need him alive, or this establishment will go to shit."

Cyrus snorted, downing a double of tequila. Jacinto rolled his eyes.

"Hey, pendejo. Sip, not shoot."

"I don't even want to be here," Cyrus grumbled. He could

be such a child. "Let's get this over with," he stood and headed for the second-floor landing.

Jacinto paced behind him slowly, taking in the people around him and enjoyed the view. They all moved out of his way, creating a path straight to the stairway. His eyes caught on an exceptionally beautiful female. She was busty, wearing a strapless dress so short that it left little to the imagination. Jacinto motioned for her to follow and she instantly flushed. His eyes connected with a male, a Shadow Wielder judging by his Wieldermarks. He was shirtless, showing off his lithe, thin body. Jacinto gave a nod and the male came to his side. Jacinto put his arms around them both.

"Now, let's go have fun, shall we?"

CHAPTER 26
STYX

STYX SIGHED AS SHE MADE HER WAY to the boardwalk. Again. Why did Aurelio insist on meeting out here? Couldn't they meet inside, where there was air conditioning? She kept her hood down, wearing her ankle length duster and mask was hot enough. She shifted her gun belt and fidgeted with her knife vest. Was she nervous? *Get a grip.* She told herself as she stared up at the waning moon, Ithea not far behind it. Styx wondered about the planet and if there was any form of life.

"Look hard enough and you may just fly there," came Aurelio's deep voice. She took in his battered self, bruising under his eye, split lip, and judging by his walk, his ribs still hurt. He looked much better than he did a few days ago.

"You're looking better," Styx said. He snorted, trying and failing to hide a wince. He stood next to her and leaned on the railing with an exhausted sigh.

"I need to talk to you about The Martyrs." Aurelio's tone made her go still.

"What about them." It wasn't a question.

"Do you know what they do? How they get their resources?" His voice sounded strained as if he was barely containing his anger.

"Yes, Aurelio, I do." Styx took a deep breath. "They call themselves the Martyrs because they are suicide bombers and terrorists. They use the guise that they're a militia that wants to protect the people. But they take out resource plants and warehouses to steal the goods." She let out a sigh. Their tactics were awful.

Personally, she wished they didn't have a contract on her head, otherwise she would've done something about them already. Aurelio opened his mouth but Styx held a hand up. "Before you ask, I absolutely do not condone what they do."

"Then why do you work for them?" he growled. "They kill and destroy the lives of anyone who doesn't join their ranks." Styx raised an eyebrow. This was personal for him.

"They are currently the best option to take down the Monarchy," she said, frustrated. "Do you think we can do this on our own?" His nose flared before he rubbed the back of his head. Styx snorted. "That's a tell, you know." Aurelio raised an eyebrow. "The rubbing of your head. You do that when you're frustrated."

"Am I that obvious?" He groaned. "These last few weeks have been hell." He closed his eyes while he Wielded a soft breeze. Styx let out a sigh as it moved through her curls. "If we can convince the Chaos Wielder to help, we won't need the Martyrs."

"Yes, we do. We need their manpower. We need the allies."

"Fuck," he grunted.

"My sentiment." Styx turned to face him. "Look, I know they're shitty fucking people. I know they do some foul stuff," she met his gaze when his eyes opened and continued, "but I promise that I will personally take them out after the Monarchy falls. I won't let them fill the power vacuum that will ensue."

"All by yourself?" Aurelio quirked an eyebrow, smirking.

"If I have to." Styx crossed her arms. "But your help would be much appreciated."

"I'll have to tell my team eventually. Especially my second, Quade." He went to rub his head and stopped himself, looking sheepish.

"Rub your head Captain, it's ok," shes aid. Aurelio gave her the finger, shake her head. "How do you think your team will handle it? Are you sure they can be trusted?"

"Yes, absolutely. Quade has been with me for over twelve years, Lilith for five. Xavia..." His eyes went distant. She saw the history they had flash through his facial expressions. "She'll be down. She hates the Monarchy." This time Aurelio rubbed his head. "Wow,

I really fucking rub my head a lot," he huffed, stuffing his hands in his pockets.

"Eh, it's a soothing method." Styx shrugged. "We all have them."

"Oh, really? What's yours?" He smirked. She wiggled a finger at him.

"No, I'm not telling you. Unlike you, I can hide my tells. My soothing methods are my own." He lifted his chin to look down at her and sucked his teeth.

"Mhm. Sure. I'll figure it out one day." Styx's watch started to blare. Aurelio gave her a nod. "I'll see you later. We head out to Malagado in two days. You have a way there?" She nodded. "Ok. Safe trip," he patted her shoulder before she disappeared.

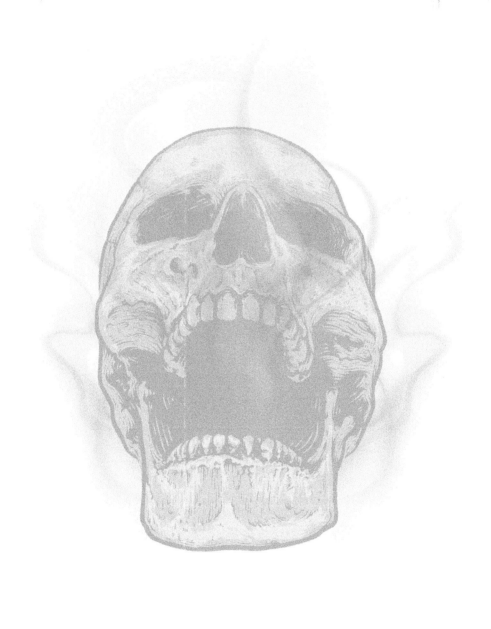

CHAPTER 27
AURELIO

THE NEXT TWO DAYS PASSED WITHOUT a hitch. The two days were much appreciated to give the team time to build up their strength for the next leg of the journey.

"Where are they?" Xavia grumbled, irritated to be up so early.

Aurelio snorted, and patted her shoulder with more force than necessary to knock her around. She hissed at him and smacked at his hand. He grinned before taking in the sight of the yacht in front of him.

Aurelio underestimated the pirate.

The superyacht must've been at least eighty feet long. It was solid black with chrome accents. From what he could see from the pier, it had a sun deck and overhead helm. It was shaped almost like a bullet, wide at the back and then narrowing to the front. In liquid silver script was the yacht's name, "Sea Demon."

Apt name, he thought.

Quade whistled as he stepped next to Aurelio, opposite Xavia.

"This one's beautiful." He stared at the yacht like it was a woman he couldn't wait to get his hands on. Of the team, he had the most experience with naval training. Despite being a Fire Wielder, Quade loved water. It always seemed like he was a bit of an oxymoron. "It probably has a complete nav helm inside and I'm almost positive that there's a garage under the stern."

Xavia peered past Aurelio to gape at Quade. He narrowed

his eyes at her.

"What?"

She just shook her head, righting herself.

"Rumor has it the yacht was hijacked from the governor and now he can't get it back without risking an uprising," a masked voice came from behind them. Lex appeared, wearing their usual attire, except without sleeves on their under armor. Water Wieldermarks took up the entirety of their right arm. It was making a lot more sense why Lex was such a good seafarer.

"About damn time," Xavia muttered, obviously in need of another cup of coffee. Aurelio held up the tumbler he prepared for her. Her eyes widened before she gave him a smile of gratitude. She took it and drank the coffee down as if it were a lifeline.

"He's right y'know." Lex motioned to Quade. "It has a three-person helm with a full navigation station that shares the space with the salon. The above deck helm is useful if you're heading in one direction and have no immediate need for the nav. Plus, it's fun when it's going forty-seven knots and the wind is in your hair."

Quade's eyes lit up with pure excitement. Aurelio hadn't seen that look in a very long time. Lex motioned for the group to follow, Ryland and Lilith joining.

"Beneath the stern is a garage large enough to house three jet skis. They're useful when you need stealth."

"I knew it." Quade snapped his fingers, elbowing Aurelio. Xavia peered at him again with mouth agape. Quade shuttered his eyes, narrowing into a scowl at her. She rolled her eyes and pushed past them.

Before boarding, introductions were made. As they boarded the swim deck, the yacht felt solid under his feet. Only a slight bob gave evidence that they were on water. Black leather couches stood in a U formation on the deck surrounding a fire pit. Tinted sliding doors encompassed the wall behind the couches. Above them was the above deck helm. Aurelio glanced at the small walking space and railing that surrounded the yacht. They'd have to sidestep to the front, the thought making Aurelio a little queasy. Storage compartments were open, showing a slew of weapons.

"You're safe to put your weapons in storage. They're waterproof. But I understand if you prefer to keep them below deck with you."

Everyone murmured, set on keeping their weapons with them. Lex shrugged and nodded toward the sliding doors. Aurelio worked hard at pulling out the knowledge he learned about yachts and naval transport.

"You retrofitted the salon," Quade said, impressed.

Directly in front, toward the front–or was it bow?–was a magnificent navigation system and what looked like weapons controls. Aurelio didn't see any weapons on the exterior and figured they must be under water or pull out from the sides. In front of the nav system were three leather chairs, the largest in the middle. Caches, some empty and some with weapons and tools, lined the left and right–starboard and port side?–and a small table with two chairs in the middle. Stairs were by the helm that led to the lower deck. Before Lex could show them the lower deck, Aurelio stopped them.

"Is anyone else joining us?" He knew they had a team. Lex shook their head.

"No, it's just me. I'm not endangering their lives. My best people are the ones I'm leaving this city with."

"Are we ever going to see who you are?" Lilith asked, gently.

Lex looked her over, obviously appreciating the view. Lilith raised an eyebrow and crossed her arms over her chest. Humor was clear in Lex's face as they took off their mask and lowered their hood. If Aurelio had a camera, he would've loved to capture the look on Lilith's face, clearly surprised by Lex's appearance, eyes roving over them.

"So, you're..."

"Non-binary," said Lex and Aurelio at the same time. Lex gave him a smile. "Alright so let's get down below so that we can get planning."

The lower deck had three cabins and two crew bunks. The master stateroom was Lex's. One guest room had double twin beds, another with one queen size, and the crew bunks that held four beds. There was a restroom in the crew quarters, one in the master stateroom, and then a general one between the guest rooms. There was a full galley, including an eat-in kitchen, that allowed for at least six individuals to sit. At the base of the stairs there was a common area, comfortable couches surrounded a chrome table with a hologram base. Everything was decked out in black with chrome accents.

Xavia opted for the guest room with the twin beds and pulled Lilith with her. Aurelio grunted, heading to the crew bunk with Ryland, giving Quade the larger room with the queen bed. He almost punched Quade for the sarcastic grin on his face. Aurelio knew what Xavia was trying to avoid so he opted to give her space.

After settling their things, they met up with Lex in the common room where the hologram of the route glowed before them.

"This is going to be about a month-long trip."

Xavia and Quade oddly huffed a sigh at the same time. They stared daggers at each other before they looked back at Lex.

"We'll be rotating between full speed and cruising." Lex looked to Quade. "I don't normally ask this, but would you be down to help at the helm?"

"Sure thing, boss." He gave a nod and Lex gave him a look of gratitude.

"If there are any storms, it'll slow us down. Thankfully we are outside of storm season so we shouldn't have too many issues." Lex shifted the map to show the coast of Ayobaí, with the coastal city of Malagado. "Once we cross the horizon line and into the planet's dark territory, we will have to cruise. We can't risk drawing attention of the sea creatures on that side of the hemisphere." Lex heaved a sigh. "We can dock a few miles south of Malagado and drive up the coast but from what I heard about the city, I don't think there's anything we can do that will allow us into the city unnoticed."

"We can decide on what to do when we're a few days out." Aurelio said, before looking at everyone. "Right now, we need to spend our time preparing for the City of Vampires. They're a ruthless lot and if we aren't prepared, we *will* die." He kept it real with them. "Go rest, eat, recharge. We'll meet back here, seven am tomorrow."

He bit back a chuckle at Xavia's groan.

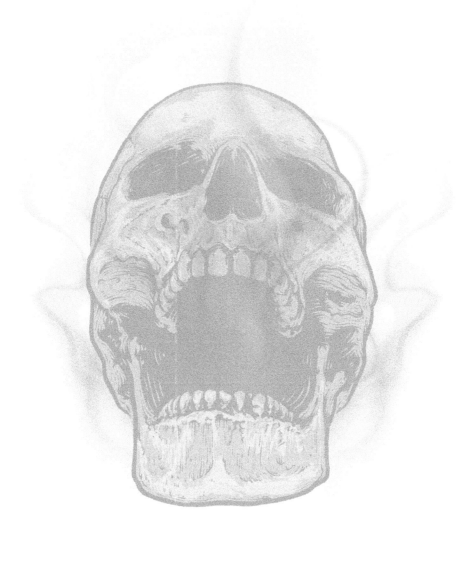

CHAPTER 28
QUADE

THE NEXT MORNING QUADE WAS lounging in the common area, tea in one hand and a book in the other. He was in sweats and a tee, barefoot. Quade was usually the first one up and used it for some quiet time to himself. He heard a shuffling of feet which brought his eyes up.

He let out a huff, seeing Xavia make her way past him to head toward the galley. She was in a pair of black cotton shorts and an oversized tee, shapely legs on display. Her curls were mussed up as if someone had run their hands through her hair. Xavia gave him the finger as she walked by, and Quade growled at her. She was such a brat and it drove him insane. She let out a chuckle as she disappeared from view, taking that fantastic ass with her. He hated how attractive she was.

As Quade finished his tea, he stood up and made for the galley to return the mug. He ran into a soft body that smelled like honey and hibiscus and immediately stiffened, his body betraying him. Xavia had been looking down and didn't see him until they collided. Her foot hooked with his somehow and they both went down with a grunt. He landed on top of her, hair falling forward. She stared up at him, eyebrows furrowed, her dark brown eyes practically black.

"You're such a fucking klutz," Quade muttered darkly. Xavia's tan cheeks darkened, ever so slightly, in a blush.

"It's not my fault that you have clown feet," she muttered back, annoyance lacing her tone. He barked out a laugh.

"Real fucking mature," Quade said as he stood up. When Xavia sat up, he pushed the back of her head causing her to let out a yelp as he walked away, leaving her on her ass. That fine, perfect ass.

A FEW HOURS LATER, THE TEAM was on the foredeck that was retrofitted with mats for sparring. Quade was in a black under armor tank and boxing sweats. Aurelio, in the same outfit, looked like he was going to throw up his breakfast.

"Of all people, I would've thought a Storm Wielder could handle the seas." Quade elbowed Aurelio. Aurelio scowled at him, grabbing the railing to steady himself.

"Storm Wielders are *especially* sensitive to the seas. We feel every little bob in the ocean, even if the yacht is solid under our feet." He took a few deep breaths. "Something about the water and rain being connected." He crouched and put his head between his knees.

Lex was at the above deck helm, monitoring the speed, using their Water Wielding to keep the ocean smooth. They were on cruise speed at the moment so that they could spar.

Grunts and the sound of a body slapping against the mat came from behind him. Quade turned to see Xavia laying out Ryland. She put her hand out for Ryland, but he slapped it away, standing with a grunt. Sweat glistened on her neck, droplets sliding down toward her breasts. He watched with keen interest as she patted herself dry with a towel. Xavia had a cocky grin on her face, another thing that drove him insane but also found sexy as hell. Was Axton torturing him on purpose? Why must the most aggravating person on Euhaven also be ridiculously sexy? She looked at him as if she could tell he was staring and gave him the finger. It was her favorite gesture for him. He was starting to believe it was a term of endearment.

"I've got next," Quade announced. Ryland looked at him, panting. "No, not you. Her." The Fire Wielder jabbed a finger at Xavia. They hadn't sparred with each other since the Academy and he was aching to give her a taste of her own medicine.*

"Fuck no," Xavia said as she flexed her fingers.

"Why? Afraid I'll mess up that pretty little face of yours?" The fire rose inside him, and he tasted smoke in his mouth.

"Aw, you think I'm pretty?" she said with a pout.

He'd give her something to pout about. He moved on the balls of his feet, quicker than a human, and threw a punch aimed for her jaw. Xavia backed up, pushing his arm in a block.

"You really want to do this?" she growled. Quade swung a hook which she ducked and retaliated with a cross punch that he blocked with his forearms.

"You punch like you're green." He crouched low and kicked her feet from beneath her. Xavia grunted, face planting with the mat. He kneeled, tossing her over, and grabbed the collar of her shirt, lifting her close. "Are you green? Did you forget what you learned in the Academy?" Quade hissed. Ire filled Xavia's eyes as she slammed her forehead against his. Fuck! She had a knack for that. It's a miracle her brain wasn't any more scrambled than it already was.

"Fuck you Quade, I'm not green," she grunted as she kick-backed up to stand. Quade stood up, blood pouring from his broken nose. Again. He snapped it back in place with a snarl.

"Well then, prove it to me." He held his hands in front of him and made a 'come on' gesture.

Xavia came at him, throwing two jabs and a hook, which he blocked, before turning to surprise him by slamming the back of her hand against his cheek. Quade's lip split and he spat the blood out while tracking her movements. She feinted before her foot came at his head in a roundhouse, unexpectedly connecting, and laying him out on the mat. It surprised Quade her foot could get that high. It meant she was flexible, and he liked flexible. *Fuck Quade, focus.*

♪ "Warning" by Martin Wave, Washyb.

He thought.

"If I hadn't left, you'd be third, asshole," Xavia hissed through her teeth as she rammed a knee into his chest, keeping him on the ground. She was about to punch him when he flipped her over onto her back, grappling with her. Quade grabbed her hands and slammed them above her head, knees at either side of her legs.

"I won't tap out," Xavia groaned as he held tighter, sliding her arms up. Her shoulders popped gently and she gritted her teeth. Her breathing increased, making her chest rise and fall not too far from his line of vision. It took all of Quade to not stare at her rising cleavage. Instead, he thought to push her limits.

"Are you going to give up?" he whispered darkly. Xavia shook her head, letting out a soft groan as he held on tighter. "Are you going to give up like you did at the academy?" She shook her head, still gritting her teeth. So, she could handle pain. Interesting. "Are you going to let your crazy ass issues get in the way?" Quade growled. "Because from what I can tell, you've got a lot of crazy in you." It surprised him to realize that he was beginning to find it hot as fuck going toe to toe with someone as wild as him.

Quade could've sworn he saw her eyes glint with another color but it was gone as quickly as it appeared. Before he knew it, Xavia bucked her hips and tossed him aside. He landed on his back, with her on top and her hands at his throat. Her nails dug into his neck and warm liquid ran down his skin from the cuts she left. Xavia was stronger than he expected. Quade grabbed her wrists, pulling her arms outward, and took a move out of her book. He slammed his forehead to hers.

"Fuck!" Xavia grunted, before he tossed her onto her stomach and pulled her arms behind her back, his knee keeping her down. A breath whooshed out of her, her cheek flat on the mat. Quade pushed his knee down further, slowly cutting off her air. Xavia refused to yield, which he begrudgingly respected. But she was a fucking brat. She'd rather pass out than yield. He let her go abruptly, standing up. Xavia let in a deep gasp of air, remaining on the floor. Quade looked around. Everyone stared at them. No one interrupted, not even Aurelio.

"Still green," he said as kicked Xavia's feet lightly and walked off the mat.

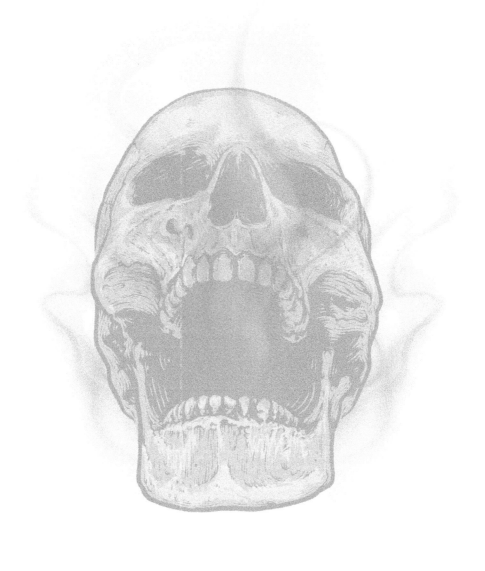

CHAPTER 29

XAVIA

XAVIA HEAVED A SIGH AS SHE stepped out of her room, freshly showered and fed. The way Quade handed her ass to her was embarrassing. Her body ached in places she didn't think possible. She made her way through the galley to the crew quarters. Xavia popped her head in to check in with Aurelio, who was not taking this trip well.

"Still haven't found your sea legs?" She chuckled. Aurelio looked up from the bunk he was laying on and grumbled something under his breath.

"How is it that you have no issue with this but I'm the one who's had some naval training?" Aurelio groaned, as he sat up slowly. He looked clammy and it was clear he just had another hurling session.

"I grew up on the coast, remember?" Xavia said. He looked at her with confusion. "I went sailing a lot before we met. I'm pretty familiar with it." She shrugged. It wasn't a memory she wanted to revisit. "I'll leave you to it. Gonna go above deck for some air."

He gave her a tight nod, sinking back down into the cot and closing his eyes. Xavia gave him a gentle pat on the head before making her way to the upper deck. Lex and Lilith were sitting at the small table behind the helm, the two of them looking thick as thieves. They both nodded to her as she exited the salon.

The sun was beginning to set, painting the sky in multicolored hues. The moon and Ithea had started to rise in the distance, and it was a breathtaking sight. The rise of those celestial beings over the ocean arrested the attention of even the most hardened among them.

The wind breezed through her curls, chilling her body. Xavia was glad she decided to throw on an oversized sweater over her black leggings, but hadn't bothered with shoes. Wanting a better view of the sunset, she moved to the top helm's lowered stairs. Xavia froze when she caught sight of Quade reclined in the middle seat, hand resting on the throttle to maintain the speed.

The yacht bobbed as it traveled over a swell. He didn't seem to notice her as she stepped softly on the deck. The sunset was even more breathtaking up here. She caught sight of Quade's profile as the wind blew those straight black strands of hair back. He looked at ease for once, without that scowl on his face. The yacht bobbed again, this time Xavia stumbled, which drew Quade's attention to her. His eyebrows narrowed and the glower instantly fell into place.

"Sorry... I'll leave," Xavia mumbled. She was *not* in the mood to bicker. He looked her over, the wind now blew his hair across his burnt sienna eyes.

"You can stay," Quade said before turning back around. She heaved a sigh of relief, moving to the railing and leaning on it, facing out. The wind blew Xavia's hair wildly around her face and she closed her eyes to it. The freedom that came with feeling the wind made her feel like she was flying. If she could have one ability, it would be flying. Xavia loved skydiving, roller coasters; the works. She slowly opened her eyes, to find Quade's on her.

"What?" she said, trying to keep the irritation out of her voice. He hit a few buttons and put the yacht on cruise control. Quade stood up and moved toward her. Xavia's pulse raised to her throat as he leaned his elbows on the railing. His burnt cedar scent was intoxicating.

"Why are you here?" Quade kept his narrowed gaze on her. Xavia raised a questioning eyebrow. "Why did you bother to come on this mission?"

"It was tasked to me by the Monarch," she said, no longer trying to keep the irritation out of her voice. She just wanted some peace. "Look, I'm not in the mood..."

"Do you even understand the risk you pose? A human bounty hunter who's an alcoholic and apparently has fugue states, I'm guessing?" Xavia's nose flared as she pushed a frustrated breath out.

"What the fuck is your problem with me?" she said, as she faced him, anger rising. Quade pushed her back against the railing, hand on either side of her body, staring down at her. His eyes practically burned through her.

"You're no good for Aurelio," he snarled. "You know that, hmm?" Quade moved his head so that she would look at him when she tried to look away.

"I'm aware. You've told me this repeatedly," Xavia said with ire. She was getting real fucking tired of this conversation.

"You tore him apart and have led him like a puppy on a leash for years." She snapped her head to him and pushed at him, but he didn't budge. "I've watched him fall apart time and time again after one of your tirades." Quade held up a hand to her face, keeping her from speaking. "You blow up and he's caught in the aftermath. And then I'm the one cleaning him up," he leaned in closer. "You don't fucking deserve him at your side." His words dripped like venom.

Xavia fought and failed to keep the tear that rolled down her cheek. She wiped it away angrily and pushed at him again, but he gripped the railing again to keep from moving. Fuck! Why wouldn't he let her leave?

"You have no idea how many times I've told him that!" Xavia snapped, keeping her voice from wavering. "I've told him over and over that he doesn't need to protect me, or try to…" Her eyes glossed a bit, blackness covering the edges of her eyesight. Really? Right now?

"No, you don't get to do that," Quade growled, grabbing her collar and tugging her. He roughly gripped her chin and tilted her to look at him. Xavia blinked the blackness away and stared at him, feeling a multitude of emotions; anger, sorrow, guilt, fury but worst of all, arousal. She gritted her teeth when he let her go and rocked against the railing.

"You have *no* idea what it's like for me," she hissed. "You have *no* fucking clue what it is like to wake up and find yourself in fucked up situations–sometimes with fucked up people–and not have one fucking memory of how you got there." Xavia seethed, channeling all her emotions into anger. She pushed at Quade again. He was rock solid, keeping her caged. "You have no idea what it's like wondering if the world would be better with you dead," she said, voice breaking. "No one hates me more than I hate myself." Xavia angrily wiped the few tears that managed to escape her eyes and looked down. "Let me go," she whispered, ready to end this conversation.

"No."

"Let. Me. Go." Xavia snapped, raising her gaze to Quade. The sun had almost finished its descent, playing with the colors of his sienna eyes. For the first time she noticed he had gold flecks throughout his irises. She wasn't sure what she expected to see in his eyes. Anger, pity? No, Quade looked at her with understanding, as if he saw her differently after her confession.

"I know exactly what it's like…" He murmured. "Well, maybe not the blackouts, but I know what it's like wondering if you're a shit stain on Euhaven and need to rid the world of the smell." Xavia's eyebrows raised in curiosity. Quade's face softened slightly, scowl disappearing. "I'm not a nice person."

She snorted, and he narrowed his eyes again. She shook her head, signaling him to continue.

"I've done some fucked up things, gotten myself in some fucked up situations, but I don't regret it." He shrugged and moved back a bit, finally giving her some space. "What does that make me?" Quade ran a hand through his hair and looked toward the horizon.

The sun had made its final descent; the stars appearing grandly in the sky. Without the light pollution of the cities, strands of star dust and nebulae of their galaxy could be seen across the sky. Low lights flared around the perimeter of the deck, giving it a light glow.

"An asshole?" Xavia said, trying to lighten the mood. The look

Quade gave her told her he was not impressed. "So... you mean to tell me that Aurelio has gotten himself stuck between two types of crazy?" With that he actually snorted, clearly trying not to laugh. He leaned against the railing next to her, body turned toward her.

"We're still not ok. You and I." Quade's tone sobered. Xavia rolled her eyes. "Your blackouts are a liability. Shit, they almost got you and Aurelio killed," he said, reminding her of their fiasco with the cage fight and Norrix. She sucked her teeth.

"My blackout helped us figure out what Norrix was." Even *she* knew the argument was weak.

"Keep telling yourself that, majnun." Crazy... He'd just called her crazy.

"Keep calling me crazy and I'll punch your perfect fucking teeth out," Xavia growled, getting in his face now. Quade's eyes dropped to her lips, causing her to flush. Flame flicked through his eyes and licked in and out of his fingers.*

"Keep up with that foul mouth and I'll show what other foul things you can do with it." His voice dropped an octave.

Heat shot down to her core, making her clench her thighs. What in Tomis's name was happening?

Xavia bit her lower lip slowly, looking anywhere but at him. Quade clasped her chin between his flaming forefinger and thumb and pulled her chin up to look at him. The fire bit at her, making her bite back a moan. "Tell me to stop," he murmured, moving close enough for their noses to touch.

Xavia could feel herself slickening between her thighs, her body betraying her. She should *not* be turned on by this male who'd spent who knows how long hating and berating her. Her mind and body warred with each other. Quade ran a hot thumb along her lower lip, popping it out from between her teeth.

"If you don't tell me to stop, I won't be held accountable for what I do next." Her breathing increased, her core pulsed.

Xavia's expression must have told him what she was too afraid to say out loud because his lips met hers. Much gentler than

♪ "Play With Fire" by Sam Tinnesz feat. Yacht Money

she thought, Quade kissed her slowly as if testing her and seeing if she was going to push him away. His lips were softer than she imagined. Xavia grabbed his shirt and, instead of pushing him away, she pulled him into her. Quade groaned and kissed her with more ferocity. His tongue licked the seam of her lips which she opened for him. Xavia couldn't help the moan that escaped her when Quade grabbed her ass to pull her closer, pelvis to pelvis. Heat–literal heat– from his hands warmed her in delicious ways. She could feel his hard on through his sweats making her core throb.

"What the fuck?"

Quade jumped back from Xavia so quickly it made her head spin. It felt like a bucket of ice was dumped over her head, the heat and arousal leaving her the moment her eyes connected with the storm grays of Aurelio.

QUADE

"FUCK…" WAS ALL QUADE COULD manage before Aurelio's fist connected with his jaw. He deserved it. What the fuck was he thinking kissing Xavia? He'd deliberately left his chin open, knowing full well that he fucked up.

Quade had gotten lost in what seemed like shared trauma. It distracted him, which pissed him off. Why did Xavia let him kiss her? Shit! Her lips. The ferocity. Fire meeting fire. He couldn't handle whatever was going on in his chest. Guilt? No, it wasn't that.

"Aurelio, stop!" Xavia yelled, attempting to get between them. Quade held out an arm to keep her to the side and shook his head.

"No, I deserve it," he grunted as another punch caught him in the stomach.

"Then I do too!" she growled, muscling her way between them. Aurelio's fist stopped just a hairsbreadth from her face. He panted hard, with a mixture of anger and pain in his eyes. Lightning cracked in the sky, lashing out at the ocean. The waves increased in frequency, rocking the yacht. His body shook as clouds formed, wind picking up. Fuck, Aurelio was going to bring a hurricane down on them if he didn't calm down.

"Cap..." Aurelio snapped his eyes to Quade, lightning cracking too close to the yacht than it should. "Be mad, but don't bring this yacht down in the process." Footsteps pounded up the stairs.

"What the—" Lex appeared, stopping cold and taking in the scene before them. While the storm above started to die down with each inhale Aurelio took, the storm that was Quade, Aurelio, and Xavia continued brewing. Lightning crackled at Aurelio's hands, Xavia panted in front of him, a palm on his chest, and behind Xavia, Quade held his hands out by his sides, prepared to move her if he needed to.

"Should I turn back around, or?" Lex had an eyebrow raised, talking to Xavia.

"It's fine. Thank you," she said, gently, with a nod. Lex narrowed their eyes at Aurelio with a 'we'll talk later' look before leaving. The night leveled out, the storm dissipating as if it never happened.

"Aurelio..."

He looked at her, raw pain reflecting in his eyes. He raised a hand to cup her face and placed his forehead on hers. Quade couldn't help the pang of jealousy that hit his gut. What the hell? His nose flared, the smell of ozone still in the air.

"I... Ah... I need a moment," Aurelio said, voice gruff. He kissed Xavia's forehead before shooting a glare at Quade. "You and I will finish this later." Lightning flared in his eyes before he turned and left. Quade let out a breath and ran a hand through his hair. He swore as he paced.

"What the fuck..." Xavia huffed before whirling to him. "You should've stopped." His jaw dropped as he stared at her incredulously. Him? *He* should've stopped?

"Are you fucking kidding me right now?" Quade's eyes

narrowed, taking in her expression. He had a feeling she didn't regret it, just felt guilty they were caught. "I told you to stop me if you wanted. You didn't." Xavia flushed. "And you liked it. Don't kid yourself." Ire grew in those depthless brown eyes of hers.

"Fuck you. You caught me in rare form."

Quade snorted, rolling his eyes.

"Yeah, right. Keep telling yourself that, brat." Xavia's eyes flared before she shoved him. She was always putting her hands on him. As much as it pissed him off, it also made him want to teach her a lesson about where she should put those hands instead. Quade caught her wrists and held them tight enough to bruise. He watched as she fought a gasp and glared at him.

"We fucked up. But don't act like it didn't make you wet," he growled as he pulled her in close. Quade watched the emotions war in Xavia's eyes. He couldn't help himself; he nipped her lip which brought out a pleasant sigh of pleasure from her. *He fucking knew it*. She could try to deny it but he knew she felt it too; this wild attraction brewing between them.

Xavia's nose flared as anger won the war. Her eyes widened slightly, her tell when she was going to do something insane. Quade ducked his head to the side before her forehead could connect with his.

"No. You're not getting me with that again." He let her go so abruptly that she stumbled. He didn't feel bad about it. Turning to leave, he paused at her chuckle and raised an eyebrow.

"I'm not the one walking off with a hard-on." Xavia pursed her lips smugly. This was dangerous ground they were walking on. His jaw ticked in frustration.

"Stay away from me," he snapped, before leaving her to fume alone.

Quade stormed into his suite, running a hand through his hair. He fucked up. He knew this. Worse was knowing that he might have catastrophically fucked up his friendship with Aurelio. He couldn't process all the complex emotions but realized he didn't feel guilty for kissing Xavia. He *did* hate the look of pain on Aurelio's face.

He faced a mirror on the wall, eyes lit with flame and smoke curling from his nose. He was a bastard, an asshole. He stared at his own scowl, years of anger fueling him, making him hate himself more.

"FUCK!" He yelled before slamming his fist into the mirror. He didn't register the pain of the glass embedded in his knuckles. Picking up a shard, he brought it to his wrist. The idea of killing himself floated through his mind once again. Playing with death, he dug in the shard just above the vein. All it would take is one slice down on each wrist and he could meet Axton in Orcus.

If I'm gone, who will be here for Aurelio? He reminded himself. He opted for slamming the shard into his thigh, biting back his groan. Pain. That was what he needed. Pain for the pain he caused.

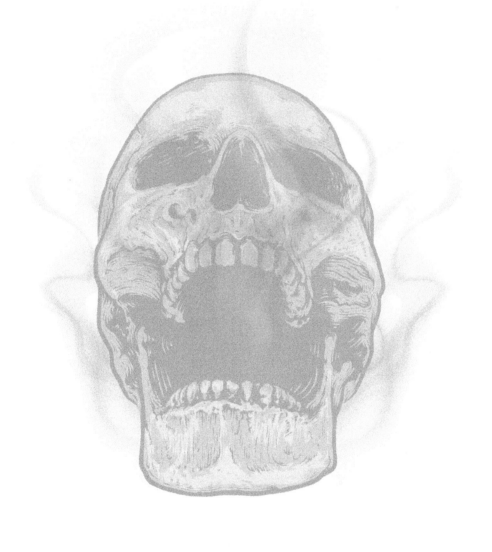

CHAPTER 30

AURELIO

THREE DAYS PASSED SINCE AURELIO caught Xavia and Quade together. Had it been going on for long? Was their ire for each other all a game? Needing to process his feelings, he'd spent the last few days contemplating everything and refused to be around them. Aurelio knew he had no right or claim on Xavia. She was a single woman who could have anyone she wanted. But *Quade?* His brother in arms? It took all his control to keep the storm inside him from breaking loose.

Aurelio panted, going through his workout regimen on the foredeck. He had finally found his sea legs and while not completely immune to the motion sickness, he couldn't continue to sit on his ass. The sun bore its full heat on his bare back as he did push-ups, sweat dripping from his nose to the mat.

"Hey," came Xavia's voice. Aurelio froze in a plank, muscles taut. He listened to her movements as she laid out in a plank, her head facing his. When their eyes met, hers seemed strained. He knew she hated planks and he wasn't sure if he should laugh or roll his eyes. He didn't break the eye contact, breath coming out in even pants while Xavia's released as short gasps. He wondered how long she would wait and was happy to let her. Her arms started shaking, sweat dripping down her nose. She had a look of determination and he couldn't help but tilt his lips into a smirk. He was about to tell her to stop when she collapsed with a huff. He pushed himself to rest on his knees, slowing his breathing.

"I'm surprised you lasted that long," he said, stifling a chuckle.

"That's what she said," Xavia groaned into the mat. Aurelio barked out a laugh, shaking his head. Axton's balls, this woman. She rolled on to her back, squinting at the sun. "I will never understand how you do those awful planks." She worked on catching her breath. As she wore only a sports bra and mid-thigh gym shorts, Aurelio couldn't help but watch as her chest rose and fell, glistening with sweat. She sat up slowly and faced him. He held up a hand when she opened her mouth.

"Don't." He stood and made his way to the salon.

"You haven't even heard what I have to say," said Xavia, hot on his heels. Aurelio shook his head, heading to the crew quarters. He grabbed a towel from a nearby rack and turned so abruptly that Xavia walked into him.

"I don't want to." He glared down at her. "I can't figure out who I'm mad at more. You, me, or Quade." His nose flared, anger raising his blood pressure. "You and I almost fucked back in the B&B." Xavia winced at his choice of words but he left all his fucks back in Silvermoon and didn't have one to give. "Then you're here sharing saliva with my best friend; my second in command!" Aurelio shook his head. "I get that I have no right to what or who you do. But it doesn't mean I have to sit here and watch." She made to say something but he moved into the bathroom and slammed the door behind him.

"YOU'LL HAVE TO TALK TO THEM EVENTUALLY." Ryland said softly while they ate. Another two days had passed and he still hadn't spoken more than a 'hi' to either Xavia or Quade. The trip took longer than they planned which meant a longer amount of time trapped on the yacht with those two. Lilith hummed in agreement, swallowing down spicy mushroom noodles.

"They haven't spoken to each other the entire week. It's all glares and scowls per usual." She pointed her chopsticks at Aurelio.

"You need to settle this, Cap. We're heading toward the Horizon Line and we need to be of one accord." Lilith narrowed those milky eyes at him.

He knew they were both right. Lilith raised her eyebrow to which he heaved a sigh and stood up. He patted her shoulder as he walked around her toward the common area.

Everyone had been below deck or in the salon due to rain pummeling the yacht. The waves were rougher, making his stomach turn. He caught sight of Quade on the couch, legs crossed with his foot on the opposite knee. He looked up from his book and stiffened when he saw Aurelio. Aurelio gave him a onceover before he sat down across from the Fire Wielder. He could see the tension in Quade's shoulders while he assessed what Aurelio planned to do. Aurelio leaned forward, resting his elbows on his knees and rubbed his face.

"I know I don't have a right to Xavia and what she does," he started.

"You don't," Quade agreed sharply, eyebrow raised. Aurelio's eyes darkened, nose flaring as he worked around his temper.

"How did it happen, Q?" he said, genuinely curious, even if it made him jealous. "I thought you two hated each other."

"We do," he said as he snapped his book close. Aurelio waited a beat to see if Quade had anything else to say. He just raised one shoulder in a shrug. Was the bastard even sorry?

"Was it consensual?"

Quade sat up, mouth open in shock, and jabbed a finger at Aurelio.

"*You* know me better than that! Why would you even ask?" he snapped.

Aurelio could admit it was a low blow. He couldn't fathom the two of them even being around each other without wanting to kill the other, let alone kissing.

"We were arguing." Quade brought Aurelio's attention back to the room. "I told Xavia what I thought of her. That she didn't deserve you and that she was a liability to this team with her unstable mind." Aurelio almost jumped from his seat at him.

"You said what?" he growled through his teeth, lightning streaking across the sky. Quade nodded.

"I told her how it is. But…" Quade's expression softened ever so slightly, slowly dissipating Aurelio's anger. "She told me how she felt about herself," he muttered, looking toward the corner of the room as if remembering the conversation. "Other than the blackouts, she could've been talking about me."

Aurelio rose an eyebrow in question. "What do you mean?"

"I told her I wasn't a nice person." Aurelio snorted and Quade rolled his eyes. "Yeah, she had the same reaction." Aurelio didn't miss the way the side of Quade's mouth tilted slightly in a smirk. "You know I've done some fucked up shit and I rarely, if ever, feel bad about it." Aurelio nodded. Quade always struggled with empathy. "There has been a time or two where I flirted with the idea of killing myself."

"Wha—"

"I just wanted to see if I could go through with it." He cut Aurelio off and shrugged again. "I don't know. There was a moment of understanding between us." He ran a hand through his hair. Aurelio had never seen Quade flustered before and he wasn't sure how to process it. "We started arguing again and then…" Quade opened his hands and spread them out as if laying a blanket in the air. Aurelio nodded.

"Do you feel guilty about it at all?" he murmured, already knowing the answer.

"No," was all Quade said before lifting his book. "I don't feel guilty for finally understanding the wildness in her and finding it fascinating." He opened the book, looking at Aurelio once more. "Somehow, I got caught in her orbit and I'm not sure if I want to pull out." Aurelio knew exactly how Quade felt. Xavia was magnetic. "But I *am* sorry I hurt you."

Aurelio was surprised by the confession. "I don't think I've ever heard an apology from you before."

"Don't get used to it," Quade quipped.

Aurelio leaned his head on the back of the couch and rubbed his face. Letting out a sigh, he took a moment to process the thought of Quade and Xavia together. In Silvermoon he would've done a lot more if Styx had given him the time of day. Was he in a position to judge Xavia for the same? There was a chasm growing between them all and he wanted nothing more than to close the gap. Emotions warred within him; jealousy, curiosity, acceptance. He couldn't imagine life without either of them in it.

He found Quade's sienna eyes on him, watching Aurelio process and come to a decision. Aurelio realized that he wouldn't try to stop them. Trying to keep them apart would be like trying to keep Euhaven from orbiting the sun. Rather than fight it, he could join them; be the Ithea to Quade's Euhaven.

"I can't believe I'm saying this… But I won't stop you two if it's something y'all want to explore. It's not within my rights. Both of you are too important to me to fuck it up for all of us."

"Alright." A man of many words, Quade dropped his eyes to the book, ending the conversation.

CHAPTER 31

XAVIA

HAVE YOU EVER SEEN THE HORIZON LINE?" Lex said, standing next to Xavia on the foredeck the next day. Everyone had come up to see the event Lex touted as one of the most beautiful sights on Euhaven. Xavia shook her head, looking off to the distance but only seeing a sunny day ahead.

"I've never been this far from the coast," she said, pushing some curls behind her ears.

"I didn't know you've sailed before, X." Lilith was standing on the other side of Lex.

"Yeah. It was a long time ago." She shifted on her feet when she looked over to Aurelio and Quade. They were having a conversation about who knows what and she felt a pang of pain in her heart. Xavia felt out of the loop and not speaking with Aurelio did a number on her. All the stuff with Quade made her want to throw up. She was not sleeping well, fighting constantly in fear that she'd black out and do something stupid. Xavia looked to her watch to find it glitching.

"Oh. We're going to be out of communications for a few hours. There's something about the Horizon Line that messes with the nav systems." Lex shrugged. "We should be ok though. I didn't see any storms in the forecast and the sea dwellers don't hover around the Line."

"Oh, look!" Ryland was at the tip of the bow, holding on to the rail. Xavia was glad he stayed with them, even if he had an attitude with her since the Dolsano. Something about her seemed to rub him the wrong way. Xavia looked in the direction he pointed and gasped softly.

Xavia had always heard of the stark beauty of the Horizon Line, that demarcation between natural night and day, and the area of Euhaven trapped in perpetual darkness. Seeing it in person was an entirely different experience. She could understand why nocturnal creatures like vampires would choose Potroya, the Dark Continent, but the humans must be something else.

Xavia's eyes widened at the sight of the darkness ahead. It felt like a wall of darkness rushed to meet them. She felt like she was looking at a rainbow in reverse. There was an arch, following the curvature of Euhaven, and they moved slowly under it. The further they moved through the arch, the darker it got.

Once they were directly under the Horizon Line, Xavia looked up. Clear sunny skies were on one side, pure midnight skies on the other. Her mouth fell open in awe. Unlike a sunset, the day faded into night like a harsh gradient. She looked ahead, and it felt as if they entered a tunnel, their surroundings getting darker by the moment. Xavia looked backward, the daylight forming a wall of light behind them. A flash in the sky made her look up again. A meteor shower! She'd never seen one with such clarity. Xavia couldn't remember the last time she felt true happiness. Tears slid down her face as she basked in the rare emotion. .

"It's a beautiful sight," a deep rumbling voice came from behind. Xavia turned her gaze to Aurelio who watched her intently. She rushed to wipe her tears but he took her hands into his. "No. You look beautiful."

His silver eyes roved over her face, as if taking in every last detail. It left her feeling vulnerable and hot. He nodded his head toward the lower deck. "We should talk." He let go of her hands but the warmth lingered.

Xavia nodded, following him. Her stomach was in knots and she fought to keep from chewing on her cuticles. They entered the guest room she shared with Lilith and she plopped on her bed, motioning him to sit.

"You can sit on her bed. She's hardly ever in here." She

smirked. Lilith spent more time crashing in the salon, hanging out with Lex. Xavia had been sleeping alone for the last few days. Aurelio chuckled as he sat with a huff. The silence in the room was palpable.

"Look, I'm s—"

"No, don't." Aurelio shook his head. He leaned forward to rest his elbows on his knees and steeple his fingers. "I spoke with Quade." Xavia blanched, pulling her knees up to her chest and resting her chin on her knees. "Don't worry, I didn't touch him." The side of his lips tilted in a smirk. "He told me about your argument…" He chuckled. "Y'all are more alike than you think." She felt her face flush and stuffed it in her knees. Yeah, she started to realize that, but it didn't make her happy about it.

"I was angry. He said all the things I already tell myself daily." Xavia muttered into her knees. Xavia felt tears pricking her eyes. "Somehow, it took a turn and I wasn't expecting it. I… don't know how I feel about it," she whispered. She felt a dip in the bed as Aurelio sat next to her. "And it's wrong on so many levels. I know that." She started rambling. "He's your best friend, I mean other than me. And he's been fighting alongside you in ways I never could. He's been there for you, cleaning up my messes and–"

"Xavia, stop." Xavia turned her head to look at him. Aurelio's eyes burned through her, silver bleeding to steel. "I can't stop you from doing what you want. I can't stop you from feeling what you feel." He moved closer, moving a strand of curls behind her ear. "But I need to know if what's been going on between us is real or just a distraction." His hand lingered, thumb tracing her jaw. She closed her eyes, liquid heat racing to her core.

She wasn't sure if she was going to regret it later, but she said, "Can't it be both?"

AURELIO

AURELIO'S HEARTBEAT WAS IN HIS THROAT as the words Xavia whispered registered. As he stared into her dark brown eyes, he wondered if this would work. Could they keep this as just a distraction? They'd been through the ringer these last few weeks; it would be a welcome distraction. But would his heart make it out in the end?

He slowly ran his thumb over her lower lip, making her shudder. "Are you sure about this?" Aurelio murmured, eyes on her lips. She let go of her knees to lean toward him.

"I'm sure," Xavia whispered before licking his thumb in a slow torturous move. He tilted her head, his hand moving to her nape, eyes still questioning. "Aurelio, I'm sure." She licked her lips, her gaze full of lust.*

Aurelio's mouth slammed into hers as Xavia straddled him. His tongue worked to gain access and she opened to him. She let out a deep moan when his hands found her ass and ground her against him. He sucked in her lower lip and bit it, making her hiss in pleasure. Xavia rocked her hips against him, making him groan. Being in sweats, Aurelio could feel every movement Xavia made against his growing erection. She took his lower lip between her teeth and nipped at it, making his cock twitch.

Xavia put a hand on either side of his face and kissed him as if it was her last chance at life. The fervor in which she kissed him had him returning it in kind. Aurelio slid Xavia's shirt over her head, watching as her breasts bounced free. They were thick and heavy, overflowing in his hands, as he brought one to his mouth. He took her beautiful brown nipple into his mouth, making her grip the back of his head, nails digging in. He groaned at the slice of pain, turning to tease her other nipple.

♪ "Skin" by Rihanna

"Shit, that feels so good," Xavia moaned, holding his head to her. He gently bit her puckered breast making her squeak in delight. "Take off your shirt and lay down," she said, authority in her voice. Aurelio looked up at her to see her eyes full of lust and with a glint of command. He slipped off his shirt and laid back, looking up at her generously thick body.

Over the years, she had filled out in the most beautiful of ways. His hands gripped her deep golden plump thighs, feeling the muscles twitch and move. Xavia pushed his hands above his head as she took in his lower lip to suck on. He groaned, cock twitching again, when she moved to his neck, biting down hard enough to make him see stars. Xavia had gotten more aggressive over the years. He remembered her as being more of a gentle lover. This was different. Pure electric.

"Shit, X," Aurelio bucked his hips against her. Xavia slowly moved down his body, her hot mouth covering his nipple. She rolled it around her tongue before sucking it. "Fuck!" A deep throated moan escaped his lips. That was a first and it felt fucking good. She moved down further, tugging at his pants to pull them off. His cock sprang free, thick and aching. Xavia looked up at him as she took hold of him.

"I'm going to suck your dick until you're begging me to let you come."

Aurelio could feel his eyes widening as she licked the tip. Fuck, she was a whole different woman.

She took him in her mouth slowly, looking at him as she did so. She wrapped her lips around her teeth and sucked him in deeper. When the head of his cock hit the back of her throat, his eyes rolled back at the sensation. Xavia started to bob, taking him in and out of her mouth. She held him at the base of his cock, hand occasionally massaging his balls. She took him as deep as she could, gagging and dripping hot saliva along his shaft as she came up for air. His hand found her hair as he lifted his hips to fuck her mouth. Aurelio stared down at her to find her watching him. The sight of his cock going in and out of her mouth made his balls clench. He could feel the orgasm building at the base of his spine.

"Oh shit, that's..." he bucked his hips.

"Use your words. Tell me what you see." She breathed, licking the underside of his shaft down to his balls. She took him back in her mouth and he groaned.

"You, baby. Watching me while I fuck your mouth." Xavia hummed in agreement. "Shit, I'm going to come," he breathed before Xavia suddenly pulled herself away from him, making him groan in protest. She had a salacious grin on her face as she stood over him to slowly drop her shorts. Sweet Etis and Sortis, her pussy was dripping with arousal. He reached up to touch her but she slapped his hands away, shaking her head.

"One second," Xavia whispered, hopping off the bed to find her robe. She pulled the tie from it and slowly walked her way to him. As she crawled up his body, his hands itched to touch her. "May I?" she asked, snapping the tie taunt.

"Yes Ma'am." Aurelio hissed as she brushed against his cock with her body. She expertly tied his wrists to the headboard. He couldn't untie himself even if he wanted to. Xavia moved to straddle his face, and he could smell her sweet arousal as she brought her pussy down on his lips.

"Before you touch me, you're going to eat this pussy first." Xavia sighed with pleasure as she started to ride his face. Aurelio hummed in approval, tongue snaking its way between her folds. He took her clit between his lips, sucking on it. Her voice rose an octave as she moaned, spreading her juices around his mouth and chin. "I'm so fucking wet for you," she gasped as he used the flat of his tongue to lap at her clit before penetrating her. She fucked his face harder, keeping pace with his tongue moving in and out of her. He could feel her tensing, knowing that she was reaching her orgasm. "Shit. I'm going to come... And you're going to drink it." Fuck. Aurelio could come on her dirty talk alone. His cock ached to be inside her.

He hummed again, focusing on her swollen clit as she started to rock against him faster. Xavia moaned loudly as she began to come on his face. He suckled on her, taking in all her juices, until she slowed. She sat back on his chest and patted him on the cheek.

"Good boy."

As she stood up again, Aurelio couldn't think straight. Did Xavia just praise him? And did he fucking like it? It was a kink he didn't know he had. It did something to the deepest parts of himself to know he satisfied her. He'd beg and grovel at her feet if it meant he'd feel like this over and over again.

Aurelio felt her pussy hovering over his cock, drawing him out of his thoughts. Xavia was on her feet as she slowly sat down, sinking herself onto his cock. He groaned as she slid up to the head of his cock before sliding him in to the hilt. Her hands rested on his chest as she rode him faster, her arousal flowing over him. As Xavia moved down, Aurelio's hips bucked up, meeting her with every stroke. She gasped as she bounced on his cock, taking him deep inside her. Fuck, he wanted to touch her and fought against the ties around his wrists. Xavia chuckled before sliding her hands up his chest to his throat. Her eyes met his, asking for permission. Damnit to Axton, if she wanted to choke him, he'd let her until he died.

"Do it," Aurelio breathed as her cunt slid up and down his cock. Xavia gave a smirk, eyes darkening, as she leaned into him, shifting to her knees. Her hands gripped his neck tight enough to surprise him. She was stronger than he expected. She moaned as she brought herself up and down. Xavia's core clenched around him, his cock aching for release. Aurelio's vision swirled as his eyes rolled back with pleasure. The sting of a light slap on his face and slight release of the hands around his throat flooded his system with endorphins. The pleasure rocked his world, making him feel as if he were floating. Never had a female owned him like this. Never had he allowed a female to take control. And holy shit, he would be lying if he said he didn't like it.

"Look at me," Xavia gasped as she bounced on him. "I want you to look at me while I fuck you and make you come," Aurelio nodded, whimpering as her hands tightened around his throat again. Rainbow stars flooded his vision as he kept eye contact with her. Her face full of pleasure and bliss, kiss swollen lips parted as she panted. Aurelio could feel his orgasm building again as he thrusted his hips up to meet each bounce she made. Xavia's core clenched around his cock, her thighs shaking slightly, letting him know she was approaching the edge. She let go of his neck enough for him to take a deep breath, that euphoria flooding him again, before she gripped him again.

"Yeah, that's it baby. Come for me," she moaned as she started to come, bringing him with her. Aurelio roared as he pumped into her, filling her pussy with his hot pleasure. Their bodies twitched as she let go of his neck and flopped down to his chest. Holy Etis and Sortis, he'd never been fucked like that. She moved gingerly to untie his wrists, which he didn't realize were aching.

"That... Was amazing," he said in between breaths, running a hand through Xavia's hair as their hearts beat together. She huffed a laugh, causing her to clench around his cock making him twitch.

"Good," she murmured, slightly moving her hips. His already hardening cock still in her as she rocked her hips. "Now flip me over and fuck me again."

CHAPTER 32

XAVIA

AURELIO FLIPPED XAVIA ONTO HER STOMACH, kisses peppered her back along her tattoo. She rose to her knees, keeping her face down on the bed. She yelped as he bit her ass before making his way to her dripping core. Aurelio dragged his tongue over her clit before sucking it in. Xavia bucked her hips, moaning louder. The sounds of his wet tongue on her pussy made her eyes roll in pleasure. It only amplified when he added two fingers, hooking them and hitting her delicious spot. *

"Fuck," she breathed. "Keep going." Xavia rubbed her cunt against his mouth. Aurelio groaned, the vibration bringing her closer to the edge. He added a third finger, pumping it in and out of her making her scream out. "I'm coming," she cried as the orgasm crested over her. She turned around quickly, Aurelio's cock right where she wanted it. She wrapped a hand around his shaft before taking the head into her mouth. Xavia moaned as she sucked him in, reaching the base of him.

"Shit, X," Aurelio moaned, hips moving in rhythm with her bobbing. She gagged as she took him as deep as she could, saliva dripping from her mouth. She enjoyed the taste of their sex on his cock. She pulled back, looking up at him. His eyes had rolled, hand resting on her head.

"Look at me and remember to use your words. I want to hear all the dirty things your mind conjures" Xavia commanded, his

♪ "Moan" by Sabrina Claudio

eyes snapped to her. She glided her teeth over the head of his dick and down the velvet smooth shaft. It wasn't hard enough to hurt, but it was enough to send a visible shiver through his body. "If you keep looking away, I'll make you regret it," she smirked when he kept his eyes on her. She watched his reaction as she slowly took him back into her mouth.

Aurelio bit his lower lip in a way that made her moan. Xavia wrapped her lips over her teeth and began moving faster, sucking him in deep enough to make him groan and buck. She pulled back. "Fuck my mouth, Aurelio." A look of surprise came over his face. She realized that he was not used to this side of her but his twitching cock told her he liked it. "Take my head, wrap your hands in my hair, and fuck. My. Mouth. Now." Xavia said, gripping him tightly enough to make him jerk and let out a moan.

"Yes Ma'am," Aurelio groaned before he wrapped her hair in his hand tightly as he thrust into her mouth. She sucked as he pumped in and out of her mouth. Her hands slid up to grab his ass, pushing him to fuck her mouth harder. He brought a second hand to her hair and drove deeper. "You look so fucking sexy sucking my dick like that," he moaned as he held her head down to the base of his cock, making her gag and saliva drip from her lips. Aurelio thrusted rough enough that Xavia knew she was going to have a delightfully sore throat.

"I'm going to come, baby," he breathed. She gripped his ass hard enough that she probably left scratches. Xavia hummed a moan as she looked up at him. Aurelio was looking at her, panting. "Can I come?" he whimpered. Her pussy throbbed at the request and she nodded. He unleashed himself, fucking her mouth deeply and thoroughly. He loaded hot streams of his orgasm down her throat and she drank what she could, excess dripping from the sides of her mouth. Sitting on his heels, he lowered himself so that she kneeled above him.

"Taste yourself on my lips," Xavia whispered as she bent and kissed him. He licked her lips, cleaning her of his cum. The way he did as she asked and kept himself lower than her spoke multitudes. Aurelio was submitting to her and damnit if that didn't pull at her heartstrings. "Hmm. You learn quickly," she said with a chuckle. He looked up at her before kissing her soft belly. She gently touched his head. "Good boy," she said as she watched his cock harden again. Oh, he liked that. Wielders had stamina to rival the Deities. Xavia turned from him and placed her hands on the headboard, bending over. She spread her legs for him to take a good look at her wetness.

"Shit X," Aurelio whispered almost reverently.

"Do you want this pussy?" she asked, looking over her shoulder. He nodded.

"Fuck, yes," he watched as she reached between her legs to play with her clit.

"Do you want to fuck this pussy?" she asked as she moaned. Xavia swatted at his hand when he tried to reach for her. "No. Not until I say," she said darkly. "I asked you a question." She dipped two fingers into her pussy. "Do you want to fuck this pussy?"

"Yes," Aurelio breathed, watching her as she finger fucked herself.

"Tell me you want to fuck this pussy," she moaned, thrusting at a faster pace.

"Baby, I want to fuck that pussy," he groaned as he watched her.

"And how do you ask?" Xavia spread her legs further.

"Can I fuck that pussy?" She slid her fingers out before putting her hand back on the head board.

"'Can I fuck that pussy' what?" She swayed her hips, his eyes tracking it with hunger.

"Can I fuck that pussy, please, Ma'am?" Aurelio's body shook with the effort to keep still. She gave him a salacious smile.

"Yes, you can fuck this pussy." He was on her before she finished her sentence, burying his cock deep into her. She cried out as he gripped her hips and fucked her like his life depended on it. "Put your thumb in my ass," Xavia commanded. Without hesitation, he reached in front of her to coat his fingers in her wetness before moving it to her puckered spot. Aurelio slowly dipped his thumb in, bringing out a deep moan from within her. He dipped it further before pumping it in and out.

"X, I'm going to come. Your pussy is too good," he groaned as he slowed his movements into an excruciating pace. His thumb matched the pace, wringing out the pleasure.

"Do you want to come?" Xavia asked as he pulled out to the head of his cock before he thrusted in her with a slap. She yelped in pleasure as he kept his thumb in her while he slowly pulled out again and thrusted in with another slap.

"Yes. I want to come," he breathed, pumping with delicious patience. She could feel her orgasm near, almost ready to crest over her.

"And how do you ask Aurelio?" Xavia said with a moan as he drove in deep.

"Can I come?" He slammed into her. "Please?" Aurelio panted.

"Yes, fuck me and come," Xavia gasped as he began to fuck her in earnest. Her orgasm crashed over her as he spilled inside. Their bodies twitched as they came down from the tail end of their orgasms. Aurelio kissed her lower back, up her spine to her shoulder. He kissed her cheek sweetly, pulling her up so her back was flush against his chest. He wrapped his arms around her waist, cock still in her, and held her tight.

AURELIO

"DID I DO GOOD?" AURELIO MURMURED into her neck. Xavia tilted her head to give him more access and placed a hand on his head. She gasped when he nipped her neck and brought his hand to her sex. Aurelio had considered himself a dominant male. He was a leader, always in charge, and the one everyone relied on to get shit done. But this experience with Xavia let him know that he didn't have to be all the time.

"Yes, you did. You were a very good boy." Xavia whispered. He ran a thumb over her swollen clit, making her breath hitch. "Down boy." There was a hint of humor in her voice, making him chuckle. Both of them groaned as they disengaged their tangled bodies from each other. He collapsed on his back with her curled to his side and head on his chest.

"When did you get so mommy-dom?" Aurelio huffed, playing with her sweaty curls.

Xavia snorted. "First, don't call me mommy." He hissed when she bit his nipple. "Second, I've always been a brat. I like it both ways but I read the energy." She licked his nipple, easing the ache of the bite. "And baby, the energy between us." Xavia let out a pleased sigh. Aurelio gently turned her head up so that he could kiss her softly.

"You definitely read the energy right," he whispered against her lips. She smiled, touching his face. Something shone in her eyes. "I'll be honest." He kissed her forehead. "I didn't think I had a praise kink." She huffed a laugh.

"Oh, you definitely have a praise kink." His mouth gaped and he mussed up her hair. "Hey!" She swatted his hands.

"What do you mean? Before today, I didn't even know I had one." He sat up on his elbows with an eyebrow raised. Xavia bit her lip, clear that she was trying to keep from chuckling. "Explain, woman!" He couldn't help the grin on his face.

"Aurelio, you always take pride when someone tells you 'Good job'." She patted his chest. "In the Academy, whenever you placed first, you glowed when the Sergeants gave you praise." He pursed his lips as he considered that. "Honestly, every time someone is impressed with you and compliments you, you perk up like a golden retriever." Aurelio swatted her head for that. Xavia laughed. "It's true!"

"I never thought about that before. I just felt pride." He traced her jawline.* His lips trailed the scar on her neck, kissing it. "It does make me feel good," he moved his thumb to her lower

---

♪ "Give" by Sleep Token

lip. "Especially when you praise me," Aurelio whispered, kissing her thoroughly, making her moan as their tongues rubbed against each other. "I like it when you tell me what to do," he whispered before kissing her again. "I like it when you tease me," another kiss. "When you take control." This time Xavia bit at his lip making him groan. "I like the bit of pain mixed with pleasure." She bit hard enough to split his lip, making him growl and pull her on top of him. Aurelio took her hands as he leaned his head back and put them on his throat. "I like it when you choke me." She applied pressure before leaning forward to kiss him.

"I like it when you submit," Xavia whispered, licking his lower lip. "I like that you listen like a good boy," Aurelio's cock twitched as he groaned. "I like that you know your place." Her grip tightened, making him see stars. "I like that you make me come." She slid her hot pussy over his cock. "I like that you beg me to let you come," Xavia slowly impaled herself, dragging out a moan. Just as he was at the edge of blackness, she released pressure flooding his system with oxytocin. Aurelio grabbed her ass in a tight hold, making her moan. "I like the pain mixed with pleasure too." She tightened her grip, this time her nails digging in. He was pretty sure bruises were going to show despite his dark skin.

"Shit, X," Aurelio breathed through the hold. Xavia began to roll her hips, sliding his cock in and out of her drenched pussy. She released enough to bring that wave of euphoria and his eyes rolled. He felt her grip on his chin.

"I like it when you look. At. Me," she said firmly. He snapped his eyes to her.

"Yes Ma'am," Aurelio breathed, moving his hips in time with hers.

"Mmm," Xavia moaned, picking up the pace. "I like it when you call me 'Ma'am'. That shit is a fucking turn on." As she began to bounce on his cock, his hips rose to match the pace. "Fuck Aurelio," she moaned, sitting up to dig her nails into his chest.

Aurelio watched her, the beauty of her, as she rocked and slammed down on him. Xavia seemed surrounded with a glow, messy curls framing her beautifully round face. She was stunning.

He turned his grip to her soft stomach, making her gasp in pleasure. Aurelio couldn't get enough of her curves; of her thickness. The heavy breasts that swayed above him. He sat up, wrapped her legs around his waist, and took one of her delicious brown nipples into his mouth. Xavia gripped the back of his head as she rocked quicker. Her pussy clenched around his cock as he grinded his hips into her.

"Fuck, baby. Please. Xavia, please," Aurelio whimpered in between her breasts with shuddering breaths. He locked his gaze with hers. He watched the ecstasy on her face; how plump her kiss swollen lips were. He hissed in pleasure when she dug her nails in. He could feel the orgasm riding up his spine.

"Do you like that? When I dig my nails in?" Xavia said, dragging a hot and pleasurable path from his scalp to his neck. "Do you like it when I bite you?" She moaned as his hips bucked in response. "Come for me when I bite you. Make this pussy come all over your dick."

"Yes Ma'am," Aurelio breathed, he picked her up, flipping her on her back and drove his cock in her. He put one leg over his shoulder. She let out a yelp of pleasure as he thrust in deep, over and over. He looked between them as he pumped. "I can watch my dick fuck you all night if I could. You're so fucking wet," he groaned. Xavia clenched, letting him know she was close to the edge. That was when she struck, biting deep into his neck. Aurelio let out a growl he didn't even know he could make, slamming into her before he released himself inside of her.

"Fuck, I'm coming!" Xavia cried out while he continued to rock his hips. Her legs were twitching from the orgasm as they slowed down enough to catch their breath. She started peppering kisses on his neck and throat. "Fuck, you have no idea what you're doing to me," she murmured, running her hands over his head and gently touching the marks she left. "You've been such a good boy, making me come like that." Aurelio slowly let her leg down before flipping her back on top of him so that she was above him, where she should always be. Her soothing touches were enough to make his limbs go languid. She continued to run her hands over him, massaging his aches and peppered kisses where she left marks. Her lips found his neck, making him groan.

"You? I'm a puddle here," Aurelio huffed a laugh, kissing her shoulder. Xavia laughed, making them groan from the rawness of her sex and the fact that he was still inside her. She touched his jaw, tilting his head up to her.

"One thing I will always do is make sure you're rewarded," Xavia kissed his forehead. "I will always take care of you and make sure you're safe," she kissed his cheek. "I will always take care of you," she whispered, before kissing him deeply.

CHAPTER 33

XAVIA

XAVIA WOKE THE NEXT MORNING with a delicious soreness between her thighs. Thoughts of the night made her smile and heat curled in her belly. They spent the night making up for lost time. She groaned as she sat up, Aurelio gently snoring next to her. She kissed his forehead before slipping on her jammies and headed to the galley. She needed coffee. She needed to process. As she got closer, she overhead Lex and Lilith talking.

"Sleep good?" Lex said with humor in their voice.

"I had to turn on music to drown out those two. They've been at it like rabbits." Lilith snorted.

"Sorry," mumbled a tired Xavia as she entered the galley. Lex and Lilith laughed, Lex grabbing Xavia by the waist and ruffling her hair. Xavia groaned, trying to duck her head. "Not before coffee!" She slapped Lex's hands away so she could fill up her tumbler with iced coffee.

"It was about time," Lilith said with a sly smile. Xavia rolled her eyes, slurping her coffee.

"So, I was right about Quade?" Lex grinned, making Xavia go warm in the cheeks. Lilith snorted around a piece of mango she was eating.

"Don't even start," Xavia groaned.

"I told you. I'm a great judge of character." Lex winked. Xavia rolled her eyes with a huff of a sigh. During one of their drinking sessions, they told Xavia that there was something between her and Quade but she refused to listen.

"I mean the sexual tension between you two can be cut with a knife," Lilith quipped. Lex snapped their fingers and pointed to Lilith.

"See?! I said the same thing." Lex high-fived Lilith. Xavia grumbled something about needing a stronger coffee before refilling her tumbler.

"I don't know what to do about it," Xavia said with a sigh. "But Aurelio, holy Tomis, things have changed. It was like he was a whole new man. It was..." She bit her tongue, looking at Lilith. "Sorry. I know he's your superior. I probably shouldn't—"

"Oh no, keep on." Lilith grinned, sipping her tea. Xavia sighed, a coy smirk on her lips.

"It was the best sex I've ever had," she chuckled. "When we were younger, I was a lot more reserved in my desires. I didn't want to scare him away." She pursed her lips. "So, I kept it vanilla, afraid of what my darker desires meant." Xavia slurped her coffee. "Twelve years changes people, y'know? So... Yeah. It was very different," she grinned. Lilith gave Lex a mischievous smirk.

"And Quade?" Lilith said, clamping her lips between her teeth to keep from laughing. Xavia gave them a dismayed look.

"Quade? Why do we keep going back to Quade? Ah..." She was once again speechless. "Where Aurelio is the quiet storm, Quade is a wildfire," she said, softly, afraid the males would hear. "We didn't take it any further than a kiss but the kiss said enough." She raised a hand to her lips. "What do I do?"

"Uh, fuck him?" Lilith said plainly. Both Lex's and Xavia's jaws dropped at the brashness of her words. Lilith shrugged. "You mean to tell me you aren't a liberated woman?" She raised an eyebrow at Xavia. "You've told me enough that I know you're not a prude, my friend."

"I... Ah..."

Lex laughed and put a finger under Xavia's chin to close her mouth. She narrowed her eyes, scrunching her nose.

"Take time to process it. Let your body do the talking." Lex said softly, smirk still playing on their face. Xavia grumbled some more about needing whiskey before washing the tumbler and placing it on the drying rack.

"I'm gonna go train. Anyone want to join?"

Lilith nodded, putting the remaining fruit and vegetables away. Lex shook their head.

"I've got helm duty. Switching with Quade." Lex wriggled their eyebrows, earning a push to their head from Xavia.

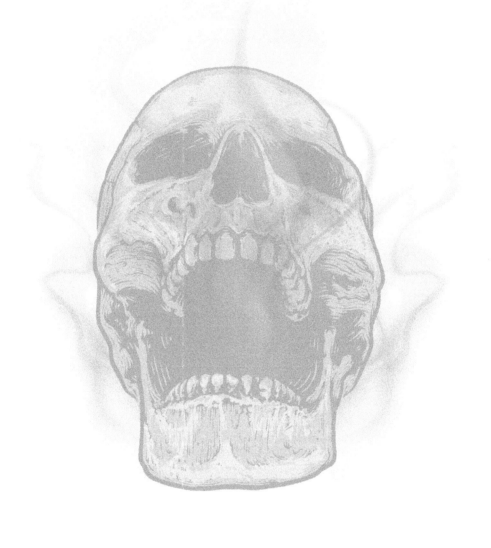

CHAPTER 34

JACINTO

YOUR EMINENCE, PLEASURE TO MEET YOU."** Norrix Aimes purred, holding his hand out to Jacinto.

The vampire looked at the pale hand extended to him, red around the nails. Norrix wore a black button up under a deep crimson vest and matching slacks. The chain of a pocket watch hung from his front pant pocket. His pure red hair was smoothed back, his blood red eyes shining. All the red made his pale skin even more stark. His style could give Cyrus a run for his money.

"Norrix." Jacinto nodded and motioned him to sit.

Norrix dropped his hand with a dark smile and sat at the conference table. Cyrus stood by the door, in a navy double-breasted suit, not looking pleased. Jacinto was not the type to wear suits and showed up in a tight white Henley with the sleeves rolled to his elbows, black jeans, and white sneakers.

"I appreciate your hospitality. The apartment you provided me and my cohort is more than ample." Norrix fixed the cuff of his shirt. "And thank you for taking the time to speak with me."

Jacinto had been caught off guard with how soon Norrix arrived in Malagado. It took him and his cohort of ten upper-level demons to arrive three weeks flat. No one ever crossed the Temisraine Ocean at such a speed. Only Wielding, or perhaps some kind of advanced science, could've done it.

"Go ahead, dime."

"I would like to enlist your help to find two people." Jacinto raised an eyebrow for him to continue. "We'd make sure your country was well compensated for it."

"Who's 'we'?" Cyrus asked from the door. Norrix raised his dark eyes to Cyrus.

"Queen Aeshma and the Kingdom of Wrath," he said, smoothly.

Jacinto leaned back, putting his feet on the table, resting his hands on his stomach. "Last time I checked, Aeshma doesn't have shit but a spot in the Dolsano Woods. Hardly calls for a kingdom."

Fury flickered through Norrix's eyes before it was tempered down.

"Queen Aeshma will reclaim what has been stolen from her," he growled.

"What can she provide for me that I don't already have?"

"Safety and the right to remain ruler in the Dark Continent," Norrix held up a chain with a dark bronze medallion on it. The medallion had an image of a half skull laid over a pair of wings. "This medallion would keep you protected while she claims the rest of Euhaven for herself." Jacinto already knew that this offer had been made to not only him but the rest of his court. Whoever took the bait, Norrix would exploit. Jacinto pursed his lips as if in thought.

"Who is it that Aeshma wants?" He almost chuckled at how sensitive Norrix was to his 'queen' being called out of her title.

"The Chaos Wielder for one," he said, while he tried and failed to cover the fury on his face. Bingo. Jacinto had already figured they wanted the Chaos Wielder, he only needed confirmation.

"What makes you think I can find them for you?"

"We know that they are meant to be here, in your capital. Who else knows the capital better than the King?"

That stupid fucking prophecy. I hate prophecies, he thought but gave nothing away as he considered Norrix.

"Hmm. And the second?"

"The bounty hunter known as Xavia Silveria," Jacinto raised his eyebrow. He had not a clue who that was. Was it the same bounty hunter that was part of the Asherite team? "I believe she is set to arrive with the other Asherites in another week or so." Norrix had some impressive intel.

"Why?"

"That is not your concern."

"The fuck it isn't. If you want my resources to find the Chaos Wielder, then I need to know why this bounty hunter is so important," Norrix bristled, eyes flaring.

"She is of interest," he said, lids shuddering as if thinking of a lost lover. Jacinto fought to roll his eyes.

"I'll consider it," he said, swinging his feet off the table. The fuck he would.

"I think it would benefit you to say yes," Norrix said, rising from his seat, a threat in his voice. He fixed his sleeves, eyes turning solid black. "I'll have you remember where your ancestors came from," he gave the vampire a feral grin, fangs elongating from his canines. "Queen Aeshma is going to move regardless. It's best to be on her side."

"I'll have an answer for you on Axton's Eve," Jacinto ignored the threat and stood to his full height, a foot taller than Norrix. He slid an invitation in the shape of a harlequin mask toward Norrix. Their gazes met, and he let Norrix see the malice in his own. Norrix's eyes widened ever so slightly. "I think it would behoove you to understand that you're not the most dangerous male in this room," Jacinto growled, voice deepening. "And you don't know shit about who my ancestors were."

Norrix took the invitation, tension releasing from his shoulders. "A masquerade?" he mused, flipping the invitation over and running his fingers over the mask.

"Old habits." Cyrus muttered and opened the door. Jacinto nodded to Norrix with an eyebrow raised.

"Shall we feed? I have an excellent female. Unless you prefer male?"

Norrix looked him over and took the peace offering.

"WHAT AREN'T YOU TELLING ME ABOUT the Chaos Wielder?" Cyrus asked sometime later. They were cleaning up in Cyrus's bathroom. Where Jacinto's was dark and moody, Cyrus's was oddly vibrant. Oranges, yellows, and browns accented the clean space. The walnut floors were smooth and warm under Jacinto's feet. One wall held a mural of the sahara with a warrior standing in the middle, the sun in the background. It was a homage to Cyrus's ancestry, before he became a vampire.

Cyrus cleaned blood off his hands, shirt rolled up to his elbows. Norrix left after a decent feed and fuck session with one of the males Jacinto provided him. Jacinto and Cyrus shared a female and opted to not get lost in a feeding frenzy. Jacinto pulled his bloodied shirt over his head to drop in the hamper.

"What makes you think I'm not telling you something?" Jacinto said smoothly. Cyrus narrowed his yellow eyes, not falling for it.

"Spare me the bullshit, 'Cin, I'm not one of your cronies," he snapped, tossing the blooded towel into the sink. As they left the bathroom Jacinto grabbed a bottle of tequila from Cyrus's wet bar. He sat on a stool, cracking open the bottle and took a swig.

"I know where they are," he said, dropping the bomb. Cyrus's head turned so fast that Jacinto thought it'd pop off his shoulders.

"¡¿Qué?!"

"I've always known. That's how I knew the Asherites would make their way here," he took another drag on the bottle. "The prophecy made it clear that The Chaos Wielder would be in the Dark Continent. It only makes sense that they'd come here to petition me, like Norrix."

Cyrus plucked the bottle from Jacinto, earning a growl, before taking a long swig. "You didn't think it prudent to tell me?" he grumbled before Jacinto snatched the bottle back.

"No, pendejo," was all he said, finishing off the bottle.

"Are you turning them over to Norrix?"

"Absolutely not." Nothing good would come from it, no matter the promises that Norrix made. "He—"

Suddenly a loud alarm blared from their cell phones indicating an emergency. They bolted to his office. Jacinto opened his laptop while Cyrus turned the HoloTV on. Cyrus let out a string of expletives before what Jacinto saw on his laptop registered. As a fair King, Jacinto allowed his people the freedom of speech and journalism. He was quickly regretting it, pissed that he wasn't notified of the news he saw before the rest of his damn kingdom.

BREAKING: DEMON OUTBREAK OVERTAKES MELHOLD. THE MONARCH OF ASHERAI HAS FLED. AESHMA, THE ANGEL OF WRATH, HAS TAKEN CONTROL OF THE CITY.

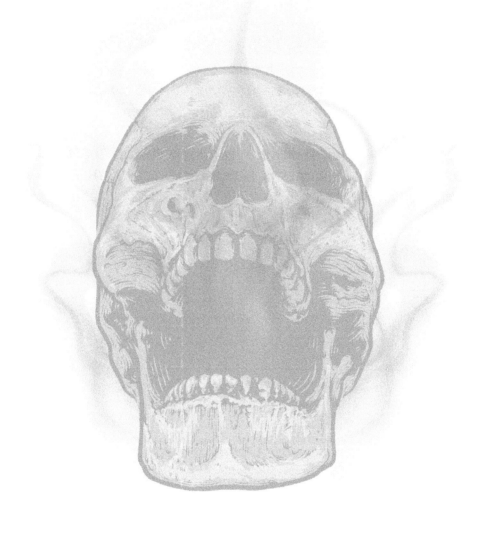

CHAPTER 35
QUADE

RYLAND, GET YOUR ASS UP." Quade shook his head, flipping a practice knife in his hands. Ryland was panting, laid flat on his back. Lilith was off to the side, watching the both of them on the sparring mat.

"Give him a minute Quade. You've been at it for hours." She was wiping sweat off her forehead, the moonlight shining off her ebony skin. The perpetual darkness was screwing with their sense of time, causing them to be cranky at each other. Lex was currently manning the helm but had been rotating with Quade so they could get their training in.

"Think those ferals will 'give him a break'?" Quade mimicked her which earned him a glare.

After the communications outage resolved itself, they received word about the feral outbreak in Melhold. They had only two more days before they arrived in Malagado. All of their original plans to arrive covertly went out the window as soon as they saw the news. They had to request an audience with the Vampire King or they'd risk never finding the Chaos Wielder in time.

"We already know guns don't work on them, so we have to get better with our close combat skills." Quade pulled out a dagger from his belt and threw it, hitting the bull's eye at the end of the mat.

"He's right Lil..." Ryland groaned as he stood up stiffly.

"Decapitation works best," came Xavia's voice as she rounded the deck, holding a bag of bamboo practice swords in her hands. Aurelio followed behind her, stupid grin on his face. It didn't get past him that Aurelio had hand marks around his neck. So, Xavia gave him a hand necklace. Fuck that turned him on. What Quade wouldn't do to return the favor.

Xavia stepped past him as she moved to the mat. Quade's nose flared as he smelled Aurelio on her. They'd been at it like rabbits the last two days and he couldn't make sense of the jealousy he felt about it. Jealousy was not in his vocabulary. He raised an eyebrow, eyes tracking her.

"No shit." Sarcasm laced his tone. Xavia scowled at him, tossing a wooden sword at him, which he caught smoothly. Aurelio rolled his silver eyes, making his way to talk with Lilith.

"None of you have sword training, other than Lex. Keeping the ferals at a distance is the best option, no?" She tossed the other bamboo swords to the others. She raised an eyebrow and Quade had to admit she was right, partially. He *did* have sword training, but Aurelio didn't know that. It was something he picked up on during a two-year recon mission. He found he loved it. "Who wants to go first?" Xavia said, deftly swinging her wooden sword to warm up her arms.*

"Let's go." Quade said, sinking into a proper defensive position; holding the sword hilt double handed, he lifted it to his temple, his body angled with one foot in front of the other. He took no small satisfaction in seeing the surprise in Xavia's face. She stepped forward, her powerful curvy legs covered in tight athletic leggings. She got into stance, her sword held low in front of her, one foot behind the other.

Quade made the first move, lunging and making a swing for her head which she parried with ease. There was a sound of a CRACK as both swords crashed into each other. Xavia moved impossibly fast for a human. Quade tried to thrust the sword into her torso but Xavia dodged it by spinning and blocking the swipe he attempted to make afterward. After ending her spin, she smacked the side of his face with the flat of the sword. Quade snarled, growing frustrated, her cocky ass smirk not helping.

♪ "The Ground Below" by Run the Jewels, El-P, Killer Mike, feat. Royal Blood

Their swords cracked against each other in a fast flurry of movement that eventually left them both panting. Xavia had laid a few more taps that would've been killing blows had they used actual swords. Quade had only managed two shots against her. He completely underestimated her, being cocky from wiping the floor with her the last time they sparred. He pushed his hair back, refusing to give up. They had another flurry of near misses and parries before suddenly, his feet were swept from under him and the point of Xavia's sword was at his throat. She panted, though not as much as him. Quade couldn't help but eye the rise and fall of her breasts before snapping his glaring eyes to hers. She smirked, a light flashing in her eyes so quickly he thought he imagined it.

"Thought I'd let the other kids play." Xavia huffed, flipping the sword away from him and holding her hand to him. Quade slapped it away, causing a bark of laughter from her, and stood up with a grunt. Shit his ass hurt. He narrowed his eyes at Lilith who was stepping up to the mat and giving him a shit eating grin. Awareness dawned upon him as he realized that Xavia led him on the entire time. Xavia could've ended it at any time. Quade glared at her and stormed off; ego bruised.

"WHERE'D YOU LEARN HOW TO SWORD FIGHT?" Xavia asked later when she found him at the top deck helm. He was watching the bioluminescent life that swam beneath the ocean's surface. In this part of the planet, most life had the glow and it made up for the lack of sunlight. Colors of violet, emerald, aqua, and magenta shimmered across the ocean. It was as if a nebula floated on the surface. Quade turned his head slightly to watch Xavia approach with two glasses filled with amber liquid. She wore an oversized long-sleeved shirt with mid-thigh cotton shorts. Fresh from a shower, her wet brown curls fell to her collarbone, longer than it was a month and a half ago. Had that much time really passed?

She slid into the seat next to him, handing him the glass. Her honey hibiscus scent accosted him and he pushed down a shudder it caused. Quade raised an eyebrow, wondering if it was poisoned. Xavia snorted as if reading his mind.

"Relax, it's not poisoned." She rolled her eyes. He plucked the glass from her and took a swig. He looked forward when she said, "It's a peace offering of sorts." She shrugged. Peace offering? For what?

"I learned back in Calñar, while on a recon mission," Quade said, answering her question. He was sent there to monitor and then possibly assassinate the Kingpin who was trying to spread his influence outside of the city.

"I was there for two years, learning from one of the best. He offered training for people to defend themselves against the Kingpin." He turned wistful as he remembered his lessons. Quade's heart was broken when his master died of natural causes.

"Master Sasori Shoyo…" Xavia murmured the name of his teacher so softly he almost missed it. He turned his head to her but she was looking off in the distance as if remembering something from her past.

"You know him?"

She nodded. "I trained under him for five years. After moving to Melhold, I went back once a month to keep up my training until he passed. I'm surprised we didn't cross paths." Xavia turned to him and it made sense why her skill was sharp. She'd been doing it far longer than he had.

"You're from Calñar?" The city was not for the faint of heart. If she grew up there, it would explain a lot about her roughness as a person. She sucked her teeth and sighed before polishing off her drink.

"Unfortunately." Xavia placed the glass in the cup holder between them and pulled her knees up to rest her chin on them. "I'm an orphan. Grew up in an orphanage. Met who I thought was the love of my life, but turned out to be a nightmare incarnate." She closed her eyes as a breeze flowed through her curls. Quade's hand itched to run his hand through them. "I got out, made it to

Melhold, and then signed up for the Academy. The rest is history."

He watched her, taking in her beauty. Xavia had a thick scar at the base of her ear that traveled down to her collar bone. Without thinking, he ran a finger down the scar, making her shudder.

"Where'd you get this?" Quade murmured, pulling his hand back and taking another swig of his drink. Xavia opened her deep brown eyes to look at him. There was something in those eyes, something dark. It was something he recognized in himself.

"Long story." The look she gave told him not to ask. He polished off his drink, dropping the glass into the cup holder and sat up a bit.

"Where do the blackouts come from?" Xavia's eyes darkened further at his line of questioning. Quade rolled his eyes. "I'm genuinely curious. Relax, not trying to bite your head off." Although he could imagine other parts of her he would like to bite, especially that lower lip of hers that she was currently nibbling on.

"I'm not sure." She pursed her lips. "They started in my late teens, early twenties. I don't know why or how they started." Xavia lifted a shoulder. "Sorry, it's not an impressive story."

"You've been having them for what, almost eighteen years?" Quade whistled when she nodded. "That'll explain why you're so rough around the edges." He meant it as a joke but it came off harsher than he intended. She dropped her knees, eyes narrowing into a glare.

"Well, fuck you. It's been my life for as long as I can remember and it's the best I can do. It's either that or sign myself into the Psych Tower," she snapped. Xavia stood to leave and he rose from his seat to catch her wrist. Flame spread from his hand to lick over hers. She gasped, turning to him.

"Wait, I'm sorry. I didn't mean to be an asshole." Wow. A second apology. Who was Quade becoming? Xavia raised an eyebrow.

"Now or ever?"

"Can you take my apology? Or will you be a dick about it?" Quade huffed. He pulled her in, watching as her breathing hitched. "Are you always a brat?" His voice dropped an octave and he watched the heat rise in her eyes.

"Sure, whatever," she grumbled as her eyes fell to his lips. A slow smirk pulled at his mouth.

"What's the peace offering for?" Quade said softly. Her tan skin flushed as she took a step back from him, pulling her hand from his. He instantly regretted asking.

"Ah... For the confusion between us. For almost getting in between your bromance with Aurelio." Xavia chewed on a fingernail, rocking a bit on the balls of her feet.

"Bromance?" He snorted. She waved a hand at him.

"You know what I mean." She turned to the railing to lean against it and watch the ocean. He took in the sight of her ample ass in those shorts, his cock awakening.

"You didn't get between us," Quade said as he walked toward her. He put a hand on either side of her, trapping her with his body. Xavia jumped, her ass pressing into him by accident.

"What?" she breathed, turning her head to look at him. He took her chin and turned her to look out to the ocean again.

"You didn't get between us," Quade said again, lips close to her ear where her scar was. He felt her shudder against him and he could feel his erection growing against her backside.

"I'm confused..." Her sentence was cut short when he placed a kiss on the scar.

"He and I have an understanding."

CHAPTER 36

XAVIA

UNDERSTANDING? THEY HAVE AN UNDERSTANDING? A whirlwind of thoughts blew through Xavia's mind, trying to understand the context. But she couldn't think straight with Quade's lips on her neck, his hardening erection against her ass, and the heat of his body enveloping her.

"Ah, what do you mean an understanding?" she breathed, her hips rocking back. Quade hummed gently, sending molten lava down to her core.

"You're your own woman. Only you have a say in who you want." He nipped her neck making her breath catch. "If you want us both, you can have us both." He bit her neck with more pressure making her knees buckle.

Wait...

"Y'all discussed this without me?" Xavia attempted to turn around but he pressed into her more, keeping her locked against the rail. She had to fight the moan that tried to bubble up her throat. She admitted to herself that she was both turned on and pissed. "If I am my own woman, then you both should've told me you had an 'understanding'." She snapped, throwing quotation fingers around 'understanding'.

"Would it have made a difference?" Quade asked, his voice vibrating through her body. He pressed into her, letting her feel how hard he was. Xavia bit back a moan. She wasn't relenting just yet. She pushed her body against his to try and push him away but he was a solid wall of lean muscle.

"No. But that's beside the point!"

"Have I told you that you're a brat?" Quade growled before sliding his hand up her nape to tangle his hand roughly in her hair and pull her head back to look at him. She let out a gasp, staring at the fire glowing in his eyes. A blend of heat and darkness shone from those sienna eyes of his, making a pulse start in her pussy. The longer she looked at him, the wetter she became.*

"And? So, what if I am," Xavia said through clenched teeth. Quade smiled darkly before crashing his lips to hers. It was as explosive as the first time, all lips, teeth, and tongues. He bit at her lower lip, making her whimper. She bit his back, drawing blood which made him ravage her mouth more. He reached forward and grabbed her wrists with his free hand, locking her hands behind her. With one hand gripping her hair and the other holding her wrists, she was utterly exposed to his every whim. More liquid heat pooled between her thighs, desire thick within her. It had been a long time since she let someone take the reins and take control.

"Do you know what happens to brats?" Quade's voice was rough and gravelly. He let go of her hair so abruptly that her head tilted forward in a snap. He moved that hand to play with the hem of her shirt before slipping inside and up the expanse of her soft belly. "Answer me," he said, tugging her wrists.

"No," Xavia lied, desire making her see stars. His hand found her heavy breast, gripping it roughly. The pain mixed with pleasure made her rock her hips, wanting more from him. His calloused fingers pinched her nipple, rolling them tightly.

"They get punished." Quade's teeth found her neck again, biting deeper than before. Xavia arched her back, a moan finally escaping her mouth. "Hmm. Yeah, there it is," he murmured against her neck. She twisted again, attempting to reach out to him. She couldn't comprehend the intense need she had to touch him. He gripped her wrists tighter, letting her know she would have bruises the next day.

Xavia let out another whimper as Quade moved to her other

breast. "No. You don't get to touch me until I say you can," he growled. Well gee, that sounded familiar. He slowly moved his hand down, gripping her stomach tightly. "You are so fucking sexy," he murmured before bringing his hand to the band of her shorts.

"Fuck..." The word came out as a whisper as he teased her by dragging a finger between the waistband and her pelvis. Quade glided it over her soft mound teasing her. The pulse in her pussy beat in sync with her heart. Xavia tried moving her hips again, wanting more from him.

"Say please," he growled, refusing to do what she wanted.

She was *not* going to say please. If she had to beg, then she didn't want it. Right? Tomis damn it.

"No." Xavia hissed before his hand shot to her chin, capturing it roughly and jerking her head back to look at him.

"No?" Quade stared into the depths of her anima. She couldn't explain it any other way. The aggression and pain was everything she needed. Pissing him off was an added bonus.

"No," Xavia said, more firmly.

He let her go abruptly and she instantly hated the feel of his absence. She wasn't going to give him the satisfaction of turning around. Xavia leaned on the railing, catching her breath. She wouldn't be surprised if her juices started to slide down her thighs, she was so wet. The sound of a belt snapping loose drew her attention as she looked over her shoulder and saw him with his belt in hand. She turned and raised her eyebrow, a thrill going through her.

"Come here," Quade demanded.

"No," she snapped. Xavia stayed where she was, even though her body wanted her to move forward. A dark chuckle escaped his lips. He came at her and she threw a punch, making his head snap back. She bit her lip, stifling a laugh as a wildness took over her. He settled his gaze on her, darkness swirling in his eyes, as he licked his bloodied lip.

"So feisty, I bet it makes your pussy wet." He repeated those words, making her core clench. *Yes, it fucking does.* She panted as she took a step back, Quade's gaze tracking her movements. "You can't run away from me this time," he growled.

She immediately turned to run for the stairs. He was upon her before she could blink, pulling her hands at her back again. This time he bound her wrists with the belt, moving in a figure-eight motion, and then buckling it. She fought against the bindings and Quade grasped the belt like a harness and snapped her to him. His hot body was flush against her back. Xavia's breaths came out in short pants, her senses heightening as her desire skyrocketed. Her aching nipples were being rubbed raw by her shirt with each breath she took. Her breasts felt heavy and she wanted his hands on her again.

Quade put a hand on her shoulder. "Kneel." She looked at him with narrowed eyes.

"Make me." Xavia attempted to scoff but it came out breathless instead. She saw the glint in his eyes. Fuck, he wanted her to snap.

"Happy to." Quade pushed her to her knees, the impact jolting pain up her legs. He slowly walked in front of her. He dragged his fingers down her jaw, tilting her to look up at him. "What happens to brats when they don't listen?" he said, slipping off his henley.

Xavia bit her lip, looking up at his powerful but slim body. Quade was obviously built for stealth and stamina. Her eyes ate up every muscle, every scar, every breath that moved his golden tanned body in delicious ways, and the sexy V peppered with hair dipping into his jeans. His Fire Wieldermarks glinted under the moonlight. His sienna eyes were dark, making her salivate. His commanding presence was enough to tip her over the edge.

He gripped her chin tightly. "What. Happens."

"They get punished." Xavia could barely get the words out. Quade let her go with a push. He unbuttoned his jeans, keeping his eyes on her. Her pussy clenched in response. Her lips parted as he pulled out his hard, thick cock and she couldn't help but lick her lips. He slid out of his jeans before gripping her hair, rubbing the hard tip along her lips.

"I can think of the perfect punishment," Quade growled when she opened for him, tongue snaking out to lick him. Without warning he pulled her to him, thrusting his cock deep into her mouth, head hitting the back of her throat. Xavia gagged before relaxing her throat. Her eyes rolled as he fucked her mouth. Saliva dripped from her mouth, down her chin. His hand gripped her hair tighter, bringing her eyes back to him.

"That's right. Look at me, brat."

Xavia whimpered. He reminded her of herself. It blew her mind. Quade groaned, pumping into her mouth, grabbing the bottom of her chin. She moaned on his cock, tasting the tang of his pre-cum. He kept his eyes on hers as he fucked her mouth.

"Fuck," he breathed, before he pulled out of her to kneel in front of her.

Quade slapped her face before gripping her jaw; not to inflict damage but to bring that pain riddled desire he knew she wanted. He held her face as he gave her a searing kiss, fire crackling from his hands down her neck. It slid into her shirt and reached her nipples with a flare, making her back arch.

"I can return the favor if you beg." Quade ripped her shirt open, the sleeves hanging by her bound wrists. He looked her over as if he would devour her. Xavia wondered how long she'd be able to hold out. She could feel her resistance crumbling.

"No," she breathed, licking her lips. Quade grabbed her hair again, free hand grabbing her breast in a bruising hold. She rocked her hips, hoping for any friction against her drenched shorts. His lips found her nipple, sucking it in tightly. Xavia's pussy clenched with need as he bit down, making her shudder.

"Fuck," she whimpered. Quade rolled her nipple with his tongue, sending jolts of pleasure straight to her core. "Fuck, Quade." She rocked her hips again. His hand slid into her shorts to tease her clit, swirling circles with inflamed fingers. She jolted in pleasure, the flame making her eyes roll.

"Say please and I'll end the torture," Quade said before kissing her roughly and deeply. His fingers dipped into her pussy, the heat of his Wielding making her cry out. Fuck. This was new for her. "Say it." He nuzzled her neck, lips barely touching her scar. His fingers slowed their pace and it was pure torture. He removed his fingers, making her whine in frustration. "So wet." He sucked her arousal from his fingers. That was her breaking point.

"Yes. Ok. Please. Please fuck me!" Xavia begged, tears of frustration leaking from her eyes. She wasn't sure if she would burn up from the desire lancing through her body. Quade smiled darkly as he moved behind her, holding on to her belted wrists. He snapped her to him, her back against his hard body, his cock rubbing against her ass.

"That's a good brat." And *she* had the nerve to call Aurelio out for his praise kink. Holy Tomis. Quade slid his hand down the front of her shorts to dip his fingers between the folds of her drenched cunt. Xavia let out a moan that she was sure everyone below could hear, but she couldn't give two fucks about it. His cock twitched against her.

"Fuck, you're drenched for me, brat." He applied pressure to her clit, making her squirm and grind herself against him. Quade let go of the belt to snake his hand up to her neck and squeeze.

"Oh shit." Xavia moaned as he slipped two fingers inside of her while rubbing her clit with his thumb. She clenched around his fingers as they pumped in and out of her. She bucked her hips, feeling that delicious orgasm dangerously close. The hand on her throat tightened while the other continued to fuck her. "I'm going to come," she whimpered.

"You're going to come?" Quade growled in her ear. She nodded, the edge so near. She almost yelled when he pulled his fingers out of her, denying her what she so badly wanted.

"What..." she breathed. He bent her over, face to the floor, lifting her hips to pull her shorts off. He bared her to him, juices dripping from her cunt.

"You come when I tell you." Oh. Shit. Xavia, was at a loss for words. Quade squeezed her ass before giving it an aggressive smack, making her jolt in pleasure. "You like that." It was a statement, not a question. He smacked her again, making her see stars. Holy. Fucking. Shit.

"Please," Xavia moaned, swaying her hips, her pussy needing to be filled. She needed him in her. "Please, Quade," she barely whispered. She could see him from the corner of her eye and saw that he was fighting with as much restraint as she. She rocked her hips back against him, feeling his cock nearing her entrance. "Please," she said as her mantra. Over and over.

Quade growled, deep in his throat, before he thrust into her, to the hilt. Xavia let out a sound that was somewhere between a moan and a scream. He was so thick, so deliciously thick. Her legs twitched as he pulled out and thrusted into her again. She could feel him hit her cervix, the sharp pain making her whimper. "You like this dick in your pussy." Again, not a question but a statement.

"Fuck, yes." She moaned as he thrust into her again, gripping her ass hard enough to bruise. She was going to be peppered with bruises and she wasn't even mad at it.

"You like it rough, brat?" Quade groaned, fucking her harder. Her eyes rolled as she nodded. "Say it," he growled. "Say you like it rough."

"I fucking like it rough." Xavia moaned, the sounds of his balls slapping against her filling the night. "Fuck me harder," she begged.

"See, brats get rewarded too." Quade gripped her ass tighter, pulling her to slam against him as he pumped. She could feel the orgasm approaching and she clenched her pussy around his cock. He grabbed the bindings, pulling her up to him again so that she was flush against him while he thrusted in and out of her. Her breasts bounced with each thrust.

"Can I come?" Xavia whimpered. Quade stilled for a moment and she was pretty sure he was surprised she asked. Shit, she knew the game. He slid a hand up to her throat, the other going between her legs to rub her clit while he slammed in and out of her again. "Please let me come," she begged. She wasn't sure how much more pleasure she could take. His grip tightened as his pace increased and she saw stars.

"Hmm. That's right, brat. Beg for me." Quade breathed in her ear before pinching her clit while squeezing her neck tighter. His cock pulsed inside her cunt which brought her over the edge. Her orgasm came crashing over her, her strained shouts loud even to her own ears. "Fuck, I'm coming." Quade let out a deep throated moan as he thrusted into her and went over the edge with her. He released his grip on her neck, the rush of euphoria overcoming her.

Quade kept a hand splayed on her stomach to keep her from tipping over while the other ran a hand through her hair, petting her. If he wasn't holding her, she would've fallen forward. Her body felt like one giant noodle. She closed her eyes to the sensation, feeling cherished in a way she never did before. It was different from what she received from Aurelio. Both equally wonderful, both dynamically different.

"Such a good brat," Quade whispered into her hair, kissing her sweaty temple softly. He moved to her neck, then her shoulders, and then kissed along the galaxy tattoo on her back. "Are you steady enough so I can remove the binds?" he murmured, his voice holding a gentleness she never thought she'd hear from him. Xavia didn't realize she was shivering until he asked. She nodded, managing to keep herself balanced as he removed the hand from her stomach to unlock the belt and unwind it from her wrists.

Her wrists and shoulders ached from being bound for... how long had it been? Quade slowly pulled out of her, making her twitch, and a soft moan left her. Xavia felt empty without him in her. He grabbed his shirt, slipping it over her. For once in her life, a male's shirt was big on her. It flowed down to her knees.

Quade pulled on his pants, taking her shorts and ripped shirt into a bundle. He knelt and scooped her into his arms. Xavia tried to protest. She wasn't the lightest person, being on the thicker side. He nipped at her nose, shutting up the nonsense she was spewing. She was suddenly feeling very tired. Elated, but very tired.

"Where are you taking me?" Xavia murmured, resting her head on his shoulder. He rested his chin on the top of her head as he began walking.

"To give you a hot bath and then my room." Her toes curled at the thought of him taking care of her. "It's your reward." His voice vibrated against her cheek. It felt good to be on the receiving end of the reward. It wasn't something she often allowed.

Xavia held onto him closer, taking in his scent of burning cedar. As a woman who'd never felt dainty in her life, Quade sure knew how to fulfill that fantasy. He gave her praise the entire walk to the room and when he helped her into the bathtub, he washed her slowly, as if she was the most precious thing in the world. After helping her out of the bath, he oiled her up, massaging her sore limbs, and soon, she was drifting off to sleep, with a smile on her lips.

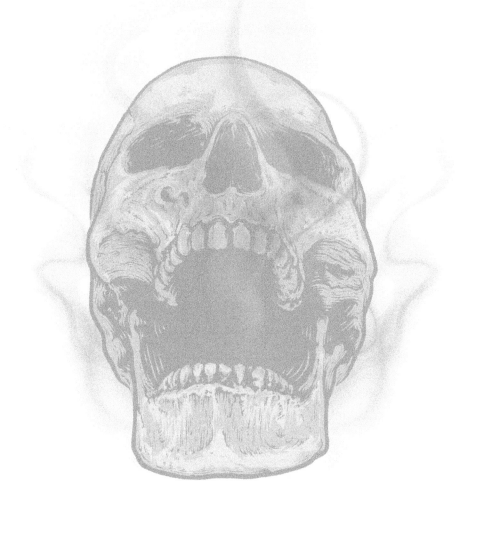

CHAPTER 37

QUADE

QUADE WOKE TO XAVIA MUMBLING in her sleep. Her body shook as if she was fighting in her dreams. She was locked in a nightmare that he wasn't sure how to wake her from. He pulled her into the crook of his arm, holding her tightly to ease her shaking. It seemed to help because her body went limp with a sigh of relief. Quade wasn't sure how long he sat there watching her but when she slowly opened her eyes to peer up at him, his heart did a tumble.

"How long have you been staring at me?" Xavia said groggily, voice full of sleep. Quade's lip twitched with a smirk.

"Not sure. You were having a nightmare," he said, voice soft. She groaned, turning to lay on her back, and ran a hand through her hair.

"Fuck, did I wake you?" Xavia covered her face with the blanket. "I should've warned you."

He snorted, pulling the blanket from her. "I don't sleep much. It's ok. It's another few hours before the rest of the ship wakes." Quade smirked. He turned to her and shifted to rest his head on his hand. He would never get used to how beautiful she was. "What were you dreaming about?" Using his free hand, he glided his fingers up and down her sternum, the lovely space between her breasts. She huffed out a sigh.

"Why don't you get much sleep?" Xavia skirted around the question.

"I'll tell you if you tell me about your nightmare." Quade drifted toward her breast, capturing a nipple between his thumb and forefinger. "Don't make me punish you," he said, voice gravelly. The way she took everything he had blew his fucking mind. He was not a gentle male. He was not a lover; he was a fucker and it was as if she didn't expect anything less. He watched as her face changed from grumpy to aroused.

"Well, I can't tell you if you keep doing that." Xavia moaned when he pinched her. He glided his hands over her neck, bruises blooming where his hands had marked her. Something territorial in him was excited to let everyone see his claim on her.

"Well, you're gonna have to try," Quade teased her, trailing her jaw before keeping his hands to himself. She turned to him, mimicking him by putting her head on her propped-up hand.

"My nightmares began shortly after my blackouts started," Xavia sighed. "They're bloody. I'm slaughtering males mostly." She chuckled when he lifted his eyebrows. "I sense they're not good males. Not in the sexy way either."

"Could they be memories of your blackouts?" Quade wondered if that was possible.

"The thought that I could be a serial killer during my blackouts would scare me into the Psych Tower," she said, narrowing her stare. "I'd like to hope I'm not out here killing people without knowledge of it."

"What's wrong with that?"

Xavia's eyebrows rose in surprise.

"I mean, if they weren't good, what's the problem with them meeting Axton early?" Quade would be lying if he said he had never killed anyone in cold blood.

"I've... uh, never killed someone before?" She said it like it should be obvious. "Wait, have you?" She held no judgment. It was clear she truly wanted to know.

"Yeah." Quade sat up, resting his head on the headboard. "My father and older brother are on the top of the list." He slid a glance toward her, seeing the shock on her face, and closed his eyes. "They were definitely not good males." He hated thinking about his father and brother.

"What did they do?" Xavia asked softly, making him look at

her. Her face was as open as he ever saw. He could fall into her dark brown gaze forever.

"They killed my mother." Quade let out a sigh. "They were drug dealers. Dealing Wielding Potions. My father was addicted. My brother did the deals and my mother and I got caught in the middle." He fucking hated Wielding Potions. They were volatile in the hands of humans, giving them temporary Wielding that drove them insane and killed them shortly after. Wielders like his parents who used the Potions were souped up like steroids. It gave them a boost in Wielding they couldn't handle and it was easy to get addicted to. Oftentimes they ended up killing themselves and anyone in the vicinity.

"Holy Tomis," Xavia whispered, sitting up next to him.

"My asshole of a father drugged my mother so they could experience the high together." Quade rubbed his face. "I was a fucking child. My brother was ten years older than me. Whenever I tried to defend my mother, they would beat me." He motioned to a scar that crossed under his pec, along his rib. "They sliced me open one day."

"What?!" Xavia ran a finger over the scar, making the hairs on his body stand on edge.

"My mother died of an overdose. Blew up the fucking house. My Wielding is the only reason I'm alive." Quade paused for a beat, listening to their mingled breathing. "I ran away and for the few years after, I trained to join the Academy. When I found out I was accepted into the Academy preliminaries, I figured I had to deal with them before I started." He risked a glance and saw she was attentive and not afraid of what he had to say. She slipped her fingers between his.

"You had to rid the world of their stain," Xavia murmured. He nodded. "I can't blame you for that. I would've probably done the same to..." She stopped herself as if not meaning to speak the last part out loud.

"The same to who?" Quade hedged. He never once cared about what someone else thought of him. Never. Somehow Xavia was making him feel things he wasn't used to feeling. He wanted to know all of her. Not just her body, but he wanted a better understanding of the mind he had mistaken as unstable.

"Um. Just this ex that I had when I was younger."

Quade could tell she was lying. "Just an ex?" He quirked an eyebrow. Xavia banged her head on the headboard in frustration.

"You remember that I told you I grew up in Calñar?" He nodded, thumb gliding over hers. "As an orphan, I was bound to get into some shit. So, I got myself wrapped up with Nicolai Sokolov." Quade started.

"Nicolai? As in Dimitri Sokolov's son? The one that died?" Xavia closed her eyes as she nodded. He swore. "What happened?" He felt fury rising in him. What did that asshole do to her? The taste of smoke invaded his mouth.

"Well, we got involved when I was fifteen. He was thirty at the time." She let go of his hand to rub her face. "He led me on, telling me I was special. The only woman in his life. You know the drill." Xavia popped her eyes open and looked at him with an eyebrow raised. Quade nodded, urging her to continue. "Shortly after I turned seventeen, he introduced me to his friend. Told me that his friend thought I was beautiful and that I should be grateful." She snapped her mouth shut, throat bobbing. Her nose flared, anger creeping up her face. "He sold me to his friend for a night." Fire sparked in Quade's hand, almost lighting the blankets on fire. "And then to another. And another." A tear fell from her eyes. Fury, white hot like an atom bomb filled him up.

"For how long?" Quade said through gritted teeth. Kingpin Sokolov was a hard man to get to. The Monarchy had been trying for as long as Quade could remember. Even when his own recon mission didn't pan out, he vowed to go back and find a way. Now, he had more fuel to do exactly that and then some.

"Five years."

He hissed a curse word.

"My blackouts started around then. My drinking did too." Quade wiped the tears from her cheeks. He had judged her for her drinking and blackouts, not knowing that her deep-seated trauma was the cause of it. He felt another unfamiliar emotion; guilt.

"At first, I thought the drinking was putting me in a coma so I wouldn't have the mental memory of... his friends." The way Xavia said 'mental' let him know that she was physically abused. That must be where her scar came from. Smoke rose from his skin, the taste of it growing stronger in his mouth. "But then I realized the blackouts also happened when I was alone." Xavia's hands shook as she looked at him, fear in her eyes.

"What is it?" Quade searched for answers in her eyes.

"You remember that Nicolai and his men were slaughtered?" Quade nodded. "I don't think I did it... But I woke from a blackout, covered in blood, with them all around me." Quade could feel the blood draining from his face.

"You don't remember if you did it?" he said softly. She shook her head.

"I hope I didn't. I mean, they deserved it but... Me? A killer?" More tears fell now. "I may be a brat, a bitch, and a fucking nuisance..." Xavia huffed a sad laugh. "But a killer, I am not," she said with as much conviction as a wolf saying it didn't have fangs. She wasn't sure, that was clear. Quade took her hand again, kissing the back of it.

"Regardless if you did or didn't. They're dead and you're alive." Their lives had so many parallels. He never thought he'd meet someone that understood what he went through and he was sure she didn't either. "Does Aurelio..."

"No." Xavia quickly responded. "No. He knows I had an insane ex. That's it."

"Why tell me?" Quade asked, pulling her closer to kiss her forehead.

"Your past is as fucked up as mine, I guess."

He chuckled, grasping her chin and giving her a searing kiss. Xavia let out a soft moan.

"Yeah, I guess."

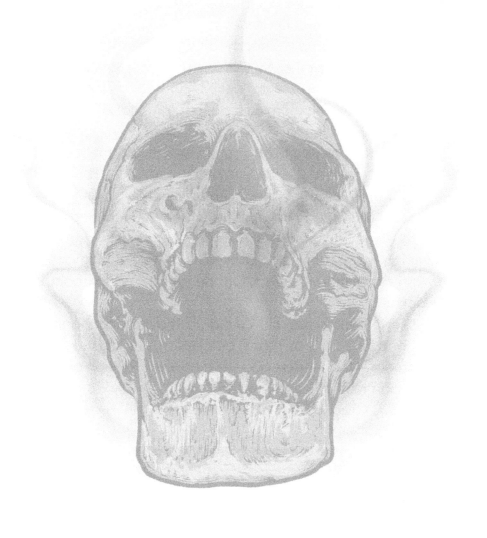

CHAPTER 38

AURELIO

DO YOU THINK THE VAMPIRE KING WILL HELP US?"** Lex asked Aurelio the next morning while inspecting the engine room; at least morning according to their watches. He held a cup of coffee in his hand and rubbed the back of his head.

"He has to. If Aeshma takes over Trezora, it's only a matter of time before she crosses the ocean for the Dark Continent." He yawned, holding a hand to his mouth to try and stifle it.

"Tired?" Lex gave him a smirk. "Xavia keep you up?"

Aurelio wished he could say it was because he spent the night with Xavia. He had mixed feelings about it. On one hand, he told them it was ok. On the other hand, he still felt jealous. It was eating him up.

"Um. More like Quade and Xavia," he grumbled before taking a gulp of his coffee.

"The three of you?" Lex raised an eyebrow, no judgment on their face. Aurelio coughed on his coffee.

"No. No, just them. They weren't exactly quiet up on the top helm," he grunted. He watched as realization crossed their face.

"Oh, that was..."

"Yup."

"And not..."

"Nope," he emphasized the P. Aurelio had been in his bunk while everyone else was taking a nightcap. It was clear that everyone heard the two of them. But with his absence, most of them thought it was Aurelio with her. Shit, he wished... A knowing look came across Lex's face.

"I thought they hated each other?" They finished their inspection and motioned for the two of them to walk. Aurelio drained the rest of his coffee, already wanting another.

"They do." He shook his head. "Or did. I'm not even sure anymore." He shrugged.

"How do you feel about it?"

"Ah…" He rubbed the back of his head and stopped at the galley to grab another cup of coffee before proceeding to the common room. "I'm not sure." To be honest, he wasn't sure about many things at the moment. He knew what he was getting himself into when he gave Quade his blessing. "I told him I wouldn't stop them. Xavia is a grown ass woman who can do what she wants." Lex gave him a pat on the shoulder, nodding with appreciation.

"Well, most males don't have that sort of emotional intelligence so I applaud you." Lex broke out into a grin, looking behind him. Aurelio turned to see Lilith coming down the stairs from above deck. He looked back at Lex with a smirk. They turned their gaze down, still smiling.

"Cap's always had great emotional intelligence. It's why he makes such a great Captain," Lilith said with a nod before Ryland popped his head in to hum in agreement. Aurelio's heart felt warm, grateful for his team, before it panged in remembrance of those he lost back in the Dolsano.

"No, that is *not* how it happened!" came Xavia's voice while they exited Quade's room. Their hands were locked together. The Fire Wielder had an actual smile on his face as he looked at her which made Aurelio bristle with jealousy. Shit. He should've prepared himself better.

The two of them stopped dead when they noticed everyone in the room. Their lips were swollen and Quade sported a bruise on his chin. Everyone looked at the pair with open mouths before looking at Aurelio. He ground his teeth, jaw ticking, as he worked to keep his frustration in check. What was he thinking? Could he really handle this? Quade's open smile immediately shut down into a scowl as he stepped away from Xavia.

"Morning..." Xavia mumbled, running out the room, presumably to get coffee.

"Cap," Quade gave a nod of acknowledgement to Aurelio which he returned.

They waited a bit for Xavia to return with a tumbler of ice coffee and a steaming cup of tea. She handed it out to Quade who took it with gratitude and then stood opposite of him, next to Aurelio. His nose flared, detecting Quade's cedar scent on her. He leaned toward her, though still looking forward.

"I am going to wipe that scent off of you later," he murmured softly so that only she could hear him. His lips tilted in a grin when he heard her gasp softly.

"Alright!" Lex said with a clap. "Tomorrow we'll be docking in Malagado. We have to decide who will be petitioning the Vampire King." They moved to the hologram console and brought up a map of Malagado. The city was massive, twice the size of Melhold. "The King is old, very old, though progressive for his kind." They swiped the map to show the tallest skyscraper at the edge of the city.

"Are we sure he's going to listen to us?" Xavia asked before taking a long slurp of her coffee.

"Aurelio mentioned earlier that he would have to if he wants to stop Aeshma from moving on the Dark Continent." Lex switched the map to Melhold which was looking worse than the last time they saw it. "Melhold is completely overrun by ferals. Somehow the officials managed to keep them trapped within the border with a Wielding shield but we don't know how long that will last. There are hundreds ravaging anyone who is left in Melhold."

Xavia sniffed, drawing Aurelio's eyes to her. Silver lined her dark eyes but she blinked rapidly to avoid tears from falling.

"We don't know if Aeshma has any control over them. If they get out, they will quickly overrun the continent," Aurelio sighed. "So, we meet with the King. We bargain in whatever way we can. The Monarch has given us the go ahead to do so." He pointed to Xavia and Quade. "We will go to the King." He turned to Lex, Lilith, and Ryland. "You scope out the city. See if there are any supporters who will help us fight against Aeshma; anything that we can use to our advantage. The contact I've been working with will be making their way to Malagado so I'll reach out to them as well." He gave them all a nod and they returned it before clearing the room, leaving Aurelio, Xavia, and Quade alone.

Xavia rocked back and forth a bit, looking between the two males. Aurelio looked her over, now noticing the tint of bruising around her neck and wrists. His hands itched to touch his own neck.

"So… I guess I'll get ready for sword lessons." She made to walk past him but he held his arm out, stopping her with a hand on her chest. Her throat bobbed with a gulp as Aurelio looked down at her. His electricity jumped from his fingers, melting into her chest and he smirked while he watched her nipples pucker under her shirt in response. Her lips parted, taking slow breaths to calm the raging heartbeat he could feel under his hand. He slid his hand up to her neck before running the pad of his thumb across her jaw.

"We have to speak, you and I. I made you a promise," his voice rumbled deeply. Aurelio could sense Quade bristling across from them. Was Aurelio being petty? Absolutely. He watched the desire in her eyes and knew he needed to get his cock in her again.

"I… Ah. The training?" was all she could say. She risked a glance at Quade, which he followed. Smoke was rising from Quade's arms as he stood there watching them. A combination of jealousy and something else played in his eyes. Was it arousal?

"C'mon now Cap. We need all the practice we can get," Quade muttered, voice taking on the edge of violence it got when he was ready to hurt someone and enjoy doing it. Aurelio didn't remove his eyes from Quade as he ran his thumb over Xavia's lower lip, making her shudder. Quade's eyes narrowed before a dark grin lifted his lips. "She's probably too sore anyway."

Aurelio took a step toward him, fist clenching. "The fuck you just say?"

"Nice hand necklace," the bastard quipped.

Aurelio snatched Quade by the shirt, bringing him to eye level. "Say that shit again asshole. I'll give you a matching one," he snarled.

"Stop it!" Xavia's voice broke through his haze. "Aurelio,

let him go." She stormed over and slapped him upside his head. "*NOW.*"

He drew his eyes to her, meeting her scorching gaze. His nose flared as he took a deep breath and let go of Quade. Xavia pushed him away from Quade, placing herself between the two of them; a hand on each of their chests. Her eyes had darkened to nearly black, standing in the middle of them. Aurelio's heart pounded as he worked to bring his flare of jealousy under control.

"I thought there was this 'understanding' between you two?" Frustration and confusion laced her tone. She started to blink furiously. "Honestly, if you can't keep your egos to yourself, then y'all can be happy with your hands," she huffed, before blinking furiously again. "Fuck!" She rubbed her eyes.

"Are you alright?" Aurelio said, concerned, ice dousing his temper. He reached out for her but she shook her head. Xavia looked at him a bit bleary eyed, eyes fluttering. She panted, as if it was a difficult task. She dropped her hands suddenly and swayed on her feet. Quade was the first one to grab her. He caught hold of Xavia's shirt and pulled her to look at him. Aurelio stood in shock when Quade slapped her gently on the cheek.

"Hey," Quade growled at Xavia. "What did I say about this?" he shook her, making her eyes flutter close. Quade gripped her chin, forcing her to look at him. "Look at me," the command in his voice made her eyes pop open. "Good brat. You're not allowed to escape." Xavia blinked more slowly and nodded. A light sheen of sweat had formed on her forehead.

"What just happened?" Aurelio took a few steps back from them, concerned and confused. What was going on?

"I pulled her from a blackout," Quade said softly, the pair still looking at each other. He breathed slowly which she matched. Aurelio rubbed the back of his head, staring at them. He'd spent time helping Xavia with her post blackout hangovers, but never saw them as they were happening. All remaining anger drained from his body as he watched them. He'd never seen Quade so... not Quade. He wouldn't say gentle or soft, but definitely not as aggressive.

"I'm sorry. Shit..." Aurelio said, drawing their attention. Quade let go of Xavia but stood close to her in an almost territorial way. She hugged herself, looking between the two of them. "I was an asshole."

"So was he," Xavia jabbed a thumb in Quade's direction which caused a spurt of flame to escape his hands. "But that's not an excuse." She rubbed her arms as if cold and glared at Aurelio. "Don't use my issues as a reason to feel sorry. And don't use me to be petty." She looked at Quade. "That goes for you too." Xavia stepped away from them and toward her room. "I'm getting ready for training." They both took a step toward her, making her give them the finger. "*Alone,*" she barked. "I suggest y'all do the same." And with that, she snapped the door closed behind her, leaving Aurelio and Quade to stare at each other.

"Fuck," they said at the same time. Aurelio rubbed his head, looking Quade over once again. He looked frustrated, running a hand through his hair. It was obvious that Xavia's near episode had dumped ice on his anger as well. They both buzzed, as if the tension still needed an outlet.

"I'm sorry," Aurelio mumbled, reaching a hand out to his best friend. "Fuck. I said I wasn't going to get in between y'all." Quade grasped his hand and their Wielding lit up as their hands connected, making them gasp and snap their hands back. They stared at each other briefly, something passing in Quade's eyes. What in Axton's name was that? Aurelio shook his hand of the odd sensation, Quade following suit.

"If it makes you feel better, I was equally jealous when you both started your marathons. I'm surprised your dick isn't raw." Quade quirked an eyebrow, humor reaching his eyes. Aurelio barked out a laugh.

"Are you... Are you actually being funny?" He'd never known Quade to make jokes. Quade shrugged, a smile slowly creeping up. Aurelio love tapped his shoulder before laughing, Quade for once joining in.

PART THREE

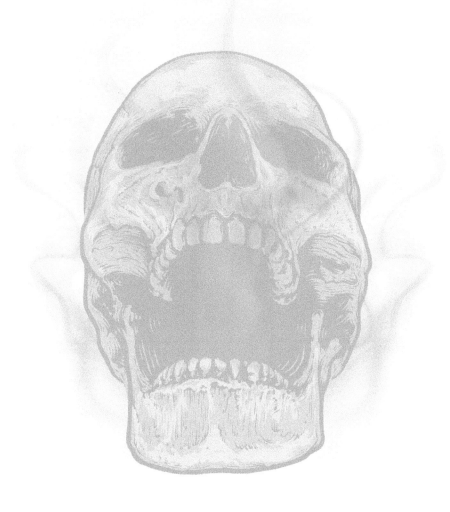

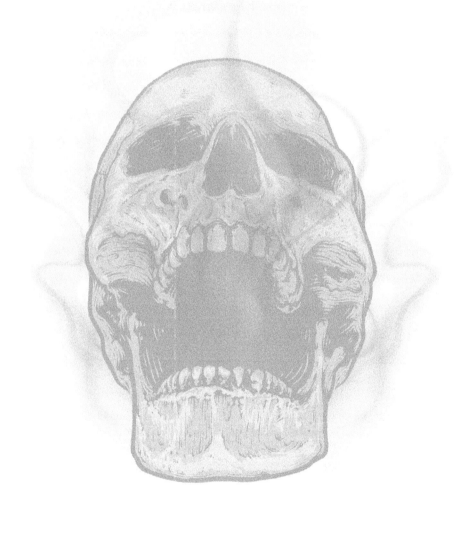

CHAPTER 39

STYX

STYX'S BREATH CLOUDED AROUND HER as she exhaled and she stepped onto the pier. The ground felt odd and solid under her. She forgot what it felt like to walk on solid ground after hiding away on a boat for weeks. Nausea turned her stomach over, making her lightheaded. Shit, maybe she should've stayed on the boat. Styx fixed her hooded black leather duster, adjusting her knife belt and thigh holsters holding her favorite twin handguns. She pulled her mask up to the bridge of her nose and shook her body, hopping in place. *Get your shit together*, she thought to herself. She had a mission and had to find the Chaos Wielder before the Asherites.

Malagado was cold and wet. What else could be expected from a city that was perpetually in darkness? Rain came down in sheets, hitting the dirty streets. It reeked. The scent of trash, urine, and other bodily fluids assaulted her nose. Styx prayed to Melvina that the entire city didn't smell this way.

She'd heard through the grapevine that the King of the Vampires had intel. She looked toward the sky-reaching tower in the distance.

It stood high above the rest but not as tall as the Monarch Tower of Melhold. Like all the other buildings, it was dark steel with dark tinted windows. Unlike the buildings, it was in the shape of a hexagon, tipping into a point at the top. She had to admit that she liked it better than the gaudy Monarch Tower. Matter of fact, other than the smell, she couldn't say she disliked the city. It was dark and gritty, like her. She could easily see herself living here if it were not for her work with the Martyrs.

Styx hopped on a motorcycle she'd 'borrowed' and made her way further into the city. The steel buildings worked as a wind tunnel, trapping the cold air and making her eyes water as she sped down the street. She pulled out her visors from her vest and slapped them on, eyeing a club with a blinking red neon sign: The Den. She slowed to a stop in front, something about the place making the hair on her arms rise.

The line wrapped around the block, but she ignored it, making her way to the entrance. Twin vampires stood at either side. They had dusty blond hair that fell to their shoulders, skin ivory pale, and yellow eyes. The only thing differentiating the two was a scar that crossed diagonally across one of the twins' face. They stared down at her as she walked up, vampires being taller and bigger than most species. It didn't matter, she could slaughter them in an instant.

"Leave your weapons," the one with the scar said, a thick Ayobían accent rolling off his tongue. People in the line groaned at her special treatment. She had that effect. She narrowed her eyes at the vampire but didn't argue as she placed her weapons in a cache that came with a key for her. As she unloaded, the one without the scar whistled.

"Ready for battle, hermosa?" He raised an eyebrow, nodding toward the cache as she snapped it shut. She shrugged.

"Rather have it and not need it than need it and not have it," Styx said before they let her in.*

She stood at the top of a landing where steps dropped down to a large dance floor. Driving dance music blared around her, oddly setting her at ease. Bodies undulated and pushed against each other as they moved to the bass of the music. It thrummed through her, making her eyes flutter in pleasure. Something about deep, heavy, bass rocked her core.

As she made her way down the steps, she took notice of the cages hanging from the ceiling. Each had a half-naked dancer in

♪ "Are You Ready" by BAD NINJA

it, gyrating for tips or more. To the right was an impressive obsidian bar with a multitude of liquor choices behind it.

A familiar coppery scent made her turn her head to the landing across the dance floor. Booths hidden within let her know that this was a blood brothel. Styx had only been in one, a rarity back in Trezora. They were well kept, despite the name. From what she knew, their workers were well compensated and taken care of. If they got sick, they were put on leave. If they died, their families were compensated. Death was a common risk. According to the few vampires she met, top blood was favored and sick blood was not good for business.

Styx made her way through the gyrating bodies around her, the smell of sweat and sex accosting her. Her instincts told her to head up to the blood brothel. Her feet were moving without much thought. As she made her way up the stairs, the pull became near unbearable. Her body told her to find the source as soon as possible. She paid minimal attention to the moans of workers and clients alike. The pull brought her to a large rounded booth, closed off with a chain and two bodyguards blocking the way.

From what Styx could see, three workers surrounded a large shadowed individual in the center. A male was on his knees before the individual, head bobbing. The females on either side had blood pouring from their necks over the male on the floor, and continued to writhe as though invisible hands touched them. Suddenly, red eyes shone through the shadow, staring at her; or through her. She didn't know. Could they see who she was?

Styx felt something that she had never felt before; arousal. Her pulse made its way down to her core. What was going on? She took a step forward but was stopped with a hand to her shoulder. Coming out of a daze she looked up to the bodyguard.

"If you want to keep your hand, I suggest you move it," she hissed through her mask. The hand on her shoulder gripped tighter, the bodyguard shaking his head. She pulled the blade she kept hidden under her nape and sliced his hand clean off. He let out a howl, eyes flashing a bright orange. The male made to advance, the other reaching for her.

"Esperar!" came the deepest and most sexy male voice she'd ever heard. The bodyguards ceased movement immediately. Styx heard a silky chuckle come from the shadows. "Let her through," His Ayobían accent made her core clench. That voice. Was it possible for a voice to make someone so dripping wet? The now one-handed bodyguard unhooked the chain with a pointed glare.

She took notice of them and realized they weren't just bodyguards. They had the Ayobían emblem embroidered on their chests, comms in their ears. Ayobían Guards? She balked, willing her feet to retreat. She wasn't ready yet. But her body refused to listen to her.

"Now, now. You can't retreat now that you're here." His voice wrapped around her, pulling her in.

The figure in the shadows pushed the male at his knees to the side before rising to his height, the full seven feet of a full-blooded vampire. He slid out of the shadows and the first thing Styx noticed was a blood covered torso. Deep bronze skin wrapped around a body made for fucking and killing. She struggled to draw her eyes from the V at his jeans, buttons undone.

Her mouth went dry as she caught his eyes on her. Red eyes sat in the face of the most handsome male she'd ever seen. Full lips, parted with fangs dripping blood over a chiseled square jaw. His skin was smooth, not a mar on it. Dark brown hair fell to his shoulders, adding to his allure. Styx felt an invisible tug, pulling her toward him, her heart hammering in her chest. She couldn't process what was happening. The pull to him was taut, bringing her feet closer against her will. What the fuck did she just get herself into?

JACINTO

JACINTO SENSED HER THE MINUTE SHE entered the club. He waited, wondering if she'd be brave enough to follow the cord of energy that seemed to stretch between them. Face obscured, purple eyes glowing in the low light, she turned in his direction. Her leather duster fell to her ankles, swaying as she walked. She wore tactical knee-high boots over form-fitting leggings. Her full figure was decorated with empty weapon holsters and knife vest, telling him that she was likely dangerous. Fuck if he didn't find that sexy. It left him pondering how this Deity of Beauty found him and what this energetic pull between them meant.

The ease with which the female sliced his Guard's hand turned Jacinto the fuck on. They were fools for not seeing her for what she was; deadly. She was blood thirsty. He stood and adjusted himself. Jacinto stepped out of the shadows and took satisfaction in the widening of her sultry eyes. What was it about her? Why was she here, in the midst of all the chaos going on? He watched her chest rise and fall as he stepped closer. Her arousal flooded his senses, making his cock twitch. If he was a better male, he'd shove the thoughts of fucking her out his head but he wasn't. If he could, he'd bend her over the closest table and fuck her till the next coming of Melvina.

"Venga." Jacinto motioned toward his office. She followed with a nod, wariness in her eyes. As they entered his minimalistic office, he motioned to the couch before his large oak desk. The furniture in the room was sleek and modern, colors of brown and charcoal accenting them. The only piece of artwork was the accent wall with a graffiti mural. He took a seat, crossing his foot over his knee.

Jacinto didn't miss the fact that her eyes tracked his every movement, including the blood that covered his body. It took everything in him to not tackle her to the ground and dig his fangs into her neck and take everything from her that he wanted. He needed to figure out what she was and why his anima called to her. While he found her attractive, even with her face obscured, the pull between them was not only attraction. It was power. That intrigued him the most.

"What brings you to The Den?"

She sat on the edge of the couch, knees slightly parted, her

268 | A.E. COSBY

guard up. Jacinto licked his lips, not hiding the fact that he found her sexy. He smirked, listening to her racing heart.

"I was on my way to see if I could petition an audience with you, your Eminence." He almost groaned at the sound of her voice, a deep alto and smooth like honey. "But I was drawn to the club. It seems that who I sought out was here." Her throat bobbed, clearly trying to figure out the energy connecting them as much as he was.

"Por favor, call me Jacinto." Her arousal swept over him and his eyes darkened. He motioned to a decanter that held his finest tequila. She shook her head and he nodded before helping himself. "I hope my current state doesn't taint your view of me." Her eyes left a hot trail down his body and he could smell how wet she was.

"I've seen worse." She raised an eyebrow. His cock hardened at the lack of fear from this female. Would it be wrong to indulge himself before finding out who she was? That purple gaze of hers dropped to his lips and he licked them slowly, watching the lust creep into those deepening eyes. He could hear her heart racing even if she didn't show a lick of it on the outside.

"I see." He took a swig of his tequila. "Well, you have my attention. What is it that you need, Señorita..."

"Styx. Just Styx." She waved off the honorific. "I assume you've heard about what is happening on Trezora?" When he nodded, she continued, "I am seeking the Chaos Wielder. I was hoping to obtain your help or resources to find them."

Jacinto sat up, dropping his foot. He schooled his face into a blank mask.

"And what makes you think I know anything about the Chaos Wielder?" He polished off his drink, placing it down with a soft clink.

"I'm not a fool to think the King of the Vampires wouldn't know the comings and goings of powerful beings on their continent," she deadpanned. His nose flared, taking in her delicious scent; honey and fresh exotic orchids. He let a smirk play on his lips.

"Why would I help you? I don't know you." Although he'd consider it if it meant keeping her around. Fuck around and find out, right?

"I am a spy and assassin for The Martyrs." Styx dropped the

name of the largest rebel system in the Bright Continent as if it were just a drop of water. If she worked for them, then she was an asset. A big one. "I know the inner workings of the Monarchy, who the senate members are, and how to take them down. I have the data to prove it." He hummed as he thought to himself.

"If you can do all this, why need the Chaos Wielder?" Jacinto murmured, standing and moving around the desk to lounge against it.

"We don't have the manpower to take down the Monarchy and their Wielders alone. We need the Chaos Wielder to take them down." Styx shifted in her seat as he crossed his arms across his bloody chest.

He was fully aware of the effect he had on her. Question was, did she realize hers on him? She stood up and the look in her eyes told him that it was against her will. Her body was speaking a different language.

"What else can you promise me if I decide to help?" Jacinto said darkly. The pull between them went taut, making him step closer to her. He wanted to touch her, just once. Although he knew that one time wouldn't be enough. Her comm watch blared startling her. He narrowed his eyes in question.

"I have to go," Styx said, shuffling forward.

He continued walking toward her, listening to her heart rate increase. There was a crackle of energy between them, making them both jolt.

"Shit, what was that?" she breathed, hand rising to her chest. So, she felt it too. She looked up at him, the crown of her head reaching his sternum. "Can we continue this conversation?" she murmured.

"What is more important than speaking to the King?" Jacinto's hands itched to touch her, tear her mask away and see what he knew was a beautiful face. His cock was aching now, the smell of her arousal telling him that her pussy was dripping wet. Her watch blared again and he could see a rising panic in her eyes.

"I don't mean to be rude." Before she could turn away, he grabbed hold of her arm tight enough to bruise. Pure fire leapt up his arm and he was sure she felt it too. She let out a gasp, a pulse on that cord of energy near unbearable. He slid an invitation in her hand.

"Let's talk at the Axton's Eve celebration." Jacinto murmured as he leaned into her. Styx nodded quickly and disappeared in a rising cloud of purple smoke, her intoxicating scent lingering to torment him.

CHAPTER 40

QUADE

THE MOOD HAD SHIFTED SIGNIFICANTLY since arriving in Malagado. Being in the City of Vampires weighed on them, knowing they were getting closer to finding the Chaos Wielder. They'd been in the city for two days when they received a request to move their lodgings into the Palacio. The King wanted to show respect to the Asherite Delegation. Quade snorted at the idea; their ragtag team was anything but a delegation. They took the invite and found themselves in accommodations that the Asherite Monarch would never afford a delegation, let alone their own senate.

Quade learned quickly that each of their suites were catered either to their Wielding abilities or origins. The furniture in Quade's suite was modern; a sleek charcoal couch, a walnut desk against a dark brown wall, sunset orange silk sheets draped over a large platform bed with ebony framing, and a stunning piece of graffiti covered one of the walls.

He hadn't spoken to or seen much of Xavia since they docked. She was still furious with him and Aurelio and made sure they knew it. Lex or Lilith kept her apprised of their plans, but she refused to meet with everyone. Fuck. This situationship between the three of them was an unwelcome distraction. He had to be the one to keep his head on straight because Axton knew Aurelio struggled with it. It was the hardest thing Quade ever had to do.

"Insane, right?" Aurelio leaned against the open door frame; arms crossed at his chest. Quade shrugged.

"A bit much, if you ask me." Quade bunked at the Guards apartments to avoid having to deal with picking furniture or decorating a space. He liked simple things. Aurelio walked over and handed him an envelope.

"What's this?" Quade opened it to find an invitation inside.

"The King requests our presence at the Axton's Eve Masquerade ball." He rolled his silver eyes. "He's making it difficult for us," Aurelio huffed, rubbing the back of his head. Quade was surprised the male didn't have a bald spot by now.

"Look, I've said this before and I'll say it again..." Aurelio groaned before the words left Quade's mouth. "We can't afford this distraction. Whatever this," he waved to the space between them, "is, we need to put it aside." Was he being a hypocrite when all he could do was think of Xavia and how he wanted to make her submit to him? The time on the boat was not enough, he needed more of her. Quade didn't know how to work through the conflict of logic and what he assumed was emotion.

"Tell yourself that," Aurelio snapped, obviously reading him.

"Fuck you. I have been." Quade glared at Aurelio, lips pursing. Aurelio gave him a look that said, *Yeah, riiight.* Quade grunted in frustration. "Do they have a training facility?" He needed to punch something.

"Yeah. The others are already there." He moved past Quade, shoulder checking him. "I am still your superior. I don't need you reminding me at every moment what my job and role in this mission is." The threat laced in Aurelio's voice came as a surprise to Quade. Was he pulling rank? This whole mission was fucking with them. He could feel the fire of anger rising in his blood as he watched Aurelio leave the suite. The taste of smoke filled his mouth as he changed into his sparring gear and made his way out.

THE SOUND OF WOOD ON WOOD let him know who was in the training center without having to look. As Quade entered, he found Lilith and Xavia sparring with their demo swords. The training center was smaller than the one at the Monarch Tower but no less sophisticated. It was mapped out the exact same way, but the atmosphere was more relaxed. Ayobían Guards sparred at a second mat at the far end of the center.

Lilith was a natural, moving like the shadows she Wielded. Quade stood in silence, watching as Xavia advanced with a lunge that Lilith barely parried. Xavia's powerful, curvy body flowed like the wind. A look of calm and peace brightened her features. She was in her element, and wore a black tank and loose cotton sweats that billowed around her legs. Lilith let out a grunt as Xavia love tapped her on the cheek with the butt of the sword. Before she could react, Xavia swung the sword, stopping at her throat.

"Work on your blind side," she said, barely panting. Lilith, on the other hand, had sweat pouring down her ebony skin, white eyes flickering as she took in gulps of air. She nodded, clasping Xavia's forearm in South Asherai fashion. "G'head get some water and then practice with Ryland." Xavia said as she looked to Ryland with compassion.

Out of them all, Ryland was not picking up the sword as well. Ever since they arrived at Malagado, Ryland had been off. The peace he found on the ocean seemed to seep out of him. He stood off to the side, looking defeated as bruises covered his arms from his failed attempts at parrying the demo swords. His head was clearly not in the game, but this mission had taken its toll on everyone, Quade included.

When he started this mission, it never occurred to him that he would fall for his best friend's ex, or that they'd agree to share. Share? That was a terrible word. More like let Xavia choose to do whatever she wanted, even if it meant the both of them. They were at her mercy.

Lex stepped on to the mat, sword at the ready. Xavia turned her head as if she could feel him watching her. She put a hand up to Lex.

"Spar with Quade. He needs work and I'm tired of laying him

on his ass." Her calm melted into ire, making him see red in response. She stormed off the mat, walking past him toward the locker room. Quade went after her, bursting into the empty locker room after her. She whirled on him, slamming into his hard body, not realizing how close he was.

"Have something you want to say to me?" Quade growled, fire licking in between his fingers. He wasn't sure what he was expecting but it wasn't the heat that he found in her dark brown eyes.

"No. Leave me alone." Xavia turned to leave but he caught her arm aggressively. Her lips parted, heartbeat fluttering in her jugular. Quade wanted to run his tongue over that heartbeat, nip at her neck, and make her moan his name. Fuck, she was a distraction. He knew he should let it go, but logic was currently drowning under his need to bury his cock in her.

"And if I don't?" His voice dropped an octave as he pulled her closer. "Are you going to stop me, brat?" He gripped her hair, forcing her to tilt her chin up. Xavia grabbed onto his shirt, a gasp escaping her mouth. Quade brought his lips to hers, teasing her mouth open as she melted into him.

He thrust his tongue into her mouth, devouring her as if he was a starved male. Her lips sucked in his bottom lip, tongue dragging across it. She nicked him hard enough to bleed. She attempted to push him away but his hand in her hair kept her in place. Ever the fighter, always tempting his temper by trying to push him away.

"Let me go," Xavia breathed. Quade licked the blood off his lip, falling deeper into the dark red he saw when he was around her. He moved his hand from her arm to circle around her throat, squeezing slowly. Her eyes rolled as she fought the desire that was clearly soaking her pussy. Her breathing increased as she turned her lust filled eyes back to him. She was his undoing. The wildness in her eyes, the sweat that glistened over her golden amber skin, her plump curves, it all became an obsession for him.

"Say it like you mean it." The deep timber of his voice rolled through his body into hers. Fuck! Quade told himself he wasn't going to let her distract him, but something about her drove him absolutely insane. It was the clashing of wild against wild, pure chaos of two animas swirling in the darkness. Only *she* understood his needs and his darkness. His cock ached as it strained against the front of his sweats.

"Let. Me. Go," Xavia said with more power through gritted teeth. The darkness in her eyes betrayed her. Quade let her go abruptly, causing her to teeter backward. She turned toward the showers, looking back at him. "Don't follow me," she growled before disappearing around the corner with an evil smirk. Those words sparked something primal in his innermost self.*

"You should've kept your mouth shut." Quade caught her, pushing her face first against the tile wall of the nearest shower. She released something between a gasp and moan as he pressed himself against her; his erection pressing against her juicy ass. He held her head to the wall, cheek flush against it. He slid his free hand down the front of her sweats, finding she wasn't wearing any panties. He leaned in, taking in her scintillating scent; hibiscus mixed with the musk of sweat. "Now I'm going to punish you for it," he whispered darkly into her ear before plunging his fingers between her folds. Her cunt was dripping as he rubbed circles around her swelling clit. She bit her lip in an attempt to keep her moan from leaving her lips.

Quade licked a line across the scar on her neck before biting down. Xavia bucked her hips, arching her back to bring her ass up against him. He slipped two fingers inside her, thumb rolling her clit. He watched her as she fought to voice her pleasure. "Moan for me," he commanded. She bit her lip hard enough to make it bleed, making him feral. He gripped her hair at the same time he pinched her clit making her jerk. "Moan for me," he commanded again. She looked at him, fight and fire mixed with dark heat in her gaze.

"Fuck you," Xavia bit out. Quade chuckled as he pushed three fingers inside her, making her eyes roll. Her juices flowed over his hand as he began to fuck her, core clenching around him. She bit down again, blood trailing down the side of her mouth. Xavia

♪ "THE DEATH OF PEACE OF MIND" by Bad Omens

shuddered against him as he picked up the pace, making it clear she was going to come.

Quade pulled out of her, watching with amusement at the look of protest on her face. He licked the blood that dripped down her chin, the copper tang driving that animalistic part of him mad. This beautiful, fierce woman turned his entire world upside down. He tugged her sweats down to her ankles before pulling her hips back enough to arch into him. He kept one hand on her head, keeping her against the wall.

"You don't get to come until you fucking beg for it and moan for me." Quade smacked her ass, holding nothing back. Xavia made a soft whimper, still holding back her moan. He repeated on her other ass cheek, leaving each one with a red hand mark. He rubbed each spot before giving her another round, making her gasp. A dark chuckle escaped his lips.

Quade turned her around, forcing her against the wall. He took her blooded lip between his, suckling on it. Her blood was intoxicating. Xavia hissed, body arching and her nipples hardening under her tank. She dug her hands into his hair, fisting it and making him groan. Quade put his fingers, wet with her arousal, into her mouth.

"Suck." Xavia looked at him as if he could see the depths of his anima as she sucked his fingers clean. She let go of him so that he could pull her tank over her head and free her breasts from the bra she wore. He gripped them hard enough to bruise, bringing out another gasp from her mouth.

"I'm not moaning for you," Xavia hissed; eyes dark, almost black.

"You're a stubborn one, brat," Quade chuckled against her neck before moving to her brown nipple to suck on. She clenched her jaw, eyes rolling while he took it between his teeth. Her body betrayed her as she grabbed his hair, holding him to her. She gripped his hair tight enough that delicious pain radiated from his scalp and headed straight for his cock. Quade pulled away from her, roughly taking hold of her jaw.

"I will fucking torture you and make you wish I had let you

come," he hissed, sliding to his knees to pull the rest of her clothes off. Xavia stared down at him, panting, as he lifted her leg over his shoulder and took her clit between his teeth. She bucked, taking a sharp inhale but refusing to moan. She was going to fucking regret it. Quade nipped her swollen bud, biting down to elicit a sharp whine. He dragged his tongue up the seam of her pussy and devoured her. Xavia grabbed his hair again as she grinded her cunt against his mouth.

"Sweet Etis and Sortis," Xavia breathed, still refusing to moan. Quade reached a hand up to pinch her nipple, wringing out another gasp. He couldn't get enough of her taste, her intoxicating scent, her hot and wet pussy. Quade put her other leg on his shoulder, holding her against the wall. She let out a squeak of surprise as she held onto his head. He spread her with his hand, giving him more access to her swollen clit while his fingers slipped inside her. Xavia made a noise that wasn't sufficient enough for him to be a moan. He felt her clenching again and he removed his fingers. He sucked on her clit before pulling away with a smack.

"Fuck Quade!" Xavia barked, frustrated.

"I told you I'd punish you," Quade said as he looked up at her. Her body flushed, thick thighs around his shoulders. He let her down as he slid up her body, kissing her roughly so she could taste herself on his lips. He grabbed Xavia's hand, dragging it into his sweats. "Pull my dick out, brat," Quade said against her lips. As though she was as desperate for him as he was for her, she pulled his cock out, stroking him as she did so. He groaned, hiking her legs around his waist.

"Wait, I'm too he—" Quade thrust up into her wet pussy, shutting up the bullshit that she was too heavy for him to hold. Xavia was an intoxicating woman. She let out a whimper as he pulled his cock out to the head and then sank slowly back in. Xavia grabbed onto his shoulders and he could hear the sound of his shirt ripping as she dug her nails in for purchase. The sharp pain of her nails came next.

"Is it torture?" Quade growled against her lips. He pushed her harder against the wall when she tried to grind her hips against him.

He pulled out to the head before driving into her. She bounced, eyes rolling. He gripped her chin, forcing her to look at him. "What did I say? Look at me, brat." Those dark, almost black eyes locked on to his as he slowly pulled out before slamming into her again. Quade watched her as those kissed swollen lips parted, bruises forming from where she bit herself repeatedly.

"Are you going to moan for me?" he hissed as he continued his slow torturous pace. He gripped her ass, spreading her more as he started to pick up the pace. He put his finger in her mouth to lick before he moved it to the puckering of her asshole and he pressed it making her gasp. "Moan for me, Xavia." There was a flare in her eyes as he said her name before she let out a moan that rocked him to his core. "That's a good brat," Quade groaned as he slammed his cock in her while placing a finger in her ass, making her buck her hips. "I'm going to fuck this one day and fill your ass with my dick," he snapped as he held on and roughly thrusted in her.

"Please. Please," Xavia whimpered as her legs started to twitch. "Fuck Quade, please." The sound of his name on her lips was his undoing. He slipped his arms under her knees, hooking them as he leaned into her and made her bounce on his cock.

"Come brat. Come on my dick," he growled into her neck.

Xavia screamed as she came over his cock, wringing out his own as he filled her. Quade held on to her as she twitched against him and shuddered. Goosebumps covered her skin as she panted and fought to catch her breath. He turned the shower on, despite still having his sweats at his ankles. The hot water covered the both of them, plastering her hair as she leaned her forehead on his.

"I'm going to let you down slowly," Quade murmured, as he slid out of her and helped her to stand. He tossed his wet clothes out of the shower before grabbing a rag and lathering it with sweet smelling soap. He washed her body, giving her gentle kisses on the bruises he left on her. He knelt, gently running his hands over her ass, marveling at his hand prints. Xavia's gaze burned through him as he stood to kiss her bloodied lips.

"I don't understand this energy between us," Quade said candidly. "All I know is that I need your wildness. I need your chaos.

I see you; you see me. I can drown in the darkness we share and meet Axton as a happy male," he whispered, before kissing her sweetly. Xavia melted against him, arms going around his neck. He sat on the shower bench, pulling her to straddle him. She slowly sheathed his already hard cock in her with a moan.

"Fire recognizes fire," Xavia said against his mouth before sucking on his lower lip. He groaned as her hips began to rock, her pussy clenching around him. "I don't know what this is, either," she breathed as he licked a hot trail up her neck. "You're a wildfire and I'm caught in the flames. But the fire doesn't hurt, it cleanses." Her words made his heart stutter. She gripped his hair, tilting his head back so she could kiss him deeply.

"Hmm. You like pulling hair, don't you?" Quade hummed, peppering kisses along her jaw, making her moan. He grunted as she pulled his hair tighter.

"Yes, I do." Xavia rolled her hips and bit his lip to make him bleed. Quade bit her back, kissing her with their comingled blood. He wrapped his arms around her, pulling her closer. She slid up and down on his cock, making him moan into her neck.

"I like seeing my marks on you," Quade said, kissing her throat and then her shoulder. She let out a moan when he gripped her ass, grinding her harder.

"I do too," Xavia said, loosening her grip on his hair. They found a slow sensual rhythm, caressing each other and learning each other's bodies on a more intimate level. His cock buried in her pussy, deep as it could go. Xavia moaned as she swirled her hips. Quade grasped her jaw.

"Open," he commanded, her mouth popping open instantly. He let his saliva drip into her mouth, making her moan as she swallowed. She was his. His and Aurelio's. They continued their slow grind. "Are we being vanilla?" Quade brought out a bark of laughter from her. He began picking up the pace, grinding her hips against him. She gasped, gripping his hair tight enough again to make him groan.

"Just this once," Xavia said darkly, matching his pace. He pumped into her wet pussy, the shower raining on them like the inferno that swept them up. He lifted her up to bounce her on his cock, making her eyes roll.

"Hey," Quade whispered, drawing her gaze to his. "Look at me when I'm fucking you," he said quietly but firmly. Xavia nodded as she whimpered. "You get a pass." He thrusted harder, her pussy tightening in response, letting him know she was getting close to coming. Their eyes remained connected as if merging their wild animas together. She raised her eyebrows in question. "You don't have to beg. Just come for me brat," he groaned when she clenched on him one last time before her orgasm crested. He pumped into her, slapping her against him, as she came.

"Come for me too," Xavia whispered against his lips, making him growl as he pumped into her and filled her. Their gazes remained locked as she pushed his wet hair out of his face. If this was what chaos felt like, he would lay down at the altar of Tomis and beseech her to continue. Xavia smirked devilishly. "Good boy." Quade barked out a laugh, swatting her ass, making her hiss.

"I'll prove to you that I'm not." She squealed when he stood up and slung her over his shoulder. "I'm going to dry you off, get you to the suite, and fuck you within an inch of your life. Then you'll see how much of a good boy I am."

CHAPTER 41

STYX

THE BIOLUMINESCENT NIGHT-BLOOMING flowers of the Malagado Cemetery held Styx's attention captive as she made her way through the gravestones. Glowing colors of lilac, magenta, aqua, and deep purple made her feel like she walked through a nebula. The cemetery doubled as a park with acres sprawling in the distance. Her combat boots barely made a sound as she trod on the dark navy grass. The air was crisp, her breath fogging through her mask. Trees towered over her, turquoise leaves glimmering as the moonlight bounced off them. She settled into an uncomfortable stillness, as if she was always meant to be here in Malagado. Styx felt like she knew the exact reason.

As she touched the flowers, her thoughts traveled to the Vampire King. What was this connection between them? It made her uncomfortable to feel such things. She had never experienced true arousal until their meeting. Her core tightened with unfamiliar intensity when she thought of Jacinto. It was obvious he was just as affected. What would they have done if she hadn't left? When she was in his presence, she found it difficult to leave. Styx couldn't allow that to happen again. It was dangerous and it left her confused; two things she didn't enjoy. She made it her life's mission to help sex workers and people who were abused. Only pain and heartache would be found there. She refused to set herself up for that.

Her comm beeped, drawing her attention from the flora and thoughts. She saw it was a message from Aurelio with a place to meet.

She sighed as she walked through the different brightly colored mausoleums, wishing she could stay longer. Aurelio leaned on one that was painted deep emerald. Floral vines crawled the walls, glowing bright enough that light was not necessary.

"Safe travels?" he said, with a smirk. Something seemed different about the Storm Wielder. Happier. She wondered what that felt like.

"I am not fit for sea travel," Styx grumbled as she sat on a bench.

"Oh, I'm not either," Aurelio snorted, sitting next to her.

"I would've thought–"

"That Storm Wielders could handle the seas…" Obviously he was told this frequently. "Nope. Common misconception."

"Well, you seem to have made it out ok." She raised an eyebrow in question. He rubbed the back of his now short, coily-haired head. It had grown over the last few weeks.

"The trip was interesting to say the least." He grinned in a way only someone in love could. Styx felt a pang in her chest. She'd never felt that way or had another feel that way about her.

Aurelio groaned, blowing warmth into his hands. "Fuck. I figured it would be cold, but not this cold." He huddled deeper into his jacket, throwing up the hood.

"I love it," Styx said, gently. "If I didn't have unfinished business in Melhold, I'd stay here."

"Fuck that. I'll be glad when I can get back to the sunny shores of Trezora."

"Well not to dampen the mood but…" Blowing out a sigh, she tapped his watch with hers. "There's new intel and you're not going to like it."

"Fuck, what is it now…" he grumbled to himself as he looked through the files. "What in Axton's balls is this?" Aurelio exploded, standing up.

"Told you," Styx groaned. "Norrix is in the city and has already presented himself to the Vampire King."

"How did you find this out?" The Storm Wielder paced. Electricity sparked at his fingertips. Styx gave him a long stare and

Aurelio rolled his eyes. "Right, you have your resources."

"Keep reading Captain."

"Just tell me."

"He knows the Chaos Wielder is in Malagado." Thunder boomed, making her flinch. Damn Storm Wielders!

"I fucking hate prophecies," he growled and motioned to her. "Keep going."

"Two of the King's governors have defected."

"Why am I not surprised? Aeshma has an appealing offer. Fuck. Does the King know?" When she shook her head, Aurelio rubbed his face and groaned. "Anything else I should be aware of?"

Styx winced, not happy to tell the next piece of information. "Norrix is trying to convince the King to hand over your bounty hunter, Xavia." Lightning blew a nearby tree apart, making her throw her hands over her head. "Melvina save us all! Fuck, this is why I rarely deal with you Storm Wielders," she barked.

Aurelio panted, eyes flaring with lightning. "That asshole has had his eyes on her since Silvermoon." He resumed his pacing, Wielding rain to quickly douse the fiery tree. "What the fuck..." He sat down with a huff, knee bouncing as he tapped a fist on it.

"Is she... The reason for your sudden change in demeanor?" Styx put two and two together. Why else would he explode—literally.

"Yeah... She is," he said softly, the lightning in his eyes dying out. "He won't get to her. My second, Quade, and I will make sure of it."

Styx nodded.

"Do you think the King will try to hand her over?"

She pursed her lips as she thought about the vampire, heat flushing through her. Thank Melvina her face was covered. "I don't think so. When I met him–"

"You met him?!"

Styx winced as thunder rumbled again. "If you don't get your Wielding under control, this conversation is over," she snapped at him like he was a child. He grimaced as he rested his elbows on his knees to calm the bouncing.

"I'm sorry. This mission has fucked with us all and it's wearing me down." Aurelio sounded as exhausted as she felt. She understood where he was coming from.

"I get that. Trust me, I do. But now's not the time to lose focus or act irrationally."

"You sound like my second... You're right," he grumbled. "So you met the King? He won't even see us. He threw us an invitation for his ball and said we'd meet after." Styx bit back her amusement at his whining.

"I met him, yes. It was... different from what I'm used to." She was too embarrassed to say more. "He's intimidating and power radiates off him as if you're standing next to a boiling furnace. I tried to petition him to help us find the Chaos Wielder." As everyone had, now that she realized it.

"What did he say?"

"Same thing. Tossed me an invitation and said to meet him afterward." She shrugged. Styx's alarm started to blare, making her jump.

"Well the King certainly has a flare for drama," Aurelio grunted as he stood up alongside Styx.

"Clearly," she muttered. "I will try to see you after the ball if I can." With that, she floated off in a cloud of purple shadows.

HAVING SNOOZED HER ALARM FOR a while longer, Styx walked into The Den, the bass thrumming through her body. As much as she wanted to avoid speaking with the King, she felt it pertinent to tell him about the turned governors. The bodyguards didn't stop her this time as she walked toward Jacinto's office. The door opened before she could knock, the cord between them taut enough to let him know she was there.

"Hello asesina," his deep bass rolled off his tongue. "What brings you here? I assumed I wouldn't see you until the Masquerade."

"Your Eminence, I have information for you," she said, her gaze slowly meeting his. She tried to ignore the way his jeans fit his slim waist and how his shirt clung to his muscular body. She tried to ignore his full lips, sharp jaw, and yellow eyes. She tried and failed. He grinned at her, as if knowing where her mind went. His fangs glistened, stained red from a recent feeding.

"Jacinto, please," he corrected as he leaned against his desk. Styx closed the door and opted to stay by it.

"Jacinto." She played with the name, having said it for the first time. A soft growl drifted on the air, making its way straight to her core. Fuck. She fought the shiver that wanted to crawl up her body. He had that grin on his face still, instantly making her irritated. The King motioned for her to sit but she shook her head. "I can't stay long." Ha! His grin dropped at that.

"Alright. What information do you have for me?"

"I have it on good authority that two of your governors have defected." Styx flinched at the wave of power that snapped her way, her chest flaring in pain. She stumbled toward him, her body moving of its own volition. She gritted her teeth as she firmly planted her feet.

"Hijo de puta! What the fuck do you mean? On whose authority?" Jacinto's eyes bled to red as he watched her stumble, taking a step forward.

"Me. I'm a spy, remember?" She grimaced, rubbing her chest and shaking her head when he tried to reach out to her. She couldn't handle him touching her. "Aeshma makes a good case. Finding out that you have defectors wasn't the issue."

"Dime, what was the issue then?" The pain in her chest eased and she noticed Jacinto's eyes had returned to yellow. He took a deep breath and said with more calm, "What was the issue?"

"Who. Finding out who defected is the issue. Do what you will with the information. It's a show of faith that I can help you if you help me." She grunted, moving backward after realizing she had taken another involuntary step toward him. Shit. She needed to leave before she got swept up. She turned to leave and a shock lit up her arm. The King's hand wrapped around her bare wrist, her jacket having slid up. "Fuck!" She snatched her hand back at the same time Jacinto hissed, his hand sparking.

"¿Qué vas a?" he asked, leaning toward her but not touching her. His hair dropped forward, smelling of freshly toiled earth, the cemetery. She narrowed her eyes, willing her body to move.

"No estoy segura," she admitted. Jacinto's eyes widened at her fluency with Potroyan. Her alarm blared, making Jacinto's eyes flare.

"You have to go." It wasn't a question. She nodded. "I will see you soon," he murmured. She stepped into her purple shadows before his hand could cup her cheek.

CHAPTER 42

XAVIA

THE SMELL OF CAR EXHAUST CLOGGED Xavia's senses, making her pop her eyes open. Where the fuck was she? Light rain fell on her face, cooling her hot body. Her vision cleared as she sat up with a grunt. Her body felt as though it had been slammed with a truck. Xavia didn't even remember leaving the Palacio. Fucking blackouts.

She heard the sounds of painful groans around her before someone wrapped an arm around her neck to lift her to her feet, putting her in a chokehold. The assailant grunted as she drove her elbow back and slammed her heel into their foot. They loosened their grip which let Xavia slam a fist backward into their groin.

"Fucking bitch!" a male voice howled in pain, vampire fangs on display, while stumbling backward.

"Who the fuck are you?" she barked. Xavia noticed there were three other vampires laying on the ground next to her, all with a limb or two missing. She pulled a knife from her vest. Wait, a vest? She looked down at herself, noticing she wore black fatigues and a knife vest. Her katanas were along her back. *What the fuck did I get into?* she wondered.

"Where am I?" She knelt to the male, snatching him by his long tawny hair, and held the knife to his throat. As she looked around, she found she was in a dirty alleyway, the smell of piss and other bodily fluids assaulting her.

"The *Barrio*," he groaned, his Ayobían accent thick, rolling the R. His yellow eyes were wide as they flicked down to the knife in her hand.

"How did I get here?" Her heart was racing, breath coming out in short pants. These blackouts were going to kill her one day. The vampire's throat bobbed as he gulped, making the blade bite into his skin.

"I don't know!" he yelled. "We were minding our business and you came along and..." his eyes shifted to the other males.

"Minding your own business, hmm? What were you *really* up to?" She wouldn't just fuck up four males for no reason, of *that* she was sure.

"We were just hanging out! I swear!" The vampire's eyes dilated, letting her know he was lying. He had a bruising ring around his eye. He must be young, not being able to cover his deception and his healing so slow.

"Liar!" came a shrieking feminine voice. Xavia's head snapped to the sound, seeing a female as she slowly stepped away from a nearby dumpster, red hair plastered to her pale face. Fire Wieldermarks lined up her one arm, making her skin seem paler. She was huffing, knuckles bruised, probably the reason for the male's black eye. Xavia started to see red as she looked back to the vampire on the ground.

"Just hanging out?" she snarled, gripping his hair tighter and making him cry out in pain. "Or trying to get laid?" She wanted to slice the male up, string him up by his hands, and watch his entrails fall out of his gut. *What in the ever-loving fuck?* she snapped to herself. She'd never been so murderous before. This explained the other males and their missing appendages. Xavia stood, putting her boot to the vampire's neck to keep him from escaping, and looked at the female.

"They were..." the Fire Wielder shuddered. "I am a worker but I still have the right to say no. And I said no. They didn't listen, so I punched one of them. Then you came along and fucked them up," the female rambled. It was obvious that any adrenaline left in her system was draining out. The vampire under Xavia's boot started to struggle so she kicked him hard enough to make him pass out. Xavia took the sweater off the passed out male and draped it around the

Fire Wielder. The female placed her forehead on Xavia's shoulder.

"What is the procedure here? What happens when males like this are reported?" Fuck. Xavia was in Malagado for political reasons. She shouldn't be fucking men up or getting her hands dirty. The female shuddered, making Xavia wrap her arm around her to keep her warm.

"The Guard is alerted. Any type of sexual assault is punishable by death, attempted or otherwise... If they're caught," she said.

"Ok, alert the Guard. These guys aren't going anywhere soon." The female did as she was told, her body no longer trembling. "Is there somewhere I can take you?" The Fire Wielder nodded toward a brothel across the street.

"There. I can go there to get someone to escort me home. These assholes caught me right as I was trying to head home. They were pissed I said no in the brothel. I should've been more careful."

"It's not your fault. Don't ever think it's your fault," Xavia murmured as she walked the Fire Wielder to the brothel. The sound of sirens let her know the Guard was arriving. The female smiled in gratitude, readying to head inside when Xavia took her forearm. "Wait. How far are we from the Palacio?" Xavia didn't even know which direction to go in.

"About twenty miles south." She nodded to the large skyscraper in the distance. Fuck. How did she get this far away?

"Thank you. Stay safe." Xavia watched the female head into the brothel and then turned toward the Palacio. Her hands shook, her nerve endings fraying and making her skittish. The adrenaline still coursed through her and she suddenly had the urge to fight. Xavia looked to the bouncer in front of the brothel. "Are there any street fights around here?"

A FEW HOURS LATER XAVIA FOUND herself banging on Quade's door. Her body ached from the three rounds of fighting she had just done.

She panted, on the verge of breaking down completely. The fights were barely a challenge and did nothing to quell the unease in the pit of her belly. It did nothing to calm the raging storm inside her mind. It did nothing to ease the hunger for pain that she needed.

The door opened suddenly, making Xavia stumble forward before Quade caught her. "Xavia? What the fuck happened?" She imagined she looked like a mess having taken a fist or two to the face and being covered in grime.

"A blackout... A fucking blackout." She kicked the door closed and grabbed his shirt to pull him into a kiss. "I fucked up," she whispered against his lips. She attempted to kiss him again when he held her shoulders.

"Talk to me. What happened?" He led her to the bathroom to turn the shower on. She stood at the doorway, hugging herself as best she could with her gear on. Xavia shook her head, tapping a finger on her elbow. She never spoke about it. She never told anyone what happened, they only saw her actions.

"No. No, it's ok. Sorry. I should leave." She turned to go.

"Xavia," Quade's voice commanded, making her still. "Come here, right now." She turned slowly and took slow steps toward him. He made quick work of helping her undress. "Get in the shower," his voice soft but charged. She nodded, body trembling as she stood under the hot spray of water. The dirt and grime dripped from her body, staining the tub.

"I'm making a mess," she murmured while Quade helped her wash up, ignoring his clothes. The shower was over before she realized and he pulled her out to wrap a soft towel around her. He sat her on the counter top, stepping between her legs and removing his wet shirt.

"What happened?" he said firmly, grasping her jaw to look at him. She told him what happened, waiting for disgust to reach his eyes but it never did.

"Not that I'm not glad to see you, but why did you come to me and not Aurelio?" Quade hedged. She understood where he was coming from. Aurelio usually was who she went to after a blackout, but this time was different.

"He doesn't understand," she whispered. "He doesn't understand the need…" She cut herself off, wondering if she should continue.

"He doesn't understand what?"

"The fights did nothing," Xavia blurted before running her hands through his hair to pull him closer.

"Did nothing?" he murmured. She pulled him closer, kissing him furiously. Desire pooled low in her belly as she scooted to the edge and wrapped her legs around him.

"It did nothing for my desire for pain," she admitted, searching his eyes for understanding. His hands found her hair, digging in and gripping. She moaned as he took her bruised lip in between his teeth and bit down. She arched into him, towel dropping and exposing her breasts.

"You desire pain?" he whispered before moving one of his hands to rub against her raw nipples. When she nodded, he pinched them, making her moan. "How much pain?" He tightly rolled her nipple between his fingers, eliciting pain and making her wetter by the moment.

"Enough to make me bleed," she moaned against his lips. He froze, making her wonder if she said the wrong thing. "Fuck. Shit. I'm sorry." She shook her head. "I–"

"Shut up," Quade growled, grabbing hold of her lower lip and gripping it tightly between his forefinger and thumb. She let out a hiss of pleasure as he made her split lip bleed freely. "Bleeding involves a lot of trust." He let her go to lick the blood off his thumb. "You really trust me that much?"

"Yes," she breathed. Xavia knew that she could trust Quade with her life. There had been a dynamic shift between them and she couldn't imagine anyone else she'd trust more with her blood. She could live in his aggression forever. It satisfied a need that she knew came from years of trauma. Her body desired to get fucked up, whether through fighting or sex. Only Quade could give her what she needed when it came to pain-fueled pleasure. He pulled her closer, letting her know how hard he was. "Yes, Quade, I trust you."

QUADE

QUADE GRIPPED XAVIA'S HIPS AS SHE voiced her trust in him. He'd had others who trusted him with their blood but the significance of having Xavia's trust blew his mind and tugged at an unknown emotion in his heart. His thumb played with her swollen and bleeding lip, watching as her gaze grew darker. He snatched her up from the counter, making her yelp, before walking to his bed.

"Thank you for your trust," he said softly. "Any hard stops?" he breathed against her lips before nipping her lower lip, making her hiss. He gripped her breasts, flames gently bouncing from his hands to her skin.

"Just don't call me 'good girl.'" Xavia said, and visibly relaxed when he nodded. He knew why it was important not to call her that.

"Safeword?" he breathed into her neck. He ran his tongue up her scar, making her shiver.

"Mangos." She snorted at his expression. "I hate them. This would be the only time I say it."

"Mangos it is." He nipped at her ear lobe before suckling on it. She moaned before she pulled back to look at him.

"And yours? Does the Fire Wielder have a safeword?" Her finger grazed over his lower lip. His tongue snaked out to lick against the sensitive skin, making her hum in pleasure.

"Sunset," his words soft. Xavia raised an eyebrow in question. "I prefer the sunrise, feeling the sun on my skin," he admitted. Her eyes grew soft as she looked at him with shining emotion.

"Well, yours is cooler than mine," she joked, making him grin.

"How do you feel about scars and wounds? I don't mind either." If he didn't establish boundaries now, he might lose himself later.

"I don't mind marks. We have medi-pills, right?" When he nodded, she gave him a dark smile. "Then wound me my Fire

Wielder," she said salaciously. He grasped her jaw, the fire in his hands softly dancing its way across it. He gave her another searing kiss as he let the fire die out. He let her go and chuckled when she whined in protest.

"Hold on," Quade said opening his nightstand. He pulled out a switchblade, sharp enough that even surface cuts made a nice bleed. He turned to her, flipping the knife in his hand. Xavia's eyes narrowed in lust and her breathing quickened. Quade glided the tip of the blade over her breasts and then between them along her sternum. She arched, nipples tight peaks.*

"This isn't too much?" Quade asked, voice hoarse with need. She popped the knife out of his hand, disarming him with a snort. His gaze trailed her hands as she glided the tip of the blade over the flesh of her stomach, right above the navel.

"No, Quade," Xavia said with a sultry grin. She gasped as she dragged it across her stomach, just enough to split the skin and make a line of blood well up. Quade watched as she rubbed her thighs together in pleasure. He leaned in to lap at the welling blood. Fuck. Her blood was addictive, making him crave more of it. He kept his gaze on the blade as she brought it to the swell of her breast and sliced just shallow enough to bleed but not deep enough to wound. He growled as he caught the blood with his tongue before sucking in her nipple. Xavia moaned as she dragged the tip of the knife down his shoulder to bicep. He hissed in pleasure at the hot pain of his skin splitting under the blade.

Vampires weren't the only ones who enjoyed blood.

"Fuck. It's like you're the mirror of me," Quade breathed as he watched her sit up to lick the trail of blood that welled up from the cut. Xavia's gaze met his as she grabbed his hair and pulled his head to the side. He groaned as she slowly grazed the knife down the side of his neck, avoiding the carotid, the warm liquid dripping down his collarbone and chest. His cock twitched as she lapped at it with a hum of pleasure before dragging the flat of the knife across his lips to smear the blood.

♪ "Hypnosis" by Sleep Token

Quade roughly grabbed her jaw, pulling her in for a hungry kiss. He moaned when she grabbed his neck and covered her hand in his blood. Growling, he snatched the knife from her. He pushed her to lay back as he dragged the tip of the knife down her body, over her soft stomach, and to her pelvis. She grabbed her breasts, spreading his blood across them, the sight making him feral.

"I need this," Xavia whispered. "I don't get this enough." She let her knees fall apart, giving him permission to run the flat of the knife up her core carefully. A moan escaped her lips as he used the flat of the knife to rub against her already swollen clit. He placed the tip of the blade at her soft mound, playing with the soft curls.

"I'll give it all to you and more," Quade said darkly, piercing the skin and making Xavia arch her back and cry out. Quade lapped at the spot of blood making her grip his hair. He rubbed his tongue over her clit before sucking it in, making her hips rise up to grind against his mouth. Quade moved back up her body, lapping at the blood at her breasts before taking her nipple between his teeth. He bit down, making her body jolt. He glided his tongue across it, rolling it and bringing out a moan. He sucked at the wound, the copper taste of her blood making him see stars.

Xavia arched into him, panting. He flipped the knife, gliding the handle down to her pussy. Quade groaned as the blade bit into his palm, the pain sending pleasure straight to his cock. He coated the hilt with her juices and rubbed it against her clit, making her hips buck.

"You like that, brat?" he growled, licking his lips of her blood. Xavia put a hand to his bloodied neck, nodding to him as she dragged his blood down her neck as if marking herself and claiming her as his. The sight of it on her was unraveling him and his body trembled as he fought to remain in control.

She opened her knees further, writhing, her eyes begging him to continue. He slid the knife toward her opening. "Like that?" Quade hissed, edging her with the handle. Xavia whimpered, eyes rolling as she tried to grind against him. He flipped the knife and placed the tip of the blade under her chin, making her eyes snap open. "Look. At. Me," Quade commanded before slicing the underside of her chin. Xavia breathed heavily as he brought his mouth to suckle at the cut. "Are you gonna be a good brat for me?" he asked, biting her neck across her scar, making her whimper. He slid the flat of the blade along her lips.

"Yes..." Xavia breathed. Quade kept his gaze locked with hers as he flipped the knife and started to push it, handle first, into her pussy. She let out a yell which he silenced with a hot kiss. She kept her gaze on his, watching as he succumbed to his dark side. The wound on Quade's palm bled freely as he began pumping the knife in and out of her, making her moan and raise her hips.

"Fuck, you're so wet. You're all over this knife and my hand," he growled, turning his gaze to his bloodied hand thrusting the knife in and out of her. She was just as dark as he was, just as unhinged, and they were mirrors of each other. There was no other way to explain what was happening between them. The darkest parts of their animas collided and he didn't know where his started and hers ended. Quade snapped his eyes to Xavia, watching her as she tried to keep her gaze on his. He smirked, pumping faster. Her hips bucked as she grinded herself against his hand and the knife.

"Please," Xavia whimpered. Quade fucked her with the knife, feeling her legs shake as she got closer to her climax.

"You want to come?" Quade whispered darkly, slowing his hand. Xavia nodded furiously, tears leaking from frustration. He licked her tears and her bloodied lips.

"Yes, please Quade. Make me come," Xavia moaned against his lips. Quade fucked her harder, capturing her mouth with his own to swallow her moans. Xavia cried out, her body shaking as she came.

Quade flipped and tossed the knife at the wall, embedding it square in the middle of a portrait of the moon. He settled his hips in between her legs, driving his cock into her pussy without wasting a moment. He filled her tightly, prolonging her orgasm.

"Fuck, Xavia," Quade breathed, putting his bloodied hand on her throat and smearing it. He took one of her legs and placed it on his shoulder, giving him deeper access into her depths. Xavia gripped his hair, making him groan and fuck her harder. He was spiraling, his control almost completely gone. Quade moved his hands to either side of her face, spreading his blood across her lips, cheeks, and into her hair. Quade tightened his fists hard enough that he could feel strands pull from her scalp. Their sweaty foreheads connected while they gripped each other. Xavia was like no one he had ever met. It blew Quade's mind when he thought about how they hated each other once but still became, whatever it is they were.

"Harder," Xavia breathed, licking her lips of his blood. Quade groaned as he slammed into her, fucking her for all that she was worth. She pulled him closer, latching to his neck and sucking on the wound she gave him. She moaned into his neck as he slammed into her roughly and deeply, control completely gone.

"Be a good brat and come for me," Quade growled before capturing her mouth in a rough kiss that was all tongues and teeth. They bit each other so thoroughly, blood pooled between their mouths as they kissed. Xavia cried out as she came, soaking him and the bed. Quade slammed into her a few more times before he came with a roar, filling her to the brim. He kissed her, less rough and more passionate, licking at her bruised lips.

"I... Can't... Even..." Xavia panted, satiated, her limbs going languid. Quade chuckled, letting her leg down slowly. He kissed and lapped at the different wounds he left on her body. They had blood smeared all over their bodies and the sheets from their intense fuckery.

"We've made a mess," Quade teased, making Xavia laugh.

CHAPTER 43

AURELIO

SO YOU'RE TELLING ME THAT NOT ONLY is Norrix in Malagado," Quade grunted, as he tried to keep up with Aurelio on their jog around the track loop. "But he's already petitioned the King, brought two governors to his side, *and* he wants Xavia?"

Aurelio nodded, breathing steady.

"Fuck!" Quade barked, stopping abruptly as smoke traveled out of his nose. He bent over, putting his hands to his knees as he fought to catch his breath. Aurelio knelt in front of him to make eye contact.

"We'll protect her. I'm just as angry as you, but we have to be level about this." For once, it was Aurelio telling Quade to keep it cool when it came to Xavia.

"I just don't know if I'd survive if something happened to her," he admitted, looking down as sweat dripped from his nose. Aurelio put a hand on Quade's shoulder, leaning in, their foreheads connecting. His stomach clenched at the closeness. What was that about?

"Hey, look at me." Quade raised his burnt sienna gaze to his. "We will protect her. It's you, me, and her. None of us will survive without each other." Quade nodded before standing with a groan. "I'm ready for all of this to be over but I have a feeling it's a far stretch."

"Xavia can't know. Otherwise, she'll try to confront him on her own. She's enough of a fucking brat to do it."

"Agreed." He slapped Quade's bare abs and nodded to

the sparring ring. "C'mon now Lieutenant, gotta stay on our toes if we're going to protect our woman." They jogged to the ring, watching as Ryland grappled with Lilith. He took down the Shadow Wielder, capturing her in an arm bar. Lilith grunted as she tapped out.

"It's our turn," Quade said with a grin, grabbing wraps for his hands while Aurelio did the same. "I'm gonna fucking own you Cap."*

"Yeah, right. That's what you said the last time Xavia laid your ass out during sword training." Aurelio barked out a laugh when Quade narrowed his eyes. Slipping out of their sneakers, they hopped onto the elevated ring. They bounced on the mat, staring each other down. In unison, they ran at each other, Aurelio slapping Quade's arm away before his punch could connect. Quade's jaw snapped with the force of Aurelio's incoming hook. Ducking, Aurelio got into Quade's guard, grabbing him around the waist to attempt a takedown. An elbow slammed down into his back, making him groan and let go. Before he could dodge, Quade's uppercut smashed into his chin, making his teeth rattle.

"You sure I'm not gonna own you Cap? Your teeth sound mighty fine rattling," He taunted as he bounced from foot to foot, shaking his arms out. Aurelio crouched and swung his foot out to trip Quade.

"Don't talk too soon, brother." He snorted as the Fire Wielder recovered. Fire lit up in his eyes, letting Aurelio know it was about to get serious. Good. They flew at each other, landing blows in the ribs, stomach, and face. A kick to his gut brought Aurelio to his knees.

"You look nice on your knees," Quade quipped, wiping blood from his newly split lip. Aurelio sniffed, blood running from his nose. They were thoroughly fucking each other up. He caught Quade by the knees, tackling him to the ground. They grappled in a flurry of grunts, elbows, and knees. Aurelio landed on top, pinning Quade's thighs with his knees. Gearing up to knock the motherfucker out, Quade caught his hands, yanked them out to the side and brought

♪ "X Gon' Give It To Ya" by DMX

his forehead up to connect with Aurelio's.

"FUCK!" Aurelio barked as the Fire Wielder bucked him off. "Took a page out of X's playbook, I see, asshole," he grumbled, rubbing his head as he got to his feet. Quade kick-backed into a stand.

"I'm sure she's taught you a thing or two about pain. Stop bitching."

That earned Quade a kick to the chin, making him stumble backward. Aurelio caught him around the waist when Quade ran at him, and tossed him backward in a suplex. They landed on their backs, breathless. Sweat poured down their bodies.

"How is it possible," Quade gasped, trying to breathe, "that one person can sweat this much?" Aurelio huffed a laugh, groaning at his sore ribs. The sounds of laughter drew their attention, making them turn in unison.

"Hey! Sparky and Flint!"

Aurelio's world narrowed as he watched Xavia walk up to them with Lex. Her face was bright with laughter and a mischievous grin. Her hair had grown long enough for her to put it up in a bun, thick scar on display. In just a sports bra and shorts, he took in every inch of her and didn't bother to hide his appreciation. Judging by the literal heat coming off Quade's body, he knew his brother was doing the same.

"Call me Flint one more time brat," Quade grumbled as he followed Aurelio in standing up.

Xavia pouted. "Aw but I like it!" Aurelio snorted at her retort. "I have a challenge for you boys." Holding out two bo staffs, the Bounty Hunter had a dark look. He knew she was up to something.

"And what's that beautiful?" He enjoyed watching her blush. Lex nudged her, amusement clear on their face. Oh, so both of them are up to something. Xavia tossed them each a bo staff, Aurelio's eyebrow lifting.

"Whoever lays the other out first..." She rocked on her feet, lips pursing. A flutter in his gut told him where this was going. "Gets the night with me." Aurelio felt the shift in the air before ducking from the bo staff in Quade's hand. Clearly, *someone* really wanted this. Fuck this, Aurelio had been taking it easy on the Fire Wielder. Not happening now. CRACK! Their staffs met in the middle. Lunging forward, Aurelio hit Quade square in the gut, making him stumble backward.

"No way you're winning this one," Aurelio said, with a grin. "Buck up." It was the only warning he gave as he came down on the Fire Wielder, flipping the bo staff across his back and grasping it with two hands. He swung, smacking it across Quade's face. Remaining firm in his footing, Aurelio effectively blocked a blow thrown his way and pushed at the offending bo staff.

"C'mon! I'm getting bored." Lex shouted, Xavia whooping next to them. Aurelio grinned, his distraction earning him an upward thrust to the chin from Quade's staff.

"Eyes on me, Cap. I'm just as pretty," the fucker said with a grin.

"You understand that I'd been taking it easy, yeah?" Aurelio growled as he twirled the staff in his hand. The Fire Wielder's eyes widened slightly. *Yeah, that's right. Remember why I'm Captain,* he thought before he moved with the speed of a gale force wind. Quade had no time to react as Aurelio landed three expertly placed blows; one to the gut, one to the side of his head, and the last to his knee. His Lieutenant crumpled to the ground with a groan. Aurelio stood over him, staff to his throat. "Have a nice night alone." He leaned in to the smoking Fire Wielder. "Flint." He ducked the fireball that came his way with a bark of laughter.

"Winner!" Xavia laughed as he jumped down from the ring and walked up to her, grabbing her behind her neck and pulling her into a passionate kiss. She melted into him, ignoring the sweat that covered his body. She bit his lip, making him hiss, before pulling away. "Remember to be a good boy tonight and you'll win a better prize," she whispered against his lips.

"Yes Ma'am," he murmured before nipping at her, making her yelp and step back. Her eyes bright with heat, she bit her lip as she walked to Quade. She leaned in and gave him a hot kiss, making Aurelio's gut clench in desire. Xavia pulled away from Quade, taking his lip with her before releasing it with a pop. Quade groaned, reaching for another kiss before she patted his head with a grin.

"C'mon Flint, it's time for sword training!" Aurelio held his stomach as he laughed at Quade's dismayed expression.

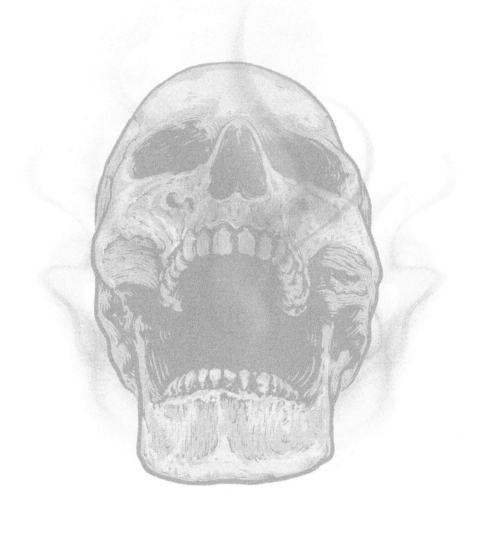

BONUS CHAPTER
QUADE

LOUNGING ON HIS BED WITH a book in hand, Quade heard a soft knock on his door. Grumbling about his peace and quiet being disturbed, he yanked the door open and stopped short. Aurelio was bouncing from foot to foot, turned away as if he planned to escape before Quade responded.

"Sup, Cap?" Aurelio froze at the sound of Quade's voice, turning slowly. The male looked nervous, electricity sparking in between his fingers. *Sparky.* Quade smirked.

"Ah. Can I ask you some questions?" Aurelio stuffed his hands into his black jeans, leather jacket squeaking with movement. "Never mind. Forget I was here. I was *never* here." When he turned again, Quade slapped a hand on the Captain's shoulder.

"What is it, man? You're tense as hell... *Sparky.*" Quade dodged before Aurelio could shove him. Quade snorted, shaking his head.

"Listen, *Flint*, I've been standing in front of your door for the last fifteen minutes wondering if I should talk to you." Quade grabbed Aurelio, pulling him into the room.

"What is it?" Quade wasn't sure if he should be concerned, amused, or annoyed.

"Xavia's coming by later..." Aurelio grunted when Quade sucker punched him playfully in the gut.

"Don't rub it in asshole."

"I'm not!" The Storm Wielder shifted from foot to foot. He was clearly nervous about something.

"Speak, Cap." Quade said sternly, making Aurelio's gaze snap to him. Oh. Xavia has taught him some things.

"I... Uh..." He rubbed the back of his head. What the fuck? Quade hadn't seen him like this since the Academy. "Xavia. She's..."

"A lot."

"Yes. That." Aurelio chuckled. "Erm. She tied me up." Quade's eyes widened. "I liked it." Aurelio took a deep breath. "She called me a 'good boy' and I almost came on the spot." He blurted out. Well shit, who would've thought.

"Well, my man." Quade thumped his shoulder. "I'm not surprised you have a praise kink." Aurelio barked out a laugh.

"What the fuck? Xavia said the same thing." He scrubbed at his face and paced. "Shit, this is embarrassing."

"Nah. What's to be embarrassed about?"

"That she tops? That I like it? And..." Aurelio dropped his hands. "I want more and don't know how the fuck to go about it." Quade stepped in front of him to stop his pacing.

"What is it that you want to know?" His Captain stared down at his feet before meeting his gaze.

"Ah, how to be a good sub?" He shrugged. "More ways to be tied up. Definitely that... and ways to explore things I've never tried."

"Only Xavia can tell you how to be a good sub. Everyone has their own preferences." Shit, Quade's were dark and not everyone was into that. "But the other things, yeah, I can help." He smiled darkly, making Aurelio blanch.

"Don't make me regret this, Q."

Quade chuckled, pulling a duffle bag from his closet. Aurelio eyed it suspiciously, making him smile wider. Oh, this was fun.

"Other than the tying, what else did you like?" Quade dropped the heavy bag on the bed, unzipping it and pulling out different carefully wrapped kits. After their blood play session, Quade went shopping. Aurelio shook his head, tapping his chin lightly.

"Why is this so hard to talk about? It's not like we haven't talked about our sexual exploits." Aurelio stepped up next to Quade to eye the kits. "It's because it's Xavia, isn't it? The fact that we're both… with her?"

"Eeeyup." Quade chuckled before opening the first kit, which contained a whip, paddle, and ball gag. Aurelio huffed a laugh.

"Oh shit. Um, no." He shook his head. "She slapped me and it was in the heat of the moment, but I don't want it to happen again." His tone hardened and Quade knew why. Aurelio's father had been a tough man with a firm hand–literally.

"I get you. So that's a nope." Quade rolled it up. "I'll ask again. What else did you like?" Quade raised an eyebrow, wondering if he would need to turn on his dom voice.

"Ahh…" Aurelio was stalling. Fuck it. He asked for it.

"What. do. you. like?" he growled, grabbing Aurelio by back of his neck. His eyes dilated, making Quade question himself. He'd been with men before but never thought of his Captain in that way. Aurelio never seemed the type. Maybe Quade was wrong.

"That. The demands," he breathed before Quade let him go. "She bit my nipples, Q. My nipples! Fuck, she bit me all over. Made me bleed." Aurelio rubbed his chest, seeming lost in the memory.

"Yeah, she loves biting." He grinned, winking. He unraveled a kit with nipple clamps and ropes. "I think this is what you're looking for." He held out the ropes to Aurelio. "They're bamboo. Durable but soft." The Storm Wielder took it, thumbs running across it. "The nipple clamps are adjustable. You'll have fun with those."

"Clamps?" Aurelio shuddered as he touched them. "Well, fuck." He turned to Quade. "Show me how to use these." He held up the ropes.

"There are a few ways." Quade plucked the ropes from him and motioned Aurelio to the center of the room. "You're gonna have to lose the jacket and shirt Cap." His Captain gave him a look before doing what he was told.

"You know, this is the only time I'll let you tell me what to do." Aurelio snapped, dropping his clothes on the bed.

"Keep telling yourself that." Quade snorted, unraveling the ropes. "Turn around, hands behind you." He bit back a laugh as Aurelio narrowed his eyes and turned. Quickly and expertly, Quade wrapped the ropes around Aurelio's wrists in a figure eight formation. Firm but not so much to lose feeling. "How do you feel?" He asked before walking in front of him.

"Vulnerable as shit." Aurelio breathed. Sweat had started to glisten on his chest and Quade would be lying to himself if he said it didn't do something to him. What in the fuck? He shook himself out of those thoughts.

"Good. That's the point." Quade leaned in, tugging at the rope to unbind it. He could feel Aurelio's breath on his face as it sped up. "Um. There's a chest harness. It's more vulnerable than this and gives her more control." he said, stepping back and seeing his Captain in a new light. Fuck, was this going to be a problem?

Aurelio shocked him by saying, "Let's try it."

"It's intimate... Just letting you know," Quade said as he started the rope wrapping process, starting around the torso. It brought him close in as he wrapped the ropes around Aurelio's shoulders and bound his arms to his body. "If you're uncomfortable, just tell me." Quade ended behind Aurelio as he finished the ropework at his wrists.

"Fuck. This is..." Aurelio seemed at a loss for words. Quade had never done something so intimate with his Captain before. It made him want to snatch those bindings, pull Aurelio to him and see if he felt the same. He opened and closed his fists, getting a handle on his impulsive thoughts. Quade would never disrespect him like that.

"Yeah, I know." Quade remembered what it felt like and he wasn't a fan. Quade made quick work to untie the ropes. "Do you want more examples?" Aurelio shook his head as he snatched his shirt and pulled it on. His body shook and Quade wondered if it was because of the nerves or if he felt the same as Quade did.

"I think I understand." Aurelio muttered, slipping his jacket on and looking down. Quade wrapped up the toys and handed them to Aurelio. He cleared his throat, causing Aurelio to look up. *Oh.* Quade thought. The male's pupils were blown and he was clearly trying to avoid Quade's gaze. Aurelio looked everywhere but him. "Thank you." He nodded and walked past Quade toward the door.

"There's nothing to be embarrassed about," Quade said as he reorganized his duffle bag. He slid his gaze to Aurelio, finding them glowing with lightning. "Just talk to her. I'm sure she's going to find this all hot as fuck" Aurelio barked out a laugh and the tension broke.

"Seriously, thank you Q."

"No problem, Cap. You've been a good boy." Quade ducked as Aurelio chucked his comm at him. "Fuck! Sorry!" They both laughed. It'd been a long time since they bonded like this.

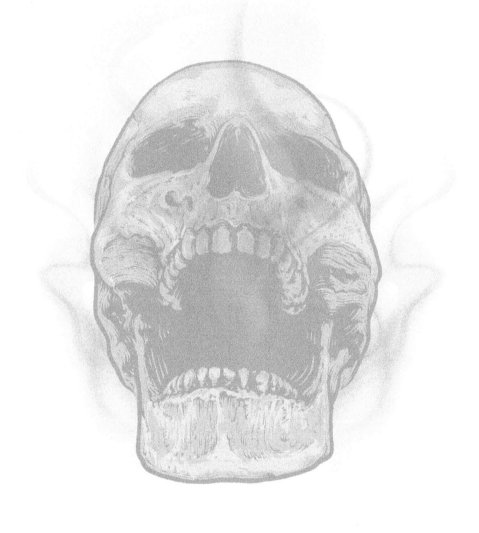

CHAPTER 44

XAVIA

XAVIA DIDN'T UNDERSTAND WHY she was nervous as she stood before Aurelio's door. It wasn't like they hadn't been together, fucking like the world was ending. Well maybe it was, or would be soon. That was beside the point. Tonight, she put some effort into her outfit, wearing clothes she hadn't worn in years. A white open button up draped over a black-laced corset top with tight navy skinny jeans forming to her thick legs like a second skin. She wore black flats; heels were never her thing. Something about this evening caused butterflies to flap around in her stomach. Xavia gently rapped on the door, hearing a shuffling before the door opened.

"Hey..." Her mouth dried, soaking in Aurelio's presence. A tight charcoal henley clung to his body, making his silver eyes brighter, black jeans that hung low on his hips, and his feet bare. He smelled of rain and fresh air, his gaze searing through her as he assessed her for his viewing pleasure.

"Fuck," he breathed before snatching her by the waist and pulling her into the room, kicking the door shut. Their mouths clashed together as he drank her in, making her moan and grab his shirt. When they finally came up for air, they laughed, foreheads connected.

"Happy to see me?" she whispered. Aurelio ran a thumb over her lower lip.

"Absolutely." He pulled himself away with a groan. "But first, I'd like to present you with..." He motioned behind him. "Food."

That was when her gaze traveled to a table filled with burgers, fries, loaded nachos, and other fried comfort food. Off to the side there was a platter of raw vegetables and salad, and an assortment of fruit.

"A man after my own heart!" Xavia couldn't hide her excitement.

"I know you're not a wine and cheese sort of woman," he said, as he pulled out a case of bottled brown ale. She pulled him into a searing kiss, making him almost drop the beer.

"You really want your prize tonight, my good boy."

"Yes Ma'am. I do."

"SHIT, THEY MAKE SOME good ass burgers," Xavia breathed, lounging back against the couch as she sat on the floor. For the last hour they had enjoyed food and conversation. It felt comfortable and warmed her heart. The food had been thoroughly ravished, bottles of beer strewn about. Aurelio sat across from her, looking equally stuffed.

"Can I ask you something?" Aurelio hedged. She took a swig of her brown ale with an eyebrow lifted. "When did you... Ah, get started with..." She grinned as Aurelio's expression turned bashful.

"BDSM?"

"Yes. Yeah. That." He rubbed the back of his head, looking at her with a glint in his eyes.

"A long time ago. I met this wonderful Mistress who introduced me to it. She's amazingly beautiful, all curves, taller than me and fond of leather and lace. I spent time as her sub." Xavia smiled wistfully as she thought about Raya. Being five years her junior, Xavia was intimidated by her. "At first, I was scared, I'll admit. My history didn't make it easy for me to trust someone with my body in that way." She nibbled at her lip as Aurelio sat next to her. "I have an affinity for pain. I knew I had to find a safe space to explore it without getting myself hurt or worse. So she taught me how it all worked and during those lessons…" Xavia flushed at the memories. "Was when we realized I was a switch. I wanted to dole it out as much as I received it. I wanted to control *and* be controlled."

"Was it… before or after you met me?"

"During… I mean, we weren't exclusive and were clear on expectations, and–"

Aurelio grabbed her hand, silencing her. "I get it. But you were never that way with me." He pursed his lips in thought. "Was it because you didn't feel safe or–"

"No!" she interrupted, gripping his hand. "It wasn't that at all. It's just… I didn't feel worthy of you. And I thought you wouldn't accept my… proclivities."

He kissed the back of her hand.

"Teach me," he said, softly, as he leaned in and kissed her where her jaw met the bottom of her ear. She shivered as he slowly moved down her neck.

"Teach you?" The words came out as a breath. He hummed in agreement, the vibration making its way down to her core. "You understand it's more than what we've done, right?" Regretfully, she pulled away to face him. His silver gaze bore into her as he nodded.

"Yes Ma'am. I understand. I trust you. I want you to know you can trust me too. We're safe together." He nipped at her lower lip before standing and helping her up.

"Aurelio, are you s—"

He led her to his bed, a stunning platform, king-sized bed. With a black frame and dark gray sheets, it fit his Storm Wielding heritage. Accents of white and navy gave the impression of a rising storm. But the bed wasn't what drew her attention. A red cloth laid across the foot of the bed, stark against the gray sheets. It was crumpled as if covering something underneath.

"So, I had a talk with Quade…"

"You did what now?" Xavia snorted. Aurelio scrunched his nose.

"Shush. I… erm," he seemed nervous. She placed a hand on his chest, feeling his heart racing under her palm. "Sorry. I'm both nervous and excited," he breathed out a chuckle.

"What's under the cloth?"

"Ok, as I was saying. I told Quade I was curious... About all of this." She'd never seen him so flustered and she found it endearing. "He helped me gather some, um toys, that I might like. He told me that only you would be able to tell me how to be a good sub and... Wait, why are you grinning like that?" Xavia tried to stop but she couldn't help it.

"You're fucking adorable, you know that right?" She grasped his chin, bringing him in for a kiss. Aurelio rubbed his head, returning her grin. His dimples were going to be the death of her. "Ok. Show me whatcha got." He pulled back the cloth to reveal a multitude of toys. "And Quade picked these out?"

"Uh, yes."

Xavia ran her hands over soft bamboo ropes, looking at him from under her lashes. Next to the ropes were shears and Aurelio's throat bobbed as she touched the adjustable nipple clamps. She made note that there were no whips or paddles.

"Seems Quade knows you pretty well." And fuck, that turned her on, making her imagine what exactly Quade showed him. "First things first. Safewords. Mine is 'mangos'. Oh, don't give me that look." She rolled her eyes.

"Ah yes. I have one..." He looked bashful again.

"You learn fast. Good boy," she winked, making him chuckle and puff up with pride. "What is it?"

"Yachts."

"Because you–"

"Hate them. Yup." They both laughed.

"Limits. I personally don't have many, if at all." She pursed her lips, wondering what he thought about that. When he didn't mention it, relief flooded through her. "Just don't call me 'good girl' and we're good. I need to know yours."

"I'm down to try most everything at least once. But I call the line with pain." He raised an eyebrow. "And I mean true pain, no smacking or spanking. Lip biting, split lips, and choking are ok though." He rubbed his face and she grabbed his wrists, pulling them down.

"It's ok. I understand. I noticed the lack of whips and paddles. I will never do anything you're not comfortable with. If anything we try makes you uncomfortable, use your safeword." Xavia was in a mild state of disbelief as he nodded and grabbed the ropes. All these years, she never thought he'd accept her lifestyle. She made all the assumptions in the world and never gave him a chance.

"May I take off my shirt?" His rich tenor drew her attention, finding his electric gaze on her.

"You may," she said as she stripped her own shirt off, leaving the corset. Aurelio held her stare as he slowly took off his henley, exposing each muscle and scar that was wrapped in dark brown skin. Her eyes trailed the perfect V that ducked into the low waistband of his jeans. Liquid heat began to pool between her thighs, soaking her thong. His abs flexed as he tossed the shirt. Her breath hitched as he handed her the ropes.

"Tie me up please?"

AURELIO

DID YOU ALREADY RESEARCH what kind you want to try? I'm assuming we're not talking about our standard headboard stuff." Xavia said as she unraveled the ropes. Aurelio itched to touch her but fought to remain patient.

"Ah yes." His throat bobbed, his erection straining against the front of his jeans. "The chest harness. Quade showed me." *That* was an interesting exchange between them. It surprised him that he felt things he'd never felt before. The heat in Xavia's gaze threatened to burn through him and he knew she imagined what it looked like. She sauntered over to him gently gliding her hand along his abs as she circled behind him.*

♪♪ "Vixen" by Miguel

"Hands," she commanded. He brought his wrists behind him, breathing increasing as she tied his wrists together. "Remember, if you get uncomfortable at any moment..." she whispered as she reached in front of him to wrap the rope under his pecs. The ropes whispered across his skin, raising goosebumps as she managed to get the ropes around his shoulders without needing him to kneel.

"This is the most intense foreplay I've ever had," he chuckled breathlessly. Xavia kissed his biceps as she moved the rope across his body to tie his arms to his torso. She ended at his back, finishing the braid and tying his wrists to the middle of his back. He gently tugged at the rope, finding it was sturdy enough to keep him from breaking free, but not tight enough to cut circulation.

"It is, isn't it?" Xavia whispered as she stepped in front of him, eyes black with desire. She ran her hands across his abs, his breath hitching. The vulnerability of his position, being at her mercy, and knowing she would never hurt him was euphoric. He flexed, watching as her breathing increased. "You're so incredibly sexy." She licked a line from his waist and up the center of his stomach. "You look so good." She knelt before him, popping the button of his jeans. "And you've been such a good boy." He groaned as she tugged his pants down and freed his aching cock.

"Fuck, baby..." He tugged at the binds, aching to touch her. She tapped his bare feet and he lifted them so she could remove his jeans.

"Do you know what good boys get?" She peered up at him, lips just barely touching the tip of his cock.

"Rewarded." He fought to keep his eyes on her as she took him into her mouth. Moving at a slow pace, he watched her as she sucked him until he hit the back of her throat. "Shit, that's a sexy sight," he breathed, body thrumming with tension. Xavia picked up the pace, gripping him at the base of his shaft with one hand and massaging his balls with the other. Every breath he took, the soft ropes rubbed tighter against his body, leaving him raw with need. Aurelio thrust into her mouth, making her moan over his cock. Each thrust matched a bob of her head. He groaned, eyes rolling. "Fuck, it feels so good." He growled when Xavia let him go with a pop.

"Eyes on me," she said and stood when he turned his gaze to her. Sweat glistened across his skin as she pulled up an ottoman. "Sit." He nodded but before he could sit, she snagged the rope at his chest. "What do you say?" Being so close to her but unable to touch her drove him insane.

"Yes Ma'am."

"Good boy." Pulling him toward her, she kissed him until he swore he saw Aether. Her tongue rubbed against his, her teeth nipping at his lips.

"Harder," Aurelio gasped between their kisses. She did as he asked, drawing blood. His cock jumped, aching to be inside her. She let him go so he could sit. Watching her as she slowly pulled her jeans down to reveal a lacey thong, he wasn't sure how much longer he could contain himself.

"Do you want this pussy?" she whispered as she turned her back to him and bent over to slip out of the soaking thong. He groaned as he took in the sight of her dripping cunt.

"Yes Ma'am." He was starting to lose his mind, the ropes making him ache in the best ways. Xavia moved to the bed to pick up the nipple clamps. She raised her eyebrow.

"How about these?" she said as she knelt in front of him. Suddenly his nipples ached for her touch.

"Fuck yes, please." Aurelio let out a deep moan as she clamped one and then the other using the lightest adjustment. The sharp bite made his back arch, driving him mad with desire.

"I'll give you this pussy if you ask nicely."

"Can you sit that pussy on my dick, please?" he said quickly, electricity sparking between his fingers but not catching on the bindings.

"That's my good boy. Always asking for permission." As she straddled him, she took his lower lip between hers and suckled on it and slowly impaled herself on his cock. She was already so wet and ready for him. Nothing could prepare him for the sensation of finally being rewarded with her soaking center.

"Oh fuck Xavia," he whimpered as she rolled her hips, sliding herself up and down on his length.

"Say my name again," she moaned as she grinded against him harder, digging her nails into his shoulders.

"Xavia," he growled, leaning in to take the soft flesh beneath her ear between his teeth. She whimpered, holding him closer as she rocked against him harder. "Xavia, shit you fuck me so good." Aurelio kissed and nipped along her scar, making her hiss in pleasure.

"Hmmm. This dick of yours is so thick. It fills me up," she gasped when he bucked into her, even with having his hands tied behind his back. "Fuck. That powerful body of yours." He was at the end of his rope, he needed to touch her.

"Yachts," he breathed, making her stop immediately. "Please, untie me." She nodded and he groaned as she slid off of him. Xavia tugged a knot and the whole thing fell from his body. Marks lined his body, his shoulders and wrists ached. She knelt in front of him, concern written across her face as she gently took the clamps off. She softly ran her tongue across each nipple, easing the ache and making him groan.

"Are you okay?" she asked as she kissed his shoulders and massaged his wrists.

"Yes. I just... I just need to touch you," he murmured, closing his eyes briefly as she drifted her hands across his torso to massage the aches. "Is that alright?" She looked up at him, emotion shining in her depthless brown eyes.

"Can you stand?" He nodded and they stood together, Xavia leading them to the bed. She crawled to the center, removing her corset. "Touch me, Aurelio."

"Yes Ma'am," he practically leapt on her, entering her as soon as he was on top of her. He hooked her legs over his shoulders, driving his cock deep into her soaking pussy. She raised her hips to meet his strokes and cried out when he tangled his hands in her hair, gripping it tightly. Her legs twitched, core clenching around him. "Fuck, baby, you're so wet. You fit my dick perfectly," he moaned.

"That's a good boy. Fuck me good," she moaned as his pace increased, pumping into her harder. Their gazes locked and his breath caught at her beauty. The ecstasy on her face, her swollen lips, her words of praise. Emotion ballooned inside of him, his climax crawling up his spine, balls going tight.

"Xavia, I'm going to come," he moaned, winding his hips and hitting the spot she loved and making her cry out. His body shuddered as he whimpered, "Can I come please?" He worked to keep his rhythm.

"Yes. Yes, fill this pussy up. Make me come." She met him, thrust for thrust. Aurelio slammed into her, making her scream as she came, bringing him with her. His body shuddered, vibrating from the force of his orgasm.

"I... have no words," he murmured before carefully putting her legs down and kissing her. It was slow and languid, a tasting of each other, all lips and tongue. Xavia nodded, humming in agreement. Aurelio pushed sweaty curls from her forehead, kissing the salty skin. They remained like that for a moment, admiring each other.

"Do you know what you're doing to me?" she said breathlessly. "I can't explain it. What this is…" He kissed her forehead.

"It's a hurricane," he whispered and she nodded. Emotion was thick in his voice and he hoped he wasn't making this bigger than she wanted. Tears leaked from her eyes. He cupped her face, thumbs catching them.

"You're my rock," she said softly.

"You're my storm," he replied before kissing her deeply. He groaned as he shifted on top of her, body sore.

"Very slowly, roll to the side," she murmured, running her fingers over the marks left by the ropes. His body trembled as he grunted, sliding out of her and tumbling onto his back. "Do you think you can stand?" The tenderness in her voice made his heart skip a beat.

"Maybe?" he snorted. Xavia smiled and kept a hand at his back as he sat up.

"Let's get you to the tub. You deserve a hot bath and a massage." The way she looked at him made his chest tight. He was safe. She was safe. Together, they were safe. He wouldn't have it any other way.

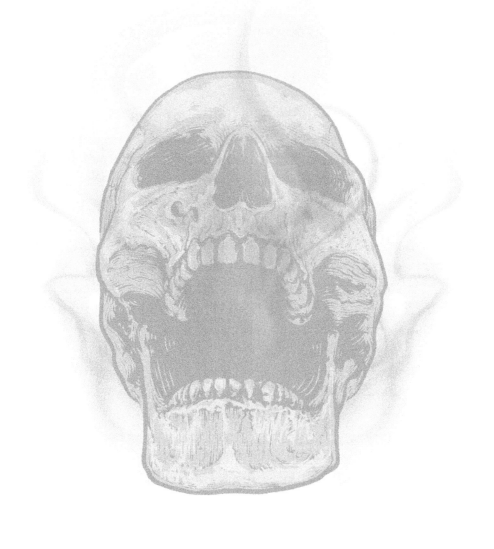

CHAPTER 45

JACINTO

THE SOUND OF PAINFUL MOANS filled the basement as Jacinto made his way to the interrogation cell. His thoughts traveled to his encounter with Styx while he walked, sneakers silent on the stone floors. Because of her intel, Cyrus was able to find out who one of the two traitors were. With that action, she solidified herself as an asset. He already knew she was resourceful. But on top of that, she was a battery of some sort. Their energetic cord was more than attraction, though that was a pleasant side effect. It was as if he was plugged in to an energy source when she was near. When she told him about his governors, he almost lost his shit due to the surge of power. Their tie was powerful enough that he felt it all the time, though not with the same strength. Jacinto doubted that she was a normal Wielder. Logic told him to stay away from her. His body said fuck logic.

Wet sounds of fists striking flesh drew him out of his thoughts. Better to get this over with.

"Fuck you! I won't tell you anything," came a deep snarl. Jacinto turned the corner and tutted loudly at the sight of Kincaid. The werewolf was strung up by the wrists, his body being used as a punching bag. An IV secured to the top of his foot pushed fluid filled with a low dose of silver to keep the wolf from shifting. Kincaid's hair was matted to his face, sweat mixed with blood covering his large body. One of his eyes was swollen shut, shallow cuts made in strategic areas to induce pain but not death. The interrogation cell was plain with gray stone walls and flooring, a drain in the middle, and a cabinet full of torture devices.

"Sure you will, cabrón. Everyone talks eventually." Cyrus flipped a silver blade in his hand, an evil smirk on his full lips. The vampire was Jacinto's best interrogator, having done so for hundreds of years. No one knew the male was the Interrogator everyone feared. If they found out, it was because they were going to die. Cyrus covered his ruthlessness well, wearing suits and keeping a level head for all to see.

The cool, calm, and collected Cyrus was kept that way through Jacinto's soothing compulsion via their sire bond by Cyrus's request. That male was not present this evening. This male wore white on purpose when he interrogated. His once white button up, rolled to his elbows, and slacks were stained with blood. Kincaid howled in pain as Cyrus sliced diagonally from collarbone to the opposite ribcage twice, leaving an X in the middle of the werewolf's chest. "Maybe I should get more creative?"

Jacinto watched in silence and leaned against the door frame, enjoying the artistry in which Cyrus worked. Cyrus lost any semblance of humanity when invaders killed his family. For his loyalty, Jacinto offered to turn him in order for Cyrus to get revenge. That was when the vampire realized he enjoyed torturing his enemies.

Grabbing a welding torch from the counter, the Interrogator walked up to the hanging werewolf. "What do you think would happen if I…" Cyrus slowly dragged his hand along Kincaid's lower abdomen, "torched right here, so close to your dick?" The werewolf jolted, trying to get away from his touch. "Come now. I'd like to find out." The smell of burning flesh clogged Jacinto's nose as Cyrus did what he promised. Kincaid screamed, eyes rolling before passing out. Cyrus turned off the torch and tossed it on the counter, sighing with disgust. "This is the third time this pendejo has passed out."

Jacinto chuckled. "Has he really not said anything?" he said as he walked around the hanging Governor. "Carajo, your work is glorious," Jacinto murmured more to himself. Cyrus had carved 'traitor' in Kincaid's back.

"He keeps passing out before we can get to the good stuff." The vampire grunted, fixing his collar as if he wasn't covered in blood. Cyrus snatched the smelling salts and held it under Kincaid's nose. The werewolf woke with a start, groaning with each heave he took. Cyrus picked the torch back up, eyes lighting with glee. "Welcome back."

"Hello Kincaid," Jacinto growled, the werewolf glaring at him. "Why did you defect? What is the demon offering you?"

Kincaid spat blood at him, landing on his white sneakers. Cyrus snarled, snatching the werewolf's long hair and searing it off at the scalp with the torch. The flame spread to the remaining hair, burning the wolf. Kincaid screamed as Cyrus doused his head with a bucket of ice water.

"Land," the werewolf dry heaved. Cyrus narrowed his eyes, waving the torch in front of Kincaid's face. He flinched away, fear permeating the air.

"What else? You have land. You have an entire fucking territory," asked the Interrogator.

"King. He'd make me king of Ayobaí... To co-rule..." Kincaid snapped his mouth shut, making Cyrus bark out a laugh.

"You'd make a terrible king. You can't even stay awake during torture." He tossed the now unlit torch on the counter, the sound making Kincaid flinch.

"Co-rule..." Jacinto mused as he pursed his lips. "Co-rule with whom?" The werewolf moaned in pain, shaking his head.

"Well... Seeing that you're never getting out of here..." Cyrus chuckled as he grabbed a silver machete and popped the button of Kincaid's jeans. "You don't have need for your dick, right?" The werewolf's body trembled as another wave of fear drenched the air. The vampire pulled the jeans down to the ankles, taking the wolf's boxers with it.

"If you kill me first, you'll never find out," Kincaid had the audacity to say.

"True. Doesn't mean I can't make it long and painful for you. We can always find out another way." Cyrus grabbed the male's cock, making him howl in pain. "I can make it easy for you. Tell us and I'll kill you quickly. Or don't. I enjoy the torture." The vampire grinned, fangs glistening in the light. Jacinto raised an eyebrow at

Kincaid, waiting for an answer.

"Ericka," Kincaid whispered, trying to breathe. Of all the people in his court, Ericka was the last one he expected to defect. Fuck.

"You're lying," Jacinto growled, taking a step forward, his power surging through the room. Kincaid shook his head, panting and closing his eye.

"I'm not. It was her idea to saddle up with Norrix," the werewolf sobbed.

"What did you give Norrix in exchange for his promises?"

"Details about where the country is weakest and best for an incursion." Kincaid had been one of Jacinto's best generals. He had the resources to provide Norrix the information he sought. If they couldn't get a handle on this, they were going to suffer the same fate as Asherai.

"Anything else?" Cyrus growled, gripping Kincaid's length tighter. The wolf cried out, more tears falling from his eyes.

"No! I swear. Nothing else!"

"¿Estas seguro?" Jacinto backed to the doorway. Kincaid nodded furiously, sobbing.

"I'm sure. Please just kill me," he whimpered. Cyrus looked to Jacinto with an eyebrow raised in question. He gave the Interrogator a slight nod.

"Wonderful!" Cyrus said with cheer, gently putting the blade of the machete to the base of Kincaid's cock, as if lining up for accuracy. The wolf tried to flinch away, only succeeding in having his dick sliced, and sobbed harder.

"Wait! You said you'd make it quick!"

"Oops," Cyrus barked out a laugh. "I lied." And down the machete went, cleanly slicing through Kincaid's cock. The werewolf screamed before vomiting on himself. Jacinto's eye twitched as Kincaid's screaming grew louder. Cyrus stood there, and waved the dismembered part in front of Kincaid's line of vision.

"Cyrus... Rein it in." Jacinto's order flowed down their sire bond, calming Cyrus. If he hadn't, the male would be there all night peeling the werewolf piece by piece. "He's given us what we need." Cyrus nodded, sobering up as he swung the machete, cutting the werewolf's head clean off his shoulders.

"We need to find Ericka."

"First, we need to deal with this ball and find out why Norrix wants the bounty hunter. We're going to need the Asherites help to take him out." Jacinto took in Cyrus's appearance. "Clean this shit up, go feed…" His nose flared as he saw the wolf's cock still in Cyrus's hand. "And for fucks safe, quema esa mierda."

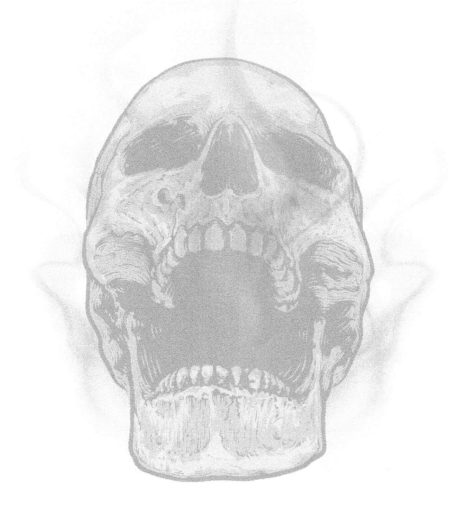

CHAPTER 46

XAVIA

XAVIA PACED IN HER SUITE as she stared at the dress laid out on the bed. The Axton's Eve Ball was that evening, the King having sent everyone something to wear. Her stomach felt like it wanted to crawl up her throat. She couldn't sift through the maelstrom of emotions that warred within her.

The thoughts of the last week flooded her. Her body was still sore, her pussy aching, from all the sex and abuse it had received. The pain was delicious, and while healed, she remembered the marks Quade left during the explosion of their animas. Xavia's thoughts traveled to Aurelio and his submission to her and it flushed her body in heat. It came so easily for him. It was as if he recognized what her anima needed and gave it all. The leader needed to be led. He needed it as much as she did.

Sweet Etis and Sortis what was she going to do about these two males in her life? It was like whiplash. The juxtaposition of the two of them had her head spinning. The fire and storm, meeting together in the wildness that was Xavia.

"You're not dressed yet?" came Lex's voice, who poked their head into the suite. Xavia shrugged before shaking her head. Her heart felt like it was going to implode, it was beating so fast. She'd never been to a ball. She'd never dressed up in fancy clothes. Except for the Monarch, she'd never met royalty. She had no clue what to expect. Not too long ago she was informed that the King wanted to speak with her personally and the thought alone made her want to throw up and hide under the bed.

"I'm in way over my head," Xavia murmured as she turned to the vanity. Yeesh. A vanity. She hadn't had one since she was a teen, during her more feminine years. Different perfumes, makeup, and oils were scattered about. It was a miracle that she remembered how to do her own makeup.

Xavia looked at herself in the mirror and barely recognized herself. Her curls were swept up in an updo that left her neck exposed. The scar she normally kept hidden was on display. Glittering pins were strategically placed to give the illusion that her dark hair had stars within them. Deep navy eyeshadow and black eyeliner made her brown eyes deeper. Her lips were painted with a purple so dark it was almost black.

"It feels like too much," she admitted, fingering the dripping crystalline earrings that matched the pins in her hair.

"I think you look beautiful," Lex said, coming further into the room. Xavia turned and her jaw dropped as she took in Lex. Their dreads were tied back at the nape, flowing to their waist. They were decked out in a cream suit that complimented their rich brown skin. Lex wore no shirt, just the jacket, allowing their chest to be slightly exposed. They looked stunning and happy. Never one to leave heritage at the door, Lex wore a choker of cowry shells around their neck.

"Me? You look stunning!" Xavia said as she looked down at herself, still in her terry cloth robe. Lex clucked their teeth.

"Stop it." A grin spread across their face. "You should see Lilith." Xavia barked out a laugh.

"That's why you're smiling so hard right now."

Lex gave a bow of their head.

"Mind if I help you?" They approached the dress on the bed. Lex whistled, taking in the stunning piece of art. "Let's get this on. I'm sure this is going to look better on you than on the bed." They smirked. Xavia begrudgingly nodded. Lex held the dress so that Xavia could step into it. As the fabric slid across her skin, goosebumps broke out. It was impossibly soft, and lightweight. She assumed it would feel heavy and cumbersome. "Holy Kutiel, Xavia. If you didn't have two males already pining after you..." Lex murmured, turning her to the floor length mirror.

Xavia's breath caught in her throat as she looked herself over. There was no way this was her, was it? The dress was sleeveless, the sweetheart bodice hugging her curves and pushing her golden tan breasts up for full view. Except for the see-through strap to hold the bodice together, the dress was backless and dipped to the small of her back, putting her large galaxy tattoo on full display. Under her bodice, the dress flowed out, swirling in colors of dark magenta, plum, and turquoise. It was a nebula, surrounding her with space and starlight. Lex held up a choker with a crescent moon and helped place it around her neck.

"Who am I?" Xavia whispered. Lex handed her a mask, black with small star shaped crystals rising from it. It was meant to cover her face to the top of her lips, the stars rising toward her hair to form a tiara. Before putting it on, a knock came from her door, making her almost jump out of her skin. Lex put a warm hand on her forearm, lending a calming energy. Aurelio walked into the room, looking down at his cuffs, fixing them. If she wasn't breathing before, she was choking now.

It was clear that Aurelio had no idea how sexy he looked. He was dressed in a navy suit that fit every muscle on his body. The dark steel vest complimented his silver eyes, making them shine. He had a fresh haircut, low on the top and shaped up around the scalp. His beard had been trimmed, framing his chin and full lips in a disastrously gorgeous way. Xavia couldn't believe that he was hers.

"Are you ready?" Aurelio said before looking up. His eyes instantly darkened as he drank her in. He looked at Lex. "Can I have a moment?" His words sounded choked, as if he couldn't breathe. Lex gave Xavia a warm smile before nodding and leaving the suite with a click of the door.

Aurelio advanced on Xavia before she could blink, his lips crashing into hers. Electricity skittered against her skin when their lips connected, making her shudder. She leaned into him, arms going around his neck. She moaned when his hands slid down her naked back to cup her ass. He smelled of petrichor, rain, and fresh air. His storm swept over her, making her heart race. He broke the hot kiss to rest his forehead on hers.

"Hey…"

"Hey," Xavia said softly against his lips. He kissed her again, filling her with molten lava that pooled in her core. Their tongues danced, teeth nipping at each other's lips. She gripped the back of his head, feeling him hardening against the front of her. He broke the kiss, seeming to have a hard time getting control of himself.

"How am I going to focus tonight with you looking so fuckable in this dress?" Aurelio murmured, hands gripping her ass harder bringing a soft gasp from her. He kissed her neck, nipping at the soft flesh. "Fuck, Xavia," he hissed as she licked up his neck. He pushed her against the vanity, sitting her on it. "Baby, if we don't stop, I'm going to fuck you in this dress." She took hold of his jaw, looking into his hot gaze.

"Then fuck me." Xavia hiked up the skirts of her dress, grabbing his hand and putting it on her dripping pussy. She didn't bother with panties. Aurelio let out a groan, shrugging out of his jacket before dipping two fingers in her. A moan escaped her lips before she bit his lower lip. His eyes never left hers as he shifted her hips closer. She heard him unbuckle his pants and then his fingers were replaced with the head of his cock. She wrapped her legs around him as he plunged inside of her. She gasped in pleasure, nails digging into his head making him moan.

"Fuck Xavia," Aurelio growled, holding her hips as he drove his cock in and out of her.

"Say my name again," she panted as he gripped her.

"Xavia," he whispered against her lips, making her buck against him. She pulled him closer, arms around his neck. "Xavia," he said louder, pumping faster. Her pussy clenched around his cock, the pleasure overcoming her. Xavia bit his neck hard enough to leave teeth marks. "Fuck, Xavia!" Aurelio growled, fucking her for all that she was worth. "Please," he said as he slowed to a torturous pace. "Xavia, please." She knew what he was asking. She gripped his chin, making sure their eyes were connected.

"Come for me baby," Xavia said as she got closer to her edge. She cried out as he picked up the pace and slammed into her, bringing her over the edge in a screaming orgasm. He released himself in her, taking her lips in a hot kiss. He pulled away, looking into her eyes, as if waiting. It was all there. What he felt. What he didn't say. The expectations. The hope. The need for approval. She smiled sweetly.

"Good boy," she whispered against his lips, making him shudder. He gripped her hips once more before they untangled from each other. They chuckled as they attempted to fix the other one up. She ran into the bathroom to make sure she was presentable; she didn't want cum dripping down her leg in front of the King. She had a goofy smile on her face as she stepped out of the bathroom but stopped in her tracks when she saw Quade enter the room.

The room felt smaller, the air sucking out of it at a rapid pace. She couldn't tear her gaze away from his even if she wanted to. Whoever dressed them knew exactly what they were doing. Quade's suit was a plum so rich, it made his eyes look like sunset during the fall. He wore a black button-up shirt with a matching plum and black corset vest. His hair had also been freshly cut, black strands combed back, beard freshly shaped up. The instant fire in his eyes made her squirm. His hands opened and closed into fists, shoulders rising and falling as he took deep breaths. She wanted those hands on her. His eyes slid to Aurelio who leaned on the vanity with a smirk. He fixed the cuff of his shirt, eyeing the both of them.*

"Don't let me stop you," Aurelio said with a raised eyebrow. The corset made Quade's hips sway as he stalked toward her, making her heart flutter in her throat. His lips crashed into hers and she opened to him in a moan while a hand of his came to her neck, thumb gliding up and down the center of her throat. His other hand was a hot trail down her back, fire from his hands leaving delicious licks of pain across her skin. Xavia ran her hands over his corset, the fabric smooth and the ribbing firm under her fingers. Fuck, seeing him in a corset made her core throb.

"A corset?" she breathed against his lips.

"Yes brat," he growled against her lips. "When we were fitted,

♪ "Dangerous Woman" by Ariana Grande

they asked my preference."

"It's sexy as fuck."

His hand at her neck tightened, ever so slightly, as he took her lip in between his teeth and bit down hard enough to make her whimper. Shit, how did her makeup stay still?

"I'm going to fuck you, right here, right now." Quade pushed her toward the bed and she let out a gasp as her ass hit the edge of the mattress.

"But… Wait." Xavia was trying to catch her breath, looking from him to Aurelio in question. What she saw, she wasn't expecting. Heat and absolute lust plagued his eyes. Quade gripped her chin and snapped her attention back to him.

"Don't look at him. You look at me," he growled. Xavia nodded and squeaked when he flipped her to bend her over the bed. He pushed her dress up over her hips, exposing her to him. He dropped to his knees. "Fuck, no panties?" Quade murmured, mouth finding her already wet cunt. She let out a moan, gripping the blankets. He spread her open so that he could have better access, the flat of his tongue running over her clit. His teeth grazed over it, making her shiver. His tongue plunged into her, bringing a moan out her lips.

"I can taste him in you," Quade said darkly. The lust in his voice took her breath away. Xavia heard rustling before she felt the blunt head of his cock at her opening. "So wet," he said before slapping her ass and thrusting into her. "My brat," he groaned as he pumped into her deliciously sore pussy. Her eyes rolled as she felt every sensation.

"Holy Etis and Sortis," Xavia whimpered before turning her head to look at Aurelio. She could see his cock straining against his pants. His steel eyes communicated with hers and she nodded. "Come here," she commanded. He walked up to her right as Quade gave her ass another slap. She licked her lips. "Dick out. Put it in my mouth." Aurelio hesitated, even though his body said otherwise. Quade slapped her ass hard enough that she knew she'd have hand prints again.

"Do what she says Cap." Quade's voice was dark and

commanding. This would be the only situation in which he could take that tone with Aurelio. Quade pulled Xavia away from the bed long enough for Aurelio to slide in and sit before her. She stopped eye to eye with him as she put her hands on either side of his hips.

"Are you sure?" Aurelio murmured against her lips. She licked his lips slowly, drawing out a groan from him. Quade slowed his pace enough for them to figure out what this meant for them. She wasn't even sure. She had storm and fire surrounding her, caught between Aurelio and Quade. They recognized the wildness that was Xavia in different ways. The emotions threatened to drown her as she tried to process it all. This moment between them was momentous. It solidified what they had and it proved she needed them both as much as they needed her.

"Do what I tell you," Xavia said, nipping his lip. It was all he needed to drop any lingering resistance, sliding his pants down to free his cock for her to take into her mouth. She licked the tip, tasting the lingering remnants of their sex, before taking him in completely. Quade gripped her ass, spreading her so that he could get a better look at thrusting in and out of her. Aurelio groaned, raising his hips while Xavia bobbed down. She wrapped her teeth with her lips as she took him in, his girth filling her mouth while Quade fucked her. She gripped the base of Aurelio's cock tightly enough to make him moan.

"Shit. Suck my dick just like that, baby," he breathed as she sucked harder. As if reading each other's mind, the two males shocked her with their Wielding at the same time. Quade danced flames along her ass, leaving a trail of hot pleasurable pain. Aurelio's hands sparked where he held her shoulder, sending shocks down her spine. She pulled away with a gasp. There was a sudden stillness as the two males looked at each other with her in the middle. Whatever was communicated between them could only be described as years of friendship and this coming together moment. Suddenly Quade slid out of her, making her yelp in frustration.

"Sit on his dick Xavia," Quade commanded, walking to the vanity.

"We're going to ruin this dress." Xavia huffed.

"Easily remedied," Aurelio said, unhooking the back and slipping it down her now naked body. He motioned for her to step out of the pooled dress and then tossed it safely on the bed.

"But the ball!" she yelped as Aurelio pulled her close.

"We can be late," Quade said from behind her, having taken a bottle of oil from the vanity. A thrill ran up her spine making her shiver. He closed in on her, sandwiching her between him and Aurelio. "Get on his dick Xavia." Xavia let out a gasp as Aurelio snatched her up and slid her on top of his cock.

"Shit, you feel so good," Aurelio groaned as he kissed her neck, running his tongue up until he bit at her earlobe, sucking in her earring and tugging it. A sharp pain shot down to her core at the tug. She rocked her hips, grinding on him. She felt Quade against her back, making her turn her head to look at him. He wrapped a hand around her throat, gripping but not roughly. Xavia squeaked when she felt Quade's oiled fingers at the puckering of her asshole.

"Didn't I say I was going to fuck you in your ass?" he growled as he slowly slid his finger in. The sensation of his finger and Aurelio's cock in her made her jerk in pleasure. When Quade added a second finger, her eyes rolled and she moaned.

"Holy Etis and Sortis," Xavia breathed, taking hold of the back of Aurelio's neck to keep herself upright.

"Bend," Quade murmured, leaning her so that her forehead rested against Aurelio's. Quade's cock teased her ass, making her gasp against Aurelio's lips. There was a slight burning as he pushed past her barrier, making her close her eyes in pleasure, before he was fully seated in her ass. Xavia was filled to the brim, her body thrumming. As if they shared one mind, both males started to move, torturing her deliciously with their slow strokes.

"Oh shit," Xavia breathed, her body flushed and hot as she writhed and moved her hips in time with them. They found a rhythm that had them getting closer to the edge. It was perfect unison between the three of them, as if this was how it always should have been. Aurelio took Xavia's hand and placed it around his throat, mimicking Quade's hold around hers. She pushed him back so that he laid on the bed, the three of them shifting ever so slightly. Aurelio groaned as she gripped him.

"Shit. Who would've thought that'd be hot to see?" Quade groaned from behind, hand tightening on her throat. Xavia moaned, the sensations taking her over. She lightened her hold on Aurelio enough for him to take a long shuddering breath. Quade did the same for her, the euphoria overcoming her. The pace picked up as Quade pumped into her, making her rock against Aurelio.

"Never thought I'd enjoy watching another male's hand around her throat," Aurelio gasped, gripping her hips tightly.

"Both of you shut up. I'm going to come if you keep talking this way," Xavia whined, tightening her grip on Aurelio at the same time as Quade tightened his. Perfect unison. They released at the same time, flooding her with pleasure. Quade moved one hand to her hip, steadying her as she rocked between them. Unconsciously, the two males locked hands, intertwining their fingers together as they held her hips. The moment filled her with so much emotion that she thought she would explode.

"Fuck, I can feel Aurelio inside you," Quade groaned, Aurelio following suit. "Come on his dick while I fill up your ass," Quade growled, fucking her harder. Tears of pure pleasure dripped down her face as Quade returned his grip to her neck tightly. She bucked between them as Quade lightened his grip enough to flood her system with that high. Xavia screamed as Aurelio thrust his hips into her. As soon as she lightened her grip on him, the three of them reached their orgasm together. She felt hot streams of their sex leaking from her, making a mess of the bed. Xavia collapsed on Aurelio, panting.

"I bet you my makeup is messed up," she huffed with a giggle. She was feeling a high she never felt before. One that could only be achieved by getting caught in the middle of these two males of hers.

"Hold our woman," Quade murmured, rubbing gentle strokes on her ass to soothe the sting of his slaps. His words made her puff up with pride. Aurelio stood, helping her wrap her arms around him. It was then that she realized her body was trembling from the pleasure. They pulled out of her slowly, making her groan at the

334 | A.E. COSBY

empty feeling.

Aurelio pulled her close, Quade coming in at her back. Quade's fire at her back, Aurelio's storm at her front. Xavia turned slightly to look at them both. She kissed Quade and he returned it sweetly, letting her know that he would always take care of her and reward her. She turned to Aurelio and took his chin to bring his lips to hers, his kiss fiercer but letting her know that he was hers to command. The males looked to each other, Aurelio seeming at a loss for words. Something communicated between them. Quade's gaze turned soft as he reached a hand to cup Aurelio's cheek.

"I'm... not sure," the Storm Wielder said softly. "I've never felt this way for a man." His throat bobbed as he leaned his forehead against Quade's. "Is it..."

"Kissing a man is the same as kissing a woman." Xavia's eyebrows lifted in surprise and Quade shrugged. She watched as Aurelio leaned in and met Quade's lips with his own. It was soft, as if Aurelio was unsure of himself. She had to stifle a moan at the sight of Quade pulling Aurelio closer, her body sandwiched tighter. Their kiss exploded, tongues licking at each other and the Fire Wielder taking the Storm Wielder's lip between his teeth. They groaned as they broke apart and turned their gazes down at Xavia. One lit up with lightning, the other with fire. She could feel their erections pressing into her and this time, she let out a soft moan.

"We're gonna be even more late, aren't we?"

CHAPTER 47
AURELIO

A SWIRL OF EMOTIONS RAN through Aurelio. It was a quiet storm, overtaking him in the best way. He had never felt attracted to a male before. It completely surprised him when he realized how attracted he was to Quade during their rope session. Had it been building over time? Was it because the three of them had formed a bond he couldn't explain? Aurelio wasn't sure but he knew he was interested in exploring more.*

Quade growled, "Yes, brat." He slipped out of his jacket, remaining in the corset that hugged his figure. Shit it made his ass look good. "Lose the shirt Cap." Aurelio was more than happy to oblige, tossing it on a nearby chair. Quade put a hand on Xavia's shoulder and forced her to her knees between them. "Stroke it." Aurelio watched, erection aching. She did as she was told, eyes up to Quade in supplication. There was something hot about watching her submit. Quade raised his fiery gaze to Aurelio. "His too," he commanded. Aurelio was speechless for a moment while Xavia took hold his cock.

"Oh fuck…" Aurelio breathed as Xavia started pumping them both, her eyes dark with desire. She watched Aurelio as she took him into her hot mouth, lips wrapping around his girth. He gripped her hair, pumping into her mouth. Fuck it, they'll fix her hair later. He shut his eyes as he groaned.

"Eyes on her, Cap," Quade growled. Aurelio's eyes snapped

♪ "Sugar" by Sleep Token

open, his gaze landing on Quade's before looking down at Xavia. Her head bobbed, cock going in and out of her mouth. Quade groaned as she pumped him faster, drawing Aurelio's eyes to her hand gripped on Quade. Fuck. The Fire Wielder gripped Aurelio's hand in Xavia's hair and pushed her harder onto his cock. "Fuck her mouth."

"Yes, Sir." Aurelio responded, with a devious smirk as Quade's eyes widened with lust. Xavia moaned, rubbing her thighs together. Aurelio thrusted harder, hitting the back of her throat while Quade held her to him. He pulled out when Xavia gagged, saliva dripping from her mouth and tears leaking from her eyes. "Ma'am, messy looks good on you." He grinned as her eyes widened.

"My turn, brat." Quade pulled her from Aurelio and drove his cock into her mouth while she jerked Aurelio off. "Fuck, yes. That's my good brat." Quade groaned. Aurelio turned his gaze to Quade, finding his already on him. "Come here," he said firmly. Aurelio could feel his heartbeat in his throat as he shifted closer to Quade. "Can I touch you?" he asked softly, bringing his lips close to Aurelio's.

"Oh shit." Xavia moaned, having popped off Quade's dick.

"Shut the fuck up. I didn't tell you to stop," he growled, pulling her back to him. Aurelio smirked as Xavia whimpered, increasing her pace. Quade looked at Aurelio, eyebrows raised in question. He appreciated that his Lieutenant asked. He respected the hell out of him for understanding that this was Aurelio's first time. He watched the fire dance in the male's eyes and nodded. "I need you to speak Cap." Quade grunted as Xavia sucked him down.

"Yes. You can touch me, Q." He was pulled in for a kiss, Quade's tongue licking at the seam of his lips. Aurelio opened for him, their tongues slowly rubbing against each other. His cock jolted in Xavia's hand as she pumped him faster in time with her head bobbing on Quade. Kissing a man was both like and unlike kissing a woman. It was more intense, the aggression fueling it. Maybe it was because it was Quade, who sucked in Aurelio's lower lip between his teeth and bit him. Aurelio moaned as he pulled Quade closer, sucking on the male's lower lip. Quade groaned as he broke the kiss.

"We only go as far as you want," he breathed against Aurelio's lips. Quade rested his hand on Aurelio's stomach, gliding over the muscles, making him flex. He was asking permission again. This was a different Quade than he knew. It was fucking sexy.

Aurelio nodded in gratitude and said, "Stop teasing me. I said you could touch me, so fucking touch me." Aurelio raised an eyebrow to a very shocked Quade.

"Don't tell me you're gonna be a brat too..." Quade growled as he slid his hand down to rest on Xavia's. Aurelio could feel her hot gaze on him, gauging his reaction while Quade took over and gripped his cock. Aurelio shuddered, Quade's grip stronger and hand more calloused. Xavia moaned around Quade's cock as she watched the male stroke Aurelio.

"Holy shit, man." Aurelio bit his lip at the sensation, trying not to roll his eyes back, hips pushing forward. He curled his fingers in Quade's hair, making him groan.

"Brat, finger yourself. You're not forgotten," Quade told Xavia while his eyes remained on Aurelio. "You like my hand on your dick." It wasn't a question. Aurelio nodded, moaning as Quade picked up the pace. "Tell me you like my hand on your dick." He gripped Aurelio, making him jolt in pleasure.

"Fuck, yes. I like your hand on my dick, sir." Aurelio couldn't help himself. He was at their mercy. Quade's eyes flared as he grasped Aurelio's jaw and kissed him for all that he was worth. Quade's tongue thrust into his mouth, making him moan against his lips. The Fire Wielder sucked on Aurelio's tongue, making him jerk against his hand. He took Quade's lip between his teeth, making him groan as he bit and pulled back with a pop. Aurelio looked down at Xavia, watching as she slid her fingers deep inside her pussy. There was a mischievous glint in her dark eyes. Quade hissed, looking down at Xavia

"Did you just fucking bite me?" He pulled out of her, grabbing her chin and pulling her up to stand. She licked her lips with a devilish smirk.

"Yes. I need one of you to fuck me right now or I'm going to scream," she whined. Aurelio almost whined himself when Quade let him go. The male locked his fingers in Xavia's hair, pulling her head back.

"Open your fucking mouth," Quade snapped. It surprised Aurelio how quickly she responded. Fuck, their energy was something else. "Cap, spit in her mouth."

"What?" Aurelio stuttered. "Why?" He'd never done that before and the thought had him aching more.

"To show her that she's ours." As Quade dripped saliva into Xavia's mouth, Aurelio found himself gripping his own cock to keep from coming right there and then. If Xavia's moan was indication, she enjoyed it as much as he enjoyed watching. Was he a voyeur? "Xavia, look at Cap." She turned her gaze to him and whimpered as she waited for him. Holy fucking shit. He could feel his gaze darkening as he hovered over her and gripped her chin.

"Are you ours?" he growled against her lips. Her eyes widened at his rare show of dominance. She nodded.

"Yes," she breathed.

"Good." He hummed in pleasure before letting his saliva drip into her mouth. Who knew this would be such a fucking turn on? Quade leaned in and joined him, the both of them making a claim on her.

"Please, someone fuck me," Xavia moaned after swallowing.

"Untie me." Quade said. She made quick work releasing him from the corset and they slipped out of their remaining clothes. Aurelio scooped Xavia up, making her squeal.

"May I fuck your ass, Ma'am?" he purred into her ear.

"Fuck, Cap. You really are a good boy." Quade groaned, watching while Aurelio dropped Xavia on the bed. The praise made him glow inside.

"Yes. Be a good boy and fuck it." Xavia made sure to snatch the oil from the nightstand and gave it to him. "Fuck it good and deep." She yelped as he pulled her on top of him, back flush with his chest. He gripped her breasts, pinching her hardened nipples and making her moan. She writhed on top of him as Quade crawled onto the bed. Oh fuck. He moved like a lion stalking its prey. Aurelio shifted Xavia forward to cover her ass in oil. Quade gripped her chin to give her a hot and aggressive kiss. Aurelio put a finger in her puckered hole, making her jolt and whimper against Quade's lips. He slid his finger in and out while Quade licked and bit at her lips. She gasped when he added a second finger.

"Fuck, so tight." Aurelio groaned before adding a third. Xavia broke her kiss with Quade.

"Aurelio!" she moaned, grinding her hips against his hard cock resting between them. "I need you to fill me up, right now," she commanded.

"Yes Ma'am." He removed his fingers, hooking his arms under knees to lift her and hover over his cock.

"Quade, put his dick in me. Please," she whined breathlessly.

"Happy to oblige." Quade wrapped his hand around Aurelio's cock, making him moan. He held it while Aurelio lowered Xavia's ass on his cock.

"Fuck." He groaned, slowly lifting her off before lowering again, allowing him to go deeper. Quade kept his hand on Aurelio's cock as he worked deeper into Xavia.

"That's it. You give it so well." Xavia moaned as Quade removed his hand so that Aurelio could be fully seated in her. He leaned her back and spread her legs further, baring her to Quade who groaned.

"Fuck."

QUADE

QUADE WAS PARTIALLY IN SHOCK at the thought he was actually doing this with Aurelio. It did something to his gut and the space where his heart should be. This bond that the three of them formed was nothing like he expected. He'd never been the relationship type but he was willing to try for them. For Aurelio and Xavia, he would try just about anything.

As Quade lapped at Xavia's clit, he watched Aurelio thrust into her ass. She grabbed Quade by the hair, digging her fingers and grinding her cunt on his mouth. He spread her, dipping in two fingers. She gasped as he sucked on her clit and added a third. He hooked his fingers, hitting the soft button that made her cry out, and her juices flowed over his hand, soaking Aurelio and the bed.

"Fuck, I can feel your fingers Q." Aurelio groaned as he bucked his hips, thrusting in her harder.

"Oh, just wait." Quade growled against Xavia's pussy as he added a fourth finger, stopping at the first set of knuckles. "Brat, you're gonna take this whole hand." She braced her hands on either side of Aurelio to slightly sit up. Xavia gasped as Quade fucked her, widening her further.

"I can't. No," she moaned, as Aurelio slowed his grind, allowing Quade to take his time. She whimpered as Quade slowly stroked her, feeling her relax as she took his fingers.

"You're taking it so good, brat." Her arousal soaked his hand as he moved deeper in her, almost to the second set knuckles. "You're so wet. You're all over me and Aurelio." At the sound of his name, Aurelio groaned and thrust into Xavia, making her yelp.

"Yes. Do it. Fuck I feel so full," she breathed. Aurelio held her as he sat up, holding her against his chest. He continued to grind his hips against her, cock driving in and out.

"Watch him, baby. Watch how good you take it." Aurelio growled in her ear, shocking Quade. By the blown look on Xavia's face, she was equally as surprised. Her pussy gushed as Quade moved deeper up to the base of his thumb. He took it an inch at a time, stretching her until his hand was fully seated in her.

"Holy shit!" she cried out, watching him as he moved inside her. Her pussy gripped him as he massaged her channel, rubbing her g-spot.

"Hmm. Come for me," Quade said, lips at her neck. He pumped gently as she clenched around him and her orgasm burst through her.

"Fuck! Quade!" she yelled as she bucked, legs shaking.

"Fuck. That's a sexy sight," Aurelio breathed, watching

Quade. "Shit, I can feel you." Quade brushed the thin membrane, grazing Aurelio's cock and feeling it twitch. Fuck, his cock ached. He slowly pulled his hand out.

"Lay back," he growled as he hovered over them in between their legs. Aurelio kept his arms hooked under Xavia's knees. Quade's mouth found Xavia's while he spread her arousal on Aurelio's lips. The male licked and sucked the juices off his fingers, making Quade groan. Fuck, he learned fast. Xavia whimpered into his mouth as she bit his lower lip and suckled on the blood she drew. He growled as he drove his cock in her, making her and Aurelio moan.

"Fuck!" Xavia screamed as Quade swirled his hips and thrusted deep inside her. Aurelio bucked his hips at the same time as Quade.

"Shit. Fuck." Aurelio bit into Xavia's shoulder and she whimpered, tears of pleasure leaking from her eyes.

"You like that, Cap? The feeling of my dick so close to yours in her pussy?" Quade growled, fucking harder and deeper. Aurelio nodded, fighting to keep his gaze on Quade. "Use your words."

"Yes, your dick feels good so close to mine, Sir," he whimpered.

"Fuck, I like it when you call me 'Sir'." Never would it happen outside of the bedroom and that gave Quade a sense of pride.

"Quade..." Xavia moaned, getting his attention. "Please. I'm going to come," she whined, moving her hips against them. Being as tall as he was, Quade propped himself on his hand, lips close to Aurelio's. Their pace quickened, Xavia gushing over them.

"Fuck, Xavia. Come on our dicks." Quade thrusted into her and captured Aurelio's mouth with his own, their kiss all tongues and teeth. He could feel the orgasm building at the base of his spine. Xavia clenched him tightly as she screamed out her pleasure.

"Shit Q." Aurelio groaned against Quade's lips.

"Be a good boy and come in her ass. Fill her up." Quade's words were their undoing as their movements became a frenzy. Xavia shuddered as she came, sobbing in pleasure. Quade captured her moans with his mouth, kissing her thoroughly and deeply. He bit her lip, making her bleed and he lapped at it.

"Fuck, I'm coming!" Aurelio roared, slamming into Xavia in

unison with Quade. They came at the same time, filling her with their cum. It overflowed out of her and over their cocks. Quade's whole body shuddered, sweat covering them all. Fuck, the King was going to be pissed at their tardiness. Too fucking bad.

"I have no words," Xavia said breathlessly. Quade helped Aurelio put her legs down. He massaged her thighs and hips. She softly moaned while Aurelio gave her soft kisses on her shoulder. Each of them groaned as they disentangled themselves, their bodies thoroughly fucked. As they sat up, Xavia rose to her knees to kiss him. "This was more than anything I've ever experienced before," she said softly before leaning behind her to pull Aurelio in for a kiss.

"I can't find the words either," Quade admitted. It was unexpected but it was glorious. He gazed at the two people who meant the most to him. He took hold of Aurelio's chin. "I didn't expect this," he murmured.

"I didn't either," Aurelio said as he leaned in and kissed Quade. The kiss was full of passion and fervor. As they broke from the kiss, they turned to Xavia and they rested their foreheads on hers.

"We're each other's," she said, emotion thick in her voice.

"We're each other's," they said at the same time.

CHAPTER 48

JACINTO

JACINTO GLARED AT CYRUS while they sat on the dais. "Where the fuck are they?" he growled. The table to his left sat Norrix with two of his demon henchmen, all wearing harlequin masks that obscured their faces entirely. The one to the right, for the Asherites, was missing three members. One of whom was the bounty hunter that Norrix so desperately wanted.

The ballroom floor in front of him was filled with patrons, citizens and politicians alike, dancing or standing at high top tables conversing. Servers carried food and drinks throughout the room, wearing black and white masks. Black sheer fabric covered the ceiling with star-like crystals sparkling to mimic the night sky. There was a raucous of nebula colors; navy, purple, and dark magenta. One could swear they stepped into space when entering the ballroom.

Jacinto unbuttoned the top two buttons of his black button up, frustrated with having to wear dress clothes at all. His shirt was tucked into a pair of black slacks which he finished off with all black sneakers. His face was obscured with a half mask on one side, covering his forehead, down to his chin. He slouched in the chair, anger seeping into his bones at having to wait.

"Ponerse derecho," Cyrus muttered, returning Jacinto's glare. The King growled, the sound vibrating from his chest. His Hand was in his element, dressed in a burnt orange suit that made his ebony skin glow, and dark brown shoes. "I assume they wanted to make an entrance?" Cyrus said, nodding to the entrance.

Two males, one the color of fire, the other of fresh storm clouds, entered. Though their masks were meant to obscure them, he knew who they were by their coloring. Aurelio, Captain of Special Forces and the Guard, and Quade, Second in Command and Lieutenant. Storm and Fire Wielders respectively. A familiar pull in Jacinto's chest made him stand up. He ignored Cyrus as he stepped down from the dais. Was she here?

The two males parted and his heart stopped as the female plaguing his dreams came into view. Even with the mask on, he knew who she was by the cord that seemed to connect them. While not as taut as the last time he saw her, he would recognize it anywhere. She was stunning in the dress that flowed around her like a nebula. Her deep golden-brown skin shone under the lights, the dress hugging her thick and generous body. Was she the bounty hunter Norrix wanted? This changed his plans. He refused to let Norrix have her. He stalked toward her, picking up on the racing of her heart. She smelled of the males beside her and sex. Was that why they were late? He mused. He sidled up to her, ignoring the males to her sides.

"Señorita Silveria, I presume?" his dark voice husky. The one to her left bristled, the Fire Wielder. He smirked as he met her eyes through his own mask. They were a different color, brown, and it confused him momentarily. Her plum colored, full lips had parted, her pulse hammering in her throat. Her throat bobbed before she nodded.

"Xavia. Pleasure to make your acquaintance," that voice, rich and honeyed. Jacinto looked her over, her hair was different too.

"No need for formality, come, please sit with us." Jacinto motioned to the table up at the dais, arm held out for her to hold. He watched her hesitate, looking at the males beside her. "I promise to return her safely to your arms, caballeros," his tone dark, begging them to deny him. He was in the mood for violence.

The Fire Wielder, Quade, clenched his jaw tight enough that Jacinto thought he was going to snap his teeth. The Storm Wielder, Aurelio, had better control. He nodded to Xavia who then took

Jacinto's arm. It felt as if someone let out a swarm of bees under his skin as her hand lit up his forearm. She let out a barely audible gasp, letting him know she felt it too. What the fuck was this between them?

"Should I address you as King or?" She peered up at him occasionally from behind her mask, slightly taller in the heels she wore.

"Jacinto is fine." He walked slowly, the males trailing behind them. "I'm glad you took me up on my invitation. Although, I was under the impression that you were working alone, not with the Asherites." He felt her hesitate and looked at her, their gazes locking. That pulling of energy tightened, causing him to lean in involuntarily. There was confusion and caution in her eyes. Her eyes fluttered a bit before she seemed to get a hold of herself, shaking her head. Something was different about her, her scent changed. "Was I wrong?"

"No, I..." Xavia's attention snapped to the far wall which held a large mural of graffiti and urban art. "Wow," she breathed. He smiled.

"Want to see it better?" Jacinto asked, startling her out of wherever her mind went. She nodded and then turned to the males behind them.

"I'll be a moment," she raised an eyebrow at Aurelio whose nose flared in frustration. Her face changed, placating almost, as she looked to Quade. His scowl told Jacinto everything he needed to know. This one was the dominant one, the other more submissive. With a nod from the Fire Wielder, they walked to the Asherite table.

"Interesting dynamic," Jacinto murmured as they walked to the mural.

"Ah. It's complicated," Xavia huffed uncomfortably.

"It's clear you're their world." She shifted, looking up at him again. "I can't say I'm surprised." That pull between them jolted, bringing them closer. Her eyes fluttered again, as if blinking some foreign object out of her eyes. "Are you okay?" She stepped away.

"Ah..." Xavia cleared her throat. "Yes. Sorry. I've only ever met royalty once. I apologize if I'm awkward." She looked away from him to take in the art before her. "Who's the artist? It looks like mixed media. Acrylic paint and spray paint?"

"Correct. I'm the artist." She snapped her head to look at him again. Jacinto laughed, running a hand through his hair. "¿Qué? I can't be an artist because I'm a king?" Color rose to her cheeks, making them rosy under her skin.

"I'm sorry!" Xavia laughed. "It surprised me. I think it's awesome." She ran her hands over the grooves of raised acrylic meant for texture. "This must've taken a long time," she murmured. She was right. It took him months to complete but it was one of his favorite pieces in the Palacio.

"Do you paint?" Jacinto asked, fighting with all his will to keep from touching her; to figure out what this bond was. It may not be as strong as it was when they first met, but it still intrigued him.

"I used to. When I was younger," she tried to suppress the sadness in her voice, waving a hand. "I don't have the time now."

"Ah right. Bounty hunter, sí?" Xavia snorted with a nod.

"Yeah," she turned to him, letting out a soft squeak at how close he was, and tripped on her heels. Jacinto reached out to steady her, catching her under her elbows. The cord between them yanked tight, making him pull her in. "What is that?" Xavia breathed, trying to understand the energy between them, rubbing her chest.

"You don't remember?" Jacinto frowned; something was definitely different. She shook her head, looking equally perplexed.

"No, I—" The sound of a champagne bottle popping drew her attention, making her jolt and lean into him. "Seriously, what the fuck?" Her eyes snapped to him. "I'm sorry. I didn't mean to..." She raised her hands to her face, clearly embarrassed. He chuckled, gently moving her hands from her face before letting go.

"I'm a king, but also a fucking person. You can speak freely around me." Jacinto raised an eyebrow. "Dance with me?"

"Oh. No. These feet don't dance." Xavia huffed a chuckle.

"Somehow I feel like that's untrue," he said with humor in his voice. She sighed with a nod and he pulled her to the dance floor just as a fast paced, rhythmic song began. The sounds of bongos and trumpets blended with trap beats playing.

"I've never heard music like this," she admired, her body instinctively moving to the beat.*

"Is music in Asherai so boring?" He feigned surprise, making her chuckle. "May I?" he asked, holding his hand out as if to take her hand in one and the other at her waist. Xavia paused, looking up to him with curious brown eyes. She nodded, having made her decision. He pulled her in, making her gasp. "It is called merengue." That was when he started to move, guiding her hips to sway in time with his. The bounty hunter laughed as he twirled her before bringing her back in. He could live for the sound of her laughter.

"It's wonderful!" she gasped, breathless. They bounced on the balls of their feet, Jacinto showing her how to step in between his at the right time.

"I told you, I'm not just a king," he said softly into her ear, making her shiver. He spun their bodies before she could respond. Xavia moved through the motions of the dance with flawless ease, as if she'd done it all her life.

"I'm learning that," she laughed as the song blended into another. They walked to the edge of the dance floor, panting. Xavia put a hand on a column, groaning. "Fuck, I'm not used to heels. I wish I could toss these." She let out a yelp as Jacinto pulled her behind the column, away from the eyes of others. He knelt in front of her and took hold of her ankle. "What–" she let out a soft moan as he pulled her shoe off to massage her foot before moving to the other.

"No one says you have to wear these," he chuckled as he stood and handed her the heels before they stepped away from the column. He nodded to his sneakers. "If I didn't have to, I'd never wear a suit again." She made to respond but locked eyes with her men and stepped away from him.

"Thank you for the dance and teaching me about Ayobaí through music," she said with a genuine smile. "I believe you wanted to have a meeting. We can do so later, after?" Reluctantly Jacinto gave her a nod.

♪ "Muñequita Linda" by Juan Magán, Deorro, MAKJ, YFN Lucci

348 | A.E. COSBY

He watched her, eyes dropping to the swell of her ass, as she walked away from him. A growl vibrated in his chest as he watched her sit between the Wielders and smile. He was going to figure out what this invisible cord between them meant. When he was near her, he felt powerful, as if she filled his cup. His gaze shifted to Norrix who had his head turned to Xavia. He nodded to his demons, two of which left the table to blend into the crowd.

"Cin." Cyrus's voice came beside him. He had also noticed what Jacinto noticed. "The spymaster left a report on Norrix." The urgent tone of his voice made Jacinto shift his gaze to Cyrus. "He's amassed a host of demons on the outskirts of Malagado in Milagros. But we have another problem." Jacinto lifted an eyebrow, Cyrus's eyes flaring. "They plan to kidnap the bounty hunter." He felt on edge, like a wolf with their hackles raised.

"Not before I do." Jacinto hissed, Cyrus raised an eyebrow in question. "She's mine."

CHAPTER 49

XAVIA

QUADE AND AURELIO WEREN'T pleased with her dance with Jacinto. They made it their business to touch her and even danced with her in between them. Briefly, as their bodies writhed together, she forgot about their mission. She lived in the bliss between her two partners. Her body became feverish as Aurelio kissed her lips while Quade kissed her neck, the three of them lost in their wild storm. When the song changed, they made their way back to the table and she plopped down, exhausted. Her feet ached, having put her heels back on.

The ballroom started to feel hot. After having her fill of food and rum, she was ready to call it a night, or at least get some air. There was something about Jacinto that had her questioning her sanity. The pull she felt to him was as if they were magnets, or two cosmic beings that were once adrift but had found each other again. It was like her energetic battery had been plugged in and lit her up. There was something familiar about him, as if she had met him before. The feeling of rightness was hard to ignore. The way her core pulled toward him as if an invisible rope had latched around her and he was the anchor. Guilt ate at her. How could she feel this when she had two amazing males at her side?

"I need some air," Xavia said to Aurelio and Quade. They had made sure to sit her between them, which both warmed her and annoyed her. It was as if they needed to prove she was theirs, as if it wasn't already evident. They made to stand but she put a hand on each of their arms. "No, it's ok. I'm a grown ass woman,

I can handle myself." She smirked, having added a knife garter before they left for the ballroom.

"I'd rather one of us go with you," Quade said, hand covering hers. Aurelio nodded in agreement. Xavia dropped her hands with a heavy thud on the table, rattling the glasses. She stood slowly, leaning with her hands on the table. She was feeling grouchy all of a sudden.

"Just because we've fucked and are figuring out all of this," Xavia motioned in a circle to indicate the three of them, "doesn't mean you have to be overbearing assholes." With that she walked away from the table, ignoring the stares of her companions.

Oddly enough, Ryland opted to leave the ball early. Maybe she should follow suit. She took a deep breath when she stepped into the cool hallway. Curls escaped her updo, falling to her collar bone. As she walked down the hall toward the restrooms, the hair on her arms stood.

Xavia... A voice clear as day spoke in her head. She stopped walking, thinking maybe she heard someone in the hall but no one was around. She shook her head, thinking the rum may have been a bit much.

Xavia... I need you to listen. The voice said. Great, did her multitude of mental health conditions now include hearing voices? She had heard this voice a time or two throughout her life, especially during hunts that were especially dangerous. The hair on her arms stood on edge again.

Xavia! You need to get back to the ballroom. The voice panicked. Her heart began beating a drum in her chest. Xavia shook her head. No. She was obviously on the verge of a break and needed to get to her suite. She started walking to the elevator.

Great Melvina! Xavia stop! The voice louder in her head.

"Get out of my head!" She yelled, picking up the pace.

Xavia, stop! The voice said with enough authority that her feet froze, as if someone else took over her body.

"Let me go!" Xavia yelled, fighting her own body. It was like walking through tar, but she finally took another step. She hit the up button, rubbing her temples as a blooming headache attacked her brain. The doors finally opened.

Xavia, look out! The voice yelled too late. The doors opened to reveal Norrix Aimes, a dark smile on his lips.

"Hello Miss Silveria. I've been waiting for you." His slimy voice was the last thing she heard before something struck her in the head, knocking her unconscious.

XAVIA!

The loud voice jolted Xavia awake. A full-blown migraine assaulted her as she regained consciousness. She raised a shackled hand to the back of her head, feeling wetness, and came away with blood on her fingers. Whoever hit her had hit her hard. Xavia opened her eyes, blinking away dark, floating spots from her vision. It was then that she noticed she was in a cell of some sort. Her hands and feet were bound by chained cuffs, bolted to the wall but the chain slackened. The bottom of her dress was tattered as if she was dragged into the cell and her hair was no longer up, all the pins removed. She felt for her knife and found it had been taken. She shuddered at the thought of someone touching her bare legs, especially because she had no panties on.

Xavia, I need you to focus. Her new companion's voice echoed in her head.

"No shit... I'm trying," Xavia grumbled. Just speaking was taking all her energy. Her head felt funky and it couldn't have just been from the blow to her head. A groan sounded to her left and she snapped her eyes to find Ryland in the cell next to her. Unlike her, his hands were bolted above his head. "Ryland?" He looked terrible. Bruises battered his face, making him near unrecognizable. His clothes had been torn, revealing burn marks on his arms and torso. He'd been tortured. "Ryland, can you hear me?"

"Hmmm..." he nodded slowly, wincing as he did so. "I'm so--..." He took a deep breath. "I'm sorry," he whispered so softly that she almost didn't hear him.

"Why are you sorry?" Xavia started to look around, wondering if there was anything she could use to defend herself. Ryland's eyes rolled and she banged the cell bars, causing him to jolt back to consciousness. "Ryland, why are you sorry?" she said louder.

"I... I told them where to find you." Tears dripped from his eyes. "They said... They said they could bring back Luc." A sick feeling dropped into her stomach.

"Who? Who did you tell?" A sob escaped from his mouth.

"Norrix. The demons." The memory came back to her, moments before she was knocked out. Norrix had made it to Malagado and found her.

"Why do they want me?" Xavia yelled. He shook his head, sobs wracking his body. "Ryland... What do they want with me?" That sick feeling started to make its way up her throat.

"I overhead them say..." He took a deep inhale, "I heard them say that they think you're the Chaos Wielder" She gagged, fear taking hold of her and clenching itself around her heart. She was only human, how the fuck could she be the Chaos Wielder?

"What? Why?" Ryland shook his head.

"I don't know." He moaned in pain, eyes rolling. This time, she let him pass out. Xavia's instincts started ringing, her body going taut with adrenaline when she heard footsteps coming down the hall and closer to her cell. Norrix appeared from the shadows, that awful smile on his face.

"Miss Silveria. I am sorry for the chains but we felt it prudent to keep you from attacking us." Xavia stood up quickly, swaying a bit on her feet.

"I'm not the fucking Chaos Wielder!" she snarled, giving him a baleful look. "I'm only a human."

"Are you though?" he raised an eyebrow. "Are you sure that you're human?" Dark crimson shadows swelled at his feet, as if lifting from the earth.

"Yes, I'm pretty sure, asshole." *Don't piss him off*. The voice said loud and clear. "I can do whatever the fuck I want," Xavia grumbled, earning a look of amusement from Norrix.

"Is she speaking to you now?" he said with delight. The shadows slithered into the cell, moving toward her. Xavia started to scoot back, as if she could somehow out run the shadows approaching her.

"Who?" she asked, not moving her eyes from the shadows.

"You truly don't know?" he chuckled, the shadows now swirling her bare feet.

Xavia, I'm sorry. The voice whispered in her head. Xavia started panting, the edges of her vision going black.

"Have you ever wondered what happens when you black out?" Norrix said, the smoke rising up to her shoulders. "How about I show you?" A sinister grin plagued his lips, the smoke stuffing itself into her nose, ears, and eventually her mouth when she screamed. Images bombarded her, memories of someone else infiltrating her mind.

She panted, looking at the litter of bodies around her. Blood covered her body while she held the bloody knife to her side. There was a thrill to the violence that made its way through her. Sokolov's men were never going to hurt Xavia again.

Xavia pulled out of the memory, gasping for air. Did she kill them? She'd never killed anyone, despite her job. Her body shuddered as another memory hit her.

She chuckled as she looked at Riddick, hanging from the wall. He'd pissed himself and begged for his life. "I don't make deals with rapists," she hissed, dragging a knife across his body. She basked in his screams and sliced open his chest. "You ruin lives. You ruin women. You ruin people who don't deserve to be ruined." The anger made her body shake as she slammed her fist into his chest, breaking through his sternum for her to grab hold of his heart. He screamed, panting, pleading more for his life. Her watch beeped and she growled in frustration. "Lucky for you, I have to go. But not without taking your heart." Sick joy filled her as he screamed while she pulled his heart from his chest.

"STOP!" Xavia yelled, her head screaming in pain. She killed Riddick? Lena said the woman was masked with purple eyes. As far as Xavia knew, she only had brown eyes. She dry heaved, her stomach doing turns.

"So, Leo. Tell me, when were you going to inform me that you're actually Captain Aurelio of Alpha Phoenix?"

Aurelio? What? It was like she was drowning and every time she was pulled under, a new memory accosted her.

"What are you doing later?" He asked, his eyes now turning steel. His voice had dropped an octave it seemed, causing her mouth to dry.

"Probably murdering someone," she deadpanned. It was her job after all. He chuckled, a dark smile crossing his lips.

"And after that? How about we have drinks?" He pulled her in a bit but not so much that it would make her uncomfortable.

"You don't even know what I look like," she said with an eyebrow raised.

"I don't have to," he murmured. She took a step back.

"Maybe next time," she said before stepping into a cloud of purple smoke.

Xavia came up for air, tears streaming down her face. Wielding? There was no way she could've Wielded. She'd never Wielded in her life! Aurelio flirted with another woman? Or was it her? How did he not recognize her?

We always wore a mask. The voice chimed in.

"Fuck you!" She yelled to the voice in her head. She felt herself get dragged down into one last memory.

"I was on my way to see if I could petition an audience with you, your Eminence," she said as she glanced over Jacinto, feeling that tug of energy between the both of them. "But I was drawn

to the club. It seems that who I sought out was here." What was it about the vampire that compelled her?

"Por favor, call me Jacinto." The deep bass of his voice flooded her with lust, sending a pulse straight to her core. His eyes darkened as if sensing where her thoughts headed. "I hope my current state doesn't taint your view of me." She drove her eyes over his body, suppressing the need to bite her lip.

"I've seen worse," she said as she raised an eyebrow. She wanted to taste the blood that had been shed all over him. She wanted to fuck him while they bathed in it. She never felt like this before. She didn't understand it...

"Please," Xavia sobbed, dropping to her knees as Norrix's cloud of smoke left her body. She leaned on to her hands, body shaking as she sobbed.

I should've told you sooner. The voice softly spoke to her.

"What the fuck is going on?" Xavia whispered, hands shaking as she sat back on her heels, staring up at Norrix. His eyes had turned wholly black, as if he fed on her fear and turmoil.

"Do you understand now?" he said with a raised eyebrow.

"No. I don't." She shuddered, her vision blurring at the edges. She fought her black out. She didn't want another one. Not after being bombarded with these memories.

Let me take over. The voice said. Xavia shook her head.

"No, no. I don't want to." She gripped her hair, shaking her head over and over.

Please. Let me deal with Norrix. I promise you'll remember everything. No more blackouts. The voice soothed a part of her, the chaotic part that wanted to thrash and fight. Let me take the torch, she said. It was definitely Xavia... but not.

"Who are you?" Xavia whispered.

I am Styx.

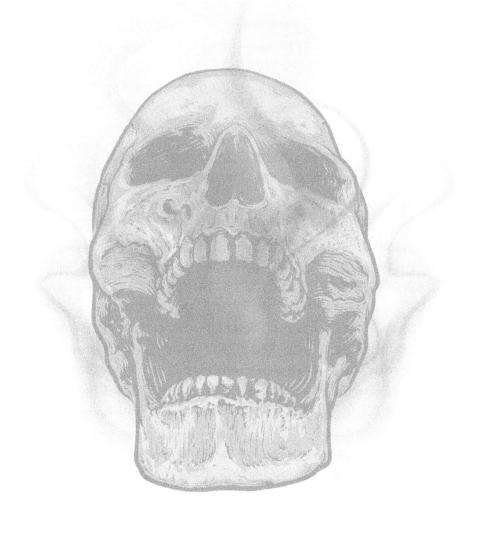

CHAPTER 50

AURELIO

WHERE IS SHE, QUADE? WE WERE supposed to make sure this didn't fucking happen." Aurelio paced inside Xavia's suite. Quade, Lilith, and Lex were all in the room, however, the Fire Wielder had smoke rising from his skin. When Xavia told them she needed air, he and Quade waited all but ten minutes before getting up to go after her. Logically, he knew he shouldn't smother her. But with the threat of Norrix taking her, he couldn't take any risks. Ten minutes was all it took for her to disappear. Did the demon get to her or was it another blackout?

"We'll find her." Quade's voice was dark with fury. His eyes had lit up into a fiery sunset when he realized Xavia wasn't in her suite. He was standing stone still by the bed they had fucked on only just a few hours earlier. Quade's hands opened and closed, fire licking between his fingers.

"Did any of you see her after she left? And where the fuck is Ryland?" It wasn't like the Earth Wielder to not be present during a team meeting.

"I haven't seen her since she walked out. Ryland left the ball early mentioning he wasn't feeling good but I haven't seen or heard from him for hours," Lilith said from the window. She was gauging the exterior courtyard for anything suspicious. Lightning flashed across the sky and the sound of thunder sounded off in the distance. Aurelio moved to the vanity, placing a hand on the smooth service. Fuck. Where was she?

"The fuck are you doing here?" Quade growled, making

Aurelio turn to see that the Vampire King, Jacinto, stood at the door. Aurelio cut Quade a glare. The last thing they needed was to piss off the king and get their asses locked up or worse.

"I know who took Xavia," Quade's fury was a candle to the roaring fire that was Jacinto's malice. The male towered over them, at least seven feet tall, and was built like a linebacker. The pure dark energy that rolled off the vampire was enough to make anyone shit their pants. But Aurelio didn't have time to cower and clearly Quade had no time for niceties.

"Who?" Aurelio took a step forward, looking up at the male whose eyes glowed red. Aurelio knew enough about vampires to know that red meant very bad things.

"The demon, Norrix Aimes."

Aurelio shook his head several times. No way. When did he get to Malagado? Fuck! The demon had read his mind and knew the plans for finding The Chaos Wielder. There was a sound of a crash as Quade threw a lamp across the room.

"Why the *fuck* does he have her?" he asked the King before looking at Aurelio. "We need to find out where he is and get her." Lilith and Lex were nodding their heads behind him. *Yeah, no shit.* Aurelio kept the retort to himself.

"Apparently he thinks your bounty hunter is the Chaos Wielder." Aurelio's heart stopped beating for a moment, his chest going tight. Xavia? The Chaos Wielder? "He's had a keen interest in her ever since your last interaction with him." Aurelio watched as Jacinto's body shook with fury. It was clear that the King blamed Aurelio. "My spies have informed me that Norrix has set up camp on the southeastern outskirts of the city. I will help you get her back."

"What's in it for you? Why do you want to help?" Aurelio asked, as he pulled up a holographic map of the city on his comms. Jacinto tapped his watch and Aurelio's map expanded to include the southern outskirts. It was right on the coast, making it easy to smuggle Xavia overseas. Red dots started to pop up, indicating a dozen demons per dot. There were at least a hundred demons. How did Norrix amass so many under their noses?

"Two things. One; I don't need this political *mierda* on my doorstep. Two; because I don't think she's as human as you all think."

Quade bristled at how the King's tone changed when speaking of Xavia. Aurelio clenched a fist, his own patience wearing thin. He took a moment to consider what Jacinto said about Xavia, and it was like he dropped a bomb and exploded Aurelio's world into a million pieces. Xavia wasn't human? Of the years he'd known her, she never indicated that she had any Wielding. She would've told him, right?

"I've known Xavia for over a decade. She's never told me about having Wielding." Aurelio refused to believe that she would keep something that big from him. He rubbed the back of his head, looking at Quade who seemed equally as perplexed.

"That's because she's not a Wielder," Jacinto said, leaning against the doorframe and crossing his arms. His dark hair flowed over his shoulder, annoyance flushing his face.

"What the fuck does that mean?" It was clear Quade had lost his patience. Aurelio stepped closer to him, shooting him a look of warning. Jacinto, the asshole, chuckled.

"Relax Firebreather, I am not sure *what* she is; but a Wielder, she is not." There was an unfamiliar look in Quade's face that Aurelio couldn't place, like he was caught off guard. He tucked that away to deal with at another time. "Get changed and meet me in my conference room." And with that, Jacinto pushed off and left.

AN HOUR LATER AURELIO AND THE others filed into the conference room in full tactical gear. Jacinto had let them retrieve their weapons and load up. On the outside, Aurelio was still, like a cloudy day without the threat of rain. He held himself together for the sake of this mission and to get Xavia back. On the inside, his storm raged. It battered against his anima, rising waves threatening to crest and drown him, lightning threatening to burn him up. Aurelio felt as if he was going to implode at any moment. By his request, they left a window open so that he could access his Wielding indoors. The voices in the room flew past his head as he tried to calm the storm that threatened to break in the sky.

"There are tunnels, leading from the Palacio to Milagros." Cyrus, Jacinto's second, was saying, drawing Aurelio's attention back to the room. Both Cyrus and Jacinto wore black tactical gear. The King and his Hand had taken Aurelio's advice and had swords strapped to their hips along with guns in thigh holsters that were loaded with hollow points to use at a distance.

"How can we be sure they didn't set up any traps or alarms?" Quade said as he gazed over the holographic map.

"You have a Shadow Wielder, yes?" Jacinto motioned to Lilith who nodded. "She can Wield through the tunnels ahead of us and disable any alarms or trip wires." Quade's eyebrows raised in question as did Lilith's. "Do you not know how to do this?" Jacinto asked, frustrated as if he was talking to children.

"No. I've never been trained to do that. I didn't know it was possible." Shadows swirled around her as she thought about it. "Is that how the demons broke our camp?" She mused out loud, looking at Aurelio.

"It makes sense. Do you think you could learn?"

She smirked, shadows escaping her hands.

"Check your comms." Lilith snorted as Aurelio quirked an eyebrow and noticed they were disconnected. Lilith was a certified genius.

"Excellent, you learn quickly," Jacinto said with a nod. "We move through the tunnels, and we will come up here." Jacinto pointed to a building a few blocks away from where Norrix was holed up. "I will send in my Guard first." The King chose five members of his Guard to form the first line of defense. The team consisted of two vampires, a werewolf, and two Shadow Wielders.

"Are we sure we can get through a hundred demons?" Lex's soft but firm voice questioned, hand gripping the sword at their side.

"The vampires alone can cut through at least half that." Quade earned a nod from Jacinto. "We only need to get in, kill that fucker Norrix, and grab Xavia." The fire sunset shade hadn't left his eyes since they first found out Xavia was taken. "If he has done *anything* to her..." he growled. Aurelio laid a hand on Quade's shoulder, his cooling wind seeping through Quade's shirt to calm his feverish body.

"Let's go," Jacinto said with a nod, seemingly just as invested as they were.

STYX

STYX PANTED AS SHE FOUGHT through Xavia's consciousness. The blackness threatened to suppress her and keep her from breaking through. Xavia had gotten stronger over the last few months, successfully blocking her gateway. With Norrix so close, Styx fought tooth and nail to gain access to the body they shared.

Let me in, she whispered to Xavia, who finally gave up the fight, sling shotting Styx to the forefront.

Pain. All she felt was pain. Her body was sore, the fog of the darkness receding as she blinked her eyes open. She caught a glimpse of her messy hair fading from brown to purple. Her vision sharpened, her heightened senses accosting her with the rank smell of the basement she was kept in. Her eyes fell on Norrix who watched with sick, lustful interest. Styx looked down at herself, taking in her tattered dress. The bruises from Xavia's sexual exploits were healed as Styx came to.

"Asshole," Styx hissed, making Norrix chuckle. Pure wrath rose within her, hotter than anything she had ever felt. Styx's rage swarmed her, became part of her energy, and fueled her. She thought of all the ways she'd disembowel Norrix.

"Ah, there she is." Norrix clapped his hands. "Hello Styx. It's a pleasure to see you again, minus the blade at my throat." He straightened his collar.

"I should've killed you when I had the chance." She would have had it not been for her forsaken timer. "But I don't have a time limit tonight. I will fulfill my mission." Styx stood, chains ringing loudly in her ears. She couldn't hide the wince at the sound. It was always disorienting when she first entered their body, she thought of it as taking up the torch. Xavia's human senses dulled in comparison to hers. The time it took to catch up depended on how hard she had to fight to gain access.

"Yes, you should've." Norrix grinned, unlocking the cage door. It opened with a loud whine that made her feel like her ears were bleeding. Styx flinched when he petted her head. "Hmm. If you weren't necessary, I'd keep you as a pet."

With her hands and feet chained, she couldn't do anything but ram her forehead into Norrix's nose. He jolted backward, holding his now bleeding nose. Black blood that smelled like carrion dripped from his nose, making her fight a gag. He snapped a hand out to grab her hair.

"I should make you pay for that." His face loomed close enough that he ran his nose across her forehead, trailing blood across it. Her eyes watered at both the smell and the hand in her hair.

"You can't do anything to me that hasn't already been done." Styx spat in his face. She'd been through enough, seen enough. Nothing surprised her. Norrix snatched her lip between his teeth, biting down all the way through her lip. She grunted in pain, trying not to move for the risk of completely having her lip torn off. She refused to scream for him. Norrix laughed, licking his lips with her blood. The hot liquid poured down her chin, aching like a fire spread from her wounded lip and into her system.

"If I was contagious, you'd turn feral with a bite like that."

Fear flooded her system at the thought. He took a deep inhale, dragging his tongue up her chin to lap at her blood. He sucked at the wound making white hot pain lance through her. Her stomach roiled, threatening to throw up the contents of her dinner.

"Yes. Fear me," he hissed as he inhaled her scent. Norrix let her go, rocking her back against the wall. Styx caught herself, her

THE CHAOS WIELDER | 363

orientation finally balancing out. "Sit tight. We are leaving in a few hours. The Queen has personally requested your presence." He made his exit, leaving her to stew. The Queen, Aeshma. The Angel of Wrath. When she was sure that Norrix was officially out of earshot, she licked her lips, the wound sealing.

"I'm coming for you," Styx said darkly as her body shifted into a haze of dark purple shadows and smoke. She caught the chains before they could make a sound, silently placing them on the ground. Keeping her body in shadow form, she slid through the bars of the cage before returning to her physical form. Sweat beaded on her forehead. Phasing wasn't something she could do for long. A glint to the right, in the opposite direction of the stairs, caught her attention. She moved on silent feet to peer into a room that held one demon guard. Of course, they'd underestimate her.

The demon wore a leather jacket, hood up, with some sort of gas mask over its face. It wore tactical pants, a machete at its hip, and three daggers on its thigh. Its back was to her so it didn't hear or see her when she slid up behind it. Before the demon knew what was happening, she slipped the machete from its belt and separated its head from its body. Black blood sprayed, splattering her face. Styx fought the urge to vomit as she took its belt and wrapped it around her waist. Using the machete, she hacked off her dress just past her calves. There was no way she was going to try running in an evening gown. Styx grabbed the demon's boots and slid them on, buckling them as tight as they would go, and sheathed the machete.

Styx turned to the hallway, moving as silently as she could with the oversized boots on her feet. When she reached the top of the stairs, her keen hearing picked up two sets of heartbeats. At least two demons stood at the door. Well, risk was her middle name.

She slammed the door open with a kick, slicing upward and successfully lopping the head off the demon closest to her. The one directly behind the door grabbed her shoulder with a snarl. Moving faster than the demon could track, she whirled on it, ducking under its arm and thrusting the machete through its thick jacket and into its heart. Styx snatched the knife from its belt to slice into its neck, spraying blood. It howled a sound so loud that she was sure everything in the building heard. Shit. She held on to the hilt of the machete while it flailed before kicking it forward to release the blade. Its head tumbled shortly after with another quick slice.

"You are not going anywhere," came Norrix's voice behind her. Fuck! She turned, gore covering her, with the machete aimed at the demon. He opened his hand and red smoke hit her in the chest, running up into her nose and making her gag. The machete fell from her hand while her mind was seized. It felt as if he dragged claws across her brain. "I think I'll keep Miss Silveria around for now." He hissed before he shot her to the recesses of the shared consciousness she had with Xavia.

Darkness covered her, a mental barrier around her. She roared as she slammed her fists against the barrier. She needed to protect Xavia. She *had* to protect her!

CHAPTER 51

QUADE

AS THEY MADE THEIR WAY THROUGH the rank tunnel, Quade ran through the last few months in his mind. He went from hating Xavia to needing her every second of the day. Now that he had her, he couldn't imagine living without her. Smoke curled around him as his body steamed. A wildfire had spread inside his mind and anima. It threatened to burn anything and everything that tried to keep her from him. Never in his life did he think he'd feel this way about anyone. Emotions didn't suit him well and he understood now more than ever why. Quade tasted smoke, his fury aching to unleash itself. He knew he had to wait and time it right.

"The alarms are down," Lilith said softly, her dark shadows encasing the tunnel before them. It was disorienting not being able to see into the depths but he trusted Lilith to guide them. Jacinto's team followed closely behind her while he and the others came up second with Cyrus at the rear. He could feel Aurelio thrumming next to him, the Storm Wielder sparking at the fingertips.

"How are you able to do that underground?" Quade murmured softly so that no one heard. Aurelio gave him a grim smile.

"I've been working on harnessing the electricity in my body." Quade raised an eyebrow in question. "Our brains and nervous systems release electrical pulses in order to communicate with the rest of our bodies." Aurelio's hands sparked again. "I found a way to use it but it's not as easy as pulling it from the sky." Quade didn't understand how Wielding worked, only that it did. The fact that

Aurelio learned new ways to Wield impressed him.

"We have to find our woman," Quade said, heart feeling as if it would explode out of his chest.

"We will," Aurelio said as they reached the end of the tunnel. Game on.

THEY SET UP A TEMPORARY BASE on the roof of a building across from the warehouse that the demons were holed up in. The roof had demons on rotation, walking with rifles. There were two entrances, one in front and the other at the back. Demons guarded both. Behind the warehouse was the dock where a yacht was being loaded with what looked like weapons, potions, and other materials. They were planning on taking Xavia to Aeshma.

"Is there a basement?" Quade asked Cyrus, who had obtained the blueprints of the warehouse.

"Yes. It used to be a jailhouse. There are holding cells underneath. The main floor is open space. I imagine most of the demons are in there." Cyrus passed them visors. "These have thermal imaging, radar, and UV vision. The demons emit a green body signature, Norrix is black with a silver shimmer, and humans or mortals flare red."

Quade liked Cyrus. He was efficient and made sure that the rest of his team was as well. Quade slipped the visors on and the warehouse lit up like fireworks. It was teeming with green figures that seemed to blend together. There was one red figure and he bristled at the sight of the black shadowy figure next to it.

"Easy." Aurelio's voice sounded in his ear comm. He was in a different position on the roof. How he knew what Quade was feeling was beyond him. After taking a full assessment, Jacinto nodded to his team.

"They will infiltrate first, taking out the guards and the ones on the dock. We wait for their signal before we move next. Let's get to the bottom floor." As they moved down the stairs, Quade's stomach turned into knots. He thought back to the one mission failure he had with Aurelio. They couldn't have another. He didn't realize he was panting until Aurelio laid a steadying hand on his shoulder and put his forehead against Quade's.

"Hey. Remember who we are," Aurelio commanded. "Alpha Phoenix." Lilith came over and laid a hand on Quade's other shoulder. Lex stepped up when Lilith nodded and laid a hand on his back. "We always complete the mission. We do not fail. We do not quit." Quade nodded. "Say it."

"We do not fail. We do not quit." Quade shook himself and they broke their huddle.

"That's sweet but we have to move," Jacinto grunted, motioning for his team to head out. They all lined up on the wall in the darkness of the building, while the King's team melted into the shadows that the Shadow Wielders formed around them. If it wasn't for the visors, Quade would not have been able to spot the vampires and werewolf in the group. It was painful waiting for them to do their part. His limbs ached to run toward that red blip he saw.

"Four down," a rough voice in his ear. The demons on the roof had lost their heads and were falling to the floor. The Guard moved like the wind; it was impossible to keep track of their positions. He caught a swarm of shadows covering the grouping of demons at the dock. Over the comms he heard the sounds of grunting, growling, and the meaty sound of flesh tearing.

"Fuck! Lorcan is down," the rough voice said with a grunt as if he was punched. There was a hiss before the shadows lifted. The werewolf, Lorcan, had lost his head in the fray but the rest of the demons were down.

"Entrance is clear," another voice.

Jacinto nodded to them. "Go!"

The blood roared in Quade's ears as he sprinted for the entrance. Tucking his rifle in his shoulder, he sprinted toward the warehouse. Two vampires waited for them before entering first. Quade was to enter right after, Lilith and Lex behind, Aurelio, Cyrus, and Jacinto bringing up the rear. The fact that the King was on this mission with him spoke multitudes. Quade was curious to find out why he was so invested in Xavia.*

After breaching the front door, it took a moment to orient themselves to the sight before them. There were at least double the number of demons than they planned for. Gunfire erupted as they took out demons with their hollow point rounds. Quade was a perfect shot, taking down one by one as fast as he could. They couldn't keep up the gunfire, the sheer number of demons overwhelming them. He risked a glance at his team and saw they had pulled their swords, weaving in and out of demons and lopping heads off of their bodies.

A fist connected with his jaw, making him stumble back. The demon before him had an arm missing, drenching the floor with black blood. Quade let the gun swing at his back before curling chains of fire and lashing out. The thing howled when the chains of flame wrapped around its neck. Quade tightened the hold of the chain in his hand until it seared right through the demon's neck. Quade kicked the head before quickly lighting several more demons on fire that had been gunning for Lilith, leaving her to slice them down.

Shadows filled the warehouse while the Shadow Wielders suffocated the demons with darkness. Thankfully the visors made it possible to see the difference between the demons and everyone else. Lightning cracked outside, flowing toward Aurelio through an open door and blasting through the demons that surrounded him. Quade caught sight of the blur that was Norrix, Xavia's red glow beside him through the floor. They were in the basement.

"Aurelio!" Quade yelled into his comm as he made his way toward them.

"I see them," Aurelio panted. Shadows lifted in one corner, a Shadow Wielder from the King's team going down. The demons seemed to be coming from somewhere they couldn't see. Quade caught the shimmer of what he assumed was a ward over Norrix and Xavia, making their job harder.

"Domination" by Kayzo, Sullivan King, Papa Roach

"I need everyone to duck," Quade hissed into the comm, smoke curling in his mouth.

"What? Why?" Aurelio barked. "We need to—"

"I know what we need to do Cap!" Quade barked back. "Get down, now!" He drew in his Wielding and began inhaling, sucking the oxygen from the top of the room. He felt a burning in his lungs, converting the oxygen into fire. Smoke curled out of his nose as he opened his mouth and roared.

AURELIO

AURELIO HIT THE GROUND AS HE watched Quade release fire from his fucking mouth like a dragon. A Firebreather. He was a Firebreather. Firebreathers were rare Fire Wielders who could convert oxygen in the air into fire, fueled by the fire in their blood. It explained his constant fury and quickness to anger. Demons in Quade's radius burned to ash, the fire white hot and all consuming. From across the warehouse Aurelio could feel the heat of it.

"Go..." Quade's voice rasped as he Wielded the fire down to keep the warehouse from exploding. "I only have one good Firebreath. It'll take time we don't have to build another one."

Quade had effectively wiped out more than half of the remaining demons. Aurelio jumped up, sprinting for Quade. He caught up to Quade who was panting, sweat streaming down his face. His eyes were lit with flame as if they were made of it. Smoke wafted from his nose and mouth. Aurelio Wielded cool wind over Quade, a look of relief covering his features at the sensation.

"They're in the—"

"Basement," finishing each other's sentences.

They moved to the doorway that led to the basement, the door completely off the hinges as if someone kicked it open from the other side. Did Xavia try to escape? They stood at the top of the stairs, red and black smoke obscuring the stairs and the basement below. The males looked at each other.

"Let's get our woman," Aurelio breathed, Quade nodding. They moved down the stairs, the stealthy and slow speed unbearable. He held his rifle up to his shoulder, pointing it before him while using his visors to help his vision. They could still make out where the two were, moving through the smoke and shadows. Aurelio's foot hit a body and he risked a glance to find that it was Ryland, throat torn out. "Quade," he whispered through gritted teeth, making Quade look down. Ryland was here the whole time. Captive?

"Now, now. Don't feel bad about the traitor Mr. Broderick," came Norrix's voice somewhere ahead of them. "He sold your precious bounty hunter out for the promise of being reunited with his love," the demon chuckled. "I was happy to do so. It just wasn't the reunion he thought it would be." Aurelio clenched his jaw, tapping Quade's shoulder to let him know to move forward.

"Aurelio! I'm not worth it!" came Xavia's voice, making his heart clench. It took everything in him to not sprint down the hallway. She sobbed, the sound shattering his anima. "I wouldn't be able to live with myself if you died." Her voice tore at him, shredding his patience.

"Brat, we're coming for you whether you want us to or not," Quade's voice shook with fury. They moved through the maze of what appeared to be an old holding area of the jailhouse. Quade and Aurelio moved as one, years of training and battle together making it second nature. They checked every cell, every guard station. It wasn't until they arrived at the deepest part that they saw Norrix holding Xavia by her wrist. She was covered in demon grime, telling him that she had tried to fight her way out. Her dress was ruined and cut at the bottom and she wore oversized boots. An empty sheath hung from her waist. Their woman was a fighter.

Aurelio felt Quade's hand on his chest, not realizing he'd taken a step forward. Tears streamed down Xavia's face and over her bruised and bloodied lip. The storm that had been brewing in Aurelio started to crest as white-hot anger flushed through him.

"Why do you want her?" Aurelio barked. He eyed the space

around Norrix, observing the wards that covered the demon and his captive. He steeled his mind, building it up iron brick by iron brick to keep Norrix from peering into it. He knew Quade was doing the same. They had been training for it after Aurelio's last encounter with Norrix.

"Well, she would make an interesting pet," Norrix said, in a tone that indicated it should've been obvious. "But Queen Aeshma wants her as she's the Chaos Wielder."

"Fuck you!" Xavia spat at Norrix. "I already told you that I'm not the Chaos Wielder!" She fought against his hold on her and gasped when he dug in, drawing blood. Norrix pulled her in, running his tongue up the side of her face, as if feasting on her fear.

"Don't you fucking touch her!" Quade took a step forward, the ward singeing his boot, before he stepped back again. Aurelio felt something brush up against the inside of his mind, like claws lightly dragging itself across the walls he put up. It didn't hurt but still made him grind his teeth.

"I see you learned from our last encounter, Mr. Broderick." Norrix sucked his teeth, looking at his nails. "You will not walk out of here," he hissed, red smoke escaping from his hands, wrapping itself around Quade and Aurelio's necks. "I don't have to get into your minds to kill you." Aurelio looked at Quade. The Fire Wielder gave him a look of confirmation.

"You forgot..." Aurelio gasped, "That wards are susceptible to lightning." Wielded lightning worked differently from standard electricity. His hands began to spark, Norrix didn't seem to notice.

"You can't Wield underground, Storm Wielder."

The smoke tightened around his neck. His vision was starting to blur around the edges. Aurelio grunted as electricity ran up his arms to shock the smoke. Norrix hissed in surprise as he snapped it back. Aurelio took a quick gulp of air before blasting at the wards with the electricity he had been building for the last few weeks. The smell of ozone filled the air as the wards started to crack and peel. Norrix growled as the ground started to shake. Quade had chains of fire ready as the wards slowly came down under the electricity.

"You will die here, Storm Wielder!" Norrix roared, the ground shaking enough to make them lose balance. Sweat beaded on Aurelio's forehead and blood dripped from his nose as he started to feel his lightning run thin. If he used it all, he would go brain dead. But he pushed himself, he would do anything if it meant getting Xavia back.

Suddenly the ceiling blasted open above Norrix and he grabbed Xavia around the waist. Aurelio's electricity snapped back into his body, jolting him backward. Xavia tried to fight against Norrix as her eyes connected with Aurelio's and then moved to Quade's. Norrix squatted before jumping through the hole in the ceiling, taking Xavia with him. The smell of fresh air swept over him, letting him know someone had blasted a hole through a wall to the outside. Aurelio panted as he grabbed Quade.

"No, you've used too much."

Aurelio gave him a look that made Quade snap his mouth shut. He Wielded the wind around them, flying them up through the hole to land on the floor beside it with a grunt. They faced off with Norrix, throwing lightning and fire at him. Norrix deflected with ease, while holding Xavia by her hair. He was too powerful. More powerful than they had prepared for.

Suddenly a blur speared Norrix, causing him to let go of Xavia. Jacinto snarled as he grappled with the demon. Xavia ran to Aurelio and Quade, sobbing. Aurelio took her into his arms, Quade coming up behind her.

"I thought I was never going to see you both again." She took several long gasps of air as she tried to get her sobbing under control.

"We're here baby. We wouldn't let them take you," Aurelio said, putting her face in his hands and looking her over. Quade softly patted her hair, leaning in.

"Yeah, brat. We're too stubborn to let you go," Quade huffed into her hair. The sounds of growls and grunts drew their attention. Aurelio moved Xavia behind him and Quade as they watched the demon and vampire battle it out.

Norrix had the upper hand, wrapping that sickly smoke around Jacinto and penetrating his mouth and nose. Jacinto let out a howl, his nose bleeding as he shook off the effects of the smoke. He lunged, sinking his fangs into Norrix's arm. He snapped his head back and forth like a shark, ripping strands of flesh off Norrix. Norrix shrieked in pain, pushing his hand into Jacinto's chest, sending him backward.

Norrix turned to Aurelio and Quade, clapping his hands. A force of energy blasted them backward, missing Xavia by a hairsbreadth. She ducked as debris flew over her head. Pain lanced through Aurelio; his shoulder was partially shredded and dislocated. He looked to Quade, who hissed, a pole jutting out of his thigh.

"Please! I need your help!" Xavia said, but no longer looking at them. "Styx!" Aurelio looked around quickly, looking for the assassin. He was left confused when he didn't see her. She bellowed, "Styx!" Xavia's eyes started to flutter as she bent over, taking long gasps. Aurelio tried to stand, arm screaming at him. His eyes widened as Xavia's hair shifted to purple, eyes melting to deep violet, and the scar disappeared from her neck.

"What...?" He heard Quade breathe. Xavia—no Styx—stood up, purple smoke swirling from her hands. She gave Aurelio a knowing look. Holy Tomis.

CHAPTER 52

STYX

FIGHTING THE MENTAL BARRIERS that Norrix used to trap Styx caused Xavia excruciating pain. But while Norrix was distracted, they mentally worked together, breaking down those walls. As soon as they fell, Styx rose to the forefront, Xavia passing the torch. Styx took a large gasp of air, her senses orienting quickly due to Xavia's permission to come up. Her purple eyes slid to Aurelio and Quade who looked at her in shock.*

"I'll explain later. Now get the fuck up." Styx waved a hand, stitching Aurelio's arm back together. She earned a howl of pain from Quade as she pulled the pole from his leg, quickly stitching it.

Look out! Xavia's voice yelled in her head.

Styx ducked as a demon flung itself at her. She kicked it square in the chest, knocking it off its feet. She grabbed it by the throat and ripped its voice box out. Styx snatched the sides of its head while it flailed and pulled the head off with a pop. She felt her shoulder jolt in agony as another demon yanked her to her feet. It slammed a fist across her jaw, making her see stars and turn. Now back-to-back with the demon, Styx reached behind to grab it by the head. She lifted her legs before snapping them to the ground and used her momentum to throw the demon overhead and slam it on the floor. She cut of its head with a quick swipe before another came up and grabbed her by the shoulder, digging into it.

A chain whip of fire encircled the demon around the neck,

♪ "Do or Die" by Magnolia Park, Ethan Park

Quade panting behind it and pulling it back. It howled and let Styx go to clutch at the chain on instinct. Styx grabbed the machete off the demon on the floor before slicing through the demon Quade was holding. The chain whip coiled at Quade's hip as he ran to her, touching her hair and face.

"Holy shit," he murmured, eyes wildfire orange. He lifted her head to look at her chin. She looked up at him, understanding why Xavia cared about him so much.

"Shit!" She pushed him behind her, getting in front of another demon, and threw up an energy shield, which she had never done before. What? The demon slammed into it, trying to crack through the ward. Quade's back hit hers as he faced off two demons. Where were they all coming from? The ground shook and the roof ripped off the warehouse. A hurricane raged above them, rain pouring down and soaking them. Lightning ripped across the sky before coming down in three successive bolts, one for each demon around them.

Aurelio's eyes glowed the color of stark silver lightning, the power of it thrumming through him. He let out a battle cry as he wiped the immediate radius of demons with his lightning. Many of them turned to ash or burned to a crisp. He sucked in a deep breath, lightning no longer crackling. Blood stung her eyes as she pushed her water-logged hair out of her face. Aurelio joined them, taking deep breaths through his nose. The rain lulled as a smirk raised on his lips.

"I knew I liked you for a reason," Aurelio panted, blood pouring from his nose. Styx snorted.

"Now is not the time Captain." Quade looked at the two of them in confusion.

"Styx was my contact this whole time. But she always wore a mask." Quade's mouth formed a surprised O. He tried to speak but a menacing roar echoed across the warehouse. Jacinto and Norrix were still battling.

"We need to help the King," Styx breathed as she watched Jacinto fight Norrix. The vampire was brutal, a wonderful flurry of chaos and wrath. Her gut clenched at the sight, worry flooding her at the thought of the King getting hurt. Aurelio nodded to both Styx and Quade and they bolted for the two. Styx took stock of the warehouse as they ran. Lex and Lilith were huddled, panting in the middle of dead demons. One vampire was left in Jacinto's team. It was just them. Only they could stop this.

JACINTO

"YOU STUPID VAMPIRE! THE QUEEN would spare you and your continent," Norrix yelled, sending a powerful blast of energy at Jacinto who stumbled back. He recovered within seconds, moving quicker than Norrix's eyes could track. Norrix's head snapped back as Jacinto laid an uppercut.

"I've been around for over five thousand years. Tyrants are always tyrants," Jacinto hissed, grabbing Norrix by his throat. "My land is my own, no one else's!" he roared as his fingers dug into Norrix's skin. His nails sharpened into claws, digging into the flesh. Norrix laughed, eyes flaring red.

The ground shook, but Jacinto rode the quake with sure feet. He caught sight of Styx with Xavia's males running toward them, trying to keep themselves balanced. He knew the bounty hunter was different but he was surprised to find that Styx and Xavia shared the same body. The power that bound him and Styx grew taut the closer she got to him.

"Your time on Euhaven is but a drop in the bucket compared to the Queen." Norrix ripped into Jacinto's abdomen, tearing through it. Jacinto let out a howl of pain as he let Norrix go. The Demon stepped back, pulling his hand out of Jacinto. Styx ran up to him, that powerful cord between them snapping tight. Blood poured from the vampire's stomach as he looked at her. Without hesitation, she sent purple smoke into him, stitching the gaping wound in record time. With a growl, Jacinto backhanded Norrix who deflected with a surge of his own shadow power.

The ground quaked violently, Norrix holding a hand to his side. The ground beside him began to cave in, a black cloud of smoke swirling in the open space.

"I never needed a boat to get in and out of your country, vampire," Norrix growled as the vortex he summoned grew larger. It was a trap. This whole thing was a trap to lure them out and eliminate them. Jacinto pushed Styx behind him as she laid a hand on his back, lighting him up with a surge of power.

"Did you think something as simple as wards would keep the Queen out?" Norrix laughed darkly and the rumbling inside the vortex morphed into the sound of boots striking the pavement.

Demons. Dozens of them flowed out of the vortex. Wielding lit up the air as the remaining Wielders did their best to kill as many demons as possible. The sounds of the hollow point guns were near deafening. It was a miracle anyone had bullets left. A wall of demons surrounded Norrix before Jacinto could rush at him. As a nearby demon attempted to claw at the vampire, Jacinto grabbed it by the head. With a single hand, Jacinto squeezed, popping its skull like an overripe tomato. He snarled, buzzing with the energy Styx still put into his body. He was fucking tired of this. He was tired of demons fucking around in his territory. He was tired of the fucking dick of a demon in front of him.

"Give me the Chaos Wielder and I won't destroy your continent," Norrix growled, voice changing. There was a female underlay to his voice, letting Jacinto know that Aeshma was speaking through him. "Give us the Chaos Wielder and I will call back my demons," they hissed.

A tendril of smoke attempted to wrap around him to get to Styx. Jacinto chuckled, holding his hand out to stop the smoke, sucking it into himself instead. He stepped away from Styx, rolling his shoulders. Norrix's eyes widened slightly as buzzing filled the air.*

Everything stood still as Wielding filled his veins. The very air seemed to be sucked into him, lightning, water, earth, fire. The many

---

♪ "Burn" by 2WEI, Edda Hayes

elements of the planet, swirling around him as his eyes glowed white. His feet lifted from the floor as a black cloak of energy in the shape of a leather duster appeared around his body. The elements swirled around his hands, turning a red and yellow so bright it could put the sun to shame. Jacinto tilted his head back, the power intoxicating. As he turned his head to Norrix, a half skull bone mask appeared on his face while a hood lifted overhead. He enjoyed the look in Norrix's face as he blanched.

"You stupid fuck," Jacinto's voice was everything and not. It was not his own but it was. It was the voice of the many. The voice of the world. The voice of the greatest beings. "I am the fucking Chaos Wielder."

"No! Impossible!" Norrix and Aeshma yelled through one mouth. Their eyes shifted to Styx, who stood far back from Jacinto. Jacinto started to carousel his hands, one over the other, as Chaos energy formed a ball in the middle of his hands. It glowed brighter with each turn, the ball getting larger.

"I was the first Wielder," he spoke. "I was the first Blessed by Tomis." The ball grew larger. "When they realized that Chaos was too much for one being to hold, they made me a vampire to hide my identity. The first of the nocturnals." The building thrummed with the power he'd built up around him. "I was made as a failsafe." A column of white-hot energy shot down from the skies directly into him, making him hiss in pleasure. "You will not win," he laughed before releasing the energy in a fury of pure chaotic power. With precise control, every demon faded into oblivion.

Norrix made for the vortex but stopped dead from an invisible force. Styx was holding her hand out, pulling the demon away from the vortex. Her eyes flared in bright purple, sweat pouring down her face. She dropped to her knees, holding her side, letting him know that she had been struck or stabbed.

Quade crawled to her, blood flowing from a wound on his scalp. Aurelio was panting, on his knees, by the edge of the vortex and trying to gather his strength. Jacinto had a decision to make; save her or kill Norrix. If he used his Chaos Wielding to destroy Norrix, Styx would get caught in the overflow. She was too close to him.

"Destroy him!" she yelled, gritting her teeth. Norrix took a step toward the vortex, Styx's grip on her power loosening and shifting forward. Jacinto's feet touched down as he made for Styx, sliding to the ground as he did so. He grabbed her by the waist, their power merging together.

"I will take what is owed!" Norrix and Aeshma yelled, pulling at the cord, dragging them forward. Styx panted in his arms; warm blood flowed from her side over his arm.

"Forget me and kill him," she panted, his hand now on top of hers, their fingers twined together.

"Silly asesina," Jacinto groaned. "It takes two." He splayed his free hand on her stomach, their energies merging as Chaos Wielding left their combined hands and slammed into Norrix. Jacinto's ears rang with the sound of Norrix's screech as the Chaos energy peeled back layers of skin and flesh. Both Jacinto and Styx yelled, as the Chaos energy flooded through them. Norrix stumbled back, skin completely flayed; only pieces of meat and bone left. The pair flew back as the Chaos snapped back into them and Norrix fell into the vortex. Jacinto turned his body so that he would take the brunt of the fall with Styx on top. They landed with a grunt, panting. The cloak he wore snapped back into his body, skull mask disappearing.

"It takes two? Really?" Styx breathed, staring down at him. Jacinto huffed out a chuckle which made him wince. His entire body hurt as if he had been rolled over by a semi-truck several times. Styx slid off of him, sitting up. Her movements were choppy as if she, too, was as sore as he was. "What the fuck did we just do?" Her eyes turned to the vortex. "And how do we close that?"

They scrambled to their feet, Styx limping toward the vortex. Jacinto was on her heels, making sure she didn't fall over. Aurelio stood, pulling her into a hug, Quade following. Styx looked at Jacinto from over Aurelio's shoulder. The look she gave Jacinto told him that she didn't feel the same for the males as they did for her— or rather Xavia.

"It's called a Convergence." Jacinto gripped his chest. Every breath he took felt like glass rubbing against his lungs. It had been too long since he last used his Wielding. Even Chaos had its limits. "It's only possible if…" A roar echoed from the vortex. Jacinto could feel the blood leaving his face. Impossible. The ground shook again and Aurelio shoved Styx into Quade. As the Fire Wielder caught her, Aurelio hit the ground, something pulling him to the vortex. It was Norrix, rasping and still holding on to life.

"I will take one of you with me," the demon hissed.

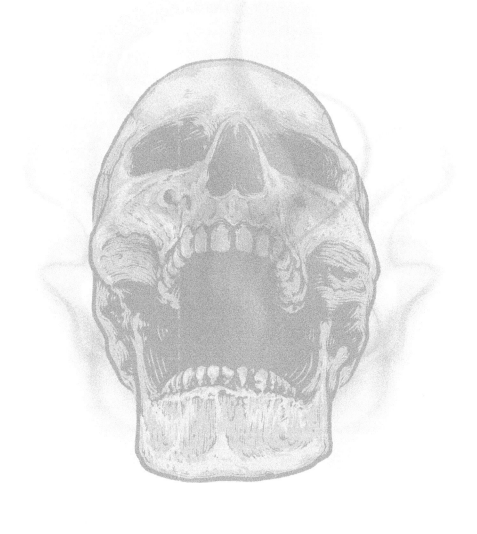

CHAPTER 53
QUADE

THE FEAR QUADE FELT WAS PALATABLE. It tasted like bile, cold metal, and all things vile. It took hold of his heart, squeezing with an iron grip. His stomach threatened to expel whatever contents it had left. Quade hated it and hoped he'd never have to feel it again. He handed a now convulsing Styx off to Jacinto as he ran to grab Aurelio's hand. Both men were heaving gulps of air as they fought against Norrix's impossible grip. How was the demon still alive? The ground shook again, fissures appearing. The building was going to collapse into itself.

"Aurelio!" Xavia wailed, having pushed to the surface. She fought weakly against Jacinto to get to them. The both of them having exhausted their Chaos and all the Wielders having exhausted their Wielding. It was futile. Lex appeared next to him, grabbing Aurelio's other hand.

"C'mon big guy!" They gritted their teeth, pulling as much as they could. Norrix was crawling up Aurelio, pulling his legs further into the vortex. Aurelio fought against the demon latched onto his legs. Another quake rocked the ground as the vortex began closing. Quade barked in pain as his knees hit the ground. Sweat pebbled on his forehead and he tightened his grip on his best friend. He couldn't lose his brother. Aurelio was the only family he really had, other than Xavia.

"I will wash Euhaven with your blood," Norrix hissed through his rotting mouth. Quade grabbed hold of Aurelio's forearm and bicep, Lex doing the same. He got one foot under him to pull harder.

Aurelio counter pulled, dragging himself out of the vortex but with Norrix on him, he was also dragging the demon out. Debris fell from the walls as the ground shook again, the vortex getting smaller. The floor on the opposite side of the warehouse caved in, crashing into the basement. Norrix yanked back with a growl, snatching both Aurelio and Quade toward him. "One is good, two is better," he snarled, sending Lex into a wall. Quade hit the floor, Aurelio now waist deep in the vortex.*

"Quade!" Aurelio yelled, catching his attention. "Look at me," he said, authority in his voice. Quade saw the look in his eyes.

"No! Absolutely no fucking way." Quade gritted his teeth, holding firm to Aurelio. The fear gripped his heart again, sending pain through his body. He knew what Aurelio planned to say; what he was going to command Quade to do.

"Quade, you..."

"Don't even fucking say it Cap!" Quade barked. He was not going to let Aurelio sacrifice himself. If it was going to be anybody, it should be Quade.

"Aurelio, no!" Xavia was yelling from Jacinto's arms. "Please, Tomis, no!" Tears streamed down her face. Silver lined Aurelio's eyes as he looked to Xavia and then back at Quade.

"You have to let me go," he said firmly. A haze covered Quade, eyes blurring as he shook his head. Another quake rocked the building, more of the floor collapsing. Norrix raised his hand, willing the vortex to close faster.

"Motherfucker... No. Not you. It should be me," Quade rasped. "You deserve to be here. You deserve her more than I do," his voice trembled. The pain lancing through his heart was overwhelming. The thoughts of their first time meeting at the Academy and every day since running through his mind in rapid speed. "I'm so sorry for being an asshole to you. I'm sorry that I was always angry about your choices. Now knowing Xavia, I see why you made those choices. Don't you fucking die on me. Not after discovering what we have," he croaked. Quade tried to fuel his Fire

♪ "Sweet Dreams (Are Made of This)" by Marilyn Manson

Wielding but found his well dry.

Time slowed.

"Think of Xavia. She can't lose us both." Aurelio winced as he looked at Xavia. "You need her. She needs you. She needs only what you can give," he hissed, the ground scraping his body as he tried to hold on to Quade. "Don't you fucking give up. Promise me you'll take care of her," Aurelio said to Quade while keeping his eyes on Xavia. "Xavia, I lo—" Suddenly Aurelio screamed in pain as Norrix punched through his back.

"NO!" Quade bellowed before his grip slipped. Xavia screamed, breaking free from Jacinto and scrambling to grab Aurelio. The light died in Aurelio's eyes as Norrix pulled his spine out of his back. Quade couldn't move as the splash of his lover's blood hit his face, arm slipping from Quade's hands. Xavia's screams sounded far away. The sounds of the chaos around them warped as if muffled. Quade watched in horror as Norrix finally dragged Aurelio into the vortex with him. He could only watch as the vortex slammed shut, rocking the foundation of his world. He froze, looking at the blood of his best friend pooled on the ground and across Xavia's face.

Time moved again with Xavia's cry ringing in his ears. Quade pulled her into his arms, tears flowing freely. He wanted to break down. He wanted to sob and scream at the world. He wanted to burn it all down. But for the woman in his arms, for Xavia, he had to try and keep it together. The building shook again.

"It's coming down! We have to get out of here," Jacinto bellowed, motioning to the others who were left. Quade scooped Xavia into his arms in a cradle hold. Her body shook as she sobbed, face in the crook of his neck.

"No. No. No." She was saying it over and over. They barely made it out of the warehouse when it collapsed in on itself. Changing the landscape of their lives forever.

IT HAD BEEN ONE WEEK since Aurelio died. Quade often found himself staring into oblivion, not eating nor sleeping. Xavia stuck around as long as she could before giving the torch to Styx. It felt odd being around Styx and he was alone and angry.

Alone in his grief.

Alone in his bed.

Alone in his room.

Angry at Xavia for escaping into herself.

Angry at Norrix for taking his only family away from him.

Angry at Jacinto for never telling them that he was the fucking Chaos Wielder.

When they first got back to the Palacio, Quade sucker punched the vampire and Jacinto let Quade take it out on him; the anger and fury.

There was a soft tap on the door, bringing him out of his thoughts.

"It's open," he said, sitting up in his bed and leaning his head back on the headboard. He was exhausted, knowing he should sleep. But every time he closed his eyes, he saw the light leaving Aurelio's eyes and sinking into the vortex. Styx walked into the room, in her typical gear of tight tactical pants, knife vest, and hooded duster. The way she moved and dressed was so different from Xavia.

He hated it. He hated that while he was grieving, Styx was walking around with Xavia hiding inside their shared body.

"I, uh… wanted to talk," Styx said, hesitating at the door. Quade motioned to the bed for her to take a seat. She stepped further in the room, hanging up her jacket before sitting.

"Is she coming up any time soon?" Quade murmured before Styx could start talking. His anger flared when she shook her head. Fire leapt between his fingers as he worked to control his temper.

"She's refusing. She's locked herself into a cage. She won't come out or come up," Styx said softly. "This has never happened before." She sighed, running a hand through her purple curls. It was hard to look at her, the woman who was Xavia but not.

"Can she hear me?" Quade said, a scowl falling on his face like a mask.

"I think so. She was never aware before when I took the torch but she's aware now. I can feel that much." Styx looked at the wall, refusing to look at Quade. He snatched her jaw and turned her to look at him. She gasped, purple eyes flaring in shock.

"If you can hear me, brat, I need you to come up here," Quade said more firmly than he felt. He gripped her chin tighter, knowing it would bruise. Styx grit her teeth, jaw grinding at the invasion. "You can't leave me here alone. You don't get to hide from this. He meant something to the both of us!" His anger was fueling faster than he could stop it. His hand moved to Styx's throat, her hand rushing up to grip his wrist tightly. It kept him from gripping, her strength considerably greater than his. "You are a fucking coward for leaving me alone, to deal with this grief alone!" He yelled, unwanted tears streaming down his face. They steamed off his hot, flushed skin. Styx's eyes fluttered, flashing brown before melting back to purple. "For fucks sake Xavia..." His anger began to cool as the grief landed on his chest like a weight.

"I'm sorry," Styx rasped. Quade dropped his hand, hanging his head. He wiped at his tears angrily. "I've tried to bring her up but she's fighting me." He knew she was trying. He was wrong for being angry at Styx but all he could see was Xavia and it tore him apart every time.

"No, I'm sorry. I shouldn't have put my hands on you," Quade said softly. "I'm having a hard time with this. I know you're not her, but at the same time you are? I mean, your face and all." He grunted as he leaned his head back against the headboard, a headache blooming across his forehead. "What did you want to talk about?" He said with his eyes closed.

"I can come back," Styx said softly. He was barely able to shake his head.

"No, it's ok. Go ahead."

"I need to tell you about my work with Aurelio." He froze as he waited for her to continue. "We were working together to take down the Monarchy." His eyes opened, eyebrows going up.

"What?" The headache flared, a throb starting in his temples. He ignored it as he watched her stand up and pace.

"We met when he caught me in the middle of an assignment. The assassination of a senator." No regret passed her features. He respected that. "Instead of arresting me, he wanted to know more. He was tired of the Monarchy and its filth." Anger flashed in her eyes. "At the time, he didn't tell me who but he wanted to find birth records for a friend of his. He didn't know who I was at the time and that I'd been trying to do the same. The Monarchy has a special interest in me and Xavia and I don't know why," Styx huffed. "Probably because of the whole part human, part Wielding stuff. Or I think it's Wielding?" She shook her head. "Anyway, we started to dive deeper. He would send me coordinates of crime lords, human traffickers, and illegal brothels that politicians frequent. I did what I always do." She looked at him then. Seeing that he was not at all phased by her actions made her shoulders sag a bit.

"So, you killed dirty politicians and shit. What did he want from you?" Quade felt like she was stalling.

"I pulled some dirty secrets from these dirty politicians," Styx said with ire. "And I found useful information that could be used against the Monarchy." She sighed. "He knew who I was working with. Who my handlers are. They own a contract on my head." She took a deep breath. "We agreed that after we took the Monarchy down, we'd take down my handlers." She stopped pacing and locked eyes with Quade. "The Martyrs."

"What in the ever-loving fuck?!" Quade exploded, getting to his feet, ignoring the pulsing headache. "Aurelio would never work with The Martyrs." He stalked up to Styx who looked up at him without a lick of fear in her face.

"I know that! He told me that," she hissed. "He said it was a means to an end. It was the only reason he hadn't wiped them off the board already." Quade remembered Aurelio having a chance to take down a major Martyr compound but had hesitated to act on it. Quade had assumed it was because of that disastrous mission they had years ago.

"Fuck... This is... Insane." Quade flopped back onto the bed, placing his forehead into his hands and rubbing his aching temples. "Why are you telling me this?"

"We need to continue where he left off." Styx plopped down next to him, equally as exhausted it seemed.

"Right... Because we're in the perfect spot to deal with this," he scoffed.

"Actually, we are. We were attempting to find the Chaos Wielder to enlist their help. Jacinto already wants revenge on Norrix for nearly destroying his territory. I am hoping he'll agree to help us with the Monarchy afterward." Quade turned his head to peer at her. He knew there was something else she wasn't saying but he let it go.

"Ok. We can do that." Quade laid back, feet hanging off the bed. "Tomorrow." He mumbled; eyes closed. "I think I'll finally sleep now."

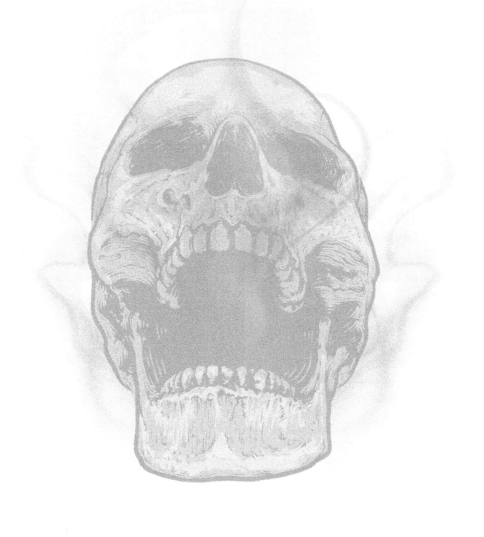

CHAPTER 54

STYX

STYX SAT IN THE PALACIO'S tea room that doubled as a garden. Night-blooming flowers glowed with bioluminescence and it invoked a spirit of calm. She could not explain how she felt about the chaos over the last few months.

For years, she fought to keep Xavia safe.

For years, she took on the burden of the heavy and hard memories.

For years, she was the one who got her hands dirty.

She knew it was inevitable; Xavia finding out about her. But the way Xavia learned about it only made it worse. Ever since the revelation, Xavia had closed herself off. After the death of Aurelio, she'd locked herself in a cage and essentially thrown away the key. Xavia was still a constant presence, sitting deep in her anima. But Styx's mind felt empty. When Styx held the torch, she could still feel Xavia's consciousness in her head. It was different this time. And she felt oddly empty because of it. Her eyes fluttered as Xavia stirred.

Styx closed her eyes, diving deeper into her consciousness to the forest that made up their inner realm. Trees reached to the sky with deep green bark and towering teal leaves. Moss covered the ground as Styx made her way down the path that led to the cabin that housed Xavia. Hibiscus trees and exotic orchids bloomed, their scents mingling with each other. The forest had grown since Xavia became aware of it. The path to the cabin took longer each time Styx dove into the forest that was their shared consciousness. Floating bioluminescent bubbles floated amongst the trees; a core memory in each one.

As Styx came up to the cabin, she noticed ivy vines snaking around it. They covered the walls, the roof, and blocked the way inside. Styx's heart broke every time she saw the cabin. More vines covered it than last time. As she approached, one vine snapped out against her cheek making her hiss and jump back.

"Xavia. Please talk to me," Styx said, her voice sounding muffled and unclear. From what she could see through the vines, the windows were lit dimly. Xavia was conscious. That was good. "Xavia. I need you. Quade needs you." Styx tried to step forward again and was whipped once more. "Sweet Melvina, Xavia!" She held her face, eyes blurring with tears.

"I can't." Her soft voice wasmuffled. Even from within the cabin, it drifted toward Styx. "I can't," Xavia said again. It became a mantra as the ground shifted underneath Styx's feet. The cabin lifted on four legs and began crawling backward like a crab.

"No! Xavia!" Styx ran, trying to keep up with the massive creature that was whisking away her other half.

"Am I interrupting?"

Styx jolted back to consciousness, a migraine blooming across her head. Styx turned to see Lex standing at the doorway. They looked as exhausted as she felt. Lex wore a denim vest over a white, sleeveless tunic that hung to their mid-thigh and white pants stuffed into tan combat boots. Lex's hair was tied back with cowry shells hanging on adornments. Silvermoon's attire of mourning. White for the purification of the anima as it passes to the Otherworld.

"No, come on in." Styx heaved a sigh. Lex and Jacinto were the only two who took the time to talk to her. Lilith, in her own grief, couldn't look at her. Quade practically hated her and could barely keep his temper in check. She felt her chin, knowing a bruise was blossoming. Lex sat next to her, passing her a steaming cup of tea. Styx murmured her thanks as she took a sip of the scalding liquid. Peppermint, chamomile, and lavender. It was loaded with honey, just how she liked it. She looked at Lex in questioning.

"I pay attention." They shrugged, looking at the flowers overhead. "I noticed the differences between you two." They sipped their own tea. Styx didn't know what to say. The others couldn't distinguish between her and Xavia. But that was to be expected. They shared the same body. The others could only see Xavia when they looked at her.

"I'm surprised. Everyone else seems to glower at me. No one lets me explain." Styx sighed, having resigned to the fact that they were not going to see her any other way.

"As someone who is non-binary, I am used to people expecting me to be one way or the other." Lex scooted closer to touch Styx's forearm. "The emotional labor that I have to do in order to get them to understand is exhausting."

"That's for sure." Styx exhaled, welcoming Lex's calming touch. It was a Water Wielder trait. "It's not only that. Lilith looks at me with pity. As if she feels bad for Xavia having to deal with me." She sipped more of the tea. "Quade, for sure, hates me. He's so angry." She rubbed her chin, drawing Lex's attention.

"Did he do that?!" They gasped, lightly touching her chin.

"Yeah... He was hoping that Xavia would hear him." Styx sighed. "I could heal it, but I feel like I deserve it."

"No, you don't." Lex said, their teeth clenched. "You don't seem to have any of Xavia's scars. Can't you heal hers?"

"No. Whatever scars she earns when she has the torch are her own." Styx sighed. She didn't understand their shared biology. "I should've exposed myself to Xavia a long time ago." Styx mumbled, looking down at her tea. "She should've known about me so that she would've been better prepared." Guilt addled her, making her stomach tight in knots. "Maybe I failed her by not letting her know."

"No, you protected her," Lex said softly, dropping their hand. "From what you've told me, you've kept her protected. She would've broken several times over if you hadn't." Styx nodded, wincing at the headache. "Have you slept at all?" Lex asked gently. Styx took a long drag on her tea, finishing it.

"I've tried." She sighed. "I've never slept before." Lex raised an eyebrow. "Well, I've always had a timer. I usually get Xavia back before she wakes, and I rest in our cabin but never sleep."

"Your cabin?" Lex inquired. Styx explained as best she could about the inner realm. "Oh, that actually makes sense," they said without judgment. Styx was grateful for them.

"There are times when I black out myself. I'll get close to the edge of returning her and then I black out. But I always remember afterward what happened. She doesn't." Styx stood to touch a purple orchid. It was so soft. "There are times where we merge. And it's chaotic. That's when we get into the worst of scenarios." She inhaled, the scent of the exotic orchid helping to soothe her aching stomach.

"Do you think she'll come back anytime soon?" Lex rose to stand next to her.

"I don't know. This has never happened before. I've never held the torch for this long. It's hard to process the ups and downs," Styx admitted. "I feel everything. I understand everything. But it's like I'm frozen, unable to do something about it." She barely slept or ate. She knew by her biological signals that she should, but she couldn't bring herself to. She'd only sleep or eat just enough to get by.

"Set a reminder like you did with Xavia," Lex suggested. Styx hadn't thought of that. "Maybe two or three times a day to start. Like, 'hey, it's time to eat.'" Lex shrugged in question.

"No, that's a good idea." Styx started putting in reminders in her comm while she spoke to Lex. "I have to learn how to adjust to this. And how to adjust to other things."

In the past, she would take the torch in order to protect Xavia when they were being trafficked. It left a scar that she wasn't sure could be healed. But the connection she felt with Jacinto was nothing like anything she felt before. It wasn't just about the instant attraction. It was something else. It had to do with him being the Chaos Wielder. She knew that much. But what did that mean for herself? She still didn't understand her own power, despite having it for so long. She knew it wasn't Wielding; it was something else. The question was, what?

"Oh, the King," Lex said, pulling her out her thoughts. Styx groaned, letting her head drop forward.

"Yes," she whispered. Lex rubbed her back, that calming

energy seeping into her body. "I don't understand it. I don't think I've ever felt aroused while having the torch. Having protected Xavia from so much, I couldn't deal. I didn't even think it was possible"

"Don't try too hard to understand it," Lex murmured before turning Styx toward them, hands on her shoulders. "You both nearly destroyed Norrix. There's clearly a power that only you two can combine. And that means you need to figure it out, but in due time." Styx bobbed her head in agreement.

"I need to find him, Lex. I need to make him suffer," she hissed. "Make him regret not dying the first time." She met Lex's gaze, which was full of determination.

"You will. We will. That motherfucker won't know what's coming," Lex murmured before nodding to Styx. "I have to go check on Lilith. Are you alright?" When Styx nodded, Lex gave her shoulder a squeeze before leaving.

Styx figured she should go talk to Jacinto. She wasn't comfortable with her instant reaction to him. It made her feel foreign in her body. Would Jacinto understand that? He seemed equally as drawn to her as she was to him. When she was around him, the rational parts of her went out of the window. Styx sighed as she made her way out of the tea room, making her way to the conference room where Jacinto had been spending his time. Before they spent any more time together on this mission, they needed to clear up a lot.

As she rounded the corner, she walked into a warm body that smelled of evergreen and musk. Styx squeaked as she turned her head up to meet the cobalt blue eyes of an Ice Wielder. She blanched, knowing that it showed on her face. What was Melvina doing to her? Why now?

The male was breathtaking. He looked down at her, standing at six feet minimum. She couldn't help but notice the light smattering of freckles across his nose and cheeks. Warm ivory skin covered a well fit muscular body. Navy Ice Wieldermarks covered his one arm in a montage of blizzards, ice crystals, and icebergs. Light golden-brown hair, peppered with grays, covered the top of his head in short waves, the sides buzzed down in a mohawk. He wore a black short-sleeved tee stuffed into comfortable looking cargo pants. A gun belt hung from his hips, knife vest covering his broad chest. There was a playful smirk on his face, a dimple in his cheek. He rubbed the short stubble across his jaw with a gloved hand.

"Whoa there darlin'. It's not often that I walk into a Deity." His eyes shone with amusement. He had an accent she couldn't place but it had a drawl to it. Styx wasn't sure of what to say at first before stepping back.

"I apologize. I wasn't looking where I was going," she said, trying to hide her embarrassment. His eyes slightly widened before he shrugged, smirk turning into a grin. What was this fluttering in her stomach?

"It happens. You have a nice night," he said before patting her shoulder and continuing on. Styx took a moment to still her fluttering heart.

"Great Melvina…"

CHAPTER 55

JACINTO

JACINTO STARED AT A HOLOGRAPHIC atlas of both the Dark and Bright continents. It gave him a panoramic view of the state of the demons movement. More had made their way into his continent and his Guard was working overtime to cut them down. His Shadow Wielders were working on a better shield for the continent, finding natural resources to amplify it.

Jacinto sighed, pushing a hand through his hair. He was currently alone, sending Cyrus to organize the Guard. Even though it'd been a week, his body had not fully recovered. He had to gorge himself on blood, a curse the Deities left on him.

"Hey," came Styx's rich, alto voice. He looked up at her, a smirk tilting his lips upward. The energy they shared changed their dynamic. He couldn't explain it. It was like two halves of an anima finally unified. The Convergence solidified it. There was a rightness to it and he felt its pull mostly when Styx held the torch. It had started to fade when Xavia held it. Such an interesting, complex puzzle. They hadn't discussed what it all meant. All they knew was that their animas desired to be close to each other.

"Hello asesina."

He came around the table and leaned on it. He ached to touch Styx but could sense her hesitancy. He could barely spend time without her presence. Just being around her was enough. The more he was with her, the stronger he felt. He could only imagine how much worse he'd feel if she wasn't there. She smelled of honey, exotic orchid and a touch of hibiscus. Styx leaned on the table next to him, their arms just slightly brushing each other. It sent a jolt up his spine and judging by her gasp, she felt it too. Styx took a deep shuddering breath.

He frowned, sensing her turmoil. "¿Estás bien?"

"Hmm. No," she said with a sigh. He remained silent to let her continue when she felt ready. She peered up at him with her beautiful purple eyes. "I feel like I'm fucking things up for Quade and Xavia," Styx said softly. "I can't convince her to come up. She's devastated. She's locked herself so tight that sometimes I can't even get to her." A tear spilled from her eye. "It feels empty in here." She tapped her head.

"Hermosa, there's only so much you can do." Jacinto captured the tear with his thumb, wiping it away. He watched as a shudder made its way through Styx's body, turning his thoughts somewhere else. He let his thumb trace her jawline, lingering on her chin just below her lower lip. Her pupils dilated as she inhaled sharply. He dropped his hand, shaking off those dark thoughts. "Learn from me. Dwelling on things you can't change will only make it worse." He'd been in his fair share of situations. Being as old as he was, there was no way he could avoid it. "Instead, what we can do is plan." He motioned to the atlas, regretfully pushing off the table to move back around the table. She stood across from him studying the map in front of her.

"The number of demons is increasing in Trezora," she hissed, resting her hands on the table. "But it looks like ferals are the same."

"My spymaster said it is because Aeshma cannot control them as well as her Death Stalkers." Styx raised an eyebrow.

"That is what they're called," he said with a shrug. That was news to him when his spymaster, Kayne, let him know. "She did something to their chemistry to keep them from making more ferals. So the Death Stalkers are the ones we have to worry about most."

"Fitting name," Styx grumbled, using her hands to move the atlas. "Potroya is seeing action too?" Her mouth gaped, looking at the red markings covering southern Vascaria, a country north of Ayobaí.

"Sí, but so far only in the northern part of Ayobaí and lower

Vascaria. They've managed to block the pass through the Loquiza Peaks." Jacinto seethed. He vowed to tear both Norrix and Aeshma apart. "Cyrus has taken the front with the Guard and they've kept the demons at bay."

"Fuck. Are we enough to stop this?" She looked at him. "Whatever this is?" She motioned between them.

"I have to hope so. Otherwise, it's a lost cause." Jacinto moved the atlas. "However, we will need an army to fight the demons while we go after Norrix and Aeshma. And my army is not enough. With Asherai taken over by Aeshma, we have to see how far her influence has spread. Do you think other countries will help us?" He raised an eyebrow. Styx pursed her lips in thought.

"Maybe Shayce." It was the easternmost country in Trezora and the furthest from Asherai. "They've always been independent and don't have a Monarchy like the other countries that border Asherai. I'm almost certain they would fight against Aeshma and her rule." Jacinto nodded, marking it with a yellow mark as a potential ally. He shifted the atlas again and pointed to Gailux, the Northern Continent. Styx's eyebrows rose. "No…"

"Yes," he said with a nod, placing a green mark on Tuthia, a western country. "They've been long-standing allies of mine. I have full belief that they'll help." Styx rubbed her face.

"Ice Wielders and yetis." She huffed a sigh. "Of course, the Vampire King would be allies with the Ice King." She rolled her eyes.

Where Jacinto was chaotic, Rizor was pure ice and cold. Being an Ice Wielder and Yeti, he had lived a long life. He was deadly and his army was practically untouchable. They went to war once, hundreds of years ago. They lost countless people and decided that an allyship would mutually benefit them instead. So, an accord was struck, they opened trade routes, and the relationship had been fruitful ever since.

"Rizor has been an ally of mine for over two hundred years," Jacinto said with a smirk. "You can thank him for our hollow point bullets. We're going to have to split up to hit both places," he said with unease. He wasn't so sure how stable the Asherai team was with the loss of their leader.

STYX

THE NEXT EVENING THE ASHERAI team, Jacinto, and Styx met in the conference room. Cyrus was up on a hologram, along with Kayne. The Asherai team had seen better days. Lex and Lilith sat close to each other, clearly having spent time mourning together. Quade looked terrible. The bags under his eyes told Styx that he hadn't slept much over the past week. There was a fury burning in his eyes, however. Good. Quade was going to need it for the next leg of the journey. Jacinto briefed them on what he thought was the best course of action.

"Of course, you'd be allies with the Ice King," Lex muttered. Jacinto pointed a thumb at Styx, who stood off to the side.

"She said the same."

Lex's lips twitched with an exhausted smirk. Styx had made sure she stood in neutral territory, close to neither Jacinto nor Quade. Styx caught the way Quade looked at her. It was always a mixture of sadness, pain, and then fury. His emotions had been run raw; Styx understood this. She could feel Jacinto tense across the room and knew he didn't appreciate the way Quade looked at her. The Fire Wielder stood to look at the atlas.

"Shayce is a good idea, however we have to tread very carefully." He looked to Styx briefly, a flare of sunset orange crossing his otherwise sienna eyes. "I've run point on a delegation there. They're..." He seemed to think of the right words to say. "Religious." Jacinto sighed looking at Styx, crossing his arms in clear frustration. She blanched looking back and forth between the males.

"What?" Styx said before sitting in a chair. "I knew they were pious. Is that a problem?" She shrugged. Quade's nose flared as he shot a glare at her.

"They're not just pious. They're cult-like zealots," he snapped.

A low threatening growl sounded in the room. It took Styx a moment to realize it was coming from Jacinto. Quade's gaze drifted to Jacinto bristling, fuming himself. She felt like she was caught in the middle of a brewing explosion and she was the bomb. "All I'm saying is that they may or may not want to help." He exhaled through his nose, smoke trailing, before he sat down again. "We have no clue how they view the prophecy. As far as I know, they're devout to the Tetrad, Tomis the most, but they could easily look to Aeshma if it fit their prerogative."

"I heard y'all need a tracker," came a smooth and familiar tenor voice from the doorway. Styx turned her gaze to the door, seeing the Ice Wielder she had run into the other day. She could feel Jacinto's stare on her as she tried to not gawk at the male. The male moved into the room, reaching out to turn the atlas to a small island off the coast of northern Potroya where the land encroached on the Horizon Line.

"Who are you?" Quade snapped, irritation clear in his voice. Amusement filled the Ice Wielder's eyes. It was as if he found the world funny and he couldn't help but enjoy it.

"Tristan Aries," he said with a nod. He caught Styx's gaze, smirk tilting his lips. Jacinto grunted, moving to Tristan and giving him a handshake and clap on his shoulder, pulling him into a brief embrace. The male returned the gesture before stepping aside.

"Tristan happens to be my best tracker and assassin," Jacinto said before looking around the room. "And he is a retired general." Styx's eyes widened slightly before she slammed the mask of nonchalance over her face.

"Why do we need a tracker?" Lex asked from their spot at the far end of the table.

"We need to find the second half of the prophecy." Jacinto said with his nose flared. Styx could tell he was exhausted, even if he managed to hide it well. "Tristan here already has a lead. Isla del Cuervo." Jacinto looked at Quade. "It might be best that you go to Shayce then. You know the country better than the rest of us," Jacinto said with a raised eyebrow. Quade nodded reluctantly.

"Yeah, sure. Adventus is our best place to start."

"Lex and Lilith and one of my nocturnals will go with you and I advise you to stop in Mutuba to pick up more Alpha Phoenix Guards." Quade started before Jacinto put a hand up to stop whatever bullshit wanted to make its way out of his mouth. "Callete. You cannot stand to be in the same room as Styx for more than a period of time." He put it plainly with a pointed glare. "She and I are stronger together than we are apart. It would be a risk to separate us. Kayne and Tristan will be joining us. After I make sure my kingdom is settled with Cyrus in place to rule in my stead, we will find the second half of the prophecy before petitioning the Ice King." Quade closed his eyes, pinching the bridge of his nose.

"And if Xavia comes back?" he said.

"I don't think she's coming back any time soon, Quade," Styx said softly. Quade's jaw clenched, the muscle ticking. "I get that this is a fucked-up situation." Styx said, getting to her feet and slamming her hands on the table. It jolted Quade's eyes open in a scowl. "If we are to honor Aurelio's memory, we need to fucking get over ourselves and destroy Aeshma." Her eyes flared. "Jacinto is right. Whatever the bond we have, it's important enough that it's going to take the both of us to defeat Aeshma." Styx crossed her arms at her waist. She couldn't promise what she would do next if Quade opened his mouth again.

"Was the prophecy incorrect then?" Lilith spoke, voice like silk. "I thought the Chaos Wielder alone was supposed to defeat Aeshma." Jacinto shook his head.

"That's why we need to find the second half. Even the Deities didn't deem to inform me of the whole of it." Yet another complication about this whole thing. Styx nodded, sinking back into her seat.

"How are we traveling? I assume flying is not an option," Lex said.

"By boat and land unfortunately," Cyrus quipped from his screen. He clicked a few buttons, pulling up Lex's yacht that looked like it was retrofitted with gun barrels and other weaponry. Lex's mouth hung open.

"Is that?" They put a hand up to their mouth.

"Sí. We upgraded her to give you better protection. You're going to have to sail around southern Trezora to get to the western coast. The engine and doppler systems have been upgraded as well. The garage will house motorcycles for land travel," Cyrus said with a nod. Three smaller yachts popped up. "This will be your escort." Lex's eyes shone, the dual turquoise and sea green eyes lighting.

"Thanks, man." They gave a nod.

"'Cin..." Another yacht pulled up on the screen, this one bigger for a full crew. "Kayne will captain the superyacht," he said, spinning it so that Jacinto could see the specs. It had all the same features as Lex's yacht with an added ward around it. "It should keep you in stealth and untraceable. We only had enough lodestones for one ward, otherwise we would've warded Lex's as well." He motioned to three more smaller yachts. "Your Guard escort."

"Good job Cyrus." He nodded.

"Keep in mind, it'll take a month to get to Isla de Cuervo." Styx let out a soft huff. She hated the last boat ride but she wasn't in charge. Maybe she'd feel differently this time. "It's roughly a two-month trip to Mutuba." There was a groan of frustration from Quade. Jacinto gave him a glare. Cyrus continued, "From the intel Kayne gathered, Aeshma is doubling down and has ceased movement for now. I imagine it has to do with Norrix's failure." Cyrus winced, a sound of a brawl coming from his speaker. "Shit, I have to go. I'll keep you posted." Cyrus clicked off. Kayne had remained silent the entire briefing.

"Have anything to add, Kayne?" Jacinto asked with a sigh.

"Nope." He emphasized the p. "When do we leave?" Styx looked to the room, assessing everyone. They were exhausted, drained, and emotionally pulled to their absolute furthest boundaries. The turmoil of the last two months showed on all of their faces. Unfortunately, there was no time to rest. They couldn't delay. The fate of Euhaven depended on them defeating Aeshma and destroying her once and for all. Styx locked eyes with Jacinto and gave a nod.

"As soon as possible."

CHAOS

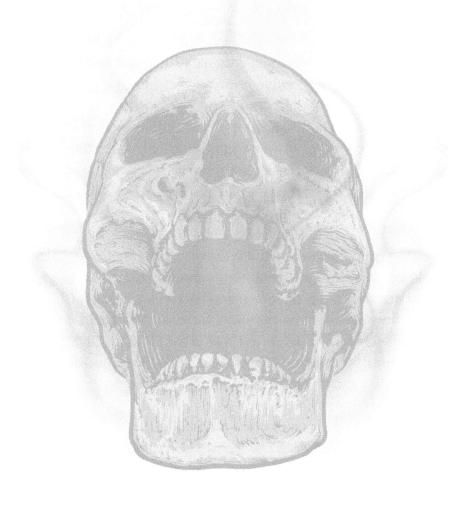

THE DARKNESS WAS ALL AROUND. It was difficult to figure out which way was up and what was down. Walking through it felt like walking through tar. It was sticky, clinging to the body and anima. The howls of wind were deafening, blowing around him like a tornado. It was chaotic, uncontrollable, and painful.

Oh, the pain. It filled every part of his being. It was as if he was torn apart and put back together to only feel pain. He fought his way through the darkness, the smell of death and decay making him gag. How long had he been stuck here? Time was irrelevant in the darkness. There was no day, nor night for there were no stars to light his way. It was just darkness. Pure, black, inky darkness.

A glimmer in the distance drew his attention. It felt impossibly far. He couldn't imagine reaching it but he knew he had to try. He had to get out of this darkness and find his way back. He couldn't remain here where fear tempted his anima to stay. He couldn't remain in the blackness where his anima would be eaten alive. Deadly snarls surrounded him as he practically climbed toward the glimmer. Things clawed at him, ripping into his arms and legs. He tried to yell but no sound came from his mouth.

The glimmer got closer. Something latched to his ankle as if to keep him back and he fought, punching it off his foot. Pain lanced through him again, his back screaming in agony. He fought to breathe through the excruciating pain as the glimmer became larger. It was a doorway. He fought against the creatures trying to keep him in the dark with renewed strength, reaching toward the light.

He tumbled through and felt himself land on a bed. It was as if his anima had been sucked back into his physical body. Keeping his eyes closed, he listened to the sounds around him. There was a faint beeping of a heart machine plus the hiss of a respirator. That's when he noticed his throat was raw and sore, filled with a breathing circuit.

His eyes popped open, the heart machine beeping quickly to match his pulse. The bright white room was blinding after being in the darkness. He pulled the circuit out of his mouth with a gag. He dry heaved but there was nothing in his stomach to vomit. He sat up, his body aching and his back screaming at him.

"Welcome back Aurelio," came the sultriest voice he had ever heard. His vision cleared as he took in the Angel before him. Skin as dark as the night, eyes as white as snow. Her skin glimmered as if starlight swirled underneath. Long white braids draped over her shoulders. Her full lips were painted with gold. She wore what looked like a gold and black warrior gown. The golden armored bodice was traced with intricate black designs that looked like old Angel Language. The dress flowed out around her sumptuous curves, landing to the floor. Wings of black and gold feathers reached the ceiling behind her. *Aeshma*. She was one of the most beautiful beings he'd ever seen. What was he doing here? Memories hit him like rapid fire. Xavia and Quade. They saw him die. He *died*.

"Where am I?" he asked, voice hoarse and raspy. He gripped his chest, heart aching. "Why did you revive me?"

"You are at the Monarch Tower in Melhold," she said with her smooth, rich voice. It felt like silk was brushing up against his skin when she spoke. "I revived you because you are going to help me bring my daughter home." Aurelio looked at her in confusion for a few moments before it dawned upon him.

"Xavia is your daughter?"*

♪ "Waiting on the Sky to Change" - Starset, Breaking Benjamin, Judge & Jury

ACKNOWLEDGEMENTS

FIRST, I HAVE TO THANK MY Ancestors and Spirit for guiding me. This novel wouldn't have been possible if I didn't answer the call and took a leap of faith. They told me it was time and I listened.

To my spiritual advisor Baba Siete, your guidance has meant everything to me. Spiritually, I wouldn't have gotten to this point without your teachings. You taught me how to listen to Spirit and the Ancestors. Without that, I'd be lost.

To my friend Toni, you have no idea how much you've impacted my life. You told me to write with reckless abandon and to follow my dreams. It was with your push that I flew at the keys and lost myself in the world of Euhaven. Your tarot deck guided me with many pivotal points in this novel. Thank you for your beautiful soul.

Many thanks to my alpha reader, Cynthia, my sweet friend and mutual lover of the dark. It was fate that we met and connected. Your help with The Chaos Wielder has been monumental. Thank you for reading, digesting, and giving me critical feedback. Our friendship has meant so much to me. You've been there for me in more ways than one.

To my amazing editor Amanda, thank you. You helped shape up the novel in more ways than one. Your feedback and suggestions helped make a big difference. Your support through the process and your patience was everything I needed.

So many thanks to my alpha reader Charli. Our late night conversations pulled me through when I was having moments of imposter syndrome. Your feedback has been invaluable and I am so grateful to have you as my friend!

To my beta readers Evelyn and Cherie, thank you so much for your support, suggestions, and commentary. It made a significant difference and helped me shape up the novel in more ways than one.

To Mara and Julia, the artistic geniuses behind my character artworks. Thank you for bringing my characters to life. I'm blown away every time I look at them.

To my friends and family, I love you. Your support has meant everything to me. Whether you were loud or quiet, I felt your presence and knew you were there for me.

To the huge bookish community on social media and off. The gathering of support that I received since starting my writing journey has been overwhelming. I've met so many great people and I am forever grateful.

To my Kickstarter supporters, thank you for your faith in me.

To my ARCs and readers, I love you all!

Thank you all for joining me on this Chaos Journey!

ABOUT THE AUTHOR

A.E. COSBY IS A PUERTO RICAN and indigenous woman obsessed with the dark and arcane. She is a bruja who honors her Ancestors and the path they've put before her. She believes with her whole chest that she lived on another planet in another life. Being an Aquarius, this is not a surprise. Having vivid dreams of this world, she invites you to experience this planet through her dark urban fantasy novels. She shares the darkest parts of her soul through her work.

She's a neurospicy comic book nerd, enjoys sci-fi and fantasy, and tattoos. Ask her how many she has. (Hint: 14). She has three minions that call her their leader and a husband that supports her dream.

You can connect with her through her website and social media channels.

hello@anissacosby.com
www.anissacosby.com
www.instagram.com/the.bookishbruja
www.tiktok.com/@thebookishbruja

CURRENT AND FUTURE WORKS BY ANISSA COSBY

THE CHAOS SERIES
The Chaos Wielder
Wrath's Daughter
Blood of Fire
Storm's War

THE EUHAVEN CHRONICLES
Death & Shadow

Milton Keynes UK
Ingram Content Group UK Ltd.
UKHW011945240823
427459UK00017B/191/J